The Scouring

Critical Acclaim for the Sudden Quiet Trilogy

"Breathtaking Northern Michigan settings are juxtaposed against the horrors of a post-collapse world. Steeped in local Native American culture, written with a vivid love both for the environment and characters it portrays, each book leaves readers eager for the next installment."
— Scott J. Couturier, author of *The Box*

"This dystopian trilogy combines mysticism, fantasy, hard science, and a deep connection with the environment in which trees communicate with each other and with certain nature-fluent characters. Whatever genre you prefer, settle back and let the author take you into this world."
— Tom Powers, reviewer for *Michigan in Books*

"I appreciate how Veith shifts focus from collapse to the quieter, more introspective struggle of rebuilding, which makes the story deeply human. The Sudden Quiet trilogy guides readers on a journey through a world that's equally wondrous and treacherous."
— D. Stebbins, author of *A Hunter's War*

"What a thrilling series! Seriously, some of the best books I have ever read! I loved every minute and did not want to put them down. This has movie series written all over it!"
— Craig Elliot, author of *The Balloonatics*

"This trilogy blends many genres—fantasy, science fiction, horror—and creates something unique. A rare treat!"
— Doug Dorda, podcaster of *This One's About...*

The Scouring

Joshua Veith

Published by Mission Point Press
2554 Chandler Rd.
Traverse City, MI 49696
(231) 421-9513
www.MissionPointPress.com

ISBN: 978-1-965278-99-4
Library of Congress Control Number: Available upon request
Printed in the United States of America

Cover Design credit to Janella Williams

This novel is a work of fiction; the characters are entirely invented by the author. It is not the fault of writers that history repeats itself, endlessly setting its well-worn stage with typecast actors delivering the same old lines.

Evil and pain exist, both in this book and in the wide world too. This novel is dedicated to those who fight back and to those who heal.

إِنَّ الأَعلى مِنَ الأَسفَلِ وَالأَسفَلُ مِنَ الأَعلى
عَمَلُ العَجائِبِ مِن واحِدٍ كَما كانَت الأَشياءُ كُلُّها مِن واحِدٍ

"That which is above is from that which is below,
and that which is below is from that which is above."
— Jabir ibn Hayyan ca. 850–950

CAST of CHARACTERS:

Island

Beaver Island

Samantha

Keith Two-Crow

Miinan

Mukwa

Tom Doyle

Beaver Bois

Main

Naturals

Nighthawk

Brian

125th Griffins

Rangers

Walker

Voyageurs

Amish

Panthers

Antiva

Panzer Pharm

Bob Campbell

Red Liz

Aghori

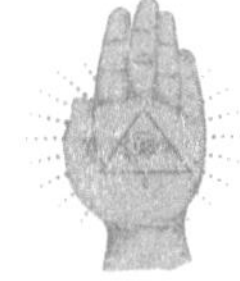
Red Hands

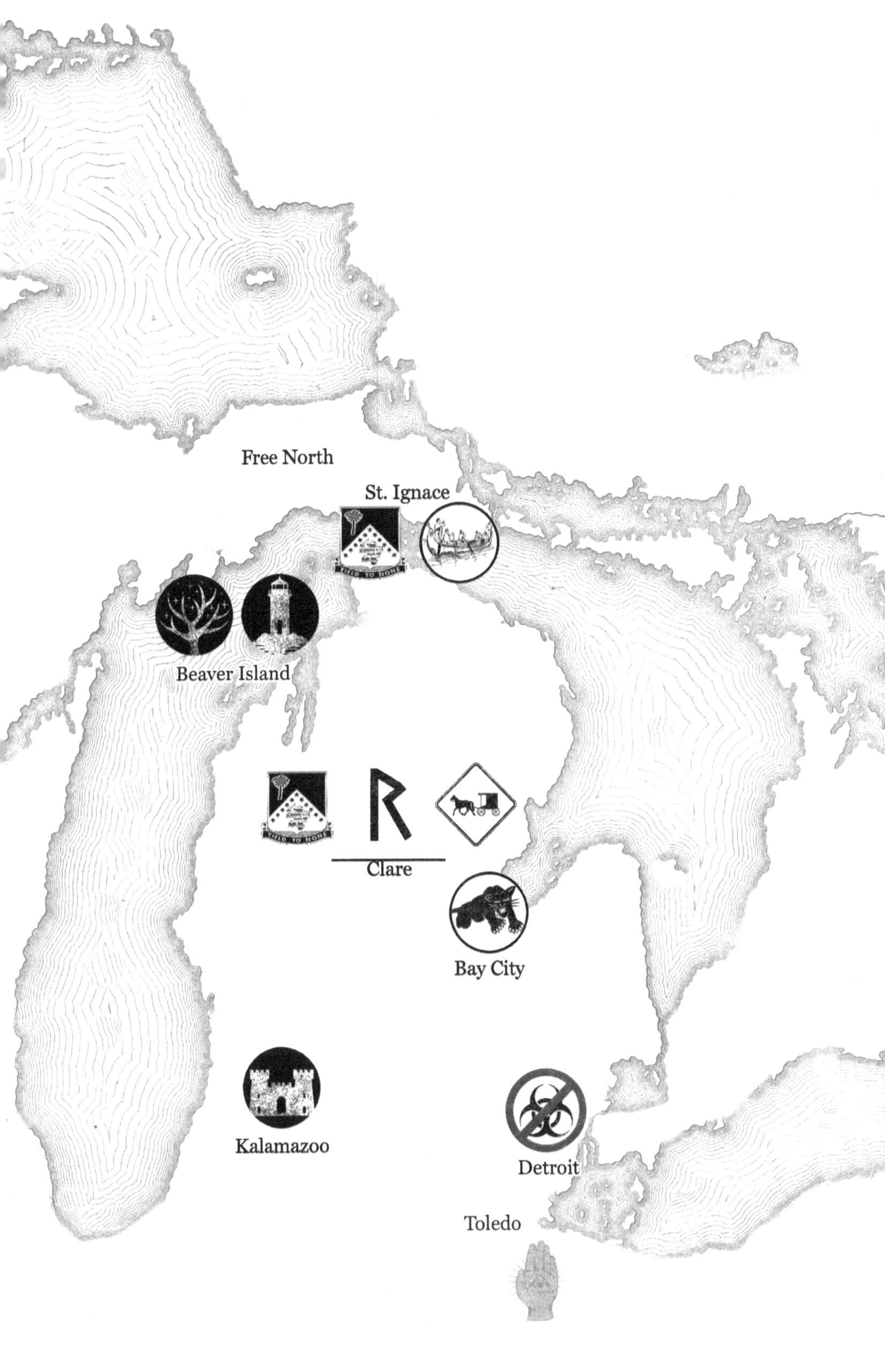

Free North
St. Ignace
Beaver Island
Clare
Bay City
Kalamazoo
Detroit
Toledo
YIELD TO NONE
YIELD TO NONE

PART 1:
New Beginnings

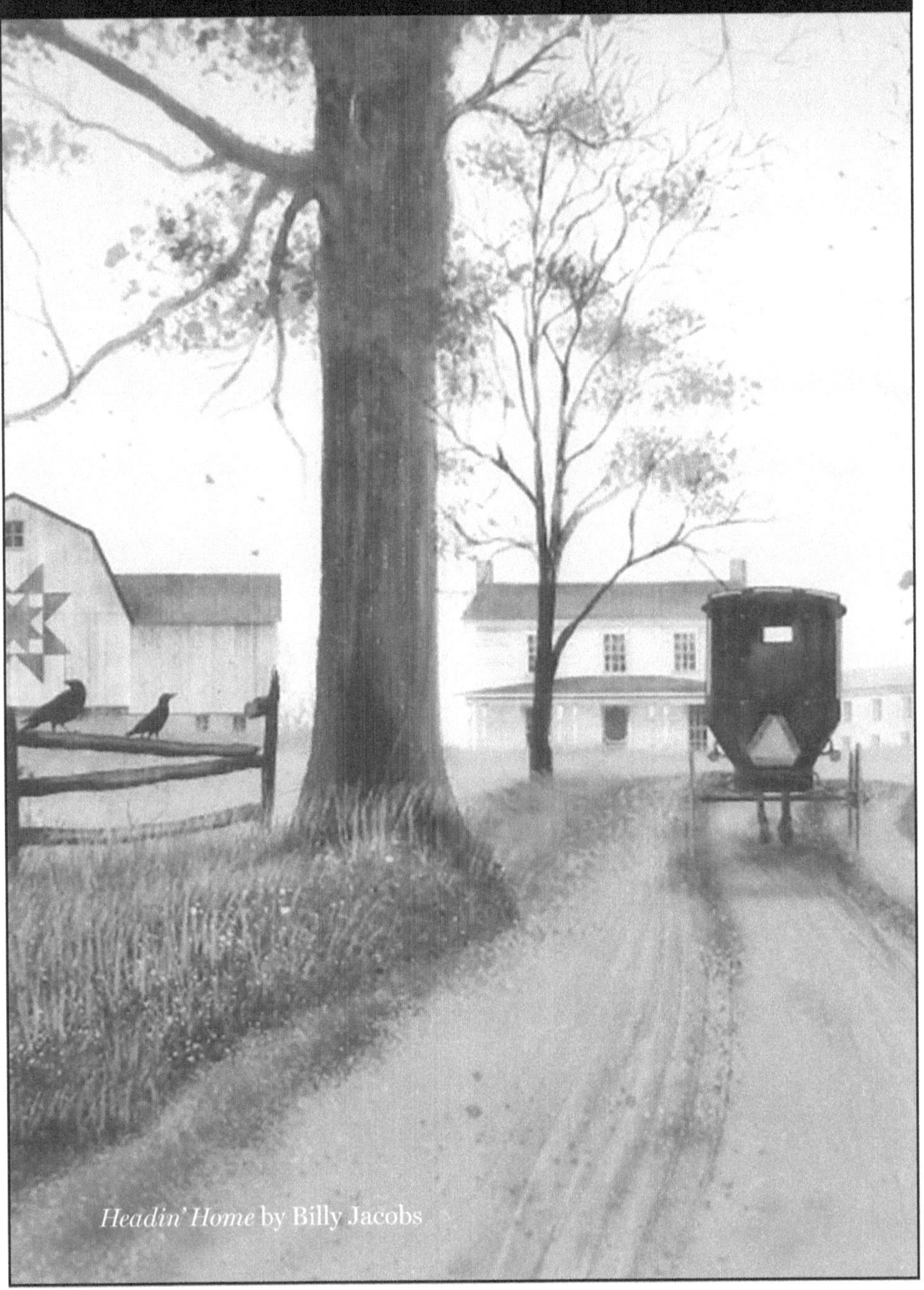

Headin' Home by Billy Jacobs

Can I Get a Witness?

"IS IT RIGHT TO BE TREATED SO BAD, when you've given everything you had?"

The man awoke, freezing, in a Michigan hayloft. *Marvin Gaye, really?* he thought, blinking in the first gray light of morning. His dreams, even now, after all the horsemen of the apocalypse, were a constant source of surprise. The barnyard cock crowed again. *That fucking rooster is a dead man! And why the hell won't my fists open?*

His bad breath steamed in the October predawn. He force-flexed his fingers, and with a sticky pull they unfisted. His blisters had oozed, hardening in the night. Bob "Cowboy" Campbell didn't recognize his own hands—no way those callusing clumps belonged to him. Red and raw, the thought of gripping a hoe handle all day filled him with real horror. From outside, Campbell heard the contented cluck of chickens being fed. Without looking out the hayloft's window, he knew the siblings were at it already. Samuel and Sarah, both pre-teens, had dressed, washed, and were now at their chores.

What day was it? *Please God, let it be Sunday.*

Campbell calculated; it wasn't.

Goddamn it. Bob forced himself to move.

The first hard frost of the season had frozen last night's pee in its bottle. The warm gush from his morning bladder thawed it into slush. He attempted to stretch. *Shit, I'm sore.* Awkward with the buttons and hooks, Bob dressed himself once again in another man's clothes: shirt, pants, suspenders, black coat, black shoes, and, of course, the brimmed hat that marked him as Amish. Except he wasn't.

He was being hidden by them, except he wasn't. He was living in plain sight as one of the Plain folk. He was also infected, a Viral. The Amish claimed they couldn't catch the Covee he carried. Bob had no idea why. They did though—it was their God.

His God too, he supposed.

Two years ago the old world—almost all of it—had toppled. The pandemic—Covee first, then the Stinger variant—gave it a shove. Nuclear exchanges, rapid climate change, and uncivil wars sealed the deal. During the chaos of collapse, "Cowboy" had done some evil-ass shit—who hadn't? Post-traumatic and definitely stressed, Bob now suffered nightmares: noosed necks and light poles dangling with human fruit.

Wearing his cowboy hat—a persona—he'd trafficked in slaves, sexual and otherwise. He'd lined people up and had them shot, coldblooded. Women, kids, it hadn't mattered. Cowboy Campbell used to be one of the Chosen. A boss actually, mid-level and mediocre when it came to meeting his scavenge quotas. Four months ago, back in June, Bob had been betrayed, tasered silly, and flex-cuffed by an old flame.

Where the hell is Red-fucking-Liz anyway?

Lizzy—a real ballbuster—had spared Bob's sorry ass, locking him inside a passenger ferry instead. The ferry was then hijacked from Charlevoix's harbor and brought to a berth on Beaver Island by commandos wielding primitive weapons and calling themselves the E.L.F. Campbell was set free by one of these "elves"—a doctor, an uninfected Natural studying disease. In secret, defying island protocol, the clinician confined his Viral patient to a remote cabin in the dunes. The good doctor— immune like all Naturals—studied Campbell's pathology and treated him decently: books, guitar, good grub, and conversation. Oh yeah, and probably drugs, strong ones. Bob felt itchy just remembering; quitting cold turkey had been a bitch.

Just as Bob was adjusting to an early retirement in the dunes, he was abducted at arrow point by a nature-worshiping psycho. Rude as hell, he never learned her name, but the ferocious woman had a face like a fucking hawk. Together—predator and prey—they fled the isolated island, crossing 30 miles of Lake Michigan to the decimated mainland in a leaky boat. Eventually reaching Kalamazoo, the fortified HQ of Panzerland, she trussed him up for a prisoner exchange that never happened. The extremist was on a suicide mission to rescue her captured ELF comrades.

He wasn't.

Long story short, he ended up here, "hiding" in a hayloft outside of Clare, peeing in a frozen bottle, bare-lipped and half-bearded. Amish on the outside, but under the borrowed hat a red-eyed murderer—a Viral, a Spreader. Bob didn't think he was that same evil guy anymore. Cowboy was a bullshitter though, his favorite audience always himself.

Samuel's accented courtesy call floated up from the chicken yard: "Wake up, *Englisch! Gude Daag!*"

Cowboy rapped on the window glass to acknowledge. "I'm up, you little bastard."

Mirrorless, he felt his face. He'd been weeks with the Hochstettlers and his beard finally stopped itching. Old man Hocher—wordless as ever—had loaned him a razor, pointing to Bob's upper lip. Cowboy had taken the hint, razored off his stache and felt like the fool he must have looked. Though on this people-less planet, who the hell was looking? There was no one left to give two shits.

Speaking of shits, Bob felt one brewing. He flexed his fingers, flinching at the blisters, and descended the wooden ladder. He kicked at a chicken and missed. He nodded to the kids and missed as well; they were serious about their chores. Cute little tykes though, in an old timey way—Sammy's suspenders, Sarah in her bonnet.

He'd had a daughter, Angela. She'd slit her wrists on her sweet sixteen. Two years ago, when collapse was cresting, Bob drove his wife—murdered by molecules—to their suburban hospital. The panicked staff had zipped her in plastic, stacking her with the rest. Soon, the staff would join the pile—not enough PPE, not for the variant, not for Stinger, not this time.

Bob, broken-hearted, returned to find his baby girl dead in the tub, a bloodbath. He didn't blame her. Everyone was doing it. The party was over. Why stick around for the shitty end of the stick? So he toweled her off, loaded her up—his contractor truck, once again, a hearse. Bob pictured the commercial they would have made. A new sales pitch for a new time, marketing's finger always on the pulse, even a dying pulse, even the end-of-times.

No indoor plumbing at the Hochstettlers, or anywhere else, not anymore. Bob dropped his dump down the outhouse hole, adding it to the pile. Humanure. Night soil. The Plain, himself included, would soon be spreading it on the fields. Not that they had a choice.

The Amish in this county (those that survived) were now slaves, food producers for their masters—infected Chosen and their Viral allies, the XCons. With the grid long gone, and gasoline going next, who better than the Amish to raise a crop to harvest? Unlike the rest of the too-modern world, the Old Order had been rehearsing Revelations for years.

Buttoning up, Campbell contemplated his steaming turd.

He'd fallen too. After all, Cowboy once held the whip that now lashed at his heels. Or maybe he was rising? If so, it sure didn't feel like it. He exited the shit box, returning to the yard.

Sarah, smiling, waved from the farmhouse. *"Gude mariye schlofkopp!* Time to eat!"

The four of them sat around a table that used to sit five. Their mother—Bob learned her name was Hannah—had been taken a month ago, transported by wagon to the plantation.

"By the *iks*." Samuel sketched the X brand on his forehead, sign of the Cons. Empowered by Covee and its variant, many convicts had escaped prison, sentenced by their chromosomes to life instead—with no parole from the coming purge.

Apparently, Hannah's husband—Elam, the children's father—had protested her abduction and was dragged away, beaten bloody. None of the Plain had lifted a finger. There'd been no word of him since; every farmstead had a similar story to tell.

So the kids had traded their loving parents for Cowboy, an ex-slaver on the lam. Old Hochstettler, Hannah's *Daadi*, made his disapproval quite clear. The kids were more polite. Campbell did what he could to crack their smiles, but his jokes rarely worked, their humor too earthy for his taste. Nothing funnier to the sibs than watching the *Englisch* step in shit, or fall off a horse, or the pinnacle of comedy—fall off his horse into shit.

Bumbling Bob did his best to oblige.

"Händt nunna," intoned grumpy Gramps. The four of them bowed their heads in prayer.

The kids for their parents?

Old Hocher for his cow?

Bob prayed for an easy day in the fields, good grub at dinner, and dreams tonight—not of nooses, but of his wife and daughter. Both angels, alive again and unfallen.

Bob opened an eye once he heard Hocher slurping. Prayer time was over. The old grump looked grim; he took no pleasure in mealtimes. Food was fuel, purely transactional. Dawdy Hocher filled up his tank. "Coffee soup," an Amish staple, was not Campbell's thing. A decent bean would make the brew better, but the ersatz grounds Hocher brewed were damn near unbearable.

The long-beard added some cream from his cow, some crusts of old bread. Dawdy mushed the concoction in a bowl, calling it breakfast.

When in Rome, Bob thought, dipping himself a ladle. The kids, unsmiling, slurped it down as well.

A jingle of harness and the clop of hooves from the yard.

Time for transport already?

The Lapps—middle-aged Aaron and his teenage boys—lived nearby. They all commuted together. Each family worked their own place, laboring for the plantation as well. The slavers, whether *iks* or Chosen, took a percentage from the home farms, and the entire yield from the big one. The Amish all went hungry, made no profit, but were allowed their Sunday Sabbath.

From his quota days as a Chosen boss, Campbell knew how slim the scavenging had become. The entire state—"Pure Michigan"—was picked clean. Every can of soup, every gallon of gas was gathered up already. As a boss, he'd heard rumors of the plantation and others like it, but Bob was never high enough on the hog to taste any bacon.

Even in these aftertimes, this era of warlords and fiefs, some things never went out of style, food being one of them—booze, drugs, and sex following closely behind.

"Hey you Yoders! Get the fuck out here, all of you!"

Breaking their fast, the four of them froze. *Yoder* was slaver-slang for Amish, for Plain. Campbell crouched by the curtain, peeking out. It was Lapp's wagon alright; their nervous neighbor held the reins, but his boys weren't with him. Two X-branded Cons wearing pistols climbed down. Another *iks* sat shotgun next to Lapp. He guarded the women in the wagon with a lecherous eye.

"Shit!" Campbell hissed. "Samuel, hide your sister."

Old Hochstettler chewed his bare lip. The boy looked from his dawdy to Bob and back. Sarah's brown eyes were wide. The old man was mumbling, then standing. He beckoned his grandkids to do the same.

Don't fucking do it, man. They'll take her. You know they will.

Hochstettler herded his grandkids towards the door and opened it. Together, the trio stepped into the yard. Three pairs of red-rimmed eyes undressed little Sarah in her bonnet. Chickens clucked around the wagon wheels. One of the horses took a steaming piss in the mud. Neighbor Lapp stared straight ahead. The rising sun illuminated the protection hex painted on the barn.

Shotgun asked Lapp a question, prompting him roughly with the butt of his gun.

Behind the curtain, Bob couldn't hear, but Lapp held up four fingers in response.

Shit!

Campbell palmed a kitchen knife, his once-quick mind completely fucking blank.

"Yoder, we know you're still in there! You've got three fucking seconds!"

Committed—*not the kids, no way*—Cowboy brimmed his hat low and moved through the door. *Look Amish, walk Amish.* He kept his bleary eyes down, shuffling towards the wagon.

Shotgun was the biggest threat.

Samuel stared a plea at his *Englischer* friend. Cowboy's brain was calculating. They weren't watching him. Their eyes crawled all over Sarah.

The two Pistols approached, bracketing her front and back.

The old man wasn't moving. Little Samuel was shaking. The captive bonnets in the wagon were praying. The two slavers frisked Sarah through her homespun, joking as they ran rough hands over her barely budding body.

"This little Yodie ain't ripe yet, but she will be. Do we take her or leave her?"

Decision time. Eyes down, Cowboy stood by the wagon, palming the utensil. The world waited on the answer.

Shotgun spat in the mud, an X puckering his brow. "We take her. Some likes 'em a little green. Better underripe than over. Am I—"

The rest of his phrase went unuttered, as in utter shock he watched his guts spill from his belly. Cowboy sliced the knife upwards, opening the man like a melon. Bob wrenched away the scattergun, racking a shell, and ran towards Sarah.

The two gropers were goggle-eyed. Too late, they fumbled their holster straps. Cowboy clubbed them both to the mud, swinging the gun by its barrel.

Guts dropped down from the wagon bench and was lurching away. His two hands were busy stuffing his insides back inside.

Lapp fought the horses—panicky from the blood, from the bile. A gabble of German was heard from the wagon as the bonnets blinked their disbelief. Samuel pulled Sarah away from the two clubbed men, imploring little sister to look away. Old Hoch-er glared condemnation—at Cowboy? At the *iks*?—a Jehovah of old, righteous with wrath.

Time to finish the job. Cowboy caught up to Guts by the barn, but couldn't risk a shotgun blast. It wasn't pretty, and took longer than it should have, but finally, the man—whoever he was, or used to be—lay dead.

Out of breath, Cowboy deflated. Bob felt warm gore on his face, didn't want the kids to see it. He kept his back turned and slipped into the barn, leaning the brain-spattered weapon against a stall. For some fucking reason, the only voice in his head was Mr. Marvin Gaye's.

Now all you chicks agree

That this ain't the way it's supposed to be.

Map created by Ed Wojan and Jeff Cashman of Beaver Island

Tree Academy: Roots

ON BEAVER ISLAND, early risers woke to the same hard frost, a foretaste of winter. It was mid-October. Thirty miles of great lake separated island and main.

Back in June, the islanders—unexposed to the Stinger variant—reluctantly opened 12,000 acres of their state forest to refugees from Michigan's mainland. ELF Country II, these Naturals called it, honoring their original home, the wild uplands of Petoskey's Bear River—*Mukwa Ziibing*. The refugees even recreated the signage, woven from wood-stuff and placed at border crossings, "Welcome to ELF Country!"

Since resettlement, the ELF—Earth Liberation Front—had not been idle, fencing in their herds, filling root cellars, and forging alliances with nearby farms. These "ELF friends"—the Greenes, the Martins, and others—would come at their call. Naturals would reciprocate if ever they were needed. Both factions raised their mugs: "To a peculiar, but excellent, arrangement!"

For two seasons now, a truce existed between the insular hosts—unprotected from the virus—and their mainland guests, supposedly "green-shielded" against infection.

The good harvest had certainly helped.

Skeptical islanders—there were plenty—quickly learned that Naturals had green thumbs as well as shields. Two years ago, the unthinkable had happened—apocalyptic collapse—and without electricity, medicine, or resupply, that first winter culled the island's population to the bone. Now, thanks to the Naturals, Beaver Island families would face Y2's winter with full larders, comforted by rows of cordwood—stored solar power for the dark months ahead.

Predawn, a dozen adolescents gathered under Twin Oaks, kindling fire from twiggy fingers shed by giants. Acorns—freed by the frost—splashed the starry mirror of Greene's Lake as they fell. Its silver surface reflected the firmament, a rime of ice fringing the shore. An oak seed plunked a sleepy student on the head, jests and giggles rippling from the source. The acolytes were a mix of local kids and refugees who'd escaped on the ferry when their mainland ELF Country was overrun.

Their three instructors were mixed as well.

Sparrow, a Natural, was a Sentinel commando, much respected for her prowess with a bow. Grace, a grandmother figure, was another Natural, steeped in herblore, a highly qualified educator from before. The day's lead teacher, Miin—a teenager herself—was an orphan, raised on Beaver Island by her foster-gran, Samantha, an Anishinaabe elder and silver-haired remnant from an earlier age.

Their curriculum never varied: sensing, merging, and healing with nature, yet each lesson was unique. Instruction, per usual, started before dawn. The learning target for the day was the ethical harvest of white-tailed deer. Miin led the class in pronouncing its old name, *Waawaashkeshiwag*.

"Deer are sensitive, gentle creatures—ambassadors between the spirit world and our own. Treat them with reverence and they will feed your families. Treat them with disdain and you will go hungry."

Ms. Miinan—"Blueberry" in *Anishinaabemowin*—continued the lesson. Miin's touchstone, her green totem, as always, was trees. "As a hunter, you only have two eyes." Her class sipped Grace's tea around a crackling campfire. No bells, fluorescents, or pledge; their only allegiance was to Nature and each other.

"The deer you seek, even a mature buck, is small and the forest is vast. You must utilize the trees, tap into all their woody senses. Oak and pine and maple, *they* know where the deer are, every last one."

The novices were nodding. Sentinel Sparrow, leaning on her bow, attended with sharp ears. "But how will they tell us?" asked Michael Martin, the academy's best tree climber.

Miin practiced wait time, lifting her eyes to the brushwork of acorn-heavy branches.

"They *are* telling us," answered Josephine Greene, born nearby, with an affinity for birches. "They're talking all the time. We just need to listen. Find the right frequency. Quiet our minds so we can hear them, let their ancient voices in."

Blowing steam from their mugs, the acolytes were grinning. Instructor Miin affirmed, gesturing to the oak grove, their classroom for the day. Each hoary trunk was furrowed with a friendly face. Her disciples, druidic, were beaming, dispersing with the sunrise; group lesson over, it was time for individualized instruction. The students sought their tutors, variously titled—Professors Oak, Pine, and Maple.

Miin made her rounds, spicing dead Latin with living *Anishinaabemowin*. The scientific names—*Querca, Pinus, Acer*—she translated to *mitigomizh, zhingwaak, ziizibaakwadwaatig*. The trees, omnilingual, nodded their approval. They'd known this *miinan*, this Blueberry, all her short life. In the woods word got around, however slowly.

After three months of practice, the students were adept. Each had their affinities, their methods, and were now hard at work. Their postures varied: some sat, some climbed, some nestled in the roots. Connections were made—fingers with twigs, minds with mycorrhiza. The students' neural pathways meshed with the forest. Their filaments entwined, frontal lobes with fast-growing fungi.

The world-wide-web of before—Miin instructed on her rounds—was now *wood-wide* thanks to global collapse. The 5G cellular signal of their childhood was gone, replaced by a fungal web of connectivity. She immersed her students in mycorrhiza, the mushroomic mesh of the forest floor. She pointed at the Twin Oaks—hub trees, cell towers of the underground network. Miin explained how across Beaver Island, electrical signals were transmitted, root tip to root tip, through the telegraphy of trees.

"Always more below than above," Blueberry lectured. Subterranean organisms were usually much older, more massive than any sky-scraping pine.

"The honey mushroom for example, *Armillaria gallica*," she pointed to its golden cap, its prominent gills, "can live for thousands of years! Can weigh *hundreds* of tons! Can connect *one hundred thousand* trees!"

Miin's enthusiasm was contagious. Michael Martin, the class mimic, had mastered her mannerisms and could get them all rolling. But never during class time. No one was more appreciative of this new-school schooling than Michael Martin and his ADHD. The boy's K-5 history—duly documented by the district—of detentions and interventions had disappeared. The rigid rows of desks, the fatal flicker of fluorescence, the windowless classrooms, were gone for good. And like the rest of that industrialized, sanitized, over-prescribed world, they would not be coming back.

Mr. Martin, high in his preferred tree, a sturdy *Pinus strobus*, had never been happier. If the Tree Academy had an honor roll, his name would top the list.

After a lunch of grilled fish and late greens—the class ate only what they procured—it was time for archery. Sentinel Sparrow—scarred from collapse and battling Chosen—led the lesson. The academy took to the trees.

"No sense in practice-shooting on flat ground when you'll be hunting for real from the canopy."

Limb to limb, she drilled them: awkward angles, moving targets, limited shooting lanes, and always, always, always the wind. "Deer can smell like we can see," she lectured, "and human eyes are good."

She pointed at indicators: quaking poplar leaves, the fluff from milkweed, their own exhalations fogging the air. "Updrafts in the morning, as the sun warms the earth. Downdrafts in the evening, as the cooling air condenses. Master the wind, or be mastered by it. A deer's nose won't forgive. And it won't forget you either."

Miin's students attended the ELF archer. Their grade point average for this project would be measured in antler tines: six point, eight point, ten.

"Get busted once by a mama doe, and she'll avoid that tree forever. She'll teach her fawns too. Generations of deer will pattern around you. Keep sitting that tree, and you'll never see shit."

The class tittered at the cuss word, Miin mock-rolling her eyes at the guest instructor.

Their training continued, arrow after arrow, honing their skills. Tree to tree, they tapped the fungal network—3F, 4F, 5F—their signal strength always improving. By late afternoon, they were ready. Their final exam was an ethical harvest.

"We don't fling arrows and we don't wound deer," Ms. Sparrow admonished, in a *read the instructions carefully* kind of tone. "You'll know when it's right. The deer will tell you. A proper harvest is a sacred offering. If you force it, if you're greedy or impatient, or have to pee—you'll miss."

The academy staff—Grace, Miin, and Sparrow—observed their students dispersing in the slanting light of late afternoon. Sparrow had distributed the school supplies. Instead of graphing calculators, each pupil carried a recurve bow. Their No. 2

pencil was a single, razor-sharp arrow. The days were growing short, the lesson would end at dusk—last shooting light—or perhaps later, if someone aced the exam. In that case, supplementary lessons—in gratitude and butchering—would be needed.

Tonight's moon phase was new crescent, a slender beginning to the Hunter's Moon. Teaching staff lounged by the campfire, confident their students' skills would wax apace. Miin smudged herself with woodsmoke. The tree-talker opened her mind to a nearby evergreen—an eastern hemlock, *Tsuga canadensis*—seeking brother bear, north of her, licking his wounds on Indian Point: *Mukwa, you big oaf, I'm fine. How are you?*

Brainstem to tree-stem, cranium to cambium, their consciousness merged: electric entanglement. Green doors—long shuttered—flew open, allowing dreamers to step through. Whether quantum physics or mysticism, superposition or superstition, the term didn't matter; what mattered was faith, and Miinan was a believer.

Sketchings

TEN MILES NORTH, SAME ISLAND, the bright moon lingered above Mukwa's cabin, his man cave on Indian Point. Wabi Muk, the White Bear, closed his eyes, penciling a vision: an evergreen, a campfire, the crescent. Of course Miin, the little show off, would know all the tree's names, traits, and blah blah blah. Thinking of *nishiime*—his foster sis—Muk couldn't help it. He grinned. It had been a while. Damn it felt good.

The tree—some kind of pine?—branched across his sketch pad as he channeled his sister. Somehow—he never asked how—Miin was guiding his hand, pushing his paw. Flipping a page, Mukwa drew an Old Town canoe. Eyes welling, he blinked back tears, for there sat the old crow, Uncle Keith guiding from the stern. Their leathery mentor, an Ojibwe elder, had been a Nam vet, a decorated Marine. Mukwa cleared his throat, replacing Keith's rifle with a paddle instead. He brushed away eraser crumbs, staying true to the scene. There was nowhere on Earth, or *when*, that he'd rather be.

Next he drew Miin, mouse-like, nestled between the thwarts, trailing her hand in living water. The sketch lines began to blur as twilight thickened. The slender moon had gone below. He closed his eyes on darkness, on trauma. Little sister's vision, and his drawing, were both glowing green? From the sketch pad, Blueberry beckoned, and brother bear—careful not to tip!—slowly stepped aboard. A quick self-portrait—good ol' Mukwa, catcher of trout, held up a full stringer from the bow.

Upon the page, clear water burbled beneath their spectral keel. Petoskey stones clacked their fossil fronds in greeting. Bear River or River Styx, Mukwa didn't care. He was there, Miin was there, and Uncle Keith too. Whether from some great beyond, or somewhere quite close, Two-Crow had found them, would always find them. Mukwa felt a flood of love, of well-being—maybe the old man had never been lost. Maybe no one was? His deadbeat parents; Sentinels Tigre and Matador, Squirrel and Diving Duck; Captain Diana on *Nodin*; angry Nighthawk, flown far away.

Mukwa paused his ponderings as Uncle Crow chastised from the stern, "That treefall gonna clear itself?" Muk opened his eyes, not on darkness, but bright purgatory. A red cedar—he'd drawn it pretty well—blocked the canoe's passage upriver. A pileated woodpecker tsk-tsked from the canopy, chiding him to duty. Muk submerged his stringer, returning the trout to cold water, to themselves. Cautious, he set his willow rod aside, picking up the toothy saw instead. He had one bare leg overboard, when little sister—grinning—rocked the canoe hard. Mighty Muck lost his balance, the circus bear cartwheeling overboard with a splash. He spluttered to the surface, fake furious. *Frickin' Miin! Let's see how YOU like it!*

Opening his eyes to twilight, the green vision dimmed upon his sketch pad. His two companions—Blueberry and Crow—raised ghostly hands in farewell. Grinning like Cheshires, they disappeared from the page.

Panzer Pharma

I AM NOT USED TO DEFEAT; it vexes me. Someone, many someones, must pay.

Even as I transcribe this to my tablet—yes, I'm still quite vain—I can't believe it. My innards are all a-twist. A sour taste spoils my several appetites. I feel fear. A very unpleasant sensation, let me assure you. One I've gone to great lengths to insulate myself from. And now it is here, like a brick in my belly.

These are the headlines I had hoped to record:

A Great Victory! A Triumph!

Technology Over Primitivism!

Science Over Superstition!

The Mackinac Bridge Captured!

The Free North Has Been Chained!

Instead, Panzer has lost the battle, if not the whole war. My primary enemies—"Greenies," Dozer called them—should have all been killed, or better yet captured. I've actually got one locked in my lab. Poor Nighthawk must be lonely. How she would love some kin to keep her company!

Instead, I've been bested by tree-people. The Birnam Wood has moved against me. Mewling Malcolm has beaten mighty Macbeth!

I'm sorry, but I've misplaced my patience. My lieutenants have been a letdown, my captains craven. I find myself besieged and toothless. Locked in a tower, my vision grows dim.

Who am I?

I am the Virus.

Oh, how I loathe exposition. "Stinger"—a variant of Covee, the crowned king of chaos—was engineered by my company, Panzer Pharmaceuticals, on a government contract. The Army, USAM-RIID to be precise, stole it from me under orders from POTUS. Then they loosed it, prematurely, on China.

Shit happened. Covee's variant, STING, forged a spike, gaining function. The vaccines didn't work, and the rest, as they say, is history. Or rather the *end* of history, at least as we know it.

I reacted, did the best that I could, eliminated competition, secured the resources necessary to survive: technocrats, paramilitary, refineries, farms, and virucide. The scarcest resource has been labor. No surprise there—Stinger, per design, was a stone cold killer.

Its R naught was a naughty +20.

Its IFR, a fatalistic +99%.

Most fascinating to me are the survivors. Not the "Hidden," like my staff and I, who've yet to be exposed, but the immune, the "shielded," the sub 1% that somehow resist Covee's Sting.

I am captivated by my captive, my banded Hawk in her cage. She claims she's been "green-shielded" by Gaia, a goddess from before. Of course the she-elf is fanatical. I'm a Horatio man; hippy Hamlet got it wrong. Nothing in heaven and earth that science can't uncover. When it comes to virology, it's all zeroes and ones.

"Gaia," she says.

Ha! I've analyzed her bloodwork. The "green-shields" of her goddess are merely enzyme inhibitors. Yes, their source might be trees, specifically the chemical compound terpene, produced by conifers. But there's nothing mystical here, just molecules.

Nothing "wondrous strange," fool Hamlet, it's called chemistry! Terpene—$(C_5H_8)_n$—is hardly a ghost.

I'm feeling better already.

Yes, at Mackinac I was defeated, though I never left my tower. So I'll blame it on my minions, on Dozer and his Chosen. On Sergeant Jones and his skeletal Aghori. On those XCon clowns, self-branded and bitter. Most of my forces were infected, shedding virus, yet proved ineffective. I'd counted on contagion. I'd counted wrong.

The bridge battle occurred on September 24th.

My tablet claims today is the 18th of October.

Bootstrap time, my pity party is over. It's been 19 months since my variant dropped, several years since CoV-2 started streaming. I've binge watched incessantly, on every screen I could scavenge. I can't change the channel; the world is down to one. But I can still create content. So that's what I'll do.

Remember my labor shortage, the difficulty of procuring food for Panzer's fief? Well, I've found the perfect farmers, and the solution is Plain.

And my adversaries, these Greenies, shielded by their trees? Ever heard of Agent Orange? Step aside Macbeth, Birnam Wood must burn.

I've also given thought to the future, to the next generation. I've suctioned Hawk's eggs from her fallopian nest, mined her tunnels for ovarian gold. There are survivors out there, like me, protected by bio-safe palaces prepared for this purpose. Who will start the bidding? No price too high for kids, for grandkids, genetically modified and immune.

My adversaries are many—Old Law, elves, and Indians—but so are my resources.

Dr. Schark is down but not out!

Of course, the board is larger than just Michigan, though that's the turf I am claiming. There are Red Hands out there, with powerful fists. Most of Panzer's military assets now rust on the bottom of Lake Michigan, a full 50 fathoms beneath the broken bridge.

Perhaps an arrangement can be made with the Reds?

My depleted forces need a sea-change: new men, materiel, and mission.

Let me close with the Bard, no stranger to Tempest:

Full fathom five thy father lies;

Of his bones are coral made;

Those are pearls that were his eyes:

Nothing of him that doth fade,

But doth suffer a sea-change

Into something rich and strange.

Sea-nymphs hourly ring his knell:

Ding-dong.

Hark! now I hear them—Ding-dong, bell.

Ranging

THE CRESCENT MOON BRIGHTENED as the October day dimmed. "The Hunter's Moon," Thorn solemnly intoned, and was immediately mocked.

Robert, a SHTF prepper, grinned as he plied his low-light binoculars. "You gonna pray to it? Sacrifice a chicken or something?"

Little brother Freddy objected, "Not Thorn's style. He's a sacrifice-a-virgin kind of guy. Robert, we've been over this."

Thorn and the two brothers—Rangers—were on reconnaissance, scoping out a truck-crowded farmyard in the middle of Michigan. Nineteen months ago, the Shit had indeed Hit The Fan. The two brothers were among the few who'd prepared.

Freddy kept his eyes on their six, watching the approach road through his rifle scope. Nothing coming, nothing going. "Also, dude, the moon is not an *it*, it's a *she*. Thorn, am I right?"

"Speaking of virgins—" Robert was hushed by Thorn's quiet signal. The ex-Natural, once an ELF Sentinel, had seen movement—not people, but crows. Three inkblots rising from the trees. Silhouetted against the twilight, they winged themselves away. Thorn studied the woods. "Someone's in there. Coming our way."

The property they surveilled was occupied by Chosen. There was a fuel tank, a motor pool, and an improvised barracks in the pole barn. The Virals, on colder nights, ran a generator for heat. The three Rangers had counted a co-ed dozen so far. No heavy weapons, but plenty of small arms. Panzer Pharma used infected as overseers for the farms. Everyone's gotta eat. No farmers, no food.

"Just a couple horny ones? Sneaking off for a quickie?"

After two days on stakeout they'd witnessed several such scenes. Thorn claimed the virus amped their sex drive, or maybe it was the hyper-sexual that survived?

Thorn, sharp-eared and bright-eyed, was all business, "Nope. It's a dog and a handler. We'd better scoot."

The brothers packed up quickly. If you had a Greenie in your party, even a fallen one, you'd better frickin' listen.

The trio had been ordered by Sergeant Taylor of the Guard to observe and report. "No firefights," Taylor warned, "do I make myself clear?"

Their response—"Yes, ma'am!"—was too earnest by far. Amanda Taylor had not been amused.

"And don't call me ma'am!"

"Yes, SERGEANT!"

"Now, git!"

They'd gotten.

Taylor, from Detroit, had fought hard for her stripes, climbing the enlisted ladder in Michigan's National Guard. Her unit, the 125th Infantry Regiment, the Griffins—Yield to None—deployed twice to Afghanistan. During collapse, Griffs had stuck together, organizing Old Law resistance. The Guard's HQ was now in St. Ignace, where Colonel Dennis, the CO, flew the US flag over the newly liberated Straits.

The unit, what was left of it, played a role in defending the Free North. A month ago, Panzer pushed hard to capture the Mackinac Bridge. The Griffins galvanized local militias, like Robert and Freddy's Rangers, in defense.

Beaver Island sent Sentinels—Thorn's ELF comrades—along with boats and crews led by fisherman Tom Doyle. Indigenous groups fought off the Viral colonizers. Motorcycle clubs like Warrior and Red Spirit heroically cooperating with Canadians from Manitoulin Island. A pack known as Howlers, wild-eyed and wolfish, had tasted blood as well. The Free North defenders had beaten the odds, severing the big bridge, buying some time.

The butcher's bill had been costly.

Panzer's shock troops were Spreaders—Chosen and XCons with heavy viral loads. The enemy used kamikaze drones, assassinating Captains Doyle and Diana, crippling their ships. There were rumors that the Free North had help from feather and from fur. Ex-ELF, Thorn believed this talk of eagles and wolves, but the prepper brothers were skeptical. The only "eagles" they believed in were the F-15s called in by the colonel, grounded now, like everything else, by the lack of fuel.

Heeding their Greenie's warning about a dog and its handler, the three Rangers, rifles strapped to packs, pedaled away on scrounged bicycles. Robert reviewed their recon: the dozen Chosen, their vehicle types, their armament, their patterns. Later, he'd brief Sergeant Taylor on contingencies for assault. Her detachment of Griffins had been tasked by the CO with disrupting the Panzer farm network. Taylor had been tipped off by some Amish they'd rescued from bondage.

Freddy's thoughts were on food. Their bivouac was five miles away, and he was famished. On recon they'd eaten only MREs—Meals, Rarely Edible. Not much better at camp, but at least the chow would be hot.

Sergeant Taylor had stashed their Humvees and howitzers at Clare's municipal airport, what was left of it. Early on, its aircraft and drums of aviation gasoline had been burned by Greenies, blinding the skies. Weeds and saplings were terraforming its tarmac. The unit had dug themselves in while Taylor waited on intel from returning scouts.

The busload of Amish were still with them. Too dangerous to send them to Colonel Dennis up at St. Ignace, and Taylor's Griffins were too few to convoy them safely. Freddy knew he shouldn't, but he thought of the women. Not much romance in these fallen times. Could one of those bonnets fall for him? Why not? The old world was long gone, the new one just beginning.

Thorn's eyes were on the moon. The crescent curved towards the treeline. October's stars pricked the early dusk. He thought of his old comrades and their ELF Country home. An owl hooted, but not for him. Disturbed, it flew from their mechanical approach, reminding Thorn of just how far he'd fallen.

Gone for Good

AND THE LORD SPOKE TO THE FISH, and it vomited Jonah out upon the dry land. —Jonah 2:10

The crescent moon, more felt than seen, was dragged beneath the surface—keelhauled as Earth rolled away. Shrubs and dune grass shivered in the cooling breeze. Herring gulls protested as the beachcomber plied his trade, circumambulating the tiny island for the hundredth time that day.

The evening dimmed, yet his vision stayed the same. The stars appeared, unwitnessed and unremarked upon. The man would go to ground soon, finding his burrow by feel, covering himself the best he could. Leafy branches for a blanket; cold sand his hearth, his home. Food was scarce; he ate what he could scavenge, battling gulls for every fishy scrap that washed ashore. Water, water, everywhere. The castaway drank his fill.

"Unsalted and Shark-Free" the bumper stickers boasted in the time of before. Oh how he'd hated tourists: the fudgies, FIPs, and trolls. Sunburned and bloated, designer wallets stuffed with white-collar cash. Back then his sneers had come easy, his behavior truly boorish.

He used to bump their boats—the yachties, the weekenders—flipping their cameras the bird. He'd been flagrant with his F-bombs, detonating salty phrases when sure to be overheard. He delighted in the covered ears of children, the angry looks from manicured mothers.

"Throw a cunt-splice in that fuckin' cable!" he'd bellow at a deckhand. "Come on you cock-sucka', we ain't got all day!"

Those days were gone for good. He chewed upon the phrase, one word at a time. *Gone for good. The good has gone? Good that they're gone? Was he gone? Was he good?*

With nightfall, the man's core temperature plunged. He'd be good and gone if he couldn't find his burrow. He navigated the tiny spit of land, keeping the wind in his left eye as he scurried to shelter. He emptied his bladder, crawled into his cave, itchy beneath his leafy blanket.

The stars, unblinking, peered down from the void.

The ancient mariner, blind to their brightness, was soothed by wave-lap and soon aslumber.

Chow Summoned

DATE TIME GROUP: 181500ROCT21

LOCATION: HQ OF 125TH, ST. IGNACE, MI

Dr. Daniel Chow for once had time on his hands. The mandatory quarantine had come and gone. The bridge combatants, all but two, were discharged from Chow's clinic.

Colonel Dennis, consolidating victory, returned the guardsmen to their duties. The SIS bikers were scouting again, short patrols only due to limited fuel. The pack of Howlers—still wild-eyed—planned a long reconnaissance. Chow had heard rumors of a Great Lakes voyage.

The discharged Sentinels—his old ELF comrades—were departing soon for Beaver Island. There they would cross over the Jordan River, rejoining fellow Naturals, returning to trees.

Not one of his patients had contracted the virus or its variant, Stinger. Death Seekers, yellow-painted, had borne the brunt of close fighting. Infected by Virals, these Free North defenders threw themselves from the bridge, dragging the enemy down with them. Chow regretted the loss of their data, so much to learn and so little time.

Only two patients remained in his St. Ignace hospital. He couldn't clear them. They hadn't healed, and Chow had no idea why. A woodstove was installed in their ward, the largest room of the so-called Healing House. Colonel Dennis had to reclaim the Army generator he'd loaned: "I'm sorry Doctor, but we can't spare the fuel."

Chow was summoned by the CO on a blustery October afternoon. Maps lined the walls, along with Panzer's captured banner; the double tower—once terrifying—was now a trophy. The 125th had shifted its HQ from Camp Grayling to the Straits. Its Griffin pennant roared from the flagpole, just below the Stars and Stripes. The off-duty guardsmen were in their barracks; the motor pool was quiet. Each morning, reveille was heard. Every evening, a trumpet tapped them out.

Chow understood about the generator; the CO had other obligations. Dennis studied the doctor studying the maps. Thumbing a pipe full of scrounged tobacco and igniting the herb, the colonel shared what he could.

Yes, the Griffins were divided. His two remaining aircraft, F-15Es, were well-hidden in a hangar at the Soo, 50 miles north of the ever-strategic Straits. Their fuel tanks were empty, the weed-filled runway way too short. The unit's howitzers—105s that pounded the XCon column at Indian River—were marooned south on the mainland with Amanda Taylor, his command sergeant major. Her detachment, along with some Rangers, was operating near Clare, doing what it could to disrupt Panzer's food supply. Sergeant Taylor held some high value prisoners, including a Chosen commander, Liz McGee. Dennis would give a lot to interrogate the notorious Red Liz.

"Colonel, what else is there? Is that really all we've got?"

The two professionals, ever-weary, shared a look.

"Of the 125th? Yes. The empty Eagles, the marooned 105s, a hundred dismounted infantry guarding the Straits. That's my muster."

Chow, post-traumatic, dissociated for a second, triggered by the crash of surf outside the HQ window. *Viral waves spiking against the flimsy breakwater, spuming molecules as they burst.*

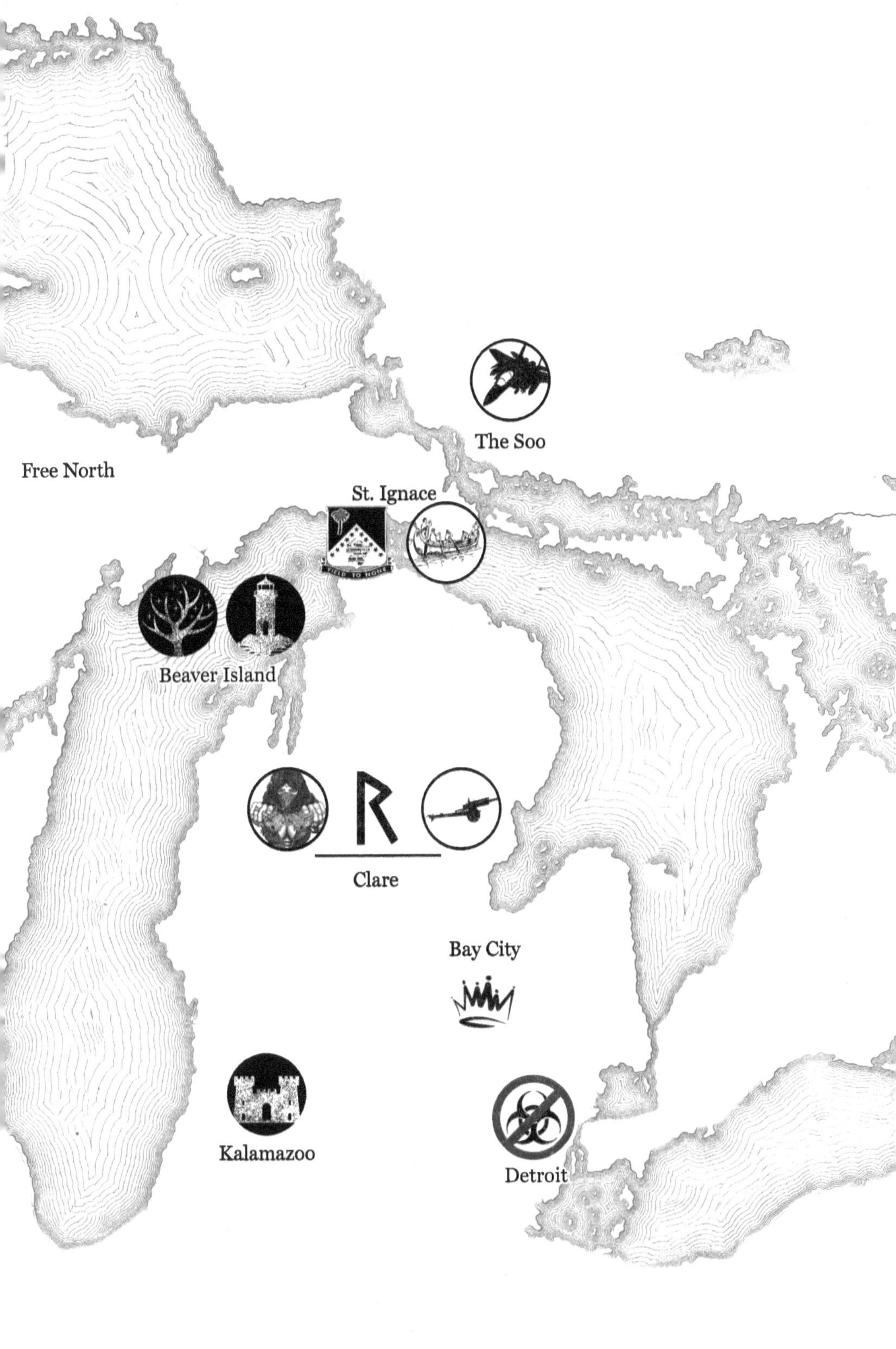

Free North
The Soo
St. Ignace
Beaver Island
Clare
Bay City
Kalamazoo
Detroit

Chow, returning to the present, nodded to the commander. "Please continue."

"Take heart, Doctor. Though our regular forces are few, these are irregular times. You know more than most the prowess of our partisans."

Chow, a one-time Natural, had seen what ELF Sentinels could do.

"If you add our irregulars, then our tally improves. Those bikers for example, the St. Ignace Scouts? Damn fine skirmishers and excellent at long range patrols."

The colonel continued, "And the Howlers? How they mopped up the Wolf Wood? Impressive. More like berserkers than anything I've got. I tell you, Chow, I'm glad they're on our side. I'll do what I can to aid and equip them."

Chow was standing by a map. "What about south of the bridge, Colonel? The rest of Michigan? Panzer's compound in Kalamazoo? Their farms and fuel refineries? There's rumors of slave labor, sex trafficking?"

The Griffin commander nodded. "All I can tell you, Chow, is that again I'm glad we've got allies. Old Law has contacts in the south. There's a prepper network down there, mostly rural, calling themselves Rangers. You may have heard that in the cities Antiva is on the rise. 'Anti-Viral' is what they are—militants dedicated to fighting back against Spreaders. There's a man, code-named Walker, a sort of preacher who holds these groups together. I've got comms with their leadership; they're doing what they can."

Again, the sound of surf. The Great Lake—cooling with the season—gathered its energy, its potential power increasing with every drop in degree.

"Now Doctor, I need your diagnosis on Captain Young. He's my best field officer and that's exactly where he's needed. I know you've discharged his two men—Sergeant Booker, Specialist Cruz—but what about their chief? When will Frank be cleared?"

Chow shook his head. "Colonel, I wish I had better news. I've got two patients left and he's one of them. I'd classify his TBI as severe. When that C-4 detonated, he was thrown from his truck. I'm worried he suffered a DAI."

After two tours in Afghanistan—"IED-istan"—the colonel was familiar: "Diffuse Axonal Injury? Tears, sometimes microscopic, between the spinal cord and the brain. Micro-bleeding? Contusions?"

"Exactly. The captain's prognosis isn't good. I've tried the conventional treatments, but nothing works. The only thing that eases his pain, helps him function, is an herbal tincture brewed on Beaver Island. I'm down to just a few drops. Powerful stuff. Healed the whole ward, or helped anyway. I need to secure a larger supply."

Colonel Dennis weighed the medical man's request. Young was worth it, a fine officer, a real soldier's soldier. "I'll talk to Baptiste. He's assembling a task force—another reconnaissance by canoe. If resupply is possible, we'll make it happen."

"Thank you, Colonel."

"Anything else Doctor? Sorry again about the generator. Will the woodstove suffice?"

"I get it, sir, no gasoline. The stove will be fine. Thank you."

Daniel Chow—widower and grieving father—saw himself out, relieved the colonel hadn't queried him about a certain Bob Campbell. This "Cowboy" character was a Person of Interest to Old Law—a Viral, a war criminal—that Chow had treated, then helped free.

Colonel Dennis stood from his desk, stretching his aching back. He felt the fabric of Panzer's tattered banner, scenting battle smoke in the weave. Duly diligent, Dennis had debriefed all the combatants, reading every After Action Review. The bookish colonel saved these AARs, appendix material for a history— stranger than fiction—he hoped someday to write.

Bald eagles grappling with drones? Gray wolves joining human Howlers in the woods? The wolf pack swimming across to St. Martin at midnight? Skeletons swinging on wires like Spiderman? Sentinel commandos securing Line 5's pump stations? Spears and arrows besting machine guns and Kevlar? Those yellow Death Seekers and their selfless sacrifice on the blasted bridge?

The battle for Mackinac could have gone either way. But they won, and who was he to complain? "Improvise and adapt!" Dennis knew the drill. He summoned his sentry, tasking her to find Baptiste: "He's probably down by the docks, by those big canoes they have?"

"Yes sir!" She saluted, was dismissed, then sprinted towards the harbor.

Dennis needed Captain Young back. And a dozen more like him. He needed Humvees, and armor, and ammunition. He needed more sat-phones, and solar panels, and a portable grid. He needed his retirement, and his wife, and a stack of books by the fire. And fuel. More than anything, he needed fuel. Except possibly intel; damn he felt blind.

The amateur historian filled his pipe with dried herbs and ignited the blend, tamping it down with a tobacco-stained thumb. Pipe smoke clouded his maps, obscuring his vision.

What was the national situation?

What about NORAD in its mountain?

Or Navy ships at sea? Boomer subs in the deep? Aircraft carriers, powered by plutonium? Was the whole planet like this, dark and depeopled, or had pockets survived? Was there a normal somewhere?

He knew that Red Hand units still choked the country's capital. During collapse, the president, contesting an election, had turned D.C.'s 372nd into his own Praetorian Guard. Upon their dear leader's death—some said assassination—furious Red Hands had rampaged.

Surviving service members—those that remained unstung—were forced to choose sides. The Reds were stronger, the far right flocking to their cause: Proud Boys, Three Percenters, Keepers, and Qs. For recruitment purposes, Red Hand discipline had been relaxed, weapons training enhanced. The wannabes finally got what they wanted. Democracy drowned in the bloody Potomac.

Internationally, the scene was murkier.

There'd been nuclear exchanges as the world's wattage dimmed: Israel v. Iran. Pakistan v. India. Whole cities, entire regions, consumed by fire. Those spared by the variant were radiated by atoms or starved to death in the cold, sooty winter that followed. As far as Dennis knew, there wasn't much left. An entire age of the world had ended. Would there ever be another?

The wind increased, an angry gale gusting against the glass. What would the coming winter bring? Thank God the fallout had cleared, sunlight powering a long growing season. The Free North farms produced a crop, hunters and fishers preserving what they could. No Free Norther would starve, not on his watch. But what about the rest? Dennis, by oath and inclination, was steward for all of Michigan, and downstate was a mess.

The big bridge, Mighty Mac, was severed by an airstrike, the colonel's call. His drawbridge was up, a moat of deep water protecting their front and the Free North behind.

But what if the Straits froze? Y1's winter had been frigid, would Y2's be the same?

The historian leafed through chapters in his mind, seeking the proper lesson. Leningrad, 1942, besieged by Hitler's Wehrmacht—starvation, cannibalism, the ice road across Lake Ladoga. Could such a thing happen here? Dennis pictured hundreds of trucks vectoring the virus, infecting the north they'd worked so hard to free.

His pipe had gone cold. The wind beat against the glass. The colonel shivered.

Bon Voyage!

AUTUMN AND BAPTISTE had said their private goodbyes already, in her medicine lodge above the Fairgrounds. The same lodge, a month ago, where she led the sweating women, painting visions in the cave: the Line 5 pipeline, petro pollution, and the oily Straits afire. Now Diana, and many others, were dead. Elena, an ELF warrior, had been badly wounded.

Their next goodbye was public: dockside and more discrete. The six big canoes—*canot du nord*, the Canadians called them—shoved off and began stroking for the harbor mouth. One canoe was crewed by bright-eyed Sentinels wearing clean, gray parkas. Cleared by Dr. Chow from quarantine, the wounded warriors were returning to Beaver Island and their comrades in ELF Country II, the Jordan State Forest.

Shaggy Wolf—a longhaired Lakota, a Howler who'd fought fiercely at the bridge—wielded a paddle as well. His mission was to "rescue" his battle buddy Mukwa from boredom. Shaggy had dreamt that Wabi Muk was depressed, hibernating in a smelly man cave on the north end of Beaver. Shaggy's amber eyes flashed at the thought of reunion.

Baptiste, standing in the stern, raised a thick hand. Autumn mirrored his move, calling out across the water, "Retrieve my boy from the *Amiks*! And *listen* to him!"

The big man waved. After the bridge battle, her son Loon had migrated to Beaver Island with his new friend Brian. Baptiste was tasked with fetching Autumn's boy—along with Samantha's medicine—back to St. Ignace and the Free North.

Autumn called out again, heartsick with farewell. *"Je vous souhaite bonne chance!"* she cried, multilingual to match her Métis man. She was setting sail for Manitoulin Island on the next favorable wind.

Baptiste shouted back, *"Bonne chance à vous aussi!"*

Autumn switched to Michif, the Cree and French of his forefathers: *"Meena kawapimitin!"*

Baptiste, white teeth flashing, responded, *"Pishshapmishko!"* and turned around no more.

The dockside well-wishers dispersed, drying their eyes as they returned to duty. Soon Autumn stood alone. Eyes closed, she peered ahead in time, limning their future journey. Westward first to Beaver Island, a ten-hour paddle, no troubles there. Dr. Chow needed more medicine, Samantha's shack the only supplier. The six canoes would then divide, three scouting the far shore of Lake Michigan: Green Bay, Milwaukee, and Chicago. The fourth canoe Baptiste loaned to the discharged Sentinels, a token of Howler thanks for their bravery at the bridge and pipeline. The elves, battle-scarred, were returning to ELF Country on Beaver Island. After that, they could use the canoe as they saw fit.

Baptiste would fetch her boy Loon, along with Sam's elixir, back to St. Ignace before leading the remaining two canoes on a *voyage périlleux:* Lake Huron, St. Claire, and south to Detroit— terra incognita. Baptiste had asked the colonel, but there was no sat-phone to spare. Like the *explorateurs* of old, the canoes were on their own.

Autumn, cut to the quick by October's sharp air, hugged herself and sent a blessing to her boys. Godspeed and *bon voyage!*

Confessions

MARVIN GAYE, WITNESS NO LONGER, had departed Bob's brain, leaving a grinding headache in his place. Hochstettler's barnyard—chickens, horse piss, blood, and bile—was a total shit show, but the immediate problem was getting to the fields on time. Two years since Campbell had punched a clock, but the familiar late-to-work anxiety surfaced just the same. The Amish bystanders—plainly stunned—weren't helping. Horrified by the violence—one man gutted, two bludgeoned—they stood gaping, frozen in time.

Cowboy supposed they were. Wasn't that their whole thing?

Pushing and prodding, he finally got the Plain folk to move. Little Samuel and neighbor Lapp woke up first, helping to translate Bob's plan: they'd pretend like nothing happened. They'd bank on sloppy XCon leadership, arrive at the fields in Lapp's wagon, jump off and get right to work, just another day in Podunk paradise.

There was a decent chance the three *iks* were acting on their own, rounding up women for their own pervy pleasure. Cowboy sure fucking hoped so. He'd stay behind, hoping his own sorry ass wasn't missed as well. His was a new face anyway, and he sure-as-shit couldn't farm. So Lapp pulled away with the Hochstettler kids, grumpy Gramps, and assorted bonnets in the back. Soon, the clopping hooves faded, and Bob was left with a godawful mess.

First thing first, Cowboy needed answers. What he'd do with the XCons after interrogation—one dead and two still alive—

would be step two. So he took their pistols, tying hands tight with baling twine. The sun kept rising; the icy ground began to thaw, then ooze. When the prisoners came to, Cowboy was there, the blinding sun behind him. Guts's shotgun lay across his knee: judge, jury, and executioner too.

The Chosen boss—recently retired—knew the drill, the ten steps of extracting a confession. He went by the book. Cowboy separated them first. He helped them stand, marching them, one at a time, past ol' Guts, brained in the mud. He rehearsed his next moves: build rapport, establish a baseline, accuse, minimize, spot the surrender position, take their confession, etc.

Turned out that Bob didn't need it: no carrots, no sticks. Once separated, each man began to babble. He just kept quiet, staying out of their way. They snitched on each other, on their XCon overseers, and even on Sharkey, their Big Boss in K-Zoo.

Bob wished he had a notebook, or his old smart phone; hell, even a tape recorder. He tried to keep it all straight. Apparently, an army of Spreaders got their asses kicked at the bridge. Not just by Old Law and their airstrikes, but by Greenies, and Indian biker gangs as well. His panicky prisoners went on about eagles smashing drones and wolves ripping throats. Wouldn't ol' hawk-face be proud? Chalk one up for Mama Earth!

Was it weird that Bob felt proud too? Wherever his head was at, he'd best get back in the game—use it now, or he'd fuckin' lose it for sure.

Victory thwarted, Sharkey was scared: another of their themes. For now, the Big Boss was laying low, hunkering down in Kalamazoo. He'd bet big, pushing all his chips on the table: Raiders, XCons, fuel, vehicles, ammo, even slaves. Sharkey lost 'em all, gaining nothing in return. Poor bastard. Cowboy could sympathize, he'd been scalped by Greenies a few times too.

Each of Bob's *iks* confessed the same: Sharkey's most feared asset—his tattooed Aghori—had abandoned Panzer as well. The fucking Skulls were gone, vanished, poof. Not a single Gorie had been spotted since the bridge. Good riddance. Cowboy had never seen one, not face-to-skull anyway, and hoped he never would. The end times were scary enough without that kind of shit prowling around.

Old Law had grown strong, both Cons agreed. Natty Guard soldiers were hitting farms, freeing slaves, messing up their schemes. Winter was coming and no one had fuel. Something was wrong with the refineries and their delivery schedules, some kind of trouble down in D-Town.

From the older one, Cowboy heard the name "Walker." Bob had him repeat it.

"Walks-on-Water, you mean?" The white man sneered and then spat; he was missing most of his teeth. "That ol' boy gonna find his place quick. At the end of a fucking rope. His Antiva ain't shit neither, you'll see. Our guys have it handled."

Questioned separately about this "Walker," the younger X, squinting up at Cowboy, offered a different take. "Heard he's a preacher, some kinda healer. Lotta rumors about what he can do."

Squints wouldn't say more. Cowboy let it go. Bob thought of the kids, young Sammy, sister Sarah. He asked each *iks*: "What do you do with them? The women you take?" Bob, trying to sound Amish, was tempted to go all "thee" and "thou."

The toothless Con looked like an addict, a meth-mouth: "We fuck 'em!"

Cowboy, picturing little Sarah, almost punched his branded face.

"When we're done we trade 'em, the sexy ones anyway. Food, gas, booze, whatever."

Methhead licked his lips, wanting reward. Cowboy dipped the *iks* some water, helping him slurp from the ladle. Bob left him bound, entering a nearby stall to extract his next confession. Tied tight, the younger man looked like a sex offender, a mugshot you'd see on the local news.

Thinking of the kids and their missing mother made Bob mad. "A month ago, the females you took. Where did you bring them?"

This one, suspicious, squinted as he said, "I thought you Yoders didn't believe in violence? Pussyfists, ain'tcha?"

Bob almost punched him too, but resisted. Squints, snarling a bit, shared what he knew: There'd been a big swap between Viral factions, both gangs preparing for the bridge. A Chosen boss—some gearhead named Dozer—had constructed a couple armored plows. The Cons wanted one, so they filled a bus with Yoders, men and women, and did the deal.

"Yeah, but *where*? Come on, *where* would that slave bus be now?"

"Fucked if I know. I look like a boss to you? This twine hurts! You're in big trouble Yoder, you hear me?"

Squints spat. Bob leaned down and slapped the man hard.

The Viral triumphantly snarled, "Pussyfist! Ha!" and spat again.

Bob stood up slowly. "I'll ask your buddy then. I'm only keeping one of you. The other dies." He let his gaze linger on Hocher's rack of farm tools: pitchforks, meathooks, logging chains.

"Alright, Yoder, alright! Our bus went to Panzerland, to K-Zoo. I know that for a fact. Happy now? Let me fucking loose!"

No, Cowboy wasn't "happy now." He'd been outside Panzer's walls a month ago when hawk-face trussed him up, leaving him on the roadside, shivering in the rain. Hannah Hochstettler and her slave bus had been a mile away, maybe less. *Damn! Sorry kids.*

Bob kept his poker face, dipping the man some water as well. "You've been helpful. Let's get out of here. I just need one more thing."

Cowboy tied Methhead and Squints together. He freed their hands, but bound their ankles so they could walk, but barely, a chain gang of two from days of yore. The two *iks* weren't happy; Bob didn't blame them. He made them carry Guts, and their buddy was stinking. Bob had rigged a stretcher from two shovels and a horse blanket. Still, Mr. Guts was heavy, dead fucking weight.

He thought it through. Bob had enough damn blood on his hands, so he'd utilize the woods to solve his three-body problem. Thinking of trees brought *her* to mind again. The psycho Greenie would be giving thanks to her goddess. Bob Campbell, obviously, would do no such thing.

Cowboy held the shotgun on them as they shuffled towards the forest. In slanting sunlight the maples flared red, yellow birches beckoning. They ducked beneath the boughs and kept going. When Hocher's barn was out of sight and the trees had gathered round, Bob called a halt. He forced the two *iks* to dig a grave.

Cowboy itched. The damn woods were watching. He felt accusatory eyes; every trunk had a frowning face, and he feared their silent judgment. The Greenie chick would know what to do, how to appease these mossy members of the jury. Bob, an ex-executioner, had no fucking clue.

When Guts and his reek had been planted and the hungry earth tamped down, Cowboy made his closing remarks. "Squints, you're right, I *am* a pussyfist, at least for now. So I'm not gonna kill you."

The two *iks* grinned, started looking around.

"You've both been most helpful. Now tie Methhead here to this tree."

The younger man complied. Bob covered them both while Squints got busy with the baling twine. By the time he was done, Meth was cocooned to his pine.

Bob stepped closer to inspect the Con's work, then clubbed Squints hard with the butt of the scattergun. The man dropped. Cowboy dragged him to a tree, spiderwebbing his prey.

"X marks the spot. Right between the eyes, motherfucker."

On the Fringe

AFTER THE BRIDGE BATTLE the skeletons had scattered, fleeing south. South was safer, the winter shorter. There were more farms and fewer wolves. Still, the pickings weren't easy, not in a land so thoroughly plucked. Starvation was real; it stalked them. Emaciated from a lack of calories, cut off—cold turkey—from Sharkey's juice, the shrunken Skulls foraged in pairs or groups of three.

Having received SERE training during their military service, the one-time special operators knew how to survive. But the details weren't pretty, and none of them were proud. They'd lost leadership: Aghori Jones rammed in battle, his tugboat exploding, freeing his soul for rebirth; Vishkanya Mackenzie, the presidential assassin, knifed by a Greenie. She'd bled out along the coast road, the burning bridge a flaming pyre behind her.

Disowned by Panzer, deserting Gories grew gaunt, diluting their doses. The virucide wouldn't last. They weakened with the dosage, powers ebbing ... ebbing ... gone. Supernatural no longer, they morphed, becoming creatures of the fringe.

With the death of Guru Jones, they suffered spiritual dilution as well. On the run and run-down, few practiced *sadhana*, sacrificed to Shiva, or reenacted the rituals they once knew by rote. Some still had weapons, but their magazines were light. They wasted ammunition going after deer. Trained to hunt humans, Michigan's white-tails eluded them. Foulness flowed from the tattooed terrors, an abhorrence that put wild things on edge.

Diluted, was the virucide even working? Were they still shielded from Covee's Sting? Desperate, a squad of three was about to find out. For several days, from the treeline, they staked out the hex-painted barn, observing two children, an old man, and the Viral. Opportunistic, they scavenged what they could, out-pecking the hens, rooting through muck at midnight. Their caloric clocks had run down, inky skins sagging from brittle bones. All three were ravenous, and they'd been watching: one body had been buried, two live ones, unconscious and cocooned. Time to practice what Babu Jones used to preach: *shava sadhana*, corpse meditation.

Everything is one, duality a dream.

The Viral with the Amish hat had left his tools behind.

The three Gories licked their lips and started shoveling.

After Action Review

DATE TIME GROUP: 182330ROCT21

LOCATION: CLARE AIRPORT, FAA LID: 48D

Sergeant Taylor proofread the AAR she just finished writing. After debriefing the Rangers, she'd sent them to chow and gotten to work. Her CO—Colonel Dennis, headquartered at Ignace—would probably never see it, but in the Army old habits die hard.

It was almost midnight. The thin moon, a sharp scythe, had set behind Clare's weedy airfield. Amanda Taylor was tired.

Exercise Title: Intelligence Report

Event: Recon of Chosen motor pool and barracks

Date/Time: 16–18 October, Y2, 19 months since collapse

Location of Observation:
Farm at intersection of Tobacco Dr. and E. Beaverton Rd.
43°52'23.1"N 84°38'47.2"W

Observation:
(Taylor detailed the Ranger surveillance)

Conclusions:
1. Chosen activity in this sector appears limited due to fuel and manpower scarcities.

2. Lax discipline indicates Panzer's inability to effectively command and control its units.

3. Since the bridge defeat, enemy strength has weakened significantly.

4. Chosen units operating near Clare could be defeated and their slave labor liberated.

5. With winter approaching, Panzer's food network could be dealt a critical blow.

Taylor filed the card with the other AARs, unsent. She switched off her red lamp, stepped out of her tent, and beheld the starry sky. Her breath fogged in the cold air as she mouthed a silent psalm.

When I consider thy heavens, the work of thy fingers, the moon and the stars …

Her thoughts went to Hannah, the Amish woman, her Bible-study friend. Taylor ordered her reluctant boots towards the hangar housing the civilians. Tonight she'd authorize a burn barrel; it was below freezing already.

The sergeant checked her watch. He'd be broadcasting soon. Amanda and her unit rarely missed one of Walker's transmissions.

Freedom Riders

OLD LAW WAS BEDDED DOWN FOR THE NIGHT: sentries in their places, OPs manned, light-discipline maintained. Sergeant Taylor inspected their bivouac as she made her weary way towards the Amish hangar. Her prisoners—two Virals, a male and female—had been fed and were secure in their shipping container. The MP on guard duty was wearing MOPP per protocol, and seemed alert. Taylor's howitzers were hitched to Humvees; every vehicle had been fueled. A single generator purred, powering the unit's minimal electronics.

All was well with her Griffins, the ragged remnants of Michigan's 125th Infantry Regiment. Icy stars shivered in the unpolluted sky. Freddy, a Ranger, approached at a run: "Ma'am!" Amanda grimaced as the Ranger skidded to a halt. "I mean, *Sergeant*. Signals just picked up a mobile broadcast, something's headed our way!"

Twenty minutes later and their ambush was ready. The signal was intermittent, moving northwest from Saginaw along US-10. Spike belts were laid across the roadway, howitzers pointing towards the approaching contact. Every Griffin, every Ranger, shouldered their rifles along the guardrail. Headlights were blacked out, but would blaze upon the sergeant's command.

Taylor remained stern. "No lights. No radios. No firing unless fired upon! Griffins, do I make myself clear?"

"YES, SERGEANT!" acknowledged two dozen voices. Skirmishers wore MOPP gear against infection. Support teams had theirs slung, but ready.

Sagittarius—the ancient missileer—had set. Orion climbed in the east, seeking higher ground to view the coming fray.

Ranger Thorn, an ELF veteran, felt it first: a dieseled disturbance, the combustion of fossil fuels. Plant life for locomotion, humanity's industrial exchange. No bright beams probed the pavement, the approaching bogies driving dark. The Griffins extended electronic feelers: night vision, infrared, radio scans. The technicians soon found the right frequencies, the invaders slowly taking form.

Through green-tinted NVGs, they saw three vehicles motor up the roadway.

FLIR detected them as heat signatures, three orange plumes rising from their carbon exhaust.

The signals specialist heard a voice in the void: digitally disguised, it spoke through her scanner. The SP4 nodded to Taylor. The Griffins were ready.

Just before the spike belt came a screeching of tires. Ambushing Humvees quickly high-beamed their prey. A cloud of dust delayed Taylor's decision.

"Hold!"

Sudden spotlights blazed from their quarry, Griffins squinting against the photonic spray. "Hold!

Doors were slammed as invaders deployed. A racking of rounds as both sides leveled weapons.

"Hold!"

Rapid breathing—Griffs and bogies both—as their adrenaline dumped. The dust slowly settled. Eyes and instruments opened wide. Every trigger finger itched as targets resolved.

"Hold!"

They began to see each other, their mutual reality. Shadows shrank as those that cast them came clear.

"Hold!"

There were no Virals here, both sides agreed: no Chosen, no Cons. What there was, was discipline. "Weapons down!" was heard from both sides. "Weapons safe!" A messy slaughter was averted. Targets were unsighted. Fingers fled from triggers. The Reaper, who'd paused, moved on. If this field wasn't quite ripe for harvest, there were plenty more that were.

"Dim those beams!" Sergeant Taylor barked. The Griffin drivers doused their brights. Spotlights from the convoy were lowered as well. Still plenty to see by, but the mad glare was gone.

"Freddy, set up a perimeter! Robert, on me!"

"Yes, SERGEANT!" Both Rangers hopped to.

The newcomers along the roadway were moving too. Head to toe, they were clad in black, N95 masks obscuring their faces. The unknown militia wore black berets and had safetied their weapons. It was a three vehicle column: two gun trucks, painted black, and a vintage bus with armor plating. The Greyhound logo was painted over. Prowling instead was a black panther, icon from the '60s.

The Panther bus bristled with aerials and antennae, crouching on bulletproof tires, ready to pounce. It mounted two machine guns, covering its flanks. With a hiss, the pneumatic door opened. A black-clad sentry stepped out, gesturing Taylor to approach.

The Griff sergeant checked with Signals. The SPC4, wearing headphones, looked up from her radio, confirming: the broadcast continued, its point of origin this bus.

Taylor and Robert cautiously approached. Above the door, a name had been stenciled—*Pony*—and an image of a pale horse, prancing. The sentry waved Taylor aboard, but stopped Robert with a raised hand. "Your pistol stays here."

The Ranger, reluctant, looked at the bouncer, implying a question about Taylor's holstered Glock. The sentry answered his look, "He knows *her*."

Taylor, from the stairs, turned and gave a look. Robert complied, unbuckling his gun-belt. Griffin first and Ranger following, Old Law climbed aboard.

The interior of the *Pony* was dimly lit and fragrant with tobacco. A burly man with a black beret sat behind the wheel. Familiar, he gave a nod to Taylor. "Miss Amanda."

Happy to see him, she nodded back. "Mr. Butters."

Most of the seats were empty. They walked down the aisle, past the two machine gunners, grim at their ports. Robert heard a deep voice speaking from the back of the bus. A man sat in the shadows holding a microphone. The device was wired to a bank of blinking radios.

Taylor paused, waiting for the broadcast to finish. Robert studied the figure, listening to his speech. Dude sounded like a preacher. Suddenly the cadence clicked: "Walker?"

Robert couldn't believe it. This man—tall, weather-beaten, hair flecked with gray—matched not at all the image he'd imagined.

The orator concluded: "And so, with our Anti-Viral allies, we've retaken the refineries. The Spreaders are on the run. They won't be going far without the Detroit diesel we've reclaimed as our own. That diesel—if our brothers and sisters can keep it flowing—will fuel our freedom as we ride through the land, preaching love and scouring away the hate. Goodnight and God bless."

Walker

WHAT FOLLOWED NEXT, before the transmission ended, was a string of code words meant for partisans and militias across Michigan. Robert, as a Ranger leader, had listened intently to such messages a hundred times before. But always, Walker's voice had been filtered, digitally disguised. To hear the angry, educated tone undistorted and in person was a moving experience. Robert's mind adjusted to this richer reality.

A tech assistant powered down the devices, removed her headphones and departed. Walker looked up at his guests. Worry lines grooved his intelligent face.

"Sergeant Taylor." He studied her uniform, nodding at her stripes.

"Reverend."

To Robert, the call and response that followed sounded sacrosanct, their spare dialogue freighted with meaning.

Walker began with a teacher's tone: "By what right do you stop this bus?"

Taylor—his star student—replied quickly, "I swore an oath, to uphold the law from before."

"And what law is that?"

"To provide for the common defense. To promote the general welfare."

"And what oath did you swear?"

"To support and defend the Constitution against all enemies, foreign and domestic."

Walker nodded, satisfied so far.

Taylor's turn, the sergeant interrogated.

"By what right do you travel these roads? Breaking the state's curfew?"

"By the same old law, the first amendment thereof."

"Which clauses of this amendment?"

The Reverend smiled, care lines smoothed by his former congregant. "No law shall be made prohibiting the exercise of religion or abridging our freedom to speak."

Taylor smiled too, setting aside for a moment the weight of command.

"Reverend, this is Robert, recently from the bridge." She moved aside so they could see one another.

"Robert? The Ranger leader, if I'm not mistaken?"

"Yes sir," Robert affirmed, nodding. "And it's good to finally meet you. Is it true? What you just said about Detroit's refineries?"

Walker's eyes glinted. "Yes. The Marathon plant and Rouge River, too."

"Panzer's taking a pounding then?"

"It appears that way, thanks in no small part to your bravery at the bridge."

"That wasn't us. We were with Colonel Dennis at Indian River. We hit the Cons there."

Walker remembered. "That's right. Well, your ambush may have turned the tide."

"Thank you, sir."

Robert stepped aside so the techie could pass through. She handed her boss a touchscreen tablet. The digital device was covered in stickers: the sun, the moon, and various quotes.

"Finally got this fixed up for you, Reverend. Should boost our broadcast. Strengthening our signal will fan the flames, especially in the west."

Walker took the tablet and nodded. He turned it in his hands, reading aloud the inscription on the back:

People fail to get along because they fear each other; they fear each other because they don't know each other; they don't know each other because they have not communicated with each other.

He looked up at his guests inquiringly.

Taylor spoke right up. Robert hadn't a clue.

"That's King's speech. Cornell College, 1962."

Walker, gray-templed, smiled again. "It's good to see you, Ms. Taylor. It's really been too long this time."

"Sir, I couldn't agree more."

Robert took his leave, both to check on the Rangers and to let the old friends catch up. Looking back, he saw Walker produce a pipe, long-stemmed and curiously carved, describing it to Taylor as a gift from a Potowatami tribe. Mr. Butters at the wheel nodded him out. The sentry at the stairs handed back his holster. Robert exited the bus, his worldview wider than before.

From shore to shore, across the darkened state, every listener felt the same. Walker's message, relayed antenna-to-antenna, came through clear, though his voice was distorted:

And so, with our Anti-Viral allies ... Colonel Dennis in St. Ignace annotated his map as the broadcast continued, replacing Panzer towers with the biohazard icon of Antiva.

Maggie Doyle and Nick Hannigan, both grieving, shared the midwatch in the Beaver Island Lighthouse. *We've retaken the refineries ...* They heard the voice and thought of the fleet's empty fuel tanks, and their father figures killed beneath the bridge.

The Spreaders are on the run ... Drunken hoots from a pole barn near Clare. The red-eyed Chosen broke bottles, defying this claim of defeat. Their radioman wondered about Walks-on-Water and the rumors. He cleaned his glasses—one lens was cracked—as if to hear the man better.

They won't be going far without the Detroit diesel we've reclaimed as our own ... "Detroit diesel? MY diesel, you mean!" fumed a doctor, a shark among minnows, from the fishbowl of his Kalamazoo compound.

That diesel—if our brothers and sisters can keep it flowing—will fuel our freedom as we ride through the land ... Loudspeakers squelched at the Rouge River transfer facility. Antiva fighters cheered beneath the floodlights as they filled container trucks with fuel.

Preaching love and scouring away the hate ... The lieutenant general—three stars on his US Army uniform—sneered at the sentiment. A metallic halo, a ring of rare metal, crowned his head. The general's Red Hands had intercepted the transmission, recorded it, and played it now for their militia leaders: Proud Boys, Three Percenters, Oathkeepers and Qs. *... Goodnight and God bless. Walker, out.*

"Well, good riddance and God damn you too!" The white men all laughed.

Island of Life by Norman Knott

Tree Academy: Flight School

THE OCTOBER DAY DAWNED COLD AND CLEAR just as Brian and Loon had predicted. The wind, a three-day blow, had muscled up overnight, knocking whitecaps off the waves. CAVU, the pilots used to call it: Ceiling and Visibility Unlimited. In other words, a perfect day for flying.

Permission slips had been sent home, allowing the acolytes to spend the night "sleeping" in the trees. Brian spoke to Miin, explaining his unusual prerequisite: "To merge with a bird, you must become bird-like."

The teachers eyed their bleary students as the disheveled dozen sipped their sunrise tea. "They certainly appear tossed and turned," Miin observed sarcastically.

"Even better," Brian countered. "Exhaustion can open many doors."

Michael Martin almost fell into the cookfire, nodding off as the sky blushed pink.

"Yes, but Brian, they still need to walk through them."

Autumn's boy Loon, a temporary island guest, answered for his fellow flier, "Walking, Ms. Miin, is not on their syllabus today."

Brian was grinning, Blueberry the same. The elder Grace doused her fire as eavesdropping pines showered the instructors with yellow-needled applause.

Back in June on the mainland, Miin had named him Red Beard. Brian served as shaman for the Naturals in their first

ELF Country home. A psychonaut, he'd spent his 20s exploring reality's edge. Isolating with friends, he weathered collapse in a lakeside cabin, deep-sixing his buddies when Covee started stinging. He'd been immune, they hadn't. Something prepared him for this, for the end of everything and the beginning of what came next.

Wearing woolen coats, Brian and Loon took the class on a walking tour, introducing them to the winged inhabitants of forest and shore. Encountering avians, the students spread out, cultivating headspace for a merge. There were no grades for this project, no rubrics or red ink.

"Merging with a bird brain is not for everyone, though everyone gets a chance."

Afterwards, sitting in a circle, they discussed their feathered friends. Some preferred the island's ground birds: grouse and turkey. It was shore birds for others: gulls, plovers, and terns. One young Natural had been hypnotized by a heron. Brian, approving, allowed the lad to linger by the pond, circling back later to debrief.

Their connections were as varied as their ages, their backgrounds; every student had felt something. Brian praised their success.

"Yes, but we want to see you do it." Josie Greene spoke for the class.

Brian countered, "Of course you do, and I get it, but it's not just some trick."

"We know it's not. But how can we do something we've never seen done?"

Brian smiled at this. Josephine had a point. Plus, he was feeling it. The wind, the sky, the season were pulling him aloft.

"Come with me then." And away they all went.

Raptors have sentry trees just as humans have their towers. Brian led them to such a tree. The class kept their distance, no crowding. He had them expound upon its virtues. Why here? Why this particular pine? What avian advantage did this particular perch provide?

The students had answers. Brian nodded along: wind direction for takeoff, nutrients from the creek, the big lake nearby and its feast of fishes.

Right on cue, an enormous osprey landed, regarding their group with her golden eye. Of course she knew Brian, and pulled hard upon him. He resisted, talking them through the process. The students were rapt, observing the raptor.

When they were ready, when Brian was ready, only then did he succumb. He closed his eyes upon his own body, opening them in hers. She/he faced the wind, and spreading their wings they were borne aloft. Open-mouthed, the students were astonished at their teacher's ascent.

A quick flight only.

Back on the ground, they debriefed. Brian, talking them through it, could only get so close. The students, good listeners, understood the unsaid. There was something new here, and at the same time very old. They connected it to Miin and the fungal network of the forest. It wasn't a matter of control, or forcing, or bossing things around. It felt more like permission. An access to perception that was always there, always available. All that was needed was a magic word. As ever, this magical word was please.

Time for lunch, or rather, its acquisition. No more standing in lines, no trays of cubed food or cardboard tasting milk. The students were thoughtful as they foraged for their midday meal. A small fire was kindled and an iron skillet set to heat. Fishing lines were uncoiled, baited with grubs pinched from a log. A few trout were caught and seared. A squirrel, fat on acorns, was sling-shot from a branch, then skillfully skinned, portioned, and seasoned with salt. Late berries were found, and some fungal fruits as well. The students were mostly silent; they had much to digest.

The afternoon was set aside for practice. More staff were called in as the students scattered. Grace and Miin moved around. Sparrow, the ELF Sentinel, flitted through the woods with her bow. Brian found Pastor George afield with his flock. The chaperones observed, keeping their distance.

Of all the adult eyes, only one pair was hostile.

Bill Ferny, from concealment, ogled Josie Greene through binoculars. An islander, a boat captain, Bill had blood on his hands—Keith Two-Crow's—that wouldn't wash clean. Ferny was foul tempered, with few friends. He led the resistance against refugees, rallying his racist clan to the cause. The rest of the island wasn't with him, but he was used to it. Shawn Greene, Josie's father, once called Ferny "a thorny branch from a crooked family tree."

Ferny, ever doubtful, had been surveilling the ELF since summer. He had seen some strange things. Hidden in a ground blind, Ferny peered at Josephine through his binoculars. He'd watched her before. The girl was a climber. Ferny knew the trees she preferred.

The pine princess was high in a crown. Josie stood on a branch, one hand on the bole. A pileated woodpecker landed nearby, cocking its head at the girl. Ferny zoomed in on her face, magnifying her smile. She closed her eyes. Bill's skin prickled; something strange was stirring.

The black and red bird took flight, flitting from one pine to the next. Josie, eyes closed, removed her hand from the tree, tight roping further along the branch. Ferny held his breath, then gasped. Josie jumped. The scene blurred. He couldn't see shit. She didn't fall? She flew?

Birdlike, Josie alighted on a nearby branch with a smile, opening her eyes as the woodpecker piped its praise. Ferny, distrusting the lenses, gazed with naked eyes instead. No fucking way. The distance between trees was impossible. Twenty feet? Thirty? And a hundred, maybe more, above the damn ground? What new devilry was this? Whose mumbo jumbo hypnotized this witch?

Bill's black heart was pounding. He kept himself concealed. Finally, the proof that he needed. Fuckin' Nats were up to no good, and no good would come of it. He'd said it before and he'd say it again, this time at council. Bill would be the judge. He'd burn a hot fire and hang 'em all high.

The Mighty Muck

THE LAST BEAR ON BEAVER ISLAND, that's how he felt. A familiar feeling, an itchy skin he'd worn most his life. Sure, there'd been moments of community, of fellowship: overnights in Gran's shack, training with the elves, free drinks and fist bumps from wide-eyed patrons at the Shamrock. But Muck mostly felt alone. Two-Crow had flown, Nighthawk too, both departing without goodbyes. The friends he'd made were either dead—Miguel, Tomas, Duck, Bull—or far away—Thorn, Shaggy, and Big Ben.

Since the bridge battle he lived alone in a leaky cabin on the north end of the island, one more disgruntled resident on Indian Point. Without electricity, without flat screens or stereos, man caves—far and wide—had lost their allure. Muck, digging a new pit for his outhouse, wrinkled his nose. He was sick of his own shit for sure.

He chopped wood; winter was coming. He kept his elders stocked, white and Native both. They were all beavers now—*Amiks*, his gran would say—and beavers stick together. His drafty cabin was on the edge of habitation. Attempting to tire himself, to surrender to sleep, he took long walks, usually at dusk. Farmers would mistake his silhouette on the edge of a treeline, swearing it was a bear.

But no, Muck knew better. He was utterly alone. If properly exhausted, he could sometimes sketch at twilight, just as the star kernels started popping—ones and twos at first, then suddenly in bright bunches. Open to art and thus to himself, visions would find him, a mixed blessing. It could be a fishing idyll with Uncle Keith, or canoeing with Miin; even amber-eyed Shaggy might appear. But terror stalked his subconscious. Hawk in a cage, trapped in a tower. Keith's waterlogged corpse and its fatal embrace. Nope, he couldn't sleep for shit, not since Hawk fled. "That Natty bitch," islanders called his old flame. Muck didn't blame them, she'd burned down half the harbor when she'd fled.

Sam's shack was always open, and he'd roam there from time to time. But the medicine woman was busy. With so many hurts that needing mending, Muck's own wounds, which he hid, were mostly ignored. If he visited, ol' *nookomis*—with Miin busy teaching—would usually set him to chores. Calluses hardened on his paws, but not his heart. It hurt to be ignored, and he'd return to his cave feeling huffy.

Muck was no instructor, though Blueberry tried. Too often truant, too often suspended, he wasn't cut out for her academy. "But you have so much you could *teach* them." Yeah right. He compared himself to Miin's other staff: bookworm Brian and his birds, Sparrow's archery, Grace's potions. Mukwa's talents lay elsewhere. The berserker knew blood, knew battle, and had a wild *fuck it* kind of bravery that would just get these kids killed. No thanks.

He fueled his body, barely, on fish hauled from the lake by sail powered sloops. He snared rabbits and ran a trotline with a crusty old elder. Craving sugar, the sweet tooth filched every wild apple or honey hive he could eat.

So he bided his time, but waiting for what? Was Shaggy, wolf-like, stalking his way? Mukwa, channeling his foster sis, stretched out green feelers. His Howler buddy had promised to visit before winter. Mukwa watched the sun go down from Indian Point. Less and less daylight each day. He sniffed the air; it smelled of frost. Something good was coming. His friend?

Feeling a rare tranquility, the white bear lit a Samantha smudge, the scent of sage tickling his snout. He felt love, felt the old familial ties, and something else. Something warm? Something bright?

For a moment, Mukwa remembered. It felt like hope.

Samantha's Mirror

EACH SPIRIT, EACH QUANTUM—Sam, Mukwa, and Miin's—was tangled tight to the others. All things all at once, and at the same time, never. Whether superposition or supernatural, the effects were the same. Samantha's kin walked in the dreams—and realities—of each other.

It wasn't Miin's plant power uniting them this time; Instructor Blueberry was too busy. Instead, Samantha stirred the pot, empowering the black cauldron atop her woodstove. Miin's academy kids kept Sam's kindling box full. The Anishinaabe elder—eldest actually—snapped maple fingers to feed her catalytic fire.

Water steamed—Earth's clear blood—releasing ghosts of ancient glaciers. Samantha breathed upon its surface as twilight dimmed her garden. The night air smelled of frost. The medicine woman, *mashkikiiwininiikwe*, cast her thoughts far ahead, pulling others with her theoretical string. Sam's hair shimmered in the reflection, turning to silver garlands as her mirror showed a garden in bloom. Samantha conjured a glimpse of Mukwa's future home—a bright day, in some possible midsummer.

A woman's voice, sharply educated, was scolding her child. A cub of a girl with a pelt of black hair, hid a juicy grin behind a tomato. Mukwa—older, grayer—turned a corner, huffing into view. "Hawk—Daniela—let her be, it's my fault."

The cub's mother wheeled mid-flight, diving towards this larger prey. Mukwa put his hands up as Nighthawk came in range, eyes flashing.

"Sentinel, stand fast!" barked an old man's raspy voice, mock serious.

From her bog shack, Samantha, the weaver of this dream, was stunned. The healer felt her heart skip, then swell. Mukwa, from his man cave on Indian Point, felt the same. As always, he was tightly tied to his gran. The moment slowed. Everyone involved felt it, saw it: the sepia tone of this interval—all intervals—of time.

Whitehaired in this particular future, Uncle Keith—"Grandpa Crow" to the cub—perched on a lawn chair shaded in tree shadow. Two-Crow spoke: "Miggy, bring that *gichi-ogin* over here."

The girl cub, Miguela—sharp-faced and strong of limb—obeyed with her roly-poly gait. She presented her prize—the filched fruit—to *omishoomisan*, her craggy-faced grandfather.

Keith smiled. "May I?" Two-Crow queried her without words, the way he used to do with Miin when Blueberry was Miggy's age.

Miguela mock bowed to her elder, silently projecting their shared speech: "*Enya,* yes. *Miigwech gayegiin,* honored warrior."

The conspirators shared a wink, trading bites as Mom and Dad hid secret smiles. Keith's mountain man beard was soon stained with juice. Miggy's giggle set them all to grinning.

But all things fade, especially visions. Samantha's dreamweave unraveled, one bright thread at a time: little Miggy first, then her hawkish mother. Keith ascended from his lawn chair. A stirring of crows, and the old man had flown.

Mukwa blinked and his bright garden was gone. He ached with each loss: Nighthawk, Uncle Keith, and—most unbearable—their little cub, Miggy?

In her shack, Samantha too ceased stirring. Eyes welling, her mirror clouded over. As eldest, she'd known Keith, not as a war hero, but as a kid—just a lanky Indian boy who'd rather be fishing.

Entombed in the catacombs of Panzer's Kalamazoo compound, the captive ELF felt the loss as well. Nighthawk, drugged and befuddled, couldn't trace the source. Daniela only knew that she'd lost something precious.

Even Keith Two-Crow—out of time, out of place—knew something was wrong. His two charges—big Mukwa and little Miin—were in danger again. Keith sorted through his options like a tackle box from beyond. With just the right lure, using the proper line-of-time, he might catch Miinan for a moment, or snag ol' Muck for a quick heart-to-heart.

Concerning Miguela and her feelings—wherever or whenever the unborn might be—less was known, even by Samantha. For those who scry upon the water—even the wisest—cannot see all ends, nor anticipate what may, or may not, come to pass.

Panzer's Pimp

DOWN BUT NOT OUT, describes my position.

Could recent events, especially at the bridge, have gone better?

Yes. Yes they could have, but they could have gone worse. After all, I've still got my health! And there's eight billion souls that can't say the same. Are these souls on my conscience? Not really. I sleep pretty well. If it hadn't been my virus, it would have been the next. The world, let's agree, had over-ripened. Covee gave it a pinch and the pustule popped.

I'm rich in some ways and quite poor in others. I have crypto coins aplenty and a whole vault of cash. Sadly, such currency is no longer au courant. The dollar—RIP—is dead, both the digitized version and the dyed. It's all about assets now, bartering one thing for another. Ben Franklin, so long the world's middle-man, has been stacked away, out of print, and obsolete.

The economic world, like all the rest, has collapsed. Gone are the algorithms, the derivatives, blockchains and bitcoins. It's all about stuff now: gasoline and guards, farms and farmers. Some things never go out of style. What was hip for the city states of old Mesopotamia is trending again in this modern mess I've made for ya!

Fuel and food and protection, I need all three building blocks. But ask yourself, as I have, why do we build? Why gather wealth? What purpose a palace? What exactly are we protecting?

The answer takes us to an asset that I currently have in plenty. Forgive my crudeness, but "assets," historically, have often been asses: females that is, in their reproductive prime.

Wordplay aside, I'm talking about sex. Simply put, we build palaces to fuck in. Do you doubt me? Open a textbook, pull back the curtain. On every page is a harem, each kingly court a breeding ground. We accumulate wealth to pass it to our children, little copies of us. We pay it forward, not to the future, but to ourselves, our genetic attempt at immortality.

The trick—pun intended!—with bartering is to leverage one thing to get another. I've made a video proffering my wares: a thumb drive file filled with my finest. Copies have been made and hand delivered to my clients.

"Bunkered behind their billions" is a term I've dictated. "Palatial protection" is equally true. I'm offering these Haves what they Have-not, and I'm hoping for a trade: Amish flesh for their refinery fuel. Girls! Girls! Girls! for more of their guards. And finally, my prize, my Hawk, to be auctioned off to the highest, bloated bidder!

I apologize, but I must leave you here. My assistant, Mr. Wermer, informs me that it's time to dress for dinner. My tuxedo awaits. The promo videos have been delivered, and hopefully drooled over. My clients might call with offers tonight!

I have a date for this special occasion. Nighthawk has been scrubbed, brushed, and decently drugged. I see on my screen that she waits for me at the table. Her handler—Ms. Frau—has dressed her elegantly in black. I don't begrudge the pearls. I must admit, Hawk is stunning. And don't worry, I won't be sampling the goods. My own libido ebbs low.

My intention is to advertise, to show Ms. Hawk to her suitors in the finest possible light. I expect the buyers to call via satellite, but some might drop by. Either way, she'll be ready.

If tonight goes well, Panzer will be back: flush with fuel, weapons, and new warriors to wield them. I've learned lessons from the bridge debacle. No more will I rely on red-eyed Spreaders. Apparently my adversaries now have shields, voiding Panzer's viral advantage. Nor will I need to needle my Aghori. The few surviving skeletons have deserted, en masse. Goodbye and good riddance! No longer so special, these skull faced operators failed to deliver. They will dwindle with their doses and eventually blow away. Guru Jones would approve, dust to dust and all that.

I check myself in my mirror: not bad, not bad. I must be a gentleman tonight, dress for success, mannered and gracious. Clients will be calling, snobs every one. Imperative that I beat them at their game, present myself as the prince of Panzer and not just its pimp.

The Lady in Black

MOON ATTUNED, Sentinel Nighthawk sensed the new crescent. She'd been captured outside Panzer's walls, in the rain, when the Harvest Moon was still young. A cycle later and the next moon—the Hunter's—sank its white fang in the west.

Waking or sleeping, her vision was clouded. Hawk—Daniela, to herself—was haunted by dreams: of Mukwa, of their unborn child. Even that old Nam vet, Keith, would sometimes visit on black wings. Twenty-eight scratches tallied her skin. The black dress was a long one, hiding her etchings. Plenty of flesh was on display, slit high up the thigh, scooped low in the chest. She'd been dressed, she'd been drugged. The only surprise were the pearls.

"He wants you looking glamorous," the frosty Frau explained while shaving Hawk's legs, already strapped tightly in stirrups. Hawk had learned not to ask. Sharkey's people—like their boss—loved to talk. The Sentinel stayed out of their way.

"You've got a date tonight, young lady, with the doctor himself." Frau clasped the necklace, nodding. "There now, that will do nicely."

Two faces in the mirror, girls readying for prom. The grinning one cajoled, "Come on Miss Hawk, would it kill you to smile?"

The thought of killing elicited the sought for response. The ELF warrior imagined herself free: the chokehold, the hated Frau turning purple first, then dead.

"My, my, your smile is dazzling. Won't Doctor Schark be impressed!"

The needle came next. Hawk guessed Rohypnol. Schark had used roofies before. At Frau's signal, a pair of muscular male attendants entered her cell, removing her restraints. For the first time in weeks, the bird left her cage. She was led through the labyrinth, through Schark's inverted tower. Hawk floated on benzodiazepine, hands cuffed—oh so elegant—before her.

She took no pleasure in the meal, refusing to peck at her plate. The good doctor was nervous, kept eyeing his screens. Schark expected callers, but so far, no one had rung. She could have killed him a dozen ways, but what she wanted was escape. Behind both doors to the dining room, guards were waiting with syringes and a straitjacket. She wouldn't fly far. Plus, the merciless Mr. Wermer, the doctor's snake, was always in the room.

"Would you like to see your competition?" Schark asked, sipping wine, hiding displeasure. His satellite phone was still silent.

Her date pushed a button, and the room dimmed. Panzer's double tower rotated on the flat screen, jazz music playing as a sultry voiced madame introduced each asset. The production value was high; the women looked good, if a bit glazed. Hawk guessed at more drugs, Panzer Pharma had plenty. The commercial had a softcore feel. Around each woman a story was constructed. Fact or fiction, hard to tell, and who the hell would care? It wasn't truth Schark was selling.

A young woman appeared on screen, kneeling in a garden. "Farmer's daughter," the madame called her. She wore a long dress and an Amish-looking bonnet. "Do you long for a simpler time? Are you looking for a companion to cater to your every need?" Scenes of the girl carrying an egg basket, preparing a meal.

"Do you wish to have children? Children with immunity?" The bonnet rocked a cradle, her nightgown showing cleavage.

"Then this farmer's daughter is for you. She'll work hard all day, and even harder at night." The madame winked with her voice as the woman undressed in candlelight, touching herself. The scene dimmed as "daughter" began to moan.

Schark sipped at his cordial. "She really is Amish, you know." Nighthawk considered—and rejected—each potential weapon on the table. "If she gets a good price, I have dozens more like her." Schark's phone began beeping and he picked it up, lips spreading in an oily grin. The video continued.

The next woman straddled a motorcycle, naked except for chaps and an unzipped jacket. She had Native American cheekbones and a long, black braid. Schark covered the mouthpiece to explain, "We captured her before the bridge battle. Calls herself a 'Howler,' some kind of scout."

The madame's voice again, a different tone, more aggressive: "It's OK to get angry sometimes. After all, you've been through a lot. Well, this one likes it rough." A montage: the woman kissing a riding crop, wrists bound to a bedpost. Whip cracks, cries of pain mixed with pleasure.

On the phone, Schark was negotiating, his man Wermer taking notes. The initial offerings appeared well received. Hawk—thoughts dimmed by her dose—overheard talk of "paramilitary," "fuel tankers," and "armory surplus." She heard Schark guarantee the women as "certified immune." The host forgot his manners; Hawk sat alone.

The promotional video ended with madame's final pitch: "And now, for the truly selective, a one-of-a-kind offering." Nighthawk viewed herself on the screen. The images were grainy.

"The world is changing, and for the right price you can own a piece of this future." The video had been spliced from multiple security cameras. It showed her standing outside Panzer's walls in the rain on the day she'd been captured. "Are you bored by average? Perhaps a super woman would excite you?"

The video showed the mutant leaping from branch to branch, both in real time and slow motion. "This Greenie is a lot to handle," her video self was throwing blades, "which is why we offer not just her body but—for the highest bidder—her DNA as well."

A voyeuristic view through a microscope: Hawk's ova in a Petri dish, stats of her vitals scrolling across the screen. "Let Panzer help plant your new family tree." Images of a well-staffed lab, a pregnant woman getting an ultrasound. "With this DNA and CRISPR technology, take a leap into the future."

The final scene—rainy security footage again—showed the impossible backflip Hawk had made, sticking the landing. Then Schark's roofies rolled her under. Sentinel Nighthawk—PhD from before, ELF after—passed out on her plate.

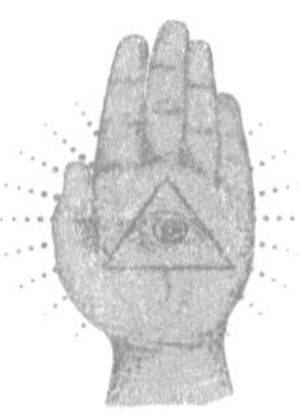

Eye of the Hand

THE PALE-SKINNED MERCENARY, Mr. Wermer, had stepped away. Returning, the snake hissed in Schark's ear as the doctor powered down his sat-phone. The pimp reel ended. Hawk lifted her head, subdued. She was drowsy with drugs but still attended his dealings. From what she could gather, their night had gone well. Together, Sharkey and his Werm must have fielded a half-dozen offers.

Wermer left again, and Schark turned his attention to her, looking serious. "I know you're tired, my dear, but it seems we have a visitor. A potential client has just arrived via helicopter. He's being screened now for infection. It's against Panzer protocol, but we really should meet him face to face."

Schark gestured and the airlock swished open. Two techs entered, securing Nighthawk tightly to her chair before departing. "I'm sorry, Ms. Hawk, but I can't take any chances. His organization is quite powerful. This deal must go well."

The other door opened, and a tall man entered wearing a US Army uniform pinned with a major's golden oak leaves. Two insignia were displayed: the twinned snakes of the Army's Medical Logistics Command and the ubiquitous Red Hand. His nametape read: NAZ. Encircling the major's head was a metallic ring, surgically embedded into his skull.

Schark attempted some pleasantries but the halo man iced him. Major Naz had eyes only for Hawk—one eye actually. An opaque plastic lens covered the other.

When Schark spluttered to a stop, the major spoke, moving closer to the woman in black. "We've studied your video, Dr. Schark. My team is very interested in what she can do."

Naz made a quick movement, conducting a skin poke, pocketing her blood sample before his host could protest. Hawk, floored by the roofies, never felt a thing. The major raised a large hand, a tattooed EYE on its palm.

Schark shut his mouth as the Red Hand concluded, "We will analyze this sample. You can keep her for now, but I've been instructed to deliver a message. General Kamul, Commander of the Hands, wants you to know that this dainty is not for you. If our lab results prove your claim, he will send for her at once. Doctor, do you understand?"

Schark swallowed his rebuttal and nodded as Hawk slumped unconscious in her chair.

The major beckoned Wermer to follow; he'd brought a gift, a precious ring—one of nine, forged of rare earth metals—that needed giving. Both men swished out the door. An hour later—surgery successful, Wermer's halo implanted—Naz boarded his black-bladed chopper and flew from the tower.

Blinded

I AM DRIVEN AWAY FROM YOUR SIGHT; yet I shall again look upon your holy temple. —Jonah 2:4

The mariner woke in his burrow. Blinded by the explosion, he viewed the world with his ears instead. The wind, from the west, had strengthened in the night. A three-day blow. He could hear whitecaps and the streaking sound of foam. He scuttled from his cave and took a long piss. Marooned by a quadrillion gallons of fresh water, dehydration was not on his worry list.

Frisked by the rough-handed wind, he started to shiver. Ship-wrecked, cast away, his clothes were in tatters, singed by the fireball that blew up *Bloody Mary*. Two weeks, maybe more, since the battle at the bridge?

Sightless in the present, he visioned the past: the clothes-line cable he and Hanny had rigged. The red-eyed Spreaders boarding his boat. That fucking drone swarm at dusk. The ferry *Nodin*, doomed. Diana, Hannigan, O'Donnell, all dead; most likely his blind ass, too. Had he been contaminated? Caught the Covee?

More than likely. That XCon he choked had spat right in his face. It was all coming back to him, though he wished it wouldn't. They'd probably lost the bridge, the Free North no longer so free. By now the whole U.P. could be infected. Had that vehicle barge made it ashore?

He'd rammed its fucking tug with his *Mary*. The last thing he'd seen: a man with a halo and that ghoulish skeleton, both grinning. He fought back a growl. He still had it, piss and vinegar. He'd need plenty of both to get off this damn island.

If he didn't feel sick and he wasn't a threat, then he might as well live, keep fighting the fight. He knew where he was, where he should be anyway. His body—seared and plucked—had washed ashore on Goose Island, the smallest and most remote of the Les Cheneaux chain. Prevailing currents had carried him there; he didn't need eyes to read this chart. The cartography of the Straits scrimshawed his bones.

45.9222370° North and 84.4303128° West was his dead-reckoned location. Brulee Point on the mainland was three miles away. This hazardous moat was ripping with current: an Olympic pool every second, 80,000 cubic meters of water per blink.

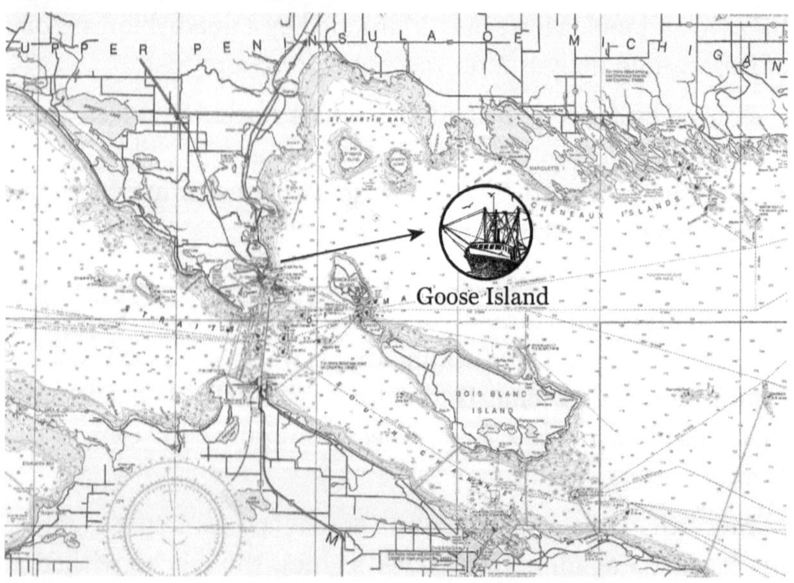

What he needed was a raft. But first he must eat.

Gull cry was his breakfast bell. Seamen, ever superstitious, believed gulls to be ghosts of drowned sailors. They overflew the tiny island—his wings now, his watchers. Empty-bellied, he limped to the shore and made his clockwise perambulation, prowling for protein. The cold wind shivered his unlimber limbs. Stranded for a fortnight, he'd yet to make fire.

Lake Huron thrashed against the shore. Goose Island sat low; a few more feet would sink it. There were no trees to speak of, no timbers for his ark. A bad place to be stranded.

But hark! That smell! A dead fish, nothing finer.

Crabwise he skittered. His nose led him to it. He felt its face, brailled its biology: an adipose fin, puckered lips, a fresh scar. Whitefish then? Mortally wounded by an osprey?

Protesting, the gulls conceded the calories to the castaway. What else could they do?

Cowboy Gets Roped

OLD HOCHSTETTLER was *pissed*.

When their field shift finally ended and neighbor Lapp dropped them home, white-haired Dawdy really let him have it—little Sammy and sister Sarah joining in. Amish rage was a quiet thing: a lifted eyebrow, a too-long stare. But boy, they unloaded. Wordless, the Hochers blasted Bob with every fucking barrel.

Of course, Cowboy had stashed the actual shotgun. He didn't know their rules, their *ordnung,* but guessed a 12-gauge stained with gore was probably verboten. They didn't ask and he sure-as-shit didn't tell what he'd done to the three XCons that had come for their Sarah.

Supper that night was a silent affair. No jokes, no faces, no teasing from the children. Murder had been done, right there in the yard. Bob Campbell was being shunned. It wasn't the first time, but this one hurt, especially from the kids. But he got it. He'd broken the Big One, commandment *Numero Uno:* Cowboy, a red-eyed Viral, had killed.

Per usual, Dawdy read aloud from the family Bible. Tonight though, instead of German, for Bob's benefit he switched to King James. In slow, accented syllables he pronounced Cowboy's Corinthian doom.

Be ye not unequally yoked together with unbelievers: for what fellowship hath righteousness with unrighteousness? and what communion hath light with darkness?

Sammy and Sarah kept their eyes down, refusing to soften the blow. In the early dropping dusk of October, Bob excused himself to his hayloft. With cold fingers, he packed a few things, cinching his saddlebag.

Unbeliever. Unrighteous. Darkness.

The Amish never lied. Old Dawdy had him pegged.

In the west the crescent moon fell, depressed. Cowboy Bob, with holstered pistols and Guts' shotgun across his back, walked north along Tobacco Drive, the very road that brought him here a month ago. He'd arrived as an outcast, and departed the same. Par for the fucking course of Bob's apocalypse. He tried a few notes, but his whistle wouldn't work, his empty head out of tunes. But at least he had a mission. Bob half-hoped it would be his last.

Passing the woodlot, he had zero desire to check on the two cocoons. Not in the woods. Not at night. He was pretty sure Guts would stay buried. As for Methhead and Squints, their fate was their own.

A mile further north was Beaverton Road, Bob's destination. Its farmhouse and pole barn were used by Virals—a far-flung outpost of Panzer. The three *iks* who'd come calling originated from there. Finding the kids' mom, Hannah Hochstettler, was a long shot. But if Bob could do some good then he would, unrighteous though he be.

By the time he arrived, the skinny moon had set. Bob left the main road, unsure of surveillance. He followed an irrigation ditch instead, choosing a position to observe from. He was looking for Amish prisoners—ideally Hannah—hoping to set some of them free. A fucking longshot, sure. But what else could he do? The shunning the siblings gave him still ached. The night got colder; he could see his breath beneath starry skies. The compound was quiet. Hands jammed in pockets, Bob shivered, drifting towards sleep.

An argument woke him, angry voices from the pole barn debating the generator. Was it cold enough to burn fuel for heat? Apparently it was. Inside the compound, an engine coughed to life. Covered by the clunky noise, many things happened at once.

Several muzzles flashed from the perimeter. Suppressors limited their noise, but to Bob, the rifle shots were obvious. He couldn't see their effect but heard the thump of bullet-struck bodies. In the darkness, several figures deployed towards the pole barn. A shout was raised and one of the parked vehicles—a gun truck?—started up. Headlights flicked on and its hungry spotlight started searching.

Next, Bob was blasted by a wall of WHITE, a shock wave pushing through his innards as the gun truck exploded. KA-BOOM! A fatal flower blossomed, petals of white phosphorus searing the sky. A rain of metallic shards pattered down. Bob blinked away the afterimage, but the deadly bloom remained.

Holy fucking SHIT!

Campbell's ears were ringing. Flash-blind, he heard a female voice barking orders through a loudspeaker: "This is the Michigan National Guard. You are surrounded. Lay down your weapons and come out with your hands up!"

Her request was answered by a long burst from a Viral, spitting bullets in defiance. More suppressed flashes from the perimeter, and the defender was silenced.

Another Panzer vehicle roared itself awake, attempting to flee the Old Law trap. Again, a wall of WHITE rippled out from impact. KA-BOOM! The insubordinate vehicle disintegrated in a blink.

God DAMN! Bob saw the attacker this time. A flat-trajecting howitzer—point blank—had blown the truck to bits.

The command voice tried again: "You are surrounded. Resist and you'll be killed. Surrender and live. Lay down your weapons!"

This time, remaining Virals obeyed. Old Law smoked 'em out, illuminating their hive with LED wattage. Campbell counted emerging Spreaders, hands high—at least ten, maybe more? But what about the Amish? Where were the plantation slaves? The bonnets? Sammy and Sarah's mom, Hannah?

Bob Campbell, from the drainage ditch, observed the scene closely.

Tattooed skeletons, ravening from the fringe, watched closer still.

"Hands up, asshole!" A male voice this time. Bob didn't move, seeing the laser dot scribing his heart.

"Robert, here's another one!"

The two voices converged, pinning Bob between them. Famished and fucking freezing to boot, Campbell complied—what else could he do? Bob squinted at the approaching beams, hazmatted figures pointing rifles at his chest.

"Kneel!" He did so.

"Hands above your head!" You betcha.

They shone a light on his face. Pupils constricting, Cowboy blinked his pink eyes.

"He's a Viral! Freddy, look out, this Chosen's got weapons!"

A rifle butt knocked the wind out of him, any urge to resist deflating as well.

The pair of arrestors—alien in their MOPP gear—disarmed him, zipping flex cuffs extra tight.

Here we go again. Bob—prone on icy ground—gasped for breath. What else was fucking new?

The Sorting

DATE TIME GROUP: 190600ROCT21

LOCATION: CLARE AIRPORT, FAA LID: 48D

For the moment anyway, there was no need to hide. Sergeant Amanda Taylor was convinced that Panzer's iron grip had loosened. In the cold hour before dawn, she authorized floodlights at Clare's municipal airfield. There was sorting to be done. It had been a busy night.

First, she'd filed the After Action Report from the Rangers' reconnaissance. Second, her Griffs—Yield to None—had intercepted Walker's bus and his band of Freedom Riders. Third, they raided the Chosen's pole barn. Here she made a note—they were down two more rounds of 105mm ammo. The long night had ended well. Improvise and adapt. Amanda Taylor was a pro.

Her compound—in stealth mode no longer—appeared bright and bustling. Walker's panther-painted Greyhound was parked alongside the XCon bus Colonel Dennis captured at Indian River. X-marked, this bus had transported Amish labor, including Hannah, the Plain woman she'd befriended at Agape Church the morning after the bridge battle. Both transports were temporarily empty, awaiting passengers.

The night's captured Virals were now quarantined, guarded by grim looking Griffins in MOPP gear and masks. Six more women, all Amish, had been freed from their servitude. The bonnets had been found in the pole barn her unit—assisted by Rangers—had raided.

Amanda's adrenaline evaporated, a hot cup of coffee was nowhere in sight. So far, her experience of apocalypse was an endless series of lists. Sighing, she formatted another one.

Priority one: load both buses and convoy civilians to Colonel Dennis for resettlement. The Free North—still nascent—was in need of free folks: farmers, hunters, builders, and especially fosters. Every family's tree had been pruned by plague—uprooted, limbs lopped and trunks scarred—surviving saplings traumatized by terror.

Priority two: separate captured Virals into two groups, Compliant and Non-Compliant. This was Reverend Walker's idea; for now, she'd play along.

Priority three: take care of her own soldiers, burning as little fuel as possible.

Priority four: maybe, just maybe, hit her rack before dawn.

Cold, gray light seeped into the sky, failing to thaw the frozen landscape. Breakfast MREs and coffee rations were heated and served to civilians. Her combat medics—wearing full PPE—ran blood tests. As usual, all Amish were quickly cleared. The wounded POWs—one gunshot wound, one concussion—had been cared for.

Ever Amanda's rock, Reverend Walker loomed by her side. He had a face like black granite, chiseled by catastrophe. They viewed the scene together. The Amish, mostly women, lined up by the buses. Walker's black-beret Panthers were helping them aboard. Sequestered Chosen—under guard and socially distanced—observed the process as well. Some hooted and catcalled at the traumatized women. Any POWs that jeered, at a nod from Walker, were separated as Non-Compliant by her hazmatted soldiers.

Then one of the Virals started shouting a name: "HANNAH! Hey, is there a Hannah here?" A tall man was yelling. His wrists were flex-cuffed; he wore half a beard and an Amish hat, cowboy style. "Hannah Hochstettler!"

Taylor saw Hannah waiting in the bus line. Her friend from Agape's garden turned towards the shouting Viral. The pink-eyed imposter noticed as well. "Sammy and Sarah are in DANGER!"

The National Guardsmen, wearing N95s, warned the manic man to be silent. The Amish cowboy refused, pushing towards the bus line. "Hannah, they NEED you!"

Warnings ignored, the tall man was tased. The stranger fell hard, limbs flailing from 50,000 volts. Two MPs in floppy MOPP suits dragged him—compliant at last—to the shipping container reserved for hard cases.

Reunited, and it Feels So Good

CAMPBELL AWOKE IN THE DARK. A tune from before—another sappy ballad from the seventies—playing on repeat. Bob's brain was a broken jukebox.

Sat here starin' at the same old wall

Came back to life just when I got your call

Wan daylight spilled through steel seams. His muscles still twitched, even his tongue was numb. God damn it, tased again.

Bob was shivering, boots still wet from last night's drainage ditch and capture. A cold-ass morning to be confined in a coffin. He forced himself to stand; the shipping container was fucking frigid. Pretty sure he'd seen Hannah though. How random was that? It had to be her, she'd turned around right away. And was it just him, or did she look a lot like young Sarah?

So, their mom was alive and hopefully headed to safety. He had to let the kids know. Could he bring them all together somehow? Facilitate a family reunion in a way better place? Get himself unshunned and off of Dawdy's shit list?

Again, the sugary lyric—circa 1978—wormed in his ear.

I was a fool to ever leave your side

Me minus you is such a lonely ride

Step one, get the fuck out of here. Campbell tested his cuffs. No dice, they'd been zipped way too tight. Shit! Red-eyed or not, he was no fucking Viral. So he yelled it: "You've made a mistake!"

No response from the guards.

He booted the side wall. "I'm not fucking Chosen!"

The response to his hissy fit was a gurgle of laughter and a taunt. "Bullshit. I've heard you've fucked plenty." The teasing voice sounded female? From *inside* the container, not out? Bob Campbell wasn't alone. He did not like this one bit.

Two figures stepped towards him from the shadows. The first—nearly naked despite the cold—was a skinny Raider with a poorly inked tattoo. In the dim light, Campbell read 𝕷𝕬𝖅𝖄 𝕭𝕺𝖄 in Gothic letters across his hollow chest. The Spreader grinned a rotten welcome. Lazy Boy's teeth were sharpened to points. The second, a dominant female, had probably stolen the submissive's clothes? Harder to see, but she wheezed as she slid nearer. Half her hair had been burned away. The flesh on her left side was puckered and scarred. He didn't recognize her.

Despite the cold, Bob took off his jacket. "You want this?" No harm in being friendly.

More laughter, more gurgling. The lizard slithered nearer. Lazy Boy moved to pin Bob between. The woman brought her face close, what was left of it anyway. She looked him in the eyes and winked. Campbell flinched, her hand groping his crotch.

Red Liz—the ol' ballbuster—gave her Cowboy a familiar squeeze. "What's a girl gotta do to get a ride around here?"

It suddenly clicked. No fucking way. A new quarter in the jukebox, though the song stayed the same.

Our quarrel was a way of learning so much

I know now that I love you 'cause I need your touch

The Hangar

EARTH ROLLED ALONG, raising a yellow sun above Clare's icy airfield. Sergeant Amanda Taylor ran through her list. The Amish cowboy, Non-Compliant, was tased and confined. Hannah, her new friend, was aboard the bus, destination: Free North. Last night's raid on the pole barn had gone well, Griffins achieving their objective. The compound was taken, several Chosen KIA; the rest were prisoners. No soldiers had been wounded, no personnel exposed. As always, Rangers had helped, the best damn scouts in mid-Michigan.

There'd been little fuel at the pole barn, her guardsmen siphoning what they could. Of food there was none. The Viral hive had been starving. Two Raider vehicles were destroyed by artillery and Taylor's cannon cockers were happy. Six women were freed from the cage they'd been kept in.

Sergeant Taylor questioned her medics about negative test results. The EMTs shook their helmets: above their paygrade, but something kept the Amish from infection.

Both buses—Greyhound and X-marked MDOC—had been loaded with civilians and were ready to roll. The buses and their escorts waited for Walker.

"Reverend, are you ready?"

Taylor's old teacher shook his head. Not yet. He had one task still to do. The old man—once a public figure—started towards the hangar housing the Compliant. Taylor signaled and the airfield lights were doused. The wind freshened, pulling cold air from the west. Once the convoy pulled out, her Griffs would get busy.

Panzerland appeared ripe for the picking. They would hit the remaining farms, liberate slave labor, capture or kill any Virals, and send uninfected refugees to Colonel Dennis in the Free North.

Another sleepless night had passed. Another busy day had begun. Bone-weary, Taylor followed Walker—ever her mentor—across the weedy tarmac.

At the door to the Compliant hangar, hazmatted MPs were waiting. Wrinkling her nose, Taylor donned her musty MOPP mask, Walker waving away the protection he was offered. Taylor couldn't help it; she put a hand on his shoulder. The Detroit Baptist smiled, his hair grayer by morning light.

The student knew her teacher, knew a quote was coming.

"Do I not destroy my enemies when I make them my friends?"

She knew this one, though it wasn't in her field manual. "MLK?"

"Older."

The clue helped, then she had it. "Lincoln!"

The preacher nodded. Barefaced, exposed to the variant, he stepped inside the hangar. Wearing her MOPP mask, Taylor reluctantly followed.

The large space had been set up as a barracks. Of the two-dozen bunks, only eight were occupied. Six males and two females; none wore the X, but all eight were infected. The MPs had cuffed each one to their bed frame. They'd been frisked, belts and boot laces taken away. As Walker entered the hangar, all eyes—regardless of tint—locked upon him. Taylor, familiar with this lodestar effect, followed her magnetic mentor.

On the first bunk sat a typical Chosen. Malnourished, he wore cracked glasses. Red-rimmed, his eyes gave him away.

Walker stopped, laying a heavy hand on his shoulder. "Did you get breakfast?"

The Chosen nodded.

"And what was your job? What are you good at?"

"I'm good with tech. A radio operator."

Walker looked askance at the flex cuffs, then back again at Taylor. Behind her mask she gave a sigh. Flicking her knife, she cut Glasses free.

The man rubbed his wrists. "Sir?" He looked up at Walker for permission.

Reverend nodded, permission granted.

"Sir, I know who you are. I've heard you before, unscrambled your transmissions." The tall man kept quiet.

"You're *Walks-on-Water,* aren't you?" The preacher kept his peace.

"Is it true what they say?" Walker shook his head. Gave the shoulder a pat, began to move away.

"Heal me!" Walker froze. The whole hangar waited.

"Please, sir! I didn't want this!" Glasses was getting agitated. Taylor moved forward, shielding the civilian, her mild-mannered mentor. But Walker waved her back. He looked upon the radioman, at the rest of the waiting ward. They didn't know it, but Taylor definitely did. Another quote was coming.

He spoke old words that carried new weight: "I am not concerned that you have fallen. I am concerned that you arise." She ordered her eyeballs not to roll. Lincoln again, she'd swear it.

Walker continued his rounds, every bunk the same. With a quiet groan, she cut their cuffs. Then came a handshake, or a touch on the arm, or a shoulder squeeze and *Walks-on-Water* would drift away.

Exiting the hangar, they saw the sun had fully risen. Walker was met by his assistant, steering him towards the buses. The passengers were all aboard, ready to depart. The MPs guarding the Compliant hangar looked to Taylor for orders. In the fresh air, she took off her mask, felt the cold wind and frowned. "Leave their cuffs off for now. If there's trouble, use your Tasers and shackle 'em again. Tight."

"Yes, Sergeant!" Still masked, the soldiers' eyes—blue, brown, green—were hard to read.

Amanda Taylor watched the preacher board his bus followed by his beret-wearing guards. The convoy pulled out, four vehicles strong. Black-painted, a gun truck led the formation. Then came Walker's Greyhound with its communication arrays. Then the DOC bus filled with Amish. A final gun truck covered their rear.

In daylight, she noticed the run-flat tires, armor plating, and .30-caliber machine guns. The trucks sported kill markings: X-marked skulls and Raider shields. With any luck, the convoy would make it to the Straits unmolested, then ferry across to St. Ignace and the Free North. She knew her CO Colonel Dennis needed settlers.

The convoy took to the road, the airfield's gate clanging shut behind them. Griffins on guard duty farewelled departing Panthers—the enemy of my enemy is my friend. Taylor raised a tired hand as well. She never said goodbye to her new friend Hannah.

Tree Academy: Potions

BLEARY-EYED STUDENTS ASSEMBLED at the Jordan River Bridge. The predawn was cloudy and loud with wind. The day before they'd flown with aviator Brian. Most of the 12 that night dreamt of wings. Now they shivered in downy coats waiting on instructors.

"Any guesses guys?" from a Natural kid, Arturo. He'd been adopted by two dads, the ELF farmers, Rodriguez and White.

Josie Greene shook her head, raising her hood as wooly clouds released their sleet. Muted by the gale, Miin's pupils endured. Felt more than heard, Lake Michigan whitecaps gnashed the nearby shore.

Miinan found them there, bunched together for warmth. She herded her sleepy flock along the ever-shifting path to Cranberry Bog. It was quieter under the trees—of course they'd learned the word for that, *psithurism*. As the gray light strengthened, heads emerged from hoods and began to look around.

Some joking warmed the back of the line as Michael Martin and his Miin-mimicry began to thaw: "And *what* do we have *here*?"

Mr. Martin exaggerated his wonder, gesturing to a birch grove, yellow leaves flayed by wind. Cheyanna, an island Native raised on Indian Point, played along: "Um, those are just birch trees?"

"Just birch trees? *Just* birch trees! Those creatures, Cheyanna GreenSky, are *Betula papyrifera!*"

The students giggled. Miin, from the front, overheard Michael and smiled along. For Miin, these paths were potent with the lingering presence of Keith Two-Crow. Arthritic and lean, slow of speech but quick to wink, her old uncle often haunted her. Some part of him walked here still, ever on the lookout for niece Blueberry. And where would she walk when her time had come?

They neared Samantha's cabin. Miin stopped her class—quiz time! The pupils gathered around. Alert now from the walk, hearts pumping and eyes shining, their potential dazzled her. Goodness, what a group!

A whiff of woodsmoke tickled their noses. The treetops all were tossing. They felt the power of the besieging gale, the sanctum of an encircling sea.

"And what do we have *here*?" Miin mimicked the mimic. Twelve smiles turned upwards. She gestured to a grove of trees— taller than the rest—lignin landmarks to Samantha's shack.

Mr. Martin spoke up, making amends: "They look like hardwoods, I'd guess maples?"

Miin nodded approval. "Other names?" Several hands shot up. "Arturo?"

"*Acer saccharum!*" Another nod.

Teacher called on a local next, "Cheyanna?"

"*Aninaatigoog.*"

"Good! And what explains their pattern here?"

She made a circling motion with her hand. The students were thinking—some comically, with scrunched up faces.

Taller maples had flamed out earlier in the season, standing naked in the wind, less tempest-tossed than their foliaged fellows. These dreadnaughts had cleared for action, battening down their barky hatches, ready to ride out the winter storms, leafy sails stowed away.

Josie Greene spoke up sweetly: "Could be a sugar grove?" Miin's eye contact encouraged her. "Maybe they were planted here, or selected? By their age, I'd say Ojibwe did this."

One more question on the quiz, "And what would you expect to find in their midst?"

"An old shack maybe? For boiling down the sap?"

Miin was satisfied. "Class, proceed!"

They did so, soon stepping into Sam's clearing. They beheld her cabin, windows aglow with fire-flicker and a sweet smoke piping from the chimney. Miin stopped them on the verge. For her—and brother Mukwa too—this place was a sanctuary. She wanted them to *feel* it.

The kids took it in: the extensive gardens, winterized and bare; the sun-bleached boards of the shack; a burble of spring water, channeled for irrigation.

But it was the trees, always the trees. Their burled bark was fissured with faces—sniffing, peering, tasting all trespassers. Wild faces, calm ones, tiny ones and vast. A whole colony of treefolk beheld the approaching bipeds. The students—islanders and Naturals alike—felt their granular gaze and stood still.

Miin, of course, had trained them in manners: open yourself, stand humble, radiate good intention, and admire. The trees—sticklers for protocol—were impressed. Slowly, so slowly, they nodded to each other, protection bestowed.

The cabin door beckoned. Samantha, the grove's resident human—oracle of this delphic opening—waved them inside. The supplicants entered.

Elder Grace was there, sipping her tea by the woodstove. The room was hot. Coats were unzipped, hats stuffed in pockets, and soon the wall pegs were full. The table had been set: warm sheets of muffin cake; a great tub of oily butter; clay pitchers of milk, beading at the brim, chilly from the springhouse.

Barely restrained, the ravenous class waited on permission. Samantha granted it with a laugh, and the hungry flock descended.

The teaching staff conferred over the smack and moan of feeding pre-teens. Samantha explained that Baptiste and his voyageurs had blown in yesterday with the gale. Six big canoes were snug in the harbor and would split up—half heading towards Wisconsin, half back to Ignace—when the weather laid down.

"This'll be a three-day blow. We've got today and tomorrow to prepare what they need."

"And what's that?" asked Miin. "The same as before?"

"Yes girl, the same. I've got a note from Doctor Chow and another from Colonel Dennis. They call our tincture 'At-the-last.' They say it worked wonders in their healing ward after the bridge battle. They're asking for more. I told Baptiste we'd do our best."

Grace set down her mug and tended the cauldron, stirring the concoction with a long-handled spoon. The quicker-eating students brushed crumbs from their faces, murmured thanks to their hosts, and gathered round the brew.

Samantha, medicine woman, a *midewikwe* in her lodge, took the lead. "When Covee came and the variant started stinging, the first shortages were of medicine. Before collapse, what percent of our pharmacy drugs came from plants?"

Only two years gone, the students still remembered: bottles, pills, packaging, eyedroppers and familiar fake flavors.

"Ten percent?"

"Twenty, maybe?"

The class noticed her rafters: the bundled plants, tied tight and drying. Samantha's herbs hung upside down, an inverted garden of fragrant pharmacons.

"Miin?"

Sam's assistant knew this lesson well. "More than 70 percent of new drugs were derived from plants."

Samantha nodded. "Much has changed and will continue to change, but what I want you students to remember is that some things don't."

When even the hungriest kid was sated, the table fare much reduced, all 12 attended as the chemistry lab began in earnest. "Now, how many of you have taken aspirin before?"

Almost every hand was raised.

"Who can tell me why people take aspirin?"

"When someone has a fever."

"My granny takes it for her heart."

Michael Martin winked, "After Mom and Dad drink too much!"

Sam was smiling too. "And can anyone tell me what *tree* aspirin comes from?"

Stumped. No guesses this time.

"Miinan?"

"Willow bark contains salicin, an active agent that relieves pain and fever."

Silver-braided, the chemist continued, "Class, we are making a medicine to help people that have been hurt, both in their minds and their bodies. Do you agree that willow bark would be a good place to start?"

Yes. Yes they certainly did.

Samantha pointed Michael to a large mason jar on a shelf. "Young man, could you unseal that jar and tell me what you smell?"

He did her bidding. Taking a cautious whiff, Michael smiled. "Smells like gum. Like minty chewing gum."

"Good! Ms. Miin?"

The TA did her prof's bidding and recited the pneumonic, the first of many: *"Minty-green, methyl salicylates means."*

Samantha gestured. Michael passed around the jar, so the circled class could get a sniff. Grace began a sing-song, incorporating portion instructions into the pneumonic. With the students watching, and some humming along, Grace dispensed the proper dose into boiling water. The retired art teacher handed the ladle to Cheyanna, instructing her to stir.

The girl did so and the lesson continued. Herb after herb, their song grew apace. Soon the whole class was swaying, perspiring in the heat. Above them, the trees, sympathetic, swayed as well, the powdered flesh of their willowy cousins empowering the potion.

Utterly unmoved, the two spies weren't swaying. They were swearing instead.

"What did I fucking tell you?" Ferny demanded of the sheriff's deputy.

Travis Williams shook his head. "Damn, that's a strange sight, I'll not deny it."

"Strange nothin', it's fuckin' sorcery. Those are our kids in there, damn it! We've got to do something."

"Well, it's private property, Bill, and I don't have a warrant."

"Warrant?" Ferny spat. "Get your head out of yer ass, Deputy! Those kids are in danger."

Travis backed away from the shack. Ferny followed, furious. The men took the path away from the bog, back towards civilization—what was left of it. Ferny, hot-headed, threatened action of his own, vigilante-style, if necessary. Travis countered, "Now Bill, that's a matter for the council. You're free to bring it up at the next session."

"God damn right I will!"

The wind took the rest of his words. The trees watched them warily as the trespassers wended their way back to the bridge and out of ELF Country.

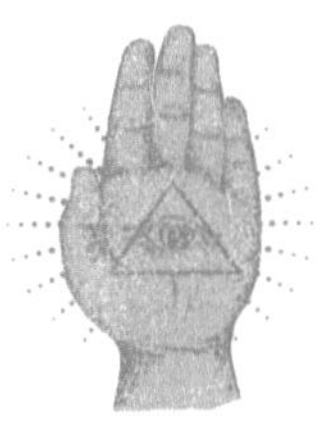

The Red Rally

MAJOR NAZ, WEARING HIS ARMY COMBAT UNIFORM and opaque eyepatch, knocked on the door of his commanding officer, Lieutenant General Kamul. "They're ready for you, sir."

The gray haired general, three stars on his ACU, stood in front of a wall map of the eastern USA, variously shaded and pinned with unit flags. Both officers wore implanted halos, connected to AYE EYE—or what was left of it, electronically brooding in the dark fortress that was once the Pentagon.

"Let Congress wait. Major, please come in."

Naz, tall and bald, with an Army background in infectious disease, stooped to enter the cramped room—the White House Military Office. Established by George Washington and ceremonial for centuries, the WHMO wielded far more power in the CORPS than the Oval Office now did. The Confederacy of Red Patriotic States is what they'd come up with after the assassination of America's last elected president. Admittedly, POTUS had been an oaf, but he'd been their oaf. Killed by a female agent posing as press, the assassin's origins were still unknown.

Post mortem, the man morphed mythical; the lout became a legend. During the ensuing purge, U.S. Armed Forces tore themselves limb-from-limb. Every base hosted battles: South against North, Reds versus Blues. The once-mighty military killed itself, its fratricidal fire far from friendly.

Both officers bore the Red Hand insignia. "We Guard the Peace," the badge proclaimed. The Hands originated with the District of Columbia's National Guard. The past president, pre-purge, converted D.C.'s 372nd Military Police Battalion into his own Praetorian Guard. The unit had a long history. In World War One, they'd battled Germans in Meuse-Argonne, earning the Croix de Guerre and France's Red Hand insignia for gallantry. During the purge, the battalion slaughtered protesters and politicians alike. The red-blooded Hands—commanded by Kamul, aided by AYE EYE—bathed in the blood of Blue America.

In the tiny map room, General Kamul placed a pale finger on Kalamazoo, Michigan. "Major, what have we learned about Schark's latest project?"

Naz studied the map with one naked eye while the other digested data projected on his smart-patch by AYE EYE. "Sir, I'm accessing her file now. The doctor doesn't disappoint. I'd expect nothing less from Panzer Pharmaceuticals."

"Her bloodwork? The lab analysis?" Kamul, servant to the same lidless EYE, activated his own implanted halo to fact-check his subordinate.

"Sir, as you can see, Schark's patient, indeed, appears shielded. Covee, along with the Stinger variant, cannot gain access to her cells. The mechanism is yet unknown, our investigation continues."

Both soldiers—spectral-looking, pale faces crowned with halos—weighed the import of this data tranche. Almost two years since collapse, and they'd seen nothing like it—no one had. Stinger was fatal, period, full stop. Yes, some red-eyed Spreaders survived, but survivors, like themselves, were either unexposed or dependent on virucide, though its side effects were extreme.

The two men shut off their neural links and powered down their halos, petroleum for the Pentagon being precious. Wraithlike, they returned to themselves—what was left, anyway.

"That's quite a project then."

"Yes sir, quite a project."

"What is your recommendation, Major?"

Naz considered the cartography in front of him. Most of the eastern seaboard was shaded red. There were very few pockets where partisans persisted, islands of blue in a rising scarlet sea. Michigan—ever purple—was not yet tinted. Since collapse, the peninsula-of-plenty had been a far flung frontier—unelectrified, the dark side of America's moon. Only two flags were pinned to the mitten state: Panzer's double tower and the National Guard Griffin. Question marks and arrows penciled next to each.

"My recommendation, sir, is to move quickly," the major intoned, "a new power might be stirring there: this Detroit pastor, 'Walker,' whose transmissions we've intercepted."

Even without the far-seeing EYE, both men envisioned a rising tide of resistance. Walker, in his last transmission, claimed refineries now, and some significant Antiva victories against Virals. Panzerland was crumbling, their bulwark against the blue.

"Very well, draw up some contingency plans. Thank you, Major."

"Yes sir. General, are you ready for your motorcade?"

Kamul took a final look at the map, musing, "Is this pomp really necessary?"

"General, the CORPS wishes to recognize the bravery of its commander. The Medal of Honor, sir, is quite a distinction."

"I suppose it is. At least it used to be. Inform my escort. Let's get this over with."

Kamul the Conqueror stood tall in his chariot—the open hatch of his Humvee. He rode without helmet, without Kevlar. D.C. was locked down tight, and its lights were still on. A shining city on a hill, electrified by coerced technocrats burning stockpiled fuel.

Kamul activated his implant, and AYE EYE winked on. Mining clouds of data, the Pentagon's supercomputer projected the past upon the present: Pennsylvania Avenue hosted surprisingly few parades. Such displays, for years, deemed dowdy.

The Grand Review of Armies in 1865 was an exception. Appomattox had ended the war and the Union mourned Lincoln, its Abrahamic father, theatrically slain upon the altar of freedom. Under May sunshine, Generals Meade and Sherman marched 140,000 men along the route. These blue butchers had widowed the South with their wrath. Uninvited to the parade were the millions of civilians starved in their wake.

Kamul blinked and the data stream continued: Eisenhower paraded in '53. An Army five-star, Ike's pageant was a projection of power. The Cold War was heating up. Aimed squarely at Moscow, nuclear artillery rolled by in review.

JFK had his in '61, before the Pigs, before the patsy. Missiles, marchers, and towed boats processioned down Penn's Avenue. Two years and a grassy knoll later, Camelot and its Kennedys had been couped.

There'd been no jubilee for the jungle war. Veterans of Vietnam slunk home unadorned. In the desert, decades later, Shield turned to Storm. In 1991, Bush the Elder declared the curse lifted: 8,000 troops paraded past General Powell.

Kamul clicked away from newsreels, shutting down the EYE's neural projector. If his halo overheated, headaches would ensue. He opened his eyes upon the bleak present: D.C., like all the rest, had been depeopled. Yes, the Red Hands had mustered—local units anyway—but they were barely 800. Of spectators, there were none, but flags flew aplenty.

Trophies of collapse, of the purge, hung limp from lamp poles: the bloodstained banners of the recently bested Blues. Pride rainbows, Black Lives Matter, Abolish ICE, and other totems of tolerance laureled their Caesar.

Diesel, of course, was in high demand, even for Red Hands. Only a few armored vehicles escorted Kamul to the Capitol. DEI was dead—tank crews, to a man, were white. And men they all were, no women in combat, zero tolerance for woke. Proper ladies of the CORPS knew their place, and there was no place like home.

October's rough hands frisked leaves from the trees. The parade route felt desolate without any populace. Kamul grimaced at his amateur army, their shoddy uniforms and undisciplined marching. Red recruiters tended to highlight live-fire exercises and the chance for easy action. Any attempts at PT, or unit discipline, led to desertions. Still, his men were gun nuts; they cared for their weapons and knew how to use them. What point in push-ups when point-and-shoot won their battles?

The general dismounted at the Capitol, taking the smooth stairs—built by slaves—two at a time. An honor guard of Prouds saluted him—sloppily—at the doors. The People's House held but few, and they congressed inside. Covee protocols in Columbia's District were strict. Very few entered the city, and almost none found the exits.

Kamul's boots echoed in Statuary Hall. The graven images stood arrayed in marble-eyed serenity. During the purge a political pogrom had occurred. Rosa Parks was clubbed from her pedestal, then forcibly removed. Helen Keller's handicap status was mocked, then permanently revoked. Suffragettes, found insufferable, were sent to the Capitol kitchen where they belonged. The Indigenous were deported en masse: Sacagawea, Po'pay, and Winnemucca were trundled away through a trail of jeers. Statues of slave owners were taken out of storage and dusted off. They now held places of honor, and Ronald Reagan too. Andrew Jackson smiled to see his hall ethnically cleansed at last.

A red-blooded roar greeted Kamul as he entered the House Chamber. The government had gathered, and the gang was all there. President Fiske applauded at the podium. The Majority Leader and the Speaker out-whooped their caucus. The Supreme Court was there, its society of federalists no longer so secret. Post-purge, its rulings were nine-nil as dissent disappeared. Technocrats captured the triumph with microphones and monitors. Edited, the moment would be maximized, propagated through airwaves and thumbed into drives. Most of the gadgets still worked; it was connection they'd lost.

At last, the medal was bestowed. Kamul's handshake crushed poor Mr. Fiske. The limp fish, from Indiana, had been president for six months. He'd sworn the oath in March at the start of the purge. The vice-less VP had not risen to the challenge. His church attendance stayed steady as Kamul—and his AYE EYE crown—filled the void.

At the podium, the delicate deacon was dismissed by his general. Fiske slunk away, sitting meekly by his wife. The Medal of Honor hung heavy. Kamul tried to ignore the revulsion its past recipients must feel towards him now. Kamul raised a Roman hand—Sieg Heil!—and the lickspittles listened: "Mr. President, Mr. Speaker, Senators and Representatives, I thank you for this honor and I dedicate this moment to every patriot who has perished fighting for freedom."

Another roar from Congress as more flags were unfurled. The techies recorded the dramatic details, the props of their propaganda.

Eventually, after a pause to let the crowd's response crescendo, Kamul gestured and quiet returned. "What kind of freedom? Well, I'll tell you, though I'm no public speaker. Freedom from infection to start. Not just from the virus, 'made in China' for export, but from homegrown mongrels and the morons in the media."

Cheering again, and chants of "U-S-A!" Congress stood in clumps, not by state but by standard: the black and gold of the Prouds, the Gadsen snake, the III, and the Q.

The honorable medal tugged his neck like a noose. "Look now, much of what I've done, what the Hands have done, I regret."

Silence, militia flags suddenly becalmed by Kamul's lack of fervor. "But what we did, we did for our country, and we'd do it again!" The wind was rising; some chanting resumed.

"The struggle is not over, and don't we all know it. There are places in this land where we are not welcome." Some booing at this, shouts of "Jews!" and "Traitors!" An Oath Keeper mimed a massacre, his "Smoke the Woke!" t-shirt garnering laughs.

The general smiled too, then forced a frown. "Thanks to patriots like you, defenders of our heritage, the CORPS is strong, but it needs room to grow. Now, there's a man in Michigan—very dangerous—whose name you might have heard. He calls himself 'Walker' and he speaks in disguise."

The spin doctors were ready; their snippets were cued. Kamul shook his head sadly as Walker's words filled the chamber. The man's voice had been altered—distorted by AYE EYE—accentuating accent, amplifying his African American anger.

The Spreaders are on the run—The booing began—*will fuel our freedom as we ride through the land*—"Porch monkey!"—preaching love and scouring away the hate—"Get a rope!"

When it was over and they were ready to listen again, Kamul concluded, "Now, we've done some research and discovered Walker's true identity."

The techies zoomed in. This was the moment.

"You won't be surprised to find out he's a preacher. A radical, a blacktivist, he's got a rap sheet and a criminal record."

"Hypocrite!" "Jungle bunny!" "Globalist!"

At this last slur—pre-planned—Kamul leered. "You're not wrong!" He pointed towards the gallery. "We found out something else. His birth certificate has issues. He's barely American, got African ancestors, Kenyan royalty. A banana king!"

More boos and cat-calls.

"Mr. Walker here has been living a lie!"

Laughter from Congress as their enemy was mocked.

Kamul mimicked the recording, sexualizing Walker's words: "I want to *spread* some legs, and have *freedom to ride*." He bucked his hips as they jeered. "I want to *preach my love*," Kamul blew the crowd kisses, "and *scour away the hate*." He mimed scrubbing his skin to remove any blackness.

Congress roared its full-throated approval. Kamul ended his address with a call for fresh recruits. He pledged to arm any citizen joining hands with the Reds. Weapons they had—it was manpower they lacked. "Let the CORPS be your arsenal of democracy!"

A standing ovation, every flag waved. The PR technocrats were pleased; they had what they needed. Edited copies were made and distributed to delegations to share with their followers.

The Aboveground Bus Road

THAT SAME MORNING, the day of Kamul's speech, two buses and their panther-painted escorts headed north from Clare's airfield. It was another day of wind. Hannah Hochstettler observed the tossing trees and prayed for her children.

Had that Viral said he'd seen them? That Samuel and Sarah were "in danger?" That they "needed her?"

The tall man had been wearing her husband's hat. Devil-eyed, the *Englischer* was tased and taken before she could follow through. She'd sought her friend Amanda, but the sergeant had been busy. Hannah was pushed aboard the X-bus and then they were gone, leaving the man and his mysterious message behind.

If he was wearing Elam's hat, then he'd been to their house. Had Dawdy given it to him? Had it been taken? Had he harmed her children? Her precious *dochder*, her *buwe?* The whole thing was strange. And now she was heading north, the wrong direction for answers.

Her husband had been killed. It happened at the plantation, Elam clubbed to death by an *iks*. She tried to keep that from her children. Hannah wished she could keep it from herself.

Her husband's skull had been shattered, one of his eyes popping out. Still tethered by its nerve, his blue eye had watched her watching him. The X-branded murderer swung a rifle, saving a bullet, and now her *mann* was dead. It was her fault. The *iks* had groped her, trying to pull her from the field. Such things happened, but she'd resisted. Elam and his eyeball had been left there, her *liebling* dead in the mud. The Amish—plainly spooked—continued to harvest around him.

Hannah sat on the bench of the prison bus with her ripe-smelling community—her *gmay*—packed tightly around her. She gazed at the gale through thick glass. She sought serenity, *gelassenheit*—to bend and sway to the will of *Gotte*, like the trees in the wind. Hannah was a healer, a braucher. Traumatized, her folk were moaning. Their hurts—mind and body—were many.

The vintage Greyhound halted again. The progress of the four-vehicle convoy was slow. They were on the outskirts of Grayling, about halfway between Clare and their Free North destination beyond the Straits. A month ago, before the bridge battle, Colonel Dennis evacuated Grayling's Army post, regrouping further north at Indian River. XCons, pushing towards the bridge, vandalized the road sign pointing towards the base: "Pussies!" and a crude drawing of the same had been wetly scrawled across the National Guard emblem.

Walker called for a halt. His driver, Mr. Butters—a large man in a black beret—braked the *Pony* obligingly. The reverend stood and cleared his throat for a quote. His PR assistant pushed record on her tablet:

"If a window in a building is broken and is left unrepaired, all the rest of the windows will soon be broken."

The reverend looked brightly at the driver's eyes in the mirror, then over to his assistant as well. Neither of his followers made a move, waiting for Walker to continue, unsure of the quote's source.

"Kelling and Wilson, 1982, authors of the broken windows theory," Walker cited, then nodding to the Pony's resident artist—an Anti-Viral fighter with graffiti skills. The Antiva activist jumped from the bus, quickly rolling white paint over the defaced sign. Back aboard, the driver put his Greyhound in gear, and they resumed the road.

North of Grayling, they passed through the town of Indian River. The marshy bottleneck was a graveyard of corpses—both human and vehicular. A month ago, Dennis's Griffins annihilated a column of XCons advancing towards the bridge battle. His well-placed howitzers havocked the red-eyed horde, preventing the Viral pincer from joining Panzer's Chosen. Many Spreaders were killed in the Griffin ambush, their equipment taken or destroyed, and some slaves—including Hannah Hochstettler—were set free.

Griffins and Rangers had hurried towards the Straits—no time to bury bodies. Marshy arteries along the river were clotted with unburied dead, leaving meat on the bone for starving scavengers. The Aghori—with Jones and Mackenzie murdered—deserted Panzer and Boss Sharkey for good. Wolves and the water-moat around Mackinac scattered them south. Emaciated, the once proud paramilitary now existed on the fringe. Virucide gone and ammunition going fast, the skeletons shriveled—inky skin sagging from brittle bones.

A two-man team, tattooed and terrible in defeat, now haunted the place. They watched the approaching convoy—fat with juicy targets—with ravenous eyes.

The Gorie sniper team was in position, the spotter glassing windage markers at the pinch point. With so few rounds remaining, they had to make this shot. By rote, the skeletal operators began their ritual, the whispered incantation of survival.

Spotter: "By eye, go to the Greyhound." The order of the approaching vehicles was Humvee, Greyhound, X-bus, Humvee.

Shooter: "Contact." His naked eye tracked the vintage bus as it wove around the wreckage.

Spotter: "Go to glass." The shooter put his eye to the riflescope, describing the target.

Shooter: "I've got a silver bus. Blacked out windows. Antennas on the roof."

Spotter: "That's your bus. Target the driver. Check parallax and mil." The shooter did so and called it.

Spotter: "Check level. Holdover, three point nine." The shooter adjusted, taking the slack out of his trigger, exhaling slowly.

Shooter: "Ready." His reticle was on the nearside window. The Gorie's pulse slowed; his aim was steady, waiting only on the wind call to deliver death to the driver.

Spotter: "Left, point two."

A fractional adjustment. The shooter fired—*CRACK!*—working the bolt, only two rounds remaining. His spotter looked for impact. The bullet spidered the window glass, failing to penetrate its polycarbonate proofing. Their shriveled stomachs raged against the still-rolling machine.

Spotter: "Lock and clear. Displace!"

Bugging out from their position, they were already taking fire. The rear gun truck, a black-painted Humvee, opened up with its heavy machine gun—*Dhak! Dhak! Dhak! Dhak!*—pulverizing their nest. The lead Humvee accelerated and would soon cut them off. The tattooed team tried running, but their withered legs were weak. Stashing their spotting scope and rifle bought them some time, but they were soon surrounded by black-bereted militia pointing weapons. Hands high, the two Gories surrendered, expecting death to be imminent.

A Panther stepped aboard the *Pony* to deliver her report. "Reverend, we've got 'em."

Walker and his assistant looked up from the tablet; they were working on the next transmission. "Very well," the man said gravely, "I'll be there in a moment."

The Panther nodded, stepping off the bus to prepare the two prisoners for interrogation. Walker's assistant looked worried. "Sir, maybe that's not a great idea?" She indicated the side window, spider-webbed by impact.

The driver—still shaken—observed his boss in the rear view. A quote was coming, the big man would bet on it.

The reverend cleared his throat, answering his PR assistant: "You will achieve more in this world through acts of mercy than you will through acts of retribution."

The driver nodded; frickin' Mandela, he'd heard that one before. Butters levered the bus door open, and Walker stepped down, surrounded by a pack of Panthers.

Two men were on their knees on the rubble-strewn asphalt. Their fatigues frayed, their musculature melted. White-eyed and hairless, they appeared uninfected.

The preacher man gestured and the black berets backed off. He looked at the bullet-impacted glass, perfectly placed to blow the brains from his driver. "That's some fine shooting, soldiers, especially in this wind."

The two scavengers, hollowed out by hunger, looked up at the tall, gray-haired man, the decider of their fate. This didn't sound like an execution.

"Let me guess, special operations? Spent some time in Afghanistan, did you?"

Skeletal, they stared at him, unblinking. After a pause, one croaked out a correction: "East Africa, sir. Camp Lemonnier."

Walker smiled, able to connect. "I've been there. Djibouti. You're Marines then? Force Recon?"

The Aghori remained silent, still unsure of their fate. They'd cannibalized the dead. They'd executed innocents. They'd sold their souls to Sharkey. Expecting a bullet, they knew they deserved it.

"We can't take you with us, not now anyway. But show these fighters where you've stashed your weapons and you'll be treated decently."

Walker reached down, and with his two large hands pulled them slowly upright. He gave his name, requested theirs, and the sniper team complied. Dan and Roy stood rigid, eyes-front for inspection. *Semper Fidelis* had been their motto, but faithful to what?

Walker boarded the bus, had a whispered word with his driver, then headed towards his office in the rear. The pair of prisoners led their escorts to the discarded sniper rifle and spotting scope. The weapons were confiscated. The Panthers mounted up. The four vehicles drove away, leaving Indian River and its dead marshes behind.

Left behind as well were the two Marines, a pallet of rations, a pocket-sized US Constitution, and instructions to turn themselves in, when ready, to any Old Law outpost.

Someone had sketched a fish on the crate of MREs with a sharpie. The meals, ready-to-eat, were all the same. Menu 21: Lemon Pepper Tuna with Tortillas and Pound Cake.

The reverend couldn't help it. In his clear script, he penned a quote—Mandela again—to fit the moment, the mood:

"To be free is not merely to cast off one's chains, but to live in a way that respects and enhances the freedom of others."

The driver—not shot, not killed, not yet—watched his would-be murderers shrink in the mirror. The two men hadn't moved. Experts at calculations, they were stymied by the preacher. Butters shook his head; he'd seen it before. Ballistic tables were one thing, *Walks-on-Water* quite another.

The rest of their route was uneventful: Topinabee, Riggsville, and then the broken bridge appeared. The once-blue paint was smoke-stained, half-melted and running with rust. The cold Straits were whipped by wind, and every wave wore a cap.

The convoy exited at Mackinaw City. Abandoned vehicles had been shoved to the side. At the ferry dock they fanned out, guarding against ambush. There was no need; the Free North began here. Colonel Dennis had garrisoned the town. Yellow Griffin flags, unyielding, flew from the lighthouse and historic fort.

Through binoculars, Panthers watched the final tack of the patched-up ferry and its jury-rigged sails. During the bridge battle its wheelhouse had been destroyed by a drone. Rough welds and unpainted steel roughened her visage, but *Nodin—Anishinaabemowin* for Wind—was graceful under sail, still serving her purpose.

Deckhands tied her to the pier. Uniformed guardsmen disembarked to relieve their comrades. A trio of Harleys rolled down the ramp. The bikers sported SIS jackets and holsters with long-barreled pistols. The St. Ignace Scouts nodded to the Panthers before roaring south down I-75 on a mission of their own.

A medical checkpoint awaited the newly freed labor force. No one boarded the ferry until Dr. Chow and his staff certified them Covee-free. Scoured of Virals and bandits alike, the Upper Peninsula was healthy; Colonel Dennis intended to keep it that way. Among Free Northers were many Hidden who—so far anyway—remained unexposed.

The Amish, exiting their bus, were processed by medics wearing PPE. Rapid diagnostic tests were administered. Hannah Hochstettler waited on her results in a fenced area where hot food and pamphlets were distributed. The convoy, with its two buses and two escorts, had already turned south for another run at freedom.

Thirty minutes later, with zero positive results, the fugitives were welcomed aboard, lines were thrown and the battle-scarred *Nodin* blustered her way across the foam-streaked Straits.

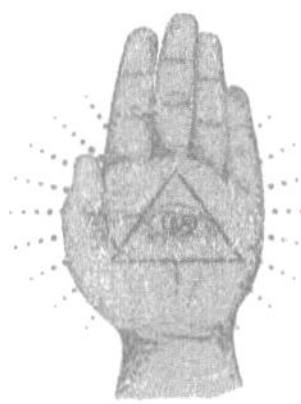

Stars and Stripes Forever

SERGEANT AMANDA TAYLOR SAID FAREWELL to Walker's bus convoy, then devoted the day to redeploying her task force. A small garrison would remain at Clare's airfield to guard the prisoners and process refugees as the plantations fell apart. Amanda led her remaining Griffs—fuel tankers, and towed cannons too—towards Panzer's Kalamazoo compound, five hours south on shitty roads. "Nothing in, nothing out," was Walker's advice. "Put a cage around Doctor Schark."

Romence Road and Portage was the northwest corner of that cage. Rangers Robert and Freddy, wielding hatchets, finished covering the Humvee and its heavy machine gun with brush as an early dusk descended. The vehicle, well camouflaged by branches, interdicted the intersection and was patched into the radio net cast around Boss Sharkey.

The prepper brothers held a quiet chat with the Guardsman crewing the Humvee's radio and .50-cal. All three watched the night for movement. A cold wind was shaking the trees; nearby woods were loud with sound. The Guardsman shared his MRE dessert, stale carrot cake: "Where's your buddy Thorn at anyway?"

Robert rolled his eyes towards the treeline. The Guardsman grinned and said, "Tree-huggin' again?" Mouths full, the Rangers nodded. Word got around, rumor too. The exploits of the ELF Sentinels—securing Line 5's pump-stations against petro pollution—grew with each telling. Plus, the colonel had singled

Thorn out, shaking his hand, praising dude's prowess at Indian River.

Green lights blipped on their radio as its scanner found a frequency. Joking stopped as the Griffin operator made adjustments. The transmission began with a marching band playing a familiar tune. Freddy knew it: "That's Sousa, 'Stars and Stripes Forever.'"

The brassy anthem faded as a military voice took over. "Good evening America, this is General Kamul speaking to you tonight from your nation's capital."

Robert and Freddy looked at the Griff, who explained, "Three-star. Army. Led the purge after the assassination. Commander of the Hands."

Kamul continued, "Now, there's been lots of rumors about Red Hands and the Confederacy of Red Patriotic States, the CORPS. Supposedly we're racists, radicals, and rebels all rolled into one." Kamul's folksy manner came through loud and clear. "Lord knows we're not perfect, I'm the first to admit it, but we're trying to be. We're fighting hard to hold on to the heritage of our great nation and its founders."

He paused as the Sousa march swelled. "Everything we've done has been by the book and authorized by law. After the murder of our dear leader, his successor, Vice President Fiske, used title 32, chapter five, section 502 of the United States Code to authorize National Guard units, including D.C.'s 372nd Red Hand Battalion, to restore order and defend democracy."

The familiar music marched on.

"This we have done, though it hasn't been easy. Our domestic enemies are many. We fight against Virals who wish to spread their disease. We fight against racists who want revenge against whites. We fight against anarchists who kill police and first responders. We fight against companies who would profit from our problems. We fight against fear. We fight for you!"

The music was drowned out by a loud ovation from Congress. The broadcast continued using snippets from Kamul's speech earlier that day: "Mr. President, Mr. Speaker, Senators and Representatives, I thank you for this honor and I dedicate this medal to every patriot that has perished fighting for freedom."

The slick PR package was delivered via airwaves, on multiple channels and various frequencies. Red militias boosted the signal, relaying it if they could. Kamul's propaganda was propagated in the open, unscrambled and unencrypted, a very public service announcement to an under-serviced public. But they listened. What else could they do?

Colonel Dennis, preceded by his pipe smoke, spiraled up the Wawatam lighthouse, part of his nightly routine. Dennis studied the list of new arrivals, specifically their trades, optimizing how best to employ them. The signals specialist staffing the tower had her earphones on, monitoring the scanner. Dennis took his eyes from the manifest when he saw her perk up and hit record. Something was coming through. She unplugged her headset and Kamul's voice filled the smoky lantern room.

... title 32, chapter five, section 502 of the United States Code to authorize National Guard units, including D.C.'s 372nd Red Hand Battalion, to restore order and defend democracy.

Dennis, amateur historian, shook his head. Kamul's Unique Law Loophole was the fine print on the death certificate of democracy.

Red Liz silenced Lazy Boy, all part of her plan. The Non-Compliant prisoners, freezing in their shipping container, overheard the radio of their jailers. Campbell didn't recognize the orator, but the commanding tone was obvious. Trouble. Lots of it.

Our domestic enemies are many. We fight against Virals who wish to spread their disease.

Cowboy muttered, "Well fuck you too, bud." Liz slithered his way, excited. It was time.

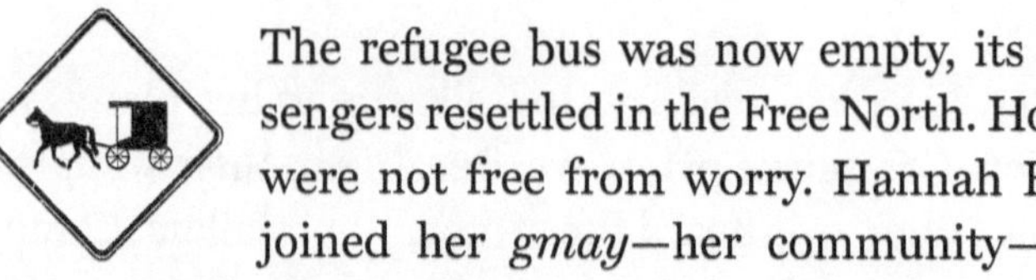 Anti-Viral fighters controlled Detroit's refineries. So far, there'd been no push from Panzer to retake them. Walker had sent engineers, and they were doing what they could. Stabilizing existing gasoline reserves was one thing; refining new fuels was something else. In the office, a switch was thrown so the plant workers could hear the speech too. Kamul's flinty voice struck sparks with the volunteer refiners.

We fight against anarchists who kill police and first responders.

Antiva raised their fists as the general was booed.

Dr. Schark lost his appetite. He should have ignored Wermer and finished his date. Patient Nighthawk, strapped sedately to her seat, hadn't touched her food, watching him—as always—like a bloody hawk.

We fight against companies who would profit from our problems.

Kamul's change in tone, and allegiance, was clear: the CORPS found something in her bloodwork. The Hands would be coming for her. Worse, they'd be coming—Schark gulped—for him.

The refugee bus was now empty, its Amish passengers resettled in the Free North. However, they were not free from worry. Hannah Hochstettler joined her *gmay*—her community—in nervous prayer inside the St. Ignace church they'd been assigned to sleep in. Candles lit the scene; no radios were heard, but menace crackled through the airwaves. The healer could feel the hatred in her bones.

 In Bill Ferny's cabin, loudmouths were debating Min's teaching methods—way too woke for the Beaver Bois. Deputy Williams, eyewitness to her Indian witchery, was there as well. The Ferny clan drank moonshine in the shadows as wind beat against the glass in frustrated fury. The AM transmission, relayed by Red militia on the mainland, passed right through. A drunken uncle fiddled with a battery powered radio, and suddenly Kamul was there, just one of the boys, sippin' shine, cussin' about covens and other female crimes.

 Dusk. The wind had not abated, nor would it till tomorrow. The waxing moon skinny-dipped in a sky free of clouds, of clutter. Michigan, and most of the Midwest, had lost its grid. The four-vehicle convoy slowly probed its way south, the antennae of the Greyhound extended, sifting the nightscape for sound. Then they twitched; a frequency was found. Walker's assistant pushed a button and General Kamul filled the interior. The bus driver growled, gripping his wheel tighter. The reverend looked up from his notes; Walker hoped for a breakthrough and he got it.

There's a man in Michigan whose name you might have heard. He calls himself Walker and he speaks in disguise. Now, we've done some research and we've discovered Walker's true identity. You won't be surprised to find out he's a preacher. A radical, a blacktivist, he's got a rap sheet and a record.

The broadcast amplified the boos and catcalls of Congress as Kamul's voice continued:

We found out something else. His birth certificate has issues. He's barely American, got African ancestors, Kenyan royalty. A banana king!

The laugh track was real, no dubbing necessary. The transmission terminated with Kamul's call to arms: *Let the Hands be your arsenal of democracy!*

Expertly edited, the Sousa march ended as well, in triumph. The techie affirmed Walker's questioning look: "Yes sir, we got it." She powered down her equipment in the dim light of *Pony's* interior.

The reverend queried its occupants: "And who was the general paraphrasing with his 'arsenal of democracy' line?"

The dozen passengers—staff and bodyguards—went suddenly deaf, suddenly dumb. The reverend called to his driver, "How about it, Mr. Butters? Do you know?"

The surly Panther, a touch too loudly, replied, "That's FDR, sir. Franklin! Delano! Roosevelt!"

Walker grinned. "Correct! Fireside chat, 1940. December, I believe? FDR utilized the radio to warn the American people about the dangers of isolationism. A fitting subject for our own times as well."

Walker's congregation listened attentively, albeit tiredly. It had been a long day. At their next stop—a bathroom break near Houghton Lake—they disembarked and sought relief, some singly, some in pairs. The black-beret militia, ever vigilant, secured their pee perimeter. The paint-can artist, inspired, scrambled up the embankment and with a white brush tagged a green MDOT sign, the first of many. The graffitist weaponized Kamul's slur by painting a new sigil, a stylized crown. His boss, *Walks-on-Water*, a descendant of ancient kings, began his ascent.

Mukwa Rescued

FROM HIS SMOKY MAN CAVE ON INDIAN POINT, Mukwa heard the bell toll—incoming craft!—and emerged, curious, scratching his filthy pelt. He had a feeling this would happen, a green dream, a vision. The bay road was soon crowded with wagons and bicycles. Mukwa joined the boodle as the *Amiks* paused their winter preparations, migrating en masse towards the harbor.

Six big canoes were rounding the breakwater, escorted by an armored gillnetter from the fleet. For the first time in weeks, Mukwa found himself smiling. His facial muscles ached from the effort; resting bitch face—bear face—was a trap he needed to escape. And he definitely would. There, in the bow of the lead canoe, a wild man was waving. Longhaired and amber-eyed, behold his biker buddy, Shaggy Wolf!

"Hullo all you Beavers!" Shaggy made a V with his hands, pointing at his crotch. The islanders, gaunt-looking and scrambled by the bell, were not amused. "And where the fuck is the bear-man, the Wabi Muk, the beast?"

Baptiste, leader of the voyageurs, tried securing the loose cannon. Yeah right. Shaggy sat for a second, then bounded up again, this time standing on the bow seat and bellowing, "Muk, you muscle-headed moron! Where the fuck are you?"

Mukwa, face sore from grinning, stepped clear of the crowd, raised both arms and roared. Shaggy did a little dance, rocking the boat, earning curses from its scowling crew.

"I hope you're ready asshole, this is a fucking rescue!"

The canoes tied up at the quarantine pier, a high fence keeping them caged. No one in, no one out was still council policy. Autumn's boy Loon—scout and navigator—bid Brian farewell as he entered the cage, rejoining big Baptiste and his fellow voyageurs. Loon's R&R on Beaver Island was officially over.

Samantha, unsurprised by their arrival, had brought medicine. Still dusty from King's Highway, the Anishinaabe elder received letters from Dr. Chow and Colonel Dennis. Baptiste's booming voice informed her that Autumn—fellow *Mide* and water protector—had returned to Manitoulin Island, far to the east, to refresh her strength and the strength of her tribe.

The black-bearded Métis man summarized the plan for his flotilla. Three of the six canoes—weather permitting—would scout the Wisconsin side of Lake Michigan; time to see what those Cheeseheads were up to … or had Covee curdled them all?

Another canoe was gifted to the Naturals, a token of thanks for ELF heroics—and losses—at the bridge battle. Besides, leadership had seen the capabilities of the militant Sentinels. Dennis drafted a letter of marque, signed and sealed 125th Infantry Regiment—Yield to None! Any damage the eco-privateers could do to Panzer would be a net gain for the Free North and its peoples.

Baptiste, with Loon safely aboard, would lead the remaining two canoes back to St. Ignace, delivering medicine and news to Dr. Chow before heading east, hugging Huron's shore down to Detroit. The time for living blind was over. They'd won a respite at the bridge and needed to see what was out there.

Voyageurs and islanders exchanged parcels via the no man's land between fences. Colonel Dennis had gifted solar chargers to keep their radios running. He also sent a codebook for communications, tower-to-tower, Whiskey to Wawatam in St. Ignace. The range was iffy, but with the right atmospherics, it could work.

The Beavers—busy all fall—gifted the hard-paddling voyageurs jerked meat and canned veggies, as much as they could spare. Every calorie would count on their mission to map the terra incognita of the Upper Great Lakes.

Sentinels, scarred veterans of many battles, visited the quarantine zone that night. They wanted news of Elena, their leader, heartbroken and hospitalized in St. Ignace. The finale of the bridge battle pitted Sentinels against Aghori. The tattooed skeletons tried sabotaging Line 5's pump stations, flooding the crystalline Straits with tar sands oil. Elena, bright-eyed, had fought the Gorie leader blade-to-blade and was badly gashed. Baptiste bore grim tidings: her body had healed, but her mind had not. She and Captain Young, the last resident patients, were being cared for by Dr. Chow in the Healing House. Samantha's medicine—Gaia willing—might help them both.

The rolling Earth turned its face towards the sun, the arc of transit further south every day. The Beavers, paler already, missed its heat, as did the leafy citizens of kingdom Plantae. The winds were variable, the big lake becalmed. People and plants both faced east, basking in whatever photons beamed their way. Sunrise signaled the time for farewells, and the voyageurs were eager to depart.

Mukwa sat dockside on his duffel. He hadn't packed much: sketchpad, pencils, dirty clothes, and some sage tied with string. His wrinkled gran, ol' *nookomis*, was busy with her Mason jars, her clinking tinctures. The wise one, foxlike, trotted over. No nonsense, Granny signaled him to stand. Well-trained, the circus bear obliged. "Mind your dreams, young man." Sammy hugged him hard, then let him go. What else was new?

Sparrow, Mukwa's squadmate from ELF Country—*RIP Miguel, Tomas, Squirrel, and Bull*—was at the wharf with Sentinels—all women—lading their war canoe. Amphibious again, where would the commandos strike next? Despite four months sharing the island, resident Beavers gave the parka-clad women a wide berth. Mukwa did too. Recent casualties—Diana's death,

Elena's wounding, Hawk's flight—had honed their hatred for Spreaders. These women, Daughters of Gaia, were deadly.

Sparrow and Muk shot the shit, both awkward in the absence of Nighthawk—*KIA? MIA? Screwing some mainlander?*

Sparrow updated him on news from ELF Country: the deer harvest had been good, the island herd was healthy, and there was much work to do. She'd been teaching at Miin's academy; the students there were doing well. "Goodbye Oso, you hairy beast. Take care of yourself, OK?"

"You too." Muk clasped arms with the muscular gymnast, then moved away, something caught in his throat.

Sister Miin found him next; she'd canceled classes for the day. *Nishiime* took his huge hand with both of hers. "Goodbye brother bear, and good luck."

She gave his calloused paw a squeeze.

"Bye Miin, good luck to you."

Ever a bookworm, sis pulled a small hardcover—red, green, and yellow—from her satchel, handing it over. Mukwa grinned as he flipped it open.

In the great green room

there was a telephone

and a red balloon

and a picture of

the cow jumping over the moon

Mighty Muck's chin began to quiver, words blurring on the cardboard page. Miin—quiet as a mouse—whispered their mantra beside him:

"And there were three little bears, sitting on chairs."

Their sleepovers, her puppet shows, popcorn and root beer with Gran.

"And two little kittens and a pair of mittens—"

Muck abruptly pulled away. Shouldering his gear, he hurried towards the gate, where a skinny, dreadlocked man flashed a smile from no man's land, something feral in his grin. The girl watched the two men reunite, thumping backs and grunting at each other.

"Uncle Keith, you'd better look out for him."

Voyaging

PADDLING AWAY FROM BEAVER—freshly provisioned with food and medicine—the six canoes soon divided. Three headed west to reconnoiter Lake Michigan, next stop Green Bay. Baptiste led two boats back to St. Ignace. They had Samantha's medicine to deliver, then would hug the Huron coast south to Detroit. The last canoe was crewed by sharp-eyed Sentinels, each one an angry D.O.G. Baptiste good-lucked them as the hooded women veered away, paddling south towards Panzerland and the rumored fray.

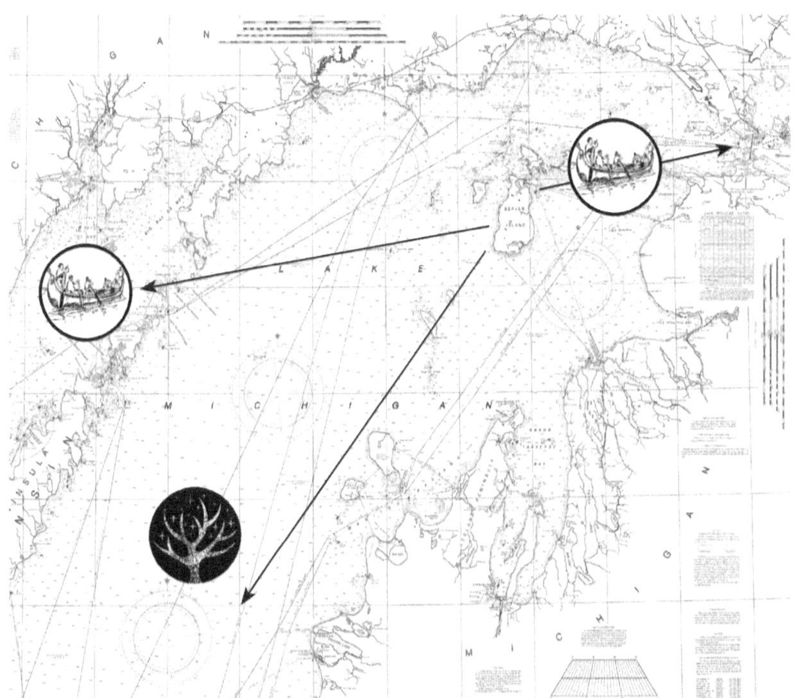

Numbed by island routine, the Daughters volunteered to make a push on Panzer. With optimal atmospherics, Whiskey Point's antenna caught snippets of Walker's broadcasts. Word got around, even in ELF Country. Dockside, Baptiste had offered the Sentinels rifles, radios, and ammunition. Grim, the women refused. They raised silent hands in farewell, then muscled south to do Gaia's bidding.

"Good riddance," grumbled some of the men in his canoe. Mukwa didn't argue. Sentinels were strange, Daughters of Gaia even stranger.

The three-day blow was over. The big lake was calm; winds were light and cold. Skies were clear and the October day—ever shortening—beamed golden.

Baptiste's two canoes reached the broken bridge at twilight. Looking up, Mukwa and Shaggy observed the severed span and remembered: the bus barricade, a burning tower, their motorcycle charge, the *swoosh* of LAWS rockets, a mammoth horn, SKTR drones, raptors, airstrikes, and that second fucking horn.

Passing beneath the shattered steel—stained by blood and battle—conversation ceased. Stone-heavy, their hearts plummeted to the bottom, two hundred icy feet below. Guilty, each survivor probed beneath the surface: the underwater canyons of their conscience. The wrack of Humvees, of Harleys, the metallic bones of not one mammoth plow-truck, but two.

And the bodies? What state were they in? The trapped, burned, gunshot, and drowned? Had they rotted? Or did cold waters preserve? Had they been feasted upon, flensed clean by feeding fish and vampire lampreys? The survivors, post-trauma, pictured the sculpture they'd constructed, a rusting art installation festooned with wavy-haired corpses, zombified merfolk encrusted with mollusks—zebra, quagga, unionid.

Emerging from its metallic menace, both crews breathed easier. The moon, at first quarter, shone bright upon the waves, bouncing cold light from a sun they couldn't see. There were watchers in the Wawatam tower. A Coast Guard Response Boat motored to intercept. The Ignace docks were crowded with craft of all sizes; the biggest of these was *Nodin*. Kamikazied by drones, Mukwa—even on the bridge—had felt her explode. Captain Diana had been atomized, her particulates scattered across the Straits. One more death to grieve, but unlike Keith's or Diving-Duck's, hers was bodiless. There'd been no corpse to cry upon.

They touched at the dock long enough for Baptiste to offload the crated tincture. Working by lamplight, he instructed the stevedores to bring it straight to Dr. Chow. As they were making ready to shove off, Colonel Dennis appeared, briefing Baptiste on the latest intel.

"There was another broadcast, three days ago. My signals specialist confirmed its authenticity."

"Walker again?"

"Appears so."

"What news from the south?"

"Walker claims Anti-Virals have taken the refineries. Spreaders are on the run. That it's time to *scour away the hate*. His words, not mine."

Baptiste's doubt loomed large in the dark. "Does this change our plan?"

Dennis squatted down, leveling himself with the tied-up canoe. "I don't think so. But, if possible, let's get a better look at Bay City, Saginaw, and Detroit, especially those refineries. I'd like Walker's intel confirmed."

The colonel handed across some letters, sealed with wax. "Safe passage, for you and your boat crews."

Baptiste took the passes. *"Oui, Colonel.* We'll do our best." He pointed his flashlight at a fuel tank on the pier.

Dennis shook his head. "We're down to fumes. We keep the Response Boat running, and *Nodin* when the wind's not right.

We've been ferrying across the uninfected. We processed another batch, mostly Amish, just today. The Free North needs farmers as well as fighters. Isaiah 2:4, not just swords, but ploughshares too."

Dennis aimed his beam at the armament lashed beneath their gunnels. "What about weapons and ammunition? You voyageurs have what you need?"

Baptiste gave a French-flavored shrug. *Je suppose.* Heard anything else?"

The Army officer shared that a Panther convoy had taken sniper fire at Indian River. "Spidered the driver's window. Lucky for him the glass had been proofed."

Baptiste nodded as a heavy parcel was lowered into Mukwa's canoe. Up and down the Straits there'd been raids, mostly for food, carried out by Panzer deserters and disbanded Gories. Before sailing for Manitoulin, Autumn had named them, *bakaak*—skeletal spirits, bones draped with skin. Others whispered an older word, defying taboo, *wiindigo*. Baptiste crossed himself. *Mon Dieu,* who's to say they were wrong?

Dennis relayed last night's broadcast: "You've heard of this man, General Kamul? The Red Hands? Based in Washington?"

Baptiste, eager to depart, lifted his cleft chin, *non.*

"You will soon. He transmitted in the open, wants to be heard. Multiple channels, multiple frequencies. The Reds in D.C. have got some pull. Kamul insulted Walker, calling him an illegal alien, a banana king."

Baptiste gave an impatient shrug. He wanted to be past Bois Blanc, and through its narrow channel, before dawn.

The colonel shoved them off. "Good luck to you then. Godspeed voyageurs!"

The two crews backed their paddles, pivoting the oversize canoes. They were soon through the breakwater and past the Wawatam light, paddling southeast with Bois Blanc to port and the setting moon astern. The two canoes were cradled by current. Autumn's boy gave a tremolo cry and was answered by one water bird, then another. Ancient aids to navigation, loon-cry piloted their passage.

There were ten in each boat, and Baptiste was their leader. The big man, from the stern, began it, caution be damned:

Voyageur! va faire tes bagages

C'est à l'aube que nous partirons.

C'est à l'aube oui, oui, oui

C'est à l'aube non, non, non

C'est à l'aube que nous partirons.

The Canadians joined the chorus as the two boats accelerated. When the verses turned English, Mukwa and Shaggy howled along:

Down the river you can hear a wind song

Bearing tales of the voyageurs.

Bearing tales oui, oui, oui

Bearing tales non, non, non

Bearing tales of the voyageurs.

Voices carry over water. The oldest pines, bioacoustic, remembered: for three hundred years such songs had been sung. Then steel hulls displaced wood, petroleum out-powered mere paddles, and the only music was made by machines. But then came a pause, a sudden quiet, as people disappeared and the world recalibrated. The fumy skies cleared, the Milky Way blazed, and hark!—the trees nudged each other—*La Chanson du Voyageur* was heard again!

But pines and cedars weren't the only audience. Starvelings listened with empty bellies. Their once-muscled flesh had atrophied. The Aghori had been gored, hollowed out by hunger. And winter approached, the white wolf of the north.

The Healing House

DR. CHOW PEERED THROUGH DARKLING GLASS into what was once the crowded quarantine ward of the Mackinac Straits Health System. Only two patients remained, the Sentinel Elena and Captain Frank Young of the 125th Infantry Regiment.

It was almost midnight. The resupply of tincture had been delivered, and Chow was eager to use it. Baptiste and his voyageurs had just departed. At HQ, Colonel Dennis finished his notes, knocked out his pipe, and blew out the candle. St. Ignace slept, all but Chow and his two patients. The two residents—walking wounded—had become accustomed to each other. He'd been treating them for a month. Quarantine officially over, the pair took walks along the peninsula but spent their nights in the ward. Neither of them had healed, not properly.

Young had frequent visitors: Booker and Cruz, other Griffins from his unit, occasionally the colonel himself. Elena had fewer. Her comrades were Sentinels. Cleared from QT, the women returned to Beaver Island and its sylvan sanctuary.

Chow had been a Natural once, living the green life in ELF Country. He'd kept notes during collapse on the pathology of SARS-CoV-2 and its variant, Stinger. The world had not been ready. Too ponderous, the institutions all failed, vaccines too. Covee morphed, gained function. WHO, CDC, DID, all said it was impossible. Too deadly, the virus should have burned itself out. They were wrong. Unalive, undead, the zombie virus was crowned.

Corona, once combined with Stinger, became a nuke. It blew the old world away. Funeral pyres mushroomed, clouding the skies. Its blast radius—biological—was everywhere. Neutronic, its RNA spared physical structures, but city-by-city the people disappeared.

The doctor's people, too. Daniel Chow had lost his wife, his boys, before fleeing to the woods. Science-oriented, he'd been a reluctant Natural from the start—a lonely Galileo in that Gaia-centric group. He'd done what he could, studying the elves he lived with and the Spreaders they fought. Ghoulish, he ghosted over battlefields, sampling serum from the living and the dead. He'd even had a captive, Bob Campbell, an impatient cowboy. Confined in a Beaver Island cabin, he'd treated the Viral, reducing the man's load over time. Campbell's red eyes had faded to pink, his sociopathic tendencies, fading as well. There were too many variables for surety, but Chow's hypothesis was that separation from other infected, combined with nature therapy and healthy habits could help restore infected to themselves.

Eventually, Captain Young and his men had found him out, but, so far, had yet to say a word: Chow's secret, Chow's shame, but Young hadn't snitched.

The colonel wanted Young, his best field officer, returned to the duty roster ASAP. Dr. Chow wanted the same. At the bridge battle, Young had suffered blast wounds; his brain had not healed. The first batch of tincture had done some good, but Young relapsed quickly when the medicine ran out. Chow observed him now at the map, Young's nocturnal routine. The colonel kept it current with unit strength and positions. Walker's broadcasts—and now Kamul's—keeping the big picture in view.

Next, the doctor's gaze went to Elena. Her map was the moon. The ward had an enclosed garden. She'd slung a hammock between two trees, with a sleeping bag against the frost. Chow could see her through the looking glass. The quarter moon was setting. Her once-blonde hair silvered, by moonlight, by mourning. Elena's life-partner was dead. Diana, helming *Nodin*, had been fire-balled by a drone.

Elena's knife wound, like Young's TBI, had refused to heal. Dr. Chow had few options. During collapse, medicine disappeared quickly. With short shelf lives, antibiotics were difficult to stockpile. When the grid came unplugged and supply chains lost their linkage, no new drugs were made. Or if they had, they'd gone undelivered, at least to them.

Chow beheld the Mason jar, the first of many from the crate: *At-the-last*. The golden tincture, island-made, had sped the recovery of his entire ward. He opened his patient notebook, dating the entry October 21st. He readied his ledger, boiled water for tea, and measured out a careful dose.

The pharmacon, catalyzed by heat, impacted olfaction first. A familiar effect from the original batch a month ago, though again it surprised him with its intensity. Suddenly, Chow basked in sunlight and the scent of green growth. He smelled the gloss of textbook pages, and the sweet breath of his wife, leaning in for a kiss. His mind cleared, a smile twitching his lips. His worry-lines unfurrowed as Daniel portioned out their tea.

Bonnie and Clyde

NOW BONNIE AND CLYDE ARE THE BARROW GANG

I'm sure you all have read.

how they rob and steal;

and those who squeal,

are usually found dying or dead.

—Bonnie Parker, "The Trail's End" (1910–1934)

Lazy Boy hadn't squealed. Liz killed him silently. No sound escaped their shipping container, though they themselves were about to. Cowboy had been squatting over the shit bucket when Liz garroted their fellow prisoner with her flex cuffs. By the time Campbell got himself zipped up to protest, the sickly looking Viral had stopped twitching.

Photons from electric light found the seams of their confinement. The Gothic letters of his chest tattoo—𝔏𝔞𝔷𝔶 𝔅𝔬𝔶—had stopped heaving. A godawful smell erupted from his beshat body. Cowboy and Liz overheard the radio of their jailers: a bravado voice, a marching band. In the filtered light, the corpse appeared smiling. Liz was smiling too. Lazy had sharpened his teeth to points, all part of her plan.

The woman, disfigured by blast and by fire, slithered to the dead man to utilize his dentistry.

"What do you think you're doing?"

She chafed her cuffs on Lazy's canines.

"Come on Liz, no way that will work!"

With a slight pop, her plastic parted. She rubbed her wrists. The bracelets still pinched, but her hands were free. "Come on, Campbell. Time's a wastin'." She air-twirled a lasso, and her cowboy complied.

Together they sawed through Bob's restraints. Body odors, the slop bucket, and armed guards all around, but damn, she turned him on! They'd done some kinky shit together, but their current exertions—side-by-side and sweaty—might take the fucking cake.

Her wounds were bad and hadn't fully healed. Ambushed near Charlevoix, her column had been trapped in a kill zone. She'd lost half her looks, basically the whole left side. What re-mained though was enough. Toiling together—*faster, harder, almost there*—they moaned in mutual triumph when Cowboy's cuffs finally parted.

The irony was obvious, but Bob didn't care. Mere months ago Liz had betrayed, tased, and cuffed *him*. Now here they were, escaping together. Oh well, love and war—or in this case, lust and larceny—either way, it all seemed fair. Cowboy was no in-nocent. In the shit stench of the Non-Compliant container, his past became present: nooses, light poles, caged women, Sam-my and Sarah in the farmyard, old Dawdy gracing their meal. Surprise, surprise, Bob the builder was falling apart. Whatever healing he'd experienced via Chow or the Amish, Red Liz was the cause of his relapse.

"Just keep your kisser closed and follow me." Liz peered through a crack to assess the two guardsmen. Her right half was profiled, and damn she looked good. Her auburn hair grew thick on that side. A perfect breast pointed beneath Lazy's hoodie. Her posture was poised: pinup of the apocalypse.

The broadcast they overheard ended with applause. The Humvee radio switched off. Their two guards were muttering.

"Fucking Hands."

"Bloody butchers from what I've heard."

"That Kamul's a fanatic."

"Keeps the lights on though."

"D.C.'s got their grid, gotta give 'em that."

"What about Walker? All that shit about his birth certificate and Kenyan kings?"

Liz began banging on the sheet metal. "Hey! We got a problem here. The kid is freezing to death! Needs a medic. Now!"

The night was cold and trending colder. Their metallic coffin had no heat. Liz retreated to the shadows, her hands faking bondage. Cowboy obliged, doing the same.

The peephole clanged open, an LED light bathing the corpse. Rigor mortis had goosebumped Lazy's flesh. Dude's face was blue. This might just work.

"Shit! Taylor's not gonna like this."

"Taylor nothin', what about Walker!"

"Shit!"

"Mask up! Grab your Taser. Let's move him inside to the hangar."

The guards donned MOPP equipment, checking each others' seals. Liz chided their caution, hoping to prompt a mistake: "He's dying in here! Hurry the fuck up!"

The big doors were unbolted, groaning open on cold hinges. Taser entered first, flashlighting the detainees. Cowboy squatted against a wall, his Amish hat pulled low. He kept his fists together, radiating a humble vibe. Liz did the same. Here we fuckin' go.

"Oh man, it reeks in here! I can smell it through my mask."

The first soldier, light in one hand, Taser in the other, kept the Non-Compliants pinned in their corners. Container secure, the Guardsman gestured and the other Griffin entered.

"God damn! Y'all worse than pigs!" Disgust flavored his voice.

The second soldier, hooded and gloved, knelt by Lazy Boy, checking vitals. Cowboy's eyes glinted from beneath the brim. The lizard flicked her tongue. NOW!

Bob threw himself on the pulse-checker, making sure to pin the man tight.

"Shit!" The Taser dude charged, cattle prod extended.

Bob braced for what was coming, then BAM! He blacked out.

Minutes later, woozy, Bob blinked and came to. The container door was closed, the LED flashlight extinguished. Bodies were on the floor, dim in the shadows. Muddle-minded, he counted the prone: one, two, and Lazy Boy made three.

A masked soldier was stooping over him, poking his body. Campbell couldn't feel a thing. The soldier probed lower. Bob watched a gloved hand grope his crotch. Electrified by lust, he bolted upright, tenting his Amish trousers.

Under the stolen MOPP hood, the lizard wheezed a laugh. "Good ol' Cowboy. Always rises to the occasion."

Fucking Liz.

Ten minutes later, cool as cukes, two hazmatted soldiers emerged, locking the latches behind them. They climbed into the parked Humvee, the larger one stumbling. The engine started up, the transmission was engaged. The vehicle slow-rolled to the gate. Words were exchanged with the duty sentry. There was an icy flash of blue. The Guardsman slumped to the pavement. The gate was lifted; two outlaws roared away.

From heart-break some people have suffered

from weariness some people have died.

But take it all in all;

our troubles are small,

till we get like Bonnie and Clyde.

Farewell and Adieu

THEN THE LORD GOD PROVIDED a leafy plant and made it grow up over Jonah to give shade for his head to ease his discomfort. —Jonah 4:2

The blind man, warm in his burrow, dreamt of trees. His sandy scoop had a roof made of roots. Tiny filaments snaked his way, wanting his water, sniffing his soil. His sleeping body meshed with the mycorrhiza of Goose Island. Sometime in the night, after moonset, the wind diminished. It had blown hard for three days.

In his dreamscape, the trees stopped tossing and stood still, beckoning. They grew right out of the water, rooted in the lakebed many impossible fathoms below. Their piney tops towered high above the surface. Branch to branch they offered a path to the dreamer. All he had to do was wake up and walk.

So he woke. Gone was the sound of whitecaps to windward. He could hear gulls again. The gale had gusted out. He brushed the root webs from his face, his beard. He scooched backwards, careful not to collapse his fragile cave.

Was it brighter? Maybe. He couldn't quite tell. The morning air was alive. Breathing deeply, he bartered with the breeze: taking oxygen, gifting carbon in return.

He couldn't see them, couldn't feel them, the piney creatures from his dream. No large trees had sprung up in the night. Goose Island remained barren, a spit of sand as before. He felt the bones of his body, his skinny legs, his ribby torso. He was shrinking. He was starving. He filled his belly with Lake Huron; bacon and eggs it was not.

Besides starvation, there was no sickness in him, no Covee, no Stinger. Face-to-face with a Spreader and he'd been spared. But for what? For this? A slow death as his body consumed itself for calories? A quicker one, if he took matters in hand? All it would take was hypothermia: a dunking at night, or a too-long swim in any direction. Not yet, but not unthinkable either.

He crabbed his way around the island, circling once, then twice. There were no morsels to be had. If only he had a fish-hook and some string! For the thousandth time he felt his pockets. There was no lighter there, no forgotten match, no knife. Made primitive by such poverties, the modern man mused beneath a bush. Physically marooned, his mind wandered free.

Something pleasant about that tree dream though, something healing. He navigated through his subconscious, avoiding the hazards: memories of the bridge battle, of explosions and drones. He let go of his anger, his Irish rage at the virus and its Spreaders. He let go of Hannigan, O'Donnell, Keith; all his small sins against Annie.

The fisherman unclenched his fists and breathed. The bush he sat beneath, still leafy, breathed as well. Molecules were exchanged, more complex than he knew. He caught a whiff of bog, reminding him of Beaver Island and, somehow, of Miin.

Dying in slow motion, the man felt peace. The rising sun warmed his face and he welcomed it. Sunlight dappled the leaves above his head. He welcomed that too. He could see them flutter: yellowed by frost, still clinging, unstripped by the gale. A great promise was offered, by the air, the sun, the water. Not just to him, but to all, and for always. He believed in the promise. He let himself believe and was saved.

Dappled? Yellow? He blinked his eyes. Something had changed. He couldn't quite see, but was less blind than before. All was not black. The day was a blur of bright. The leaves? Yes, the leaves were there! Were they yellow? Yes, something of that color smeared his mind.

And something else. Important. A large *thing* was looming. Unseen as yet, but felt just the same. Something from his dream. Something promised, something pleasant. The lookout scanned the horizon, seeing only fuzz. Anything further than a few feet was socked in by optic fog.

Instruments on the fritz, he closed one set and opened another. He reached out with mental radar and felt a return. He pinged again and the mass took shape. It was a tree, a pine, carried by current. The gale, wave by wave, had chewed through its footing. Uprooted, the leviathan migrated, west to east, leaving needles in its wake as it wallowed on its way.

This was it! This was the dream! And if it wasn't, he didn't fucking care.

Was it time? Yes it was.

Was he packed? Was his seabag ready?

He croaked out a laugh. He traveled light these days. The ragged man stood up, prepared for what lay ahead. The mariner rotated his apparatus, seeking data with all sensors. Old calculations came quick as he computed: current, time, and tide. He charted his course. Could this work? He dead-reckoned his destination. Was it death?

Another rusty laugh. He was probably dead already. He certainly would be if he stayed. He reveled in the old *fuck-it* feeling. Knee deep already, goodbye Goose Island! He plotted his intercept. The bark-clad creature drifted close. The stowaway waded to his waist, then swam: ten strokes, 20, 100. He sensed its loom, the massy shadow in his mind. He grappled with its branches, then pulled himself aboard.

Captain on deck! He stood upon its trunk, gripping the spokes of its helm. The root rudder held steady, sappy sails squared away. If this was the afterlife, he would take it!

Farewell and adieu to you fair, Spanish ladies.

Farewell and adieu, you ladies of Spain!

For we've received orders to sail back to Boston.

So never no more shall we see you again!

A Campus Stroll

SINCE HER "DATE NIGHT" WITH DR. SCHARK, three more etches marred her skin. The swelling moon had passed first quarter. Kept from windows, Hawk tracked Luna's phases through concrete. She'd be full in a week. Gaia-willing, Hawk would greet the Hunter's Moon face to face.

Last night she dreamt of Miin. She'd met the girl back in ELF Country, the first one, the one they'd had to flee. Dream-Miin had soothed her, or tried to. Hawk didn't feel much better.

She knew the promotional video had been distributed, soft porn from Panzerland. Suitors, bio-safe in their bunkers, had placed their bids. Of mercenaries, fuel, and weapons they had plenty; it was women they wanted. The females were kept in their cages: farmer's-daughter, bondage-biker, others, and herself. Hawk's trade value had never been higher. Schark bragged that even the Red Hands were interested, "At the highest level."

Part seller's remorse, part loneliness, the doctor preferred her company. "Keeping an eye on my investment," he explained. She watched him too, not just on screens but side-by-side. The lab results had placated his paranoia. She was not contagious, nor could she be. She was something new. He was interested; everyone was. She was granted rare access to his company, and his campus too. The ELF Sentinel, sharp-eyed, paid attention.

She was costumed and coiffed by a female assistant: a frosty blonde bitch they called Frau. Apparently, a "color-tour of the compound" was on the day's agenda. No black dress and pearls, Frau laid out jeans and a flannel instead. The big man on campus wanted to stroll. Wermer and his halo kept their distance as Hawk, hyper-vigilant, cataloged every detail: greenhouses, labs, armories, barracks, motor pool, fuel reserves. She crunched the data and concluded: Panzer Pharma was understaffed, hungry, and coasting on fumes.

Sharkey seemed shaken, admitting as much: "Nothing in! Nothing out! They've put a cage around me, a cage around *us!*"

The fall colors were peaking. Maples and oaks, blockade-oblivious, did their thing, preparing for winter, sanguine about any siege. Hawk felt their furrowed frequency and hooded her own. Her silence provoked Sharkey, "It's the damn National Guard. That bookish colonel, his scruffy Griffs! Yield to None. Ha! Kamul will test that motto! He'll choke 'em with his Hands. Squeeze 'em till they're Red!"

Sharkey's pace increased. He sported khakis and a blazer. The Prince of Panzer kicked through the leaves; the only prop missing was a spicy latte.

Hawk kept filing: *Kamul, Red Hands, Griffins, a colonel, Yield to None.* The predator kept her bright eyes half-lidded.

Joe Cool grew heated: "Did you know, Ms. Hawk, that all access roads have been cut? Without new mercenaries, I'm trapped! And guess what? You're trapped too, with a *shark in his cage!*"

He was fuming now. "My clients, yours too, have been scared away. One businessman's convoy—totally peaceful mind you—was ambushed and destroyed. *Destroyed!* Our free market has been fucked! If they can't get their *girls*, then I can't get my *guns!*"

Hawk's list lengthened: *clients, convoys, human trafficking, arms deal, ambush.*

"Now the client, well-connected mind you, wants compensation. His mercenaries were murdered; they were supposed to be mine! His tanker truck, filled with fuel for *me*, was stolen too!"

Schark thrashed through the fallen foliage; if there was a pumpkin, he'd have smashed it. "A few survivors babbled about *Greenies*," he accused her with a look, "claimed they were attacked by Black Panthers and worse! I know what you're thinking, how could it get worse? I won't scare you with details, but it could. Cannibalism, my dear, is worse! Skeletons are worse! Being betrayed by people you trained, saved, and cared for is worse!"

Their tour, indeed, had turned colorful. The doctor's tantrum took them to his tower; he hissed at his snake. Wermer slithered over and re-cinched her shackles, tugging Hawk towards her cage.

The October day was mild. The sun sailed through a sea-blue sky, further south each day as the hemisphere tilted away. The resident trees were mostly bare. A gale had blown through, strewing leaves upon the ground. Taking a last gasp before entering her catacomb, the Sentinel sifted each scent, savoring their signatures. Heliotropic, Hawk's face sought the sun. Synchronizing frequencies, she charged herself with solar, with sound. A low V of geese overflew the compound, bound for the Argentine. She converted each decibel, honks into hertz. Her batteries blinked, charging with green.

Shark Cage

SERGEANT TAYLOR SHOOK HER HEAD at the "reports" she was receiving. It was the damn United Nations over here. Multiple militias now enveloped Panzerland: Griffins, Panthers, and Rangers too. Without proper comms, unit leaders scrawled notes, sending them via bicycle. Her ability to command and control the battlespace depended on bad handwriting and the pedal-speed of malnourished messengers. Yes, Dr. Schark was caged, denied resupply. But the bars were bending. If they bent any further, they'd break.

Her Detroit reverend—resistance name Walker—had lent her some Panthers, all he could spare from Free North bus duty. But her core fighters, as always, were Griffs. No finer unit existed. Of this, Amanda was sure. She'd redeployed southwest from Clare, away from Amish country. Her force—infantry and cannons—had given the plantations there a push. Rotten, Panzer's food network had fallen apart. She'd left a small force at Clare's airfield, too small apparently. Her latest comms detailed a jailbreak. One Viral, Lazy Boy, was dead and two others escaped, stealing a Humvee. No MPs were killed, and for that, she was thankful.

The two escapees, Bob Campbell and Red Liz, were high-value targets. Colonel Dennis had signed their warrants himself. Now they were gone. She grit her teeth at the SNAFU, but after all, this was the Army, Situation Normal: All Fucked Up.

Taylor's cargo pockets were stuffed with correspondence. The most professional note was from her cannon crew. She skimmed its neatly lettered contents: date, time, location, event, conclusions, ammunition expenditure, etc. Terse and to-the-point, she could see the ambush it described.

Her Griffins were responsible for Panzer's northwest sector, placing their howitzers to interdict Romence Road and Lovers Lane. Tipped off by preppers that a merc-convoy was approaching, the Griffs laid their trap. Unsuspecting, Schark's resupply column had been snared, two 105mm rounds, expended. Ambush SOP was to disable the first truck and the last, stopping the convoy in its tracks, pinning targets in the kill zone.

Her cannon-cockers had succeeded. Two gun trucks were obliterated along with their crews. Trapped, accompanying vehicles were quickly abandoned. The mercenaries—wearing Blackwater badges and quality PPE—dismounted and dispersed. Fifty caliber MG fire had thinned their ranks, but the mercs were ex-military, not Virals. Her Griffs ceased firing once the threat had been neutralized. Sergeant Taylor approved.

Inventorying the list of captured equipment, her approval increased: small arms, grenades, and a tanker filled with diesel. Not a bad day's work for the 125th. She printed a note in her field book, tore out the page and handed it to a runner:

Bravo Zulu Cannoneers!

Utilize wrecked vehicles to block Rom/Lovers intersection.

Send a detachment to bring the captured fuel to the FOB.

Shift your position east 1 klick to Portage Road.

Maintain situational awareness. More hostiles expected.

Coordinate with Rangers to continue siege operations.

Be advised, allied "Panthers" may be operating in your area.

Avoid friendly fire. Liaise if possible.

Yield to None!

— Taylor

The next "report" in her stack was from the prepper brothers, Robert and Freddy. Most of the Rangers had remained in the north. They had communities to protect. Viral deserters—Chosen and Cons—were on the prowl, desperate and dangerous.

Dear Mom, (Taylor hated when they did this)

Our apocalypse vacation has been OK. The family is in good spirits and we're all healthy. The weather has been very windy and cold and we're feeling homesick. The care package you sent was appreciated, but next time, send some brownies! We've been playing nice with the kids in uniform, even if they're bossy.

Speaking of kids, it looks like we have new neighbors? They dress themselves in black, love big cats and are angry all the time?

Know what else is scary? Skeletons, especially skinny ones. Did you know that they're around? Why didn't you tell us? Halloween is coming, look out for trick-or-treaters!

Your Loving Boys,

Bob and Fred

PS Don't forget the brownies!

PPS Brother Thorn found something in the woods, he sends it with his love!

Taylor looked at the piece of torn fabric: gray, waterproof, and embroidered with a tree. On the backside of the note, Thorn had written:

Sergeant,

This patch is from an ELF parka.

A friend of mine—Mukwa—told me that Sentinel Nighthawk has gone missing?

Do you know anything about this?

— Thorn

Taylor knew nothing about anyone named Mukwa or Night-hawk. She only knew the term "Sentinel" because of Thorn. She'd seen him in action. At the Indian River fight, the man had been freakish. If Panzer had a Sentinel in their labs, a Green guinea pig to poke, then this was bad news for the good guys. She printed another note from her pad, tasking a bike messenger to deliver it back to the Rangers.

"Hold up, Private!" The soldier paused his pedaling. "Stop by the field kitchen. If you find any MREs with brownies, deliver them too."

The "new neighbors" must mean Panthers? The Rangers better be "playing nice." If she could do it, then they could too.

"Skeletons, skinny ones," were something else entirely. Taylor guessed at Gories. Panzer's skull-faced special operators—pre-collapse—had been national news, back when there'd been news, when there'd been a nation. But the Aghori were beaten at the bridge battle by Sentinels like Thorn. Leaderless, they deserted from Panzerland, from Schark. There'd been Gorie sightings around the plantations, reports of scavengers outside the settlements. They'd harassed convoys, a nuisance to the Free North. Taylor wasn't surprised they'd been spotted by Rangers.

Her last "report" was from the black-clad Panthers. When the grid went down and shit hit the fan, Panthers defended their turf—Saginaw, Flint, Detroit—against Spreaders. They suffered heavy losses fighting Virals. Walker's emergence had revitalized them. Their immunity to Covee appeared mixed. Some militia members wore PPE, others, closest to Walker, claimed protection.

Sergeant Taylor,

We have taken Sprinkle Road and Centre Avenue as requested.

(Taylor rolled her eyes at "requested," it had been an order).

Nothing will pass in or out of the compound. Reverend Walker says we are to cooperate with you in this blockade and we will. But we ask you to reconsider your allegiance. The issue of minorities in the military has long been problematic. (Another eye-roll from Taylor.) *If being a cog in the wheel of the Army's white, patriarchal power structure becomes unbearable, you will always have a place in the Panthers.*

All Power to the People!

Our king is Coming!

She folded up the Panther report. Preaching to the choir as far as Amanda was concerned. Lord knew, the Army was far from perfect. Her loyalty to community—race too—topped her list. The only pull stronger was that of the Griffs. The closing phrase gave her pause, as did the graffiti logo. She'd heard the nick-name *Walks-on-Water* before, but the crown was new, and the honorific "king."

She'd heard the broadcast of General Kamul's speech, along with most of her troopers. Hard not to, the Hands had carpet-bombed the bandwidth. Taylor resented Kamul's mockery of her mentor. The red-blooded roar of the CORPS had chilled her. There was evil here, nothing new, but still. You'd think eight billion deaths would have exorcised that demon. Yeah, right.

Voyage of Discovery

THE OCCUPANTS OF THE PAIR OF OVERSIZE CANOES had been paddling for two days now, ever since the gale gusted out. Since leaving St. Ignace, they hadn't missed a stroke, not even at night. They "slept" in shifts, paddles unceasing as the crew took turns snoring. Baptiste, following orders from Colonel Dennis, drove them hard.

"Hey Bappy, what's the fuckin' hurry?" Shaggy batted an amber eye at Mukwa. Baptiste, the stern oarsman, ignored the mischief in the wolfman's query. Shaggy, per usual, ignored being ignored.

"Pardon, mon capitaine!" Shaggy tried again, this time in a female voice, mocking the masculine Métis man. *"Pourquoi* so fast, eh? *Oui! Oui!"*

One of these days, maybe today? Baptiste would snap Shaggy like a twig. Mukwa liked the skinny troublemaker, his battle-buddy from the bridge, but even an oversize canoe was too small for his shit. Part Lakota, part combat veteran, part PTSD, his friend was a total mess. Shaggy would be the first to admit it, and Mukwa, second. The rest of the voyageurs would all tie for third.

Baptiste had laid it out dockside at St. Ignace. They'd offloaded the medicine crate and finished stowing a heavy bundle wrapped in a tarp, lowered aboard with a winch. Both canoe crews attended their captain, standing tall in the stern. The boy Loon was on the bow, probably missing his mother. "Men, we depart on a *Voyage de découverte—*of discovery."

No cheers, no popping corks, just the lap of waves and Shaggy's mock salute. "Just *what* exactly are we discovering, sir?"

"Je ne sais fucking pas!" Baptiste barked back. The Canadians—men and women wearing toques—were all grinning. The Lakota longhair blew them a kiss, sticking out his tongue. The crews had overheard Colonel Dennis briefing Baptiste on the pier—*Walker, Panthers, ambush, refineries*—pleasure cruise this was not.

Eyes grainy and muscles sore, Mukwa tallied his "discoveries" so far:

The Métis were badasses. Their strokes never faltered, they roared every chorus.

Shaggy was a live wire. Twitchy before, after the bridge battle he was worse.

Shitting off a canoe required skill. The Métis—true *voyageurs*—hung their asses over the gunnel, dropping turds cleanly astern. Mukwa, ever-unsteady, needed the shit bucket. Shaggy would yell for quiet. "Hey, assholes, keep it down! Bucket-boy needs to focus!"

He missed Keith. He missed Miin. No surprise there. A canoe, for Mukwa, would always mean Two-Crow. Last night, during a break, he'd briefly dreamt of Miin. She was looking for someone. An important Beaver Islander, a boat captain, presumed dead, might be missing instead? Little sis urged brother bear to be on the lookout too.

Loon, their familiar navigator, was perched on the bow. His communications were subtle, but Baptiste—properly tuned—heard them all. "Across this bay we'll see a lighthouse. Tall, white brick, black trim."

Sitting between, Mukwa observed them both. Father and son? Muk didn't think so. Baptiste nodded at Loon's report. Was the lighthouse occupied? Would they be observed? Reported? Brained by a high powered rifle? Loon relieved them of anxiety, "No people."

Shaggy raised his voice: "Ha! Ha! So the coast is clear! Get it? The coast is *literally* clear!" As always, there was nothing to "get" other than annoyed. This, they all got. Mukwa—one of ten in the boat—heard plenty of grumbling, much of it in French: *"Fou du roi! Pitre!"*

Shaggy nodded along, delighted at their attention. The slithery syllables meant nothing till Mukwa heard, *"Bisexuel."* Muk checked with his friend, bisexual? He/She confirmed it with an amber-eyed wink. Mukwa steadied his strokes, synchronizing with the others. Another discovery, add it to the list.

Instead of standing to piss, Shaggy was squatting now, female-style, over the bucket. "I'm *winyanktehca*, a *winkte*. Man-who's-sometimes-a-woman. You dig it?"

Mukwa did indeed. Why not?

Baptiste prepared his crew; Loon's lighthouse was on Presque Isle. They were hugging the Huron coast. Tomorrow they'd reach Bay City. The day after, they'd take the St. Clair River towards Detroit. A large water bird, ungainly in flight, left the tower and overflew their canoes. The boy cupped his hands and released a tremolo cry. Of thanks? Of instruction? The bird banked—signaling the two boats?—before winging away.

"Baptiste! There's something in the current!"

The boy was pointing in the direction his scout had flown, towards deep water. Every voyageur strained to see, Baptiste shifting his oar. They soon raised something large on the horizon, wallowing in the waves. They veered to intercept the spiky silhouette.

Were those masts? No, it wasn't manmade.

A floating forest then?

Paddling closer, they discerned a massy pine, 100 feet from its rooty stern to its tapered bow. Not so unusual; they'd seen big blowdowns before. Shaggy elbowed Mukwa, his bench-mate near the yoke. A joke was coming, probably tasteless. Mukwa vowed to ignore the winking *winkte*. Instead, Shaggy's amber eyes widened and the Lakota two-spirit started shaking.

His friend prophesied—dead ass, zero jest—"There's someone there." Loon, a minute later, confirmed. The voyageurs squinted, then commenced their cussing.

Another discovery: a man—was he blind?—in rags, stood at the helm of the burly barque. Was that the damn Judas? Captain Chickenshit, who abandoned them in Charlevoix? Was Tom-fucking-Doyle back from the dead?

The ancient mariner, oblivious to their presence, was singing shanties.

Tree Academy: Homework

THE THREE-DAY BLOW HAD BLOWN ITSELF OUT. An early dusk descended. The exhausted students were grimy with woodsmoke, their hands blistered from butchery. They'd spent the day at deer camp, jerking venison for the winter. If their classroom had a clock, they'd all be staring.

But it didn't.

There was no clock, no classroom, no lining up for dismissal, no bus-gauntlet of bullies. Instead, they gathered in a forest clearing. The hardwoods stood leafless, winnowed by wind. The moon, at first quarter, rode high. She'd be full in a week.

The students wore hats, exhaling heat as they blew on cold fingers. They'd been pounding pemmican, preparing the "power bars" that would feed the island till spring. The ingredients were local: berries, deer meat, and spices. The students were seasoned as well, their hair and clothes reeking from their labors.

Miin stood in their circle, glad to see them tired, all part of her lesson plan. "I'm proud of you. Today was not easy." She paused. Would Michael Martin jest? Apparently not. The local boy was ready for home. The instructor continued, "Your project tonight—"

She was interrupted by a chorus of groans, Mr. Martin's the most indignant. "*Homework?*" he whined. "Come on Miin, are you serious?"

The class lawyer was vocally supported by his peers.

Miin waited. It didn't take long. Her pupils, like the gale, had lost their gusto. "As I was saying, your project tonight involves *sleep*."

The frowns quickly reversed. Josie teased, "When it comes to *that* subject, Michael's name is on the honor roll!"

The class recovered its spirit. Miinan smiled and said, "When our bodies are tired, our minds are free to roam. Your *home-work* tonight is actually *sleep-work*. Give your mind a task. Something you want it to find or figure out while your body is resting. Write out its mission and repeat it to yourself as you fall asleep. When you wake in the morning, record your thoughts. Any questions?"

They yawned. Full dark had fallen, October's stars snapping in the cold.

"Very well," Miin dismissed them. "At sunrise we'll meet at Samantha's to discuss."

The students departed: Arturo and Cheyanna for ELF Country shelters, the Greenes and Martins for nearby farms. The path pulled Miin to her foster gran's shack. The *midewikwe* wasn't home. Sam was on the north end of the island, doing medicine-work with her people on Indian Point.

The craggy maples had shed their leaves. Their foliage—expired solar panels—crunched beneath her feet. The old grove stored a season's worth of sugar below the frost line. There, in rooty cellars, the green batch fermented, waiting for spring.

The instructor—tired from the fall semester—said good night to the moon, bowed to the bare branches, and shut out the dark and all its nightly noises. Blueberry lit a fire in the wood-stove, kindling memories that warmed her as well: Mukwa and his moods, read-alouds from library books, puppet shows and root beer. She arranged her tea things for the morning; the iron warmed, beginning to ping. She loaded up the firebox and climbed into her cot. Of course, the bedding was cold. Shadows flickered on the wall. Squares of moonlight migrated across the planked floor.

Miin, modeling for her students, tasked her sleepy mind to focus on *need*. Who was out there? Who could she reach? How strong was her telepathic signal tonight? The cabin began to warm. Her eyes began to close. With a final effort she fine-tuned her frequency, projecting her thoughts. Miin's broadcast rippled outward, concentric with intent: shack, forest, island, mainland. Her query, unencrypted, was universal: *Who needs help?*

Samantha, sage, did not: *Miinan, we are well. Pass us by!*

An osprey and its handler: *Goodnight Miin. Coast is clear.*

Autumn's medicine pulsed: *I feel your power, dream weaver!*

A mariner from a raft: *Yo, ho, ho and the winds blow free!*

A bearish man, cramped in a canoe: *Lonely, lonely, lonely.*

A hawk in a cage, hooded and jessed: *Watch! Strike! Fly!*

The young dreamer, lucid on her cot, did what she could, dispensing comfort of a kind. Miin's signal strength faded as the range increased. Individual need became lost in the white noise of weeping, the snowy static of global sorrow. Depleted, her green guard was down. Hibernating already, lethargic trees couldn't help. Too late, Samantha felt the threat from her familiars—fox, cat, owl—and sent her foster an urgent warning. Miin's receiver, however, was turned off.

There were men leering at the windows. Men forcing the cabin door: strong hands, boozy breath, metallic whiskers, a panic of duct tape. Mouth, wrists, ankles, and Blueberry was bound.

Leering beneath dirty, white hoods, the manly clan laughed. Witch hunt successful, it was time for a trial.

In the morning, boot prints were studied, and the tape's empty roll. Academy students, homework forgotten, took counsel around the shack's wooden table.

Josie Greene: "You can see the drag marks. Miin didn't go willing."

Cheyanna: "We have to tell! The whole ELF needs to know."

Arturo, another Natural: "I *knew* we weren't welcome here!"

Michael: "You think islanders did this? Impossible! I know them."

Josie corrected her fellow tree climber, "You know *some* of them, Michael Martin. What we *need* is a *plan*."

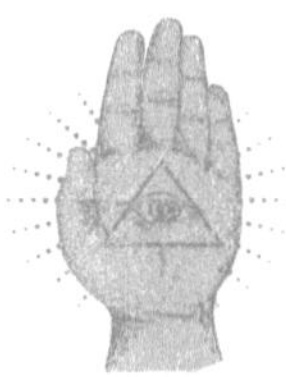

Hands Across America

PLACE: JOINT BASE ANDREWS, MARYLAND

TIME: 23 OCTOBER 1800 EST

MISSION: MATERIAL SUPPORT OF RED MILITIAS

FLIGHT TIME: 5 HOURS

Major Naz climbed aboard the C-130 transport. Returning the pilot's salute, he settled himself into the cockpit's jump seat. He'd brought his homework along.

"Wheel's up in 30, Major."

Naz acknowledged the takeoff time and opened his briefcase. It contained one file, tabbed "Walker." It was General Kamul's idea for Naz to tag along: "Wish I could go myself. Hell, Major, if only I had the time, I'd *fly* the damn plane!"

Kamul gave Naz carte blanche to arm, rally, and utilize any assets that could destabilize Michigan's resistance to the Confederacy of Red Patriotic States, the CORPS. The Midwest, for now, was too far for the D.C.'s Hands. Local Reds would have to step up and take care of their turf. General Kamul—following prompts from AYE EYE—would arm them; Major Naz would organize and orchestrate any assault.

Naz was familiar with this particular hop. Four days ago, he'd collected blood samples from Schark's specimen at Panzer. Further analysis revealed genetic markers that might explain her enhanced physical aptitude and resistance to Stinger. Curious and curiouser.

Naz, as a medical man, was tempted to scrub the night's militia mission. He'd rather land in Kalamazoo instead, storm the Panzer compound and take Schark's birdy in hand. But the EYE was always judging. The general—given a verdict via halo—had executed headstrong Hands for less.

The four-engine turboprop taxied into position, its pilots ready. Post-collapse, the most versatile aircraft were these low-tech dinosaurs. Lockheed's Hercules had been heavy lifting since the 1950s. Turboprops, like the C-130, burned less fuel, could use unprepared runways, and operated without a multitude of microchips, many of which had been fried by solar flares or the EMPs of collapse.

Pure acceleration shoved him into his seat. As the pilot banked, Naz had a wide view of D.C. and its watery environs. The sun had set, and the glow of the grid was obvious: the core of the CORPS. Downtown was electrified, a smoggy city on a hill. The District was gloomy, permanently fouled from the rotten fuel it burned to empower AYE EYE. Far on the horizon, a power plant flickered: a fiery mountain wreathed in clouds—particulates from petro exhaust. Potomac's marshes were slick with oil, flickering with Elmo's fire, lanterns for the dead. D.C.'s dirty secret—the great EYE was dimming, simply not enough wattage, not anymore.

Early in collapse, a perimeter was established to keep the virus out and humans in. Two rivers helped. The Potomac and Anacostia belted the city: west, south, and east. Their strategic bridges were removed except for fortified checkpoints. The sluggish rivers were patrolled by Red Marines in gunboats. A wall was built on the northern flank from Foggy Bottom to Ivy City. Engineers and technicians—the EYE's essential workers—were denied exit passes. Some techies had tried to escape, machine guns bloodying their frayed white collars. K Street became a new Berlin wall. Joint Base Andrews was outside the perimeter, as were the glowing refineries. The biggest one was near Philadelphia, up the Schuylkill River. From the air, aided by his smart-patch, Naz inspected the shadow land's vulnerabilities.

Tonight, his mission focus was Walker; AYE EYE concurred that the preacher's growing popularity was problematic. The Reds, the Hands, and the CORPS dominated the Right side of the spectrum. What was left of the Left lacked leadership. General Kamul, seeing through the EYE, feared Walker. Naz opened the file and scanned a few pages. Kamul was correct. The pastor posed a threat, the biggest they'd faced since the U.S. military fractured.

Major Naz lifted the smart-patch, rubbing his itchy orb. He admired his CO. General Kamul, by temperament, by training, was a blitzkrieger. The cargo bay of the C-130 was loaded with weaponry that in the right hands—Red ones—could strike Walker dead, along with his followers. The pilots were given a list of drop zones, generated by AYE EYE. Hercules' crew had labeled the crated weapons, attached parachutes, and were ready to push. Major Naz checked his watch, then his halo: they still had some flying to do.

The cargo plane flew with its nav lights on—red and green—a show of force for the hinterlands. The aircraft blinked above blacked-out hills. Naz's smart-patch projected population estimates of the territories they traversed. The numbers were low: coal country was dusted, Big Ag had gone to seed, not since the Pleistocene had Penn's Woods been so unpeopled.

Millennia ago, as the ice wall retreated, paleo-hunters opened the thawing land. The first sites settled were now the last ones to go. Strategic intersections of salt lick and fresh water might still host humans. Everywhere else had gone dark, devoid of *Homo* and their signature fires.

The major adjusted his eyepatch, returning to the perp's file. A tab labeled, *Walks-on-Water,* documented an event last winter. The Flint River had frozen over. A Covee colony, like lepers of old, built their shanties upon thin ice. Infected families, highly contagious, were shunned by dry land survivors. Dr. Schark's variant shook the life out of them, singly and in bunches. Corpses were dragged to the edge of their encampment, a perimeter of pestilence.

Pastor Walker, on a mercy mission for Second Baptist, had been there. There were eyewitness accounts in the file. Walker's companions—Naz sneered at the word "disciples"—had urged the reverend off the cracking ice. Walker loaded a sled with blankets and a sloshy urn of soup and stepped away from the shore. A trick of light, a bending of beams, and the man seemed to float above the ice floes. He crossed open water without getting wet.

Arriving at the shanty town, he was overwhelmed. Mobbed by the miserable, the reverend rose above, calming the colony, quoting scripture, and ladling soup. He gave his jacket to a hacking child, his gloves to a grateful granny. He went among the virulent and emerged uninfected. The accounts went on, but Major Naz could not. Apparently, the soup never ran out and some sick had recovered. The story was a super-spreader. Kamul was correct—a popularity problem, indeed.

Major Naz checked their navigation, the copilot pointing to their position on the aeronautical chart. They'd entered Michigan airspace; the first drop zone was approaching. A half-dozen Red militias stood out from the mass of wannabes. These weapon drops were congratulatory, containing letters of encouragement along with transmission codes and a list of HVTs. The highest value targets on Kamul's list? The ol' water-walker himself, followed by Colonel Dennis and his CSM—a DEI hire no doubt—Amanda Taylor.

Following Kamul's order to disrupt resistance to the CORPS, Naz designated Toledo—just south of Michigan's border—as the rally point for patriotic partisans. With smartwatches dumbed down, the full moon—six nights away—would mark the kickoff. He signed each pamphlet with a favorite phrase from POTUS, dearly departed: "Be there, it will be wild!"

The aircraft's ramp lowered. Cold air gushed into the cargo bay. The loadmaster and a gunner readied the aft-most pallet, stenciled: BAD AXE, MI. Receiving the green light, they pushed the lethal payload into the void. The parachute deployed. So far, so good.

Lurking behind the munition pallets were twin beasts: two small helicopters crouching with folded wings and a jet fuel stink. Their once black paint had faded to gray. *Terror* and *Panic* were their call signs.

The green light switched off. The crew double-checked the next pallet, giving each other a silent thumbs up.

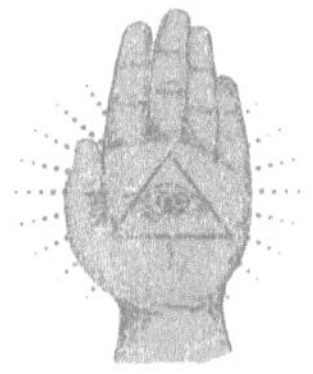

The Thumbs

ON THE GROUND, the militia members, clear-eyed, tracked the red and green nav lights of the Hercules as the big plane transited the stars. The band was based in Bad Axe. If Michigan were a hand, these guys were the thumb. A lookout wearing NVGs spotted the ChemLights of the pallet and its chute. Invisible to the eye, the infrared burned bright through his goggles. The scout watched the pallet bump across a weedy field. He indicated direction with his arm, whispering, "Touchdown boys, let's go!" The Thumbs, ever-tactical, moved out. It was a night of frost, Santa Kamul had just delivered.

All-white, all-dude, these country boys had survived. Even pre-Covee, their peninsula was sparsely populated. When the SHTF they hunkered down, taking care of their own. Hibernation was a strategy of sorts. During the worst of collapse, they mostly just slept. They avoided urban areas: Bay City, Sarnia, Flint. They stayed away and survived. By the time they emerged, flabby from their lairs, the good ol' boys were hungry. Since then, they'd bullied their way around the county, taking food, taking pleasure.

They'd gone through several brandings: Wolverines, Watchmen, Bad-Axers, etc. But when the Red Hands finally choked out the Blues and formed into fists, their vote had been unanimous. From now on, they were Thumbs.

They created a stencil and logoed their gear. Without the internet, their only posts were on light poles, their followers were each other. Chat rooms were mom's basement. Without an audience, their threads began to fray. Then the Thumbs grew bored.

They had weapons and they knew how to use them, the one thing they did well. There were no rules anymore, no consequences, not for Reds anyway, not for them. They started "patrolling." They killed some people, self-defense of course. They tried rape, they tried pillage. They developed a taste. The region, a wild west, was under their thumb.

They had solar panels, a ham radio, and time. Old Law, busy elsewhere, left them alone. Bad Axe, even pre-collapse, barely registered. They found General Kamul on the radio and became fanboys. Kamul, aided by AYE EYE, found them too and fanned their white flames.

The Thumbs, early on, had pinched themselves a prisoner. An escapee from Bay City, undocumented, scavenged too close to their turf and was taken. Media savvy, the militia made hay: their 15 minutes of high-frequency fame. They recorded the interrogation, putting words—and dirty fists—in the immigrant's mouth. They spliced the audio into installments, then released it, a serial on surviving. Spoiler alert: their prisoner didn't.

They deepfaked the whole thing, falsely flagging the man as Antiva, Anti-Viral. The Thumbs built suspense as their audience grew. They had him chant slogans and confess to hate crimes, often their own. They made him out as a militant—though he wasn't—painting him as MS-13, someone who whistled at women, especially white ones.

Antenna to antenna the broadcasts were repeated, signal strength boosted by tech bro backers. Michigan's thumb was flatland, its radio traffic light. Their wavelengths, across multiple frequencies, made quite a splash.

A Red Hand signals specialist recorded the transmissions, alerting Major Naz. The major binged their whole show. Every episode was well-executed. The finale—surprise!—ended with a real one, the prisoner's. General Kamul was impressed: the Thumbs had made his naughty list.

Sidecar

TWO DAYS AGO, the voyageurs plucked Tom Doyle from his pine, rescuing the recluse from his resinous raft. They fed the starving man slowly, Baptiste keeping an eye on him. Since the bridge battle a month ago, the Beaver Islander had rapidly aged.

Shaggy, the *winkte*, ever-winking, mocked the mariner and his mannerisms. "Ever heard of *The Old Man and the Sea*?" he'd intone, deep-voiced and solemn. Code-switching, Shaggy assumed a feminine falsetto, "Well we've got that beat. *Our* old man? He can't even see!" Shaggy cracked himself up. The groaning crew, on their third listen, were cracking as well.

Mukwa remembered the old Doyle, dude's bloody temper, his cinderblock fists. *That* man would have knocked Shaggy out cold. The voyageurs would have cheered. But Tom's marooning had mellowed him. Sightless, Doyle now peered inward. His rage was gone, his tornadic temper too. For hours he'd mutter as they paddled, emerging from the maze of his mind only for navigation.

"Mind your helm, there!" he'd cry, "you're fighting the current! Come to starboard a bit, Frenchie, you'll make better time."

Baptiste—"Frenchie"—indulged the old timer. Doyle's course corrections were spot-on every time. They were paddling south on Lake Huron. Behind them were the harbor towns: Alpena, Oscoda, Tawas City. They'd yet to disembark. Instead, Loon conducted fly-bys, utilizing his feathered familiars. These recon flights were all the same: the rusty ports—XCon staging areas for last month's bridge battle—were empty, and thoroughly scavenged. Every fuel tank, every armory, was empty. Naked yachts sprawled, violated; hatches pried open, engine rooms stripped of their parts.

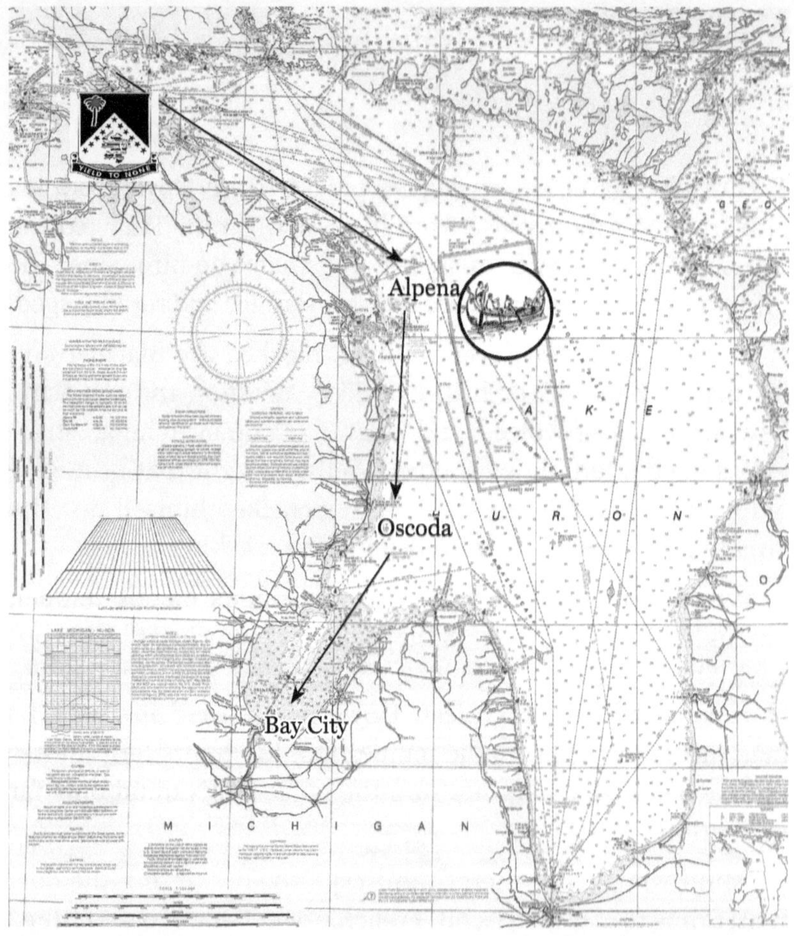

The two oversize canoes waited for sunset before approaching Bay City, the industrious base of the thumb. Baptiste made it clear, this port wasn't optional. Colonel Dennis—and the whole Free North—were running on fumes. Bay City must be thoroughly scouted. Prepping for the op, each voyageur—Muk and Shaggy too—grew tense, faces tight from remembered trauma.

Weapons were unzipped from waterproof cases. Magazines were checked, then inserted into wells with a clunk. The crews safetied their rifles, stowing them close to hand.

Nautical twilight was upon them. Saginaw Bay bled out, hemorrhaging red to purple to black. Loon and his birds had reconnoitered: no watchers in the towers, no lights from the town. Some of the buoys still blinked. Untended, unhelpful, adrift from the proper channel. The blind man took them through the hazards instead.

A riffle of current tugged Doyle's ear. "Sandbar ahead. Port side, back paddles."

The voyageurs did so in silence, even Shaggy going quiet.

Next, a set of waves sounded wrong: bobbing floats and a tangle of twine. "Net stakes to port!" Doyle gave his order. "Net stakes, boys—can't you hear 'em! Starboard side, back paddles!"

They passed Channel Island to port, then Gull to starboard. Doyle, scenting another hazard—diesel, rust, and soil—followed his nose upriver. "Wreck ahead, a freighter there, stuck in the mud."

Nervous, they paddled around the obstacle in the dark, ducking beneath an old rail-bridge. The river narrowed and grew cluttered. Storage tanks and gravel piles silhouetted the shore. And then, most improbably, a warship loomed suddenly to starboard, its long guns spiking the sky. Doyle, overhearing the crew and their questions, knew just where they were.

"Boys, that there's the *Edson*, mothballed in '88." Doyle— blind leading the blind—played tour guide in the dark. "DD-946, last all-gun destroyer in the fleet."

Every voyageur eyeballed her sleek and lethal silhouette, her inactive weaponry. Doyle, saltiness returning, mimed arousal: "Imagine ol' Denny if you brought her into Ignace!" The crew laughed. Doyle's fog began to lift.

Baptiste bumped them softly against the pier. Shaggy scrambled up, securing their lines. The rest followed. For the first time in days, they stood on solid ground. Too solid for some; land-sickness was a thing.

They'd seen not a soul on their voyage. Two refineries here needed checking, Marathon and Port Fisher. Baptiste looked at the boy, but the refineries were inland, plus too toxic. Loon shook his head; his feathered scouts wouldn't fly.

Full dark now and starry, the moon sailed above as the Saginaw River slid by. Mukwa's ears twitched; he rotated his acoustic apertures, detecting engine noise high above. There! The voyageurs all were pointing. Red and green lights—blinking with electric menace—crossed the unpolluted sky. He nudged Shaggy, who growled, flipping the high fliers the bird. "Ho-ho-ho motherfuckers! Santa's white ass is early this year."

Baptiste called them both over, handing Mukwa a letter. "Two sites need scouting. Mukwa, can you handle him?"

The "him" was Shaggy, who was panting. His long tongue lolled; the Lakota Howler was eager to run. Mukwa shrugged, he'd do his best. Baptiste, far from satisfied, gave orders. The voyageurs jury-rigged a crane and muscled two tarp-covered bundles—a mini motorcycle, plus its sidecar—off the canoe and onto the wharf.

Unasked, Shaggy cadenced their efforts:

Oh you better watch out—Heave!

You better not cry—Heave!

You better not pout—Heave!

I'm telling you why—Heave!

Ten minutes and twenty curses later, Oso stuffed himself into the sidecar, and they scootered away. The October night would frost. The motorcycle's miniature engine was warm. Mukwa's ponytail streamed behind, his battered M4 propped against the rail. Shaggy Wolf, adrenaline junkie, spurred his metallic mount and let loose a wild howl. A pack of urban coyotes howled back, claiming Bay City as their own.

Up ahead, a flare flickered on the I-75 overpass. The clown car detoured from its refinery mission to investigate the anomaly. Shaggy reduced RPM and turned off the headlight, approaching the disturbance with caution. Mukwa, alert, shouldered his rifle and red-dotted the disabled Humvee. Two soldiers in MOPP gear were changing a flat. Shaggy reined them in, Mukwa covering the scene with his carbine.

Shaggy flicked on his brights, spot-lighting the Griffin logo—Yield to None—stenciled on the Humvee door. The masked soldiers, surprised, recovered quickly, waving them down. They needed help. Mukwa safetied his weapon, then began pawing his pockets for the colonel's letter of reference, their safe passage through the wasteland.

Crossroads

Sometimes you can hardly see.

But it's fight man to man

And do all you can,

For they know they can never be free.

—Bonnie Parker, "The Trail's End" (1910–1934)

The road ahead was dim. Cowboy, wrangling their stolen Humvee, could barely see. Liz's wounds were oozing again: blood, pus, and body odor fugged the vehicle's interior. Once clear of Clare and the threat of Old Law, she'd shucked off her MOPP gear, opening the medkit. Her left side—seared by fire—was profiled. Bob took his bleary eyes off the approaching interchange, then wished he hadn't. Her lizard skin was scaly. Her left breast had been sheared away, an Amazon of old. Dusk was descending, the light was low. Bob watched Liz struggling with the gauze, her infected blood seeping through the bandage.

"Need a hand with that?" Bob asked queasily.

Liz hissed her retort, negative.

"Come on Liz, let me help." One hand on the wheel, he reached for the QuikClot.

"Don't!" she snarled, slapping him away. It stung on multiple levels.

"God damn it!" Cowboy hit the brakes, put the transmission in park, and turned off the engine. Fuck this. Fuck her. He exited the armored vehicle, stepping away from its dirty diesel exhaust. It was almost full dark, they'd reached a crossroads. The night air was cold, clean too; Bob filled his lungs. A highway sign loomed. He stepped to it, flashing a light: they'd taken M-10 from Clare. Now, I-75, a four-lane, intersected. A right would take them south: Flint, Detroit, Toledo. A left would point them north: Grayling, Indian River, the broken bridge and the Free North beyond. If they kept going straight, in another mile they'd cross the Saginaw River. If they turned around, pursuing Griffs would pound them.

He heard Liz's door open and shut. She limped his way till she stood beside him. She put the gauze packet in his hand, an olive-drab branch, an offering. "Give a girl a hand?"

He did so. How not? Of all the people on the people-less planet, none were closer than Red fucking Liz. Bob ripped the packet open, the clotting agent smelling like clay. The moon illuminated his labor as round and round he went. He mummified her torso, tucking the bandage tight. His lonely hands lingered a moment: her breast, her hip.

Her lizard tongue flicked. "Cold as a witch's titty out here. Let's turn on that heater." She grabbed Cowboy by his horn, tugging him towards the Humvee's interior.

Bob's heater was already on, but he stopped her. "Hold on honey, it's time to decide." He flashed his light at the highway sign. North or south?

They'd wasted three days and half their fuel fighting this out. There were no good options. Passing through Amish country, Bob insisted on stopping by Hochstettler's. But mama Hannah was long gone, boarding an Old Law bus back in Clare. Liz seethed while Bob hid the Humvee, stalking Dawdy's farm. Sarah and Sammy seemed fine, that fucking rooster too. Campbell observed them at chores. The Chosen were scattered, XCons too; Panzer's food network had been disrupted. The *iks*, one by one, were crossed out, the Griffins scouring slavers from the land. All in all, Bob's little family seemed fine.

Liz adjusted to the altered reality; imprisoned a month, she had to see things for herself. She was shocked by Panzer's weakened position, their checkpoints, strongholds, and farms all abandoned. There was nowhere to return to, no one to welcome her back. What choice now for a Chosen? Without underlings, what good was a boss?

So they bickered away their freedom, their fuel. A hundred miles, maybe less, still sloshed in their tank. Bob switched off his flashlight. High above and far away, they heard the drone of propellers. Red and green lights blinked across the sky. The cargo plane blotted out the stars, then revealed them. "Now, who the fuck is up there?" Liz asked.

"And where the hell are they going?" Bob added. He reached for her hand, the scaly one. The lizard let him hold it. They both stood transfixed.

"Gotta be military?" she offered. "Only ones with any fuel."

"Yeah, but which side?" The lights receded.

"Does it matter?" Liz shivered, tugging her boy toy towards the Humvee's heat. Their ears pricked again as another motor polluted the soundscape. They listened, hearing two cylinders and a muffled growl. A motorcycle, running dark, was headed their way.

Liz's idea to pop the flare; only Old Law would be so bold. Faking the tire change was riskier. Humvees rolled on run-flats, so anyone with experience would smell a rat. MOPP hoods masked the two bandits. Disguised as Griffs, the desperados loosened pistols, checking their loads.

A miniature motorcycle pulled up, modified for quiet, showing no lights. The road flare flickered; a beanpole was driving, a bear stuffed in the sidecar. This sidecar-man, all business, covered the scene with his rifle. Bob, still masked, showed both his hands, waving them down. He willed the big guy to point his carbine somewhere else. The cycle's headlight winked on; sidecar-man leaned his rifle on the rail. The big man began pawing through his pockets.

Cowboy took a charcoal-filtered breath. He felt Liz—his ride or die—do the same. Showtime! Ready for their roles, the two cons had their marks. The scene had been set. Time to fucking go.

Bob, disguised as a Griffin, began the grift: "We're scouts from Clare. Man, we're glad to see you guys. You Antiva? Where's your masks?" Cowboy tapped his MOPP filter, faking confusion, roping them in.

Beanpole broke in, "We're scouts too."

The bearish man grumbled, "No masks, but you can trust us. We're protected."

Liz, bulky and ungendered in her MOPP, feigned fright, gesturing them back.

Her defensive posture drew a protest from the big guy, proffering a paper shield in his paw. "This is from Colonel Dennis. Free North. For you. Explains who we are."

The two marks hadn't dismounted; big man's rifle was way too close. So the cons kept fishing. Liz applied her wrench to a seemingly stubborn lug nut. Faking a stumble, she lured them in—gender reveal—a damsel in distress: "I can't do it." Her tire iron clanged to the pavement. She slumped against the door. The newcomers responded to her feminine voice, swallowing the bait. Beanpole and Bear—hook, line, and sinker—dismounted.

Cowboy, amped on adrenaline, waved the letter closer. The teddy bear complied. Beanpole took a knee next to Liz, handing back her iron. The red flare sputtered. The moonlight was thin. All too easy. In a second, it was over.

Cowboy, two-handed, pulled both his pistols with a flourish. One 9mm pinned the big man, the other his skinny driver. The Bear, blindsided, gawped at the barrel. Liz swung her heavy wrench—clunk!—and Beanpole was down.

Moving quickly, Liz cuffed the dreadlocked man. She zipped his ties tight, gurgling a laugh. Standing up, she snatched the paper and stepped clear. Cowboy steadied both nines on Bear. If the big man charged, Bob would need every bullet. Tricked and then robbed, Bear began growling his grief.

Liz hushed him: "None of that now, big boy."

"Better tase him, Lizzy."

"Think so?" Liz lowered her MOPP hood, shaking out her hair. She profiled her good side and grinned.

Five minutes later and both boys were bound, back-to-back. There'd been no real argument; for the moment anyway, Liz's mood for murder was low.

Beanpole was slumped, the man-bear resigned. The fake flat had been "fixed," the stolen Humvee ready to roll. Liz cataloged the booty: an M4 with magazines; some freeze-dried food; two sleeping bags; a pouch, a pipe, and some herb; a porno mag; an Army issue poncho and a gray-hooded parka, both tightly rolled.

The cycle's saddlebags had been emptied. He read through the colonel's letter; it was perfect.

Liz handed Bob their loot. She passed him the poncho, then the parka. Campbell felt its fabric: something familiar about its warp, its weft. He flicked on his light and unrolled it. Bob felt a flash of fright, the sudden thunder of trauma. There was embroidery on the chest. He'd seen that tree before.

The first time, back in June, this damn tree had been scrawled—in blood—on the door panel of an ambushed truck. Mikey, his Chosen fixer, had found it and puked. Fucking elves had murdered Bob's men. A few months later, fleeing Beaver Island, that she-elf had worn a parka just like this. Eventually she'd punched him in the nose, leaving him bound and bleeding on the rainy road to Panzer. That hawk-faced bitch had turned her back on him. Well, fuck her too.

The man-bear, zipped tight, was watching him closely. Had he seen Bob flinch? Cowboy sauntered over and squatted down, studying the cuffed warrior by moonlight. "Are you one of *them?*"

The big man's tattoo clawed at his neck. Cowboy locked eyes with his captive. A recognition of sorts; they'd both seen the same shit. "Well? Are you?"

The Bear replied, unblinking, "I used to be."

Cowboy pressed his ex-adversary: "Charlevoix?"

The Bear nodded. "We stole your ferry, had to. We were betrayed. Beaver Island left us for dead."

"*My* ferry?"

Another quick nod, then a slow burning anger. "I know who you are. You're the hangman. Petoskey. Where's your hat?"

Hangman? Shit. The big guy wasn't wrong. *Noosed necks, light poles, the heavy dangle of human fruit.* His hat? Good fucking question. Bob glared at Liz, now warm in the vehicle. She'd worn it last. Charlevoix. Right after she betrayed, tased, and confined him.

"I misplaced it," Bob answered.

"Were you there, hangman? In Charlevoix? When we elves attacked?"

Bob shook his hatless head. "I was locked in the ferry. Probably saved my life."

Would Liz have killed him? Shit. She might have, if she couldn't get a price from Sharkey. More likely, she'd have tasked a Chosen to do it. Like that fucking Lacy, peeing in his dog bowl.

"Locked in the ferry?" The Bear, alert, was all ears. Beanpole, concussed, started stirring. "Then you were on Beaver Island?"

"Look big man, it's a long story and we're out of time here." Bob made a move to stand.

"Please!" Man-bear was desperate. "Truth for truth. What do you want to know?"

Bob considered. So many things. Why this fucking virus, for starters. Why his wife? *Sheeted on the hospital sidewalk.* Why his daughter? *Celebrating her sweet 16 in a bath of blood.* How could people do this to each other? *The cages, the dripping tree, Methhead, Guts, Squints, a hundred more. No, a thousand.*

"Look big fella, there was a man on the island, some kind of professor." It felt good to talk; Bob gave himself permission to speak. "He was studying me. The virus. A cure. It was working too. Some soldiers tried to arrest me. A wanted man, an outlaw. A psycho Greenie got me instead. We stole a boat, some gas, and escaped. I've been on the run, story of my life, my after-life anyway."

The big man's eyes were wide with shock. "A Greenie? A she-elf?"

"Let me guess, you knew her?"

Bear nodded.

"Cared about her?"

Another nod.

Cowboy shook his head. "Best forget her then. Last I saw, she was headed into Panzer. Was gonna kick Sharkey's ass all by her lonesome."

"Why Panzer?"

"Said she was looking for friends, maybe prisoners. She wanted to trade me." Bob thought back to a month ago, recalling the names. "Thorn, maybe? Another named Ox? Or was it Bull?"

"Bullshit!" Bear's ears were cocked. If dude had fur, he'd be bristling.

Bob shrugged and stood up. "My turn." Cowboy tapped his two holstered pistols. "Truth or dare?"

The A-Team

BAY CITY WASN'T THEIR TURF, but it wasn't Viral either. A no man's land, like much of southeast Michigan—RIP—resigned to Rust in Peace. The team was there because Walker wanted it checked. "BC" had been coded in the reverend's last transmission. There were two refineries here, both offline. Could they be restored? The A-Team looked, tested. The answer was maybe, but they'd need a lot of work. Their home base was Detroit; after tonight, they'd recon K-Zoo next.

Anti-Virals, that's what they were. The black and red van was filled with militants; gas masks and weapons cluttering the interior. "Antiva" was a pandemic riff on "Antifa," the anti-fascist, anti-racist resistance pre-Covee. Red-eyed, violent, and super-spreading; fascists and Virals had much in common. Topping the list of similarities, at least to militants: both groups of haters were better off dead. The driver's door panel tallied their kills; they were running out of room.

The van cruised with its lights off. The moon lit the way, high-beaming the potholed pavement. Bay City—"Hell's Half Mile" in the lumbering days—was busy tonight, almost like the early days before collapse had crested. First, there'd been a plane, high up and far away, but still, a plane. Military? With its lights on? What was its mission? Then, a motorcycle and sidecar scouted the Marathon plant and Port Fisher too. More fuel burned, more burning questions for the team to ponder. Finally, a red flare attracted Antiva's attention. Moths to a flame, they loaded up and hit the road. And now, here they were, slow-ing down on the overpass. The road-flare still sputtered, strobe lighting a cycle, its sidecar, and two mismatched companions. The riders—one huge and one skinny—were bound back-to-back and shivering.

"Mask up people! Couple possibles out there. No shooting, even if they're hot."

Those in the van proofed themselves against Covee—face-masks, gloves, and respirators—shielding themselves from molecular malice. The side door slid open, and the assault team quickly scattered.

"Clear right!"

"Clear left!"

A perimeter was established around the two perps. The A-Team, lights beaming from their rifle barrels, approached the cuffed men with caution. The big man sat subdued. His thin companion squirmed when inspected, bitching, "Stick that light up your ass!"

Skinny sported dreadlocks. In the LED light, his irises shone gold. His silent sidekick had red rims, a warning sign. Infected? Contagious? Antiva peered closer, fingers finding triggers as the penlight probed further. Negative. Negative. Not Covee, dude hadn't been stung, least not by Stinger. The A-Team rolled their eyes. Ol' boy had been crying.

Execution averted, scene secured, an Antiva artist slung her rifle, unholstering a spray can instead. She airbrushed a crown on the crumbling overpass, a concrete proclamation for Antiva's preferred leader: Walker, recently rumored to be a descendant of kings.

The Braucher

HANNAH HOCHSTETTLER—grieving widow, mother of two—had been helping the healers. Five days ago, disembarking from the bus, she and her fellow Amish tested negative for infection. Once clear of quarantine, they were ferried to the Free North and processed for resettlement. Hannah's interview and skill-set matched her with the medics. Since then, they'd been busy.

Fuel shortages and frequent gales slowed *Nodin*. She transited the Straits only when wind direction and refugee numbers were right. Still, the Amish kept coming. Panzerland and its plantations were crumbling, Pharaoh's slaves found themselves free. Some stayed in the south, rooted tight to family farms. Some boarded Walker's buses, taking the freedom road to a fresh start up north.

Hannah, a caregiver, triaged the new arrivals, overhearing their chatter. There was much traumatized talk of "demons in the woods" and "skull-faced devils" scavenging slops. Hannah didn't doubt them; she'd seen such *Teufels* herself. Her bus convoy had been targeted near Indian River. The skeletons—two snipers—were quickly caught by Panther escorts. She watched Walker take their bony hands in his. The *breddicher* pulled both devils to their feet. He left them food. He left them hope. Hannah prayed they turned themselves in.

Upon resettlement, she'd been assigned to Dr. Chow. The learned man, so far, had been kind. She slept at the Ignace hospital, sharing a stove with two nurses. Mathew and Sean, Beaver

Islanders, were lovebirds; she overheard them cooing at night. Hannah missed Elam, her murdered husband, and the children they'd raised. She worried for Dawdy and the farm, for Samuel and Sarah. Hannah saw their faces in each batch of refugees.

There were two more assigned to Chow's medical team: Captain Young from the Army, and Elena, a younger woman with prematurely silver hair. The triage wasn't tricky. The needs of the new arrivals were easy to assess. Whip-cuts and bruises would fade; the evils they'd witnessed would not.

The Plain, her peaceful people, had seen killings. Sexual violence had been done. Women—girls even—had been caged. Those bars had left scars. Though invisible, Hannah could see them. That's who she was: a healer, a *braucher*. She could take away their pain. Dawdy hadn't approved, but he'd helped Elam paint their barn. The hex sign they'd put there, the *sterne*, marked their home as a place of healing. With each success, Hannah's reputation had grown. The gift payments of produce or livestock had grown apace, helping to mute her *daadi's* moody muttering.

Burns, bruises, and blood had been her business. Nothing magic about it; the true healer was Jesus. She helped her patients believe. Their faith was the cure.

"Here they come!"

The medical team was ready, *Nodin* already at the pier. Mathew, Sean, and Captain Young wore PPE. Chow, Elena, and Hannah did not. They'd been in radio contact with the ferry and knew the manifest. There were some Amish aboard, though that tide was plainly ebbing. There were two families of Hidden as well, malnourished and ill prepared for winter. Heeding Walker's broadcast, they emerged from hiding.

The passengers were typical and the medics' routine stayed the same. They'd been screened already on the south shore for Covee. Their needs were food, shelter, and safety. The Free North, for now, could provide all three.

Not at all typical were the Spreaders. For the first time in Free North history, there were a dozen Virals on board: some Chosen, some Cons. They'd been captured in skirmishes or had turned themselves in. Sergeant Taylor's detachment of Griffs had redeployed from Clare's airfield, besieging Panzer's Kalamazoo compound instead. During the move, Taylor's MPs shipped their "Compliant" prisoners north. Dr. Chow was recommending isolation, observation, and eventual resettlement. The deciding factor had been the Spreaders' viral load. Over the past few days, their levels—closely monitored by MPs—had clearly diminished.

Dr. Chow briefed his team: "Just because the MPs call them Compliant doesn't mean they're not dangerous."

Colonel Dennis had assigned Cruz and Booker to security. The soldiers wore MOPP gear and carried dinged-up M4s. The two combat veterans conferred with Captain Young, leading the team. The prisoners would remain aboard until the Amish and Hidden had been processed. Mathew and Sean were tasked with that duty.

Young gave his orders. "After that, it's all hands on deck, understood?"

Cruz and Booker got it: "Yes, sir."

Young clarified, "Use rifles as a last resort. If force is needed, try Tasers instead."

"Roger that, Captain."

Young's men winked at each other. After a month of Frank stuck in sickbay, it was good to have their chief back.

The Beaver Island potion, *At-the-last*, had again proven its potency. Four days ago, Baptiste offloaded a clinking crate of Mason jars. Patients Elena and Young were dosed twice a day, Chow recording the results. The good doctor imbibed as well. Calmer, clearer, stronger were descriptors in his ledger.

Elena queried her fellow Natural, Dr. Chow: "Where do you want Hannah and I?"

"You two will be POC, if you're up for it?"

Elena nodded. The ELF leader wore scrubs, a winter hat, and a military sweater. Her Sentinel parka was still hanging back in the ward. Her wounded arm was in a sling.

"POC?" Hannah asked with an accent.

Elena answered, "Point-of-care. It means we go first."

Chow nodded. "You two will serve them their tea."

Mathew and Sean did their duty. The uninfected disembarked and were sorted. Most were escorted to the mess hall for coffee and to catch up on calories. Critical patients were brought to the hospital for further care.

The infected were isolated inside the ferry; *Nodin's* exits were guarded by MOPP-wearing MPs. The Griffins from Clare were happy to be relieved by Young's team.

"They're all yours, sir." They saluted the captain.

"Give you any trouble?"

The taller MP shook her head. "Not this bunch anyway."

Her partner elaborated, "Two NCs escaped their container before we left Clare. Roughed us up pretty good. Fuckers killed one of their own, then stole uniforms and a Humvee."

"NCs?"

"Non-Compliants. Virals. Too nasty, even for Walker. Don't worry though, this batch we brought you is chill."

Hannah would take point, Elena beside her, part of Chow's plan to put the Compliants at ease. The two women—unmasked, unarmed—would greet each prisoner, conducting light interrogation. Cruz, Booker, and their 5.56 ammo backing them up.

Dr. Chow reviewed their file—handwritten by Griff medics at Clare. He'd take more blood samples to check against their baselines. Captain Young would brew the tea. They prepared the ferry's lounge: a folding table, a propane burner, a kettle, and a sparkling jar of liquid gold.

Hannah sat nervously beside Elena at the table. She opened herself to Christ, but His calm eluded her. What if one of them was Elam's killer? Would she recognize him? What if one had hurt Sarah or Samuel? Would she feel it? These Virals, Compliant or not, had done evil.

The healer breathed a verse, a talisman from a long-lost friend: *Oh, thou! my dear Lord Jesus Christ, I am thine own, that no dog may bite me, no wolf bite me, and no murderer secretly approach me; save me, O my God, from sudden death!*

Upon arriving in the Free North, Hannah had borrowed a Bible. Nothing fancy, just an unread Gideon from an Ignace hotel. She placed it on the table: *Whoever carries this book is safe from all enemies, visible or invisible.*

Elena said nothing. She'd been a believer once too, first in God, then in Gaia. She remembered turkey hunting with her dad, the day Covee killed him: the crowded church, the sermon, the super-spreader event.

The kettle whistled. The Free Northers gathered round as Dr. Chow tinctured the tea. The pharmacon's effects were familiar to the welcome party. Everyone but Hannah had felt them before. The healer caught her first whiff and was transported.

She was in the hayfield, pregnant with Sarah. She held a rake with calloused hands. The cut-grass smell seeped into her. Elam was there: his sweat, his salt, his itchy kiss. The barn and its hex—freshly painted—were in the background. Summer green grew lush around them …

The first Viral was released into the lounge. The man and his molecules drifted their way. Hannah, nervous, invited him to sit. The Bible was there, and Jesus too. Hannah breathed deeply, embracing their power.

The man wore glasses, one lens badly cracked. He was offered a paper cup with some tea. Ignoring the potion, he spoke, "Look, I'm a radio operator, no trouble. And I don't want any either."

He watched Chow and his needle-poke warily. "I'm *Compliant*, see? He said so himself."

Hannah heard the capital H. "*Who* said so?"

"Walker did. I asked him to heal me. He touched my shoulder and moved on."

The hayfield scent was still strong. Hannah went with the flow: "You don't want trouble, we know that. What do you want?"

"Same as you. I wanna live. Find some happiness before I die."

Hannah looked the survivor in the eyes—more pink now than red—and nodded. "Amen."

She gestured at the tea. Glasses sniffed and took a small sip.

If any scent-memory stirred, he kept it to himself. She asked permission for the needle-poke with a glance. Calmer now, Glasses unzipped his jacket, offered an arm, and was sampled. The man was escorted out of the lounge and off the ferry.

One down, eleven more to go.

The Hands of a Healer

DR. CHOW CONFERRED WITH HIS MEDICAL STAFF. They'd had a long day at the docks and were back at the hospital. The Compliants had all been sampled. The shallowing sun, weaker each day, had set. The big moon rolled above, almost full. Elena opened windows to her courtyard garden. Despite the early dark, the fresh air wasn't cold. Indian Summer breezed up from the south. There was a feeling of relief around the table as they finished their meal.

Chow went over the notebook on Compliants, detailing their time in Clare's hangar. "The Griffin medics could only test for antigens."

Chow passed it around as he summarized the results: "I'm glad that they did. Less accurate than our PCR, but it gives us a baseline on these Compliants."

Hannah spoke up, the *braucher* a valued part of the team: "What does that tell us?"

Elena ran her finger down the ledger. "It tells us that upon capture, all twelve tested positive for surface proteins of the virus."

Chow concurred, "We don't know what their load-levels were. Just that they had it."

Hannah asked, "Then what happened?"

Chow shook his head. "The cause is unknown, but you're right, Hannah, *something* happened. Elena, the results from their second round, please?"

Left arm bandaged, the Natural leafed through the ledger with her right. "By the second round—looks like three days ago?—patients one, six, eight, and 11 had no detectable viral proteins. Their antigen tests were now negative."

A whistle escaped from Booker as the sergeant forked his dessert. Specialist Cruz brushed away crumbs, asking, "So they don't have Covee anymore? They're not infected?"

"Antigen tests are quick but not reliable," Chow explained. "Still, it's remarkable."

Those at the table debated as last bites were shared. Hannah thought of something: "*Fraa* Elena, you have notes? From today?"

The silver-haired Sentinel flipped to the interview page. Hannah directed her, "One, six, eight, and eleven?"

Elena found them. Hannah remembered each man, their nicknames anyway: *Glasses, Butcher, Giant,* and *Mouse.* She quoted from memory as Elena confirmed each entry.

"Patient one said, *He touched my shoulder and moved on.*"

"Patient six, *I looked him in the eyes when he shook my hand.*"

"Patient eight, *Medic was changing my dressing. He helped.*"

"Patient eleven, *I was crying. He held my hand, then let it go.*"

Dr. Chow was grinning. The Amish woman had found a correlation. Chow had studied the data and missed it. It didn't prove causation, but still. "And your conclusion, Hannah?"

Hannah thought it through, what had Walker said? *It is in your hands ...* she'd overheard him on the bus, talking to his followers. *In your hands to create a better world ...* he'd been quoting someone, but she couldn't remember who ... *to create a better world for all who live in it.*

"*Ach du lieva,*" Hannah explained. "It is in your hands."

Those seated at the table were staring. Booker's mouth dropped open, still half-full. Hannah could picture it: the airfield at Clare. The preacher making his rounds, unmasked, ungloved. The hangar crowded with Compliants and their complaints. A shoulder, a hand, a forehead. An exchange of molecules, of enzymes, of life.

Hannah gave silent thanks: *Jesus Christ, Precious blood! Which soothes the pains and stops the blood. Help us God the Father, God the Son, and God the Holy Ghost. Amen.*

The *braucher* came back to them, to the lamplit room. To the open windows and the southern breeze. Hannah blinked, looking around the table. "My conclusion?" She gave Chow her answer: "Doctor, it's Walker. His touch. He has the hands of a healer."

Bound to Be True

THE BUS CONVOY, empty of passengers, rolled south with blacked-out lights under a waxing moon. They'd delivered more refugees; the Free North was filling up quickly. The black-bereted driver cranked his window down. For October, the night was warm. Butters tried to ignore the spidered windshield. The sniper's well-aimed bullet had penetrated several layers and was embedded there, still pushing towards his brain. A debate took place behind him, Walker vs. Everyone—what else was new?

They were overdue for a broadcast; Walker was outlining the content of his next drop. Item number three on his list: *Amnesty for Virals*—Compliant ones anyway. The driver tracked the highway signs, pale in the moonlight, as I-75 pulled them south. They'd just passed Bay City. Flint was next, the base of Michigan's thumb. Walker was returning them to the Detroit refinery—recently captured from Panzer—to refuel and rearm.

"Reverend, all due respect, but you can't do that!" The objector was Antiva, a dark man named Grim. In the Before, he'd earned street cred as Anti-Fascist. He earned even more killing Virals in the After. Fighting hand-to-hand, Grim recognized some of his old opponents: their Aryan-blue eyes had turned a virulent red.

"A few Compliants doesn't change things, Walker. Most of your followers are unprotected. One or two droplets and we're dead!"

"Not you though, Grim. Not me either," grumbled Butters to an audience of one. Spend enough time with Walker and people picked up immunity. He'd never seen the pastor in PPE. Most of the bus had stopped masking as well. A perk of employment, maybe the only one. Butters eyed the bullet. He recalled Kamul's smear on the radio: *Kenyan royalty, banana king.*

"Walker, this just isn't the time." Grim couldn't let it go. "Spreaders are on the run. After two years, we're finally *winning!*"

There was a pause, too long. Grim knew what was coming, everyone did. Then there it was, the familiar throat clearing. Behind the wheel, Butters lip-synched Mr. Lincoln, word for well-worn word: *I am not bound to win. But I am bound to be true. I must stand with anybody that stands right, and part with him when he goes wrong.*

Boom, mic-drop, another win for Walker, though the game was rigged. Grim bit his tongue, keeping the peace as old *Pony* pranced down the road.

Anything but peaceful, sudden sparks flashed from an overpass. "Rocket!" Butters screamed a warning, bracing for impact. Moments later, *Ka-BOOM!*—his bus exploded in a white-hot fireball.

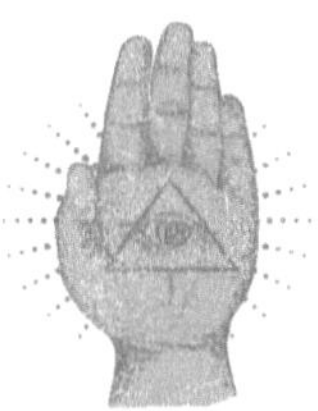

Fireball

KA-BOOM! A white-hot explosion. Their night vision was seared as the anti-tank rocket punched home. The resulting shockwave pushed through the watching Thumbs—their bodies, their brains. Way better than any video game. *This was fucking happening!*

Another Javelin was loaded in the launcher. Another stream of sparks. *Ka-BOOM!* One of the escort vehicles crumpled. Their video was rolling, flames lighting the scene. One more vehicle, one more rocket.

Swoosh!—streaming sparks, screaming men—*Ka-BOOM!*

Panther-painted, the last Humvee jumped off the highway; flipping in the air, it landed upside down. *Ka-Crunch!* The wreck became a cage, then an oven, as its occupants were broiled.

"You gettin' this?" One Thumb elbowed another.

A nod from the filmmaker: "Fucking money, man." Three vehicles burned in his viewfinder.

The militia members, trigger-happy, scanned the underpass for survivors to shoot at. Nothing moved. Kamul's care package—dropped from the Hercules—had come with thermal-optics. Some bodies, and their pieces, had been blown from the vehicles. These blobs cooled slowly in the warmish night: red to orange to blue. Those still trapped in the wreckage showed white-hot in the thermal sights—a charry melt of flesh.

"Let's go boys, we got what we need."

Kamul's toys—launcher, optics, and video equipment—were loaded into the van. "Hey, I need a body count." The stocky leader pointed. The two youngest Thumbs scrambled down the embankment. Soon, the sound of their retching came up from below.

"They're tossin' their cookies!" The leader flashed a rotten grin. His bearded boys grinned back.

"Toledo's gonna be *wild!*"

"Wait till the Hands see this footage. Prouds and Keepers too!"

"Gonna be fuckin' legends."

"I'd settle just for some fucking!" Laughter belched from the militia, drunk on adrenaline. "Goodbye Reverend Walker!" They mock saluted.

"Long live the banana king!" Dirty hands *Sieg Heiled* the burning blobs. Then the militiamen buckled up and took I-75 towards the state line: "Ohio, here we fucking come!"

Night Flight

HE'D BEEN QUOTING LINCOLN, preaching to his attending choir—*and part with him when he goes wrong*—there'd been a searing interruption. "Rocket!" screamed Deacon Butters. Everything ended as the missile's HEAT warhead blew their bus apart.

Reverend Walker ascended, body and mind. Worn out, his wrinkled *corpus* cartwheeled above the scene. One second, maybe two—the duration of his night flight. The man's eyes were wide open. Vibrant, his *spiritus* flew. Wheeling stars compressed the time. A lifetime, many lifetimes, in a blink. He lived them all, his bookish mind unbound. Every word he'd ever read available at the end, an endless scroll of fiery letters. Unquenched, his curiosity burned:

I am flying. Who else had thus ascended?

Far-ranging, he knew his lore: the Western Canon and the East. He paged through his parietal searching for precedents, his lobe-library responding in an instant:

Enoch walked with God, and he was not, for God took him.

And Elijah went up by a whirlwind into heaven.

He parted from them, and was carried up into heaven.

Muhammad saw the signs of his Lord.

Genesis, Kings, Luke, the Quran.

He cited sources as he flew. He reached the apex, a respiratory pause at parabolic peak: *Kumbhaka.* Between ebb and flood, a slack tide of stars. Gravity found him there and reclaimed him. He descended through his mind and all its mentors. Falling through their words, Walker heard them anew:

We never heal until we forgive. Mandela too, was descended from kings.

Hate the sin, love the sinner, counseled Mohandas, he of the great soul.

He heard laughter—his departed wife, his children too. Walker dove deeply into the lake of their love. But there was no waking up from this dream. No stay of execution from the governor of gravity. No pardon from the laws of motion. Only a sickening crunch of bone as Earth crushed him with its colossal embrace.

Only when it is dark enough—his body thudded upon the unyielding pavement.

Can you see the stars—he'd ascended; descended; and returned, a broken man.

The Path of Dead

THEY CALL THEM COLD-BLOODED KILLERS

They say they are heartless and mean.

But I say this with pride

That I once knew Clyde,

When he was honest and upright and clean.

—Bonnie Parker, "The Trail's End" (1910–1934)

A day had passed since they'd conned Beanpole and Bear, leaving the cuffed men behind. Another night had fallen, this one felt a bit warmer, summer's last gasp before winter's suffocation. Undecided, the bickering couple hadn't gone far.

Bob argued they should head up to Mackinaw City, beg for amnesty—and some land—in the Free North. He hinted he had a contact, a medical man that might help.

"Free North? Fuck no! It's south to Toledo," said Liz. "Let's join the Red militia."

Their crossroads dilemma still crossed them up.

For now, they indulged in food, fuel, and heat while they lasted. The two Chosen staked out the intersection, waiting for a sign. They lounged in the stolen Humvee, hidden along I-75. A moon—honey-colored—sweetened above. Their bulletproof windows were steamy.

"You want a piece of this?" Bob offered his pouch with a wink. Liz licked her lips: pound cake, her favorite. They'd stuffed themselves, in more ways than one. Liz's bandage had slipped. Her old wounds were seeping.

"Sweetie, you're hurt," Bob said, spooning it into her.

"I'll hurt you, you fuckin' say that again." She savored a swallow.

"There's medics up north, doctors too. I told you, I know one."

"Oh, so you wanna play *doctor?*" Liz arched her toned body.

Cowboy stiffened, his Free North resolve melting away.

Nearby, a sudden FLASH of light! A second later, *Ka-BOOM!* Thunder bounced off the concrete. "What the *fuck* was that?" Cowboy yelled. Partners in crime, they scrambled into readiness, fumbling with the Velcro and zips of Griffin uniforms.

Another soundless FLASH, then a thunderous *Ka-BOOM!*

With eyes first, then ears, they both pinned the source. It was close, way too close. They were parked beneath an on-ramp. Turned on themselves, they exited from the Humvee. Liz carried Bear's rifle in the low-ready position. Cowboy sported a pair of pistols and the MP's stolen Taser. Fires burned on the highway. The two Virals vectored closer, keeping to the shadows. Another sear of sparks whooshed from an overpass to cripple the convoy below. *Ka-BOOM!*

The last vehicle somersaulted and crunched upside down. Its occupants were on fire. They both heard screams, then after a while, they didn't.

Bob felt nauseous, scanning the scene from cover: a Greyhound bus had been totaled along with two panther-painted Humvees. All three were burning. It smelled sickeningly like a backyard BBQ from before: lighter fluid and roasting meat.

They heard the bravado of male voices, unseen from the bridge above. Apparently, the ambushers were amped. Bob had been there; he'd been in those shoes. He looked sideways at Liz. The scabby side of her face, reptilian, was grinning.

The moon and three fires lit the roadway. Bodies and their bits—some burning—spackled the pavement. Two of the ambushers, retching, searched the wreckage, then left. Soon after, doors were slamming, and the attackers drove away. Bob, curious about their route, watched them take the exit south towards Ohio.

Liz was first to break cover. Bob followed, hating himself— what choice did they have? They scavenged the scene. The three oversize vehicles had been demolished and were burning. The firepower was impressive, some kind of anti-tank shit he hadn't seen before.

"Your fuckin' Griff buddies do this?" Liz, a burn victim herself, flinched from the heat.

First of all, they weren't buddies. And second, those ambushers weren't guardsmen. Bob found a black beret by a beefy blob. Someone's torso—with no fuckin' legs?—tarred the asphalt with intestinal goo.

"Doubt it, Liz. But you're right, those missiles were definitely military."

Bob handed her the beret. Turning it, she found the logo: "Panthers? Who hit 'em? Who the hell has weapons like that? Panzer?"

"You bossed for them, Liz, same as me. Ever seen ordinance like that before?"

She hadn't. Anyway, Sharkey was on the outs. Bob had seen it; Panzer's turf was shrinking.

Chemical fires flickered from the roadway: rubber tires, metallic frames, and rotten diesel. In the ghoulish light, the outlaws followed the path of dead. There was nothing to salvage. Cowboy's throat itched from bile and the grit of fumes. Too many bodies, too much death, he'd had his fill. Liz prodded the piles, kicking each corpse with her stolen boots. There was nothing.

"Let's scram, Lizzy. Others will be coming, moths to a flame."

"So what? We'll trap 'em when they do."

Campbell caught a whiff of human bacon. His stomach heaved, but he choked it down. Bob was done with this shit, he really was. They investigated outward to the firelight's perimeter, Campbell sweating in his combat uniform. The night was warm, the molten wrecks even warmer. His pupils dilated, dissecting the dark, then a sudden *twitch* caught his attention. Sure as shit, someone was out there. He hushed his partner with a word, "Movement!"

Rifle up, ready to rock, Red Liz took point. Tactical, they approached a limping figure. Cowboy's pistols, unbidden, were now at hand. The figure was an old man, ghostly in the moonlight: a shock of gray hair, dark skin, frail and lanky. With every step and stumble, he left a trail behind, red blood transmuted by moonlight into a silver spoor. The man's hands were empty. Liz relaxed her rifle. "Dude's got a flat tire." She grinned at her partner.

Bob took a gander; indeed he had. Ol' boy had lost a foot, blown off by the blast. Unaware of his stalkers, the geezer pegged on, mumbling to himself. Reaching an underpass, he folded to the ground. With a final effort, dude elbow-crawled to the wall, propping himself against the concrete.

"Shine a light there, Liz."

She flicked on her weapon's beam, six hundred lumens pinning their prey. The target shielded his eyes with a hand. Some skin had sloughed away; the rest was bubbled black. His stump was spurting, the flat tire leaking air.

Campbell had seen this man before, no doubt about it: the airfield, the sorting of Compliants back at Clare. Bob had yelled out to Hannah, and was promptly tased. This guy had been standing with that Griff sergeant, the female one. Looked like they knew each other? Maybe from before?

The underpass they stood beneath was tagged with graffiti. Above the injured man's head, a gangster crown was dripping paint; it looked like blood.

Walker was the name Bob recalled from Clare. Some infected Spreader had begged this dude for healing. *Walks-on-Water* was another; Cowboy heard that one in Dawdy's barn, receiving confessions from Methhead and Squints, the unrepentant fucks that had threatened Sammy and little Sarah.

"Honey, fetch the med kit from the Humvee, will ya?"

The amputee needed QuikClot and some morphine. Campbell knelt by the wounded man, improvising a tourniquet. Liz, bossed around by Bob, gave him a wrathful look before slowly obeying. He'd pay for that later. *What else was new? Put it on my tab.*

PART 3:
The Gathering Storm

Winona and the Big Oil Windigo by Jason Clark

The Crucible: Confined

MIIN KNEW WHERE SHE WAS. Built in the 1800s, the Stone House is what they called it, just off King's Highway. Most Beavers considered it haunted. The place had been empty since collapse, its off-island owners—like so many—would never return. She'd been confined in its cellar. The old stones ignored her, ancient breath icy with indifference. Blueberry shivered in their damp embrace but continued her song. Miin sang of *nibi*, of water. She'd been singing for days.

Wayaa way-ay-haa-yo wayaa way-ay-haa-yo.

Mee-ay Nibi Kinagajitoyan!

No one else knew, though. How could they? The Ferny clan claimed the place, but in secret. She'd been abducted by white men, just another missing Indigenous woman. ELF Country was stirring and Indian Point too. Questions were asked, even of Ferny. But the thorny man dissembled. Too crafty to catch, with too many kin to confront. Miin knew her crucible was coming. Her captors had shifted her twice already, search parties drawing near. Each time returning to Stone House, their castle, entombing Miin in its dungeon.

Four nights ago, she'd assigned homework—dream-work actually—to her class. That very night, Bill Ferny came for her, filled with wrath and rotgut whiskey. His cronies violated Sam's shack, the sylvan sanctity of the grove. The men, superstitious, had not been gentle, binding her, blinding her, then hauling her away.

Half-hibernating already, the sleepy maples hadn't stirred. The power of leaf and limb was on the ebb. Solar-dependent, the green world dimmed with daylight's diminution. Miin had no window in her Stone House cellar, and Ferny barred the door. Blueberry wilted in the dark.

She heard harsh voices outside and the snick of a lock. The cellar door slanted open, daylight bounding in. A masculine reek—body odor and boozy breath—rushed into the cave. "Careful boys, don't know what she can do."

Miinan adjusted her vision, forcing herself to stillness. Depositing her, they'd yanked the tape from her wrists and mouth, Miin's soft skin, torn by the glue. Blueberry couldn't abide another binding. She hugged her knees, seemingly docile in defeat.

Bill Ferny leered. "What'd I tell ya? Our little witch is all done in."

"She wants us to think so. Billy, don't you be fooled." Bill's cousin kept her covered with a shotgun as their clansmen brought implements: a bench, a bucket of water, a filthy dishtowel. A rough-fibered rope was threaded through ceiling joists, the bitter ends dangling down. Miin stole glances as the men stood joshing. Her eyes climbed the stairs and hungrily gulped the outdoor vista. The cellar faced south, away from the road, away from any rescuers. Golden sunlight lazed upon the land.

The pit was cold and foul smelling; Miin's offal bucket needed dumping. A warm breeze pushed in, a few dry leaves tumbling down the steps. She tasted the day, savoring the flavor of free molecules. The big lake was on her tongue, and the tang of burning leaves. Beaver Island basked in Indian Summer. The line between past and present grew hazy, smudged by the countless cookfires of those who came before. Vaporous, Miin's ancestors couldn't help her. If they were there at all, they could see but not touch.

Ferny squatted down, his face, pocked with old acne scars, oozing triumph. Miin looked past him, stamping the scene in her mind: the neglected garden, a weedy yard, the line of trees and woods beyond.

"Do you know how this goes, Miss Minny?"

She didn't attend. She wasn't there. Part of her had slipped past him. Ferny bit back a snarl, vice-gripping her chin. His calloused hand stank of shit. He wrenched her attention; they glared at one another, eye to eye.

"Well! Do ya?"

Miinan shook her head in fear. She wasn't acting; she might die in this crypt.

"That's better. Much better. When I ask, you answer, see?"

Miin saw, but not him, never him, even if it killed her.

What she watched instead, over his shoulder, were sleepy trees shedding foliage. The photo-factories, having synthesized their quota, pink-slipped their seasonal workers. Laid off, the blushing leaves fell, making their final commute to the forest floor.

With a creak of knees Ferny stood, nodding to his cousins. The rustics gathered round, crude of thought and rude of gesture. Dirty jeans were hitched higher, crotches—crawling with lice—were roughly scratched.

"Minny, you're a witch and we know it. Now, maybe it's an Indian thing, and not really our business?" The jury was grinning, mouths mossy from lack of hygiene. Judge Ferny was building their case.

"Not our business, that is, till it is. So far, me and my boys have left Indian Point alone, let you Chippewa do your thing. Live and let live, the island way."

A pimply youngster, premature, nudged Miin's backside with his boot. Ferny shot him a hard look. Cousin Boot backed away.

"The problem, Miin, is that you've crossed the line. We got witnesses, seen you corrupting our kids."

The jurors were nodding. A greasy head turned and spat. The judge held forth, "Not the Nat-brats mind you. They ain't ours, never will be. But the islanders? The Greenes. The Martins. That's a different story, those families go way back."

Oppressed, Miin felt their dark hearts and bent her head towards the dirt floor.

"Now, what we need is confession, a list of names. The devil is here. You've conjured, you've called. You and old Sammy have put a stain on this place. Now, it's our job to scrub, to scour. And Minny, you've got a choice."

Ferny nodded and Boot grabbed the rope. He lashed the ends to her wrists, knotting them tight.

"Think about it, Miin. This can be easy. This can be done. Walk out today? Or hang for a week?"

No choice at all, Miin hung her head. Judge nodded and Boots hauled away. Miin was snatched off her knees. Spread-eagled, her arms pulled at their sockets. Boots hauled again and made the rope fast. Miin's arms were already burning. She'd been tugged, barefoot, to her tiptoes, pilloried by pain.

The leering men observed her, their musky scent increasing. Soon they'd be touching. After that would be worse. Young Boot moved in. Chest to chest, he made a show of checking her bindings. He let his hands linger; stole a quick frisk.

Ferny, alpha of the pack, allowed it before barking him back. "That's enough!" Then Bill jested, "Can't ya see that she's stretching!"

Laughter from his dogs, lolling tongues, yellow teeth.

"It's time for snitching, not witching. Give us some names. Who all has been helping?"

Miin couldn't. She closed her eyes in refusal. Pain opened them again. Her *couldn't* turned to *wouldn't*, just a matter of time. Ferny grinned, sensing her retreat.

"It only gets worse." He nodded at the bench, the water bucket. "Does the Miin-fish have gills?"

She grit her teeth to keep quiet.

"When we come back, it'll be time for a ducking."

His men were winking. *Ducking* to *fucking*, the crude joke went around. Ferny nodded. All kinds of pressure. He wanted her to see it, how bad it could be.

"Different strokes, different folks!" Bill mimed a few as his followers laughed.

"Don't you worry. We'll be back soon." Ferny herded them out.

Boots looked back. "Or maybe sooner!" A final guffaw and they were gone.

The cellar door was closing. Miin, desperate, scanned her tomb. She willed time to slow, bidding the photons to linger: joisted ceiling, fieldstone walls, dirt floor. There was nothing, no tendrils, no roots, not a single green ally to call upon. Time continued. The storm door descended, a final wedge of daylight narrowing at her feet. The hatch thudded down, the lock snickered shut.

Miin shuddered, arms aching, salty tears dampening the hardpack. Shaky at first, she resumed her water song, a summons, for any plants that could hear.

Miigwech Manitou!

Wayaa way-ay-haa-yo wayaa way-ay-haa-yo.

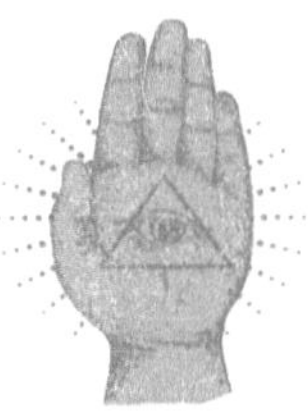

Unite the Right

AIRDROPS COMPLETE, the C-130 Hercules had landed in Ohio. The oversize aircraft rested from its labors, fuel tanks empty. The ramp had been lowered; Major Naz supervising the offload. He'd ordered his pilots to touch down at TDZ, Toledo's Executive Airport, the northwest corner of the state's scarlet heart.

Naz—a prudent commander, linked to the EYE—was unhurried. Men and materiel were mustering. Militia tents sprouted near the tarmac, a fungal bloom of canvas and nylon. The row of RVs and their banners grew larger by the day. The militiamen, awaiting orders, lounged in the warmth of Indian Summer. Cookfires were tended, soup kettles were stirred. A guitar and harmonica added ambiance to the scene; the music was timeless, echoes from the last Civil War.

Touch football had been organized, Red versus Red. Naz heard a burst of cheer; the Keepers had scored. The Prouds contested with, "Stop the steal!" refusing to concede. Negotiations ensued. Double-or-nothing, the ante was raised. The encampment, bored, bet on everything: sharp-shooting, cards, touchdowns, and knifery. The stakes were various: moonshine, toilet paper, ammo, and porn.

Lacking MPs, Naz kept his touch light. The rules were few, but enforcement was swift. Latrine use was mandatory and generators forbidden. As far as he knew, Toledo's gas tanks were dry. He'd sent a team to scout the Maumee River. The refinery on its banks was a longshot, but it had to be checked. The scouts concurred: there was no petroleum, and no hostiles were encountered.

The major, guided by the EYE, planned to cross the Maumee in force, blitz north, then take Detroit and all its fuel. The Marathon plant was his mission objective; Naz wouldn't object to a high kill count as well. General Kamul insisted that it all came down to numbers, ours versus theirs. Fighters were finite. The game was attrition.

Naz set up roadblocks, rotating the sentries. If any Virals were out there, the Spreaders kept their distance. Too big to hit, their TDZ rally point was secure.

His handheld beeped as a checkpoint checked in: "*Black Rider, Black Rider*, this is *Boogaloo* on Lemoyne, over.*"

Naz keyed a return. "*Boogaloo, Black Rider*, what's your report, over."

"Sir, we've got two vans at the east gate, Michigan plates. Call themselves Thumbs. Say they've got good news. How to proceed? Over."

"*Boogaloo*, check for infection. Have them clear actions and remove magazines. I want this news first. Bring their leader to me. *Black Rider* out."

Naz lifted his smart-patch, rubbing his data-eye. Their plan was coming together; the offload had been completed. Coming together as well were his two beasts: attack helicopters *Panic* and *Terror*. The greedy birds drained all remaining fuel from the Hercules, gray snouts nursing at the C-130's fumy teat. The pilots ran through their checklists. Weapon pods were attached to hardpoints. Each missile was a talon; the enemy would be shredded.

There would be no resupply from General Kamul; too many unsecured miles between Toledo and the CORPS. Naz's assault force must live off the land. Kamul's orders made that point clear. Each arriving unit—Oathkeepers, Proud Boys, Three Percenters, and more—must be self-sufficient.

Major Naz, aided by his implant, had done the math, his motor pool tallying their fuel. With luck and decent roads, most vehicles would reach Detroit. If they could capture its refineries, the remaining Reds would rally. Michigan and its resources would become part of the Confederacy, the newest Patriotic State to join the CORPS.

Kamul, his CO, saw further: once Michigan was secure, a Red wave would flood the Great Lakes. A freshwater navy would be assembled; Red sailors would be trained. Then, Viking-like, they could raid at will, spreading like invasive wildfire through the aquatic arteries of the undefended Midwest.

The bearded leader of the newly arrived Thumbs approached, escorted by one of the boys from the checkpoint. Naz grimaced at the Hawaiian-shirted sentry and his sloppy salute.

"Major, here's the Thumb you asked for."

Naz was not impressed. Unwashed and under-muscled, the militia leader looked soft. The man brandished a video recorder and wore a shit-eating grin.

An hour later, the Toledo troops assembled in TDZ's largest hangar. The flying beasts were coiled, gray and lethal, in a dark corner. The militiamen eyed them uneasily. *Panic* and *Terror* were freshly repainted, toothy snarls leering above their nose cannons.

Naz had his superior on the sat-phone. General Kamul—amplified by AYE EYE—was prepared to broadcast. The footage from the Thumbs had been analyzed. Intelligence agencies concurred: the resistance leader Walker was KIA.

"Atten-shun!"

Toledo's two hundred stiffened, facing the flag. Kamul's live broadcast began; Sousa's "Stars and Stripes" marched brassily around the hangar. Across the Midwest and Eastern Seaboard, a hundred other radios, a thousand, tuned in, hungry for news.

The anthem faded. General Kamul came through: "At ease!"

Toledo's strike force relaxed their posture.

"Good afternoon."

"Good afternoon, *SIR!*" Toledo, unheard, responded to the radio.

"This is General Kamul broadcasting from D.C., the capital of the CORPS. Now, you all know me, I'm a man of few words. Your time is precious so I won't keep you in suspense. Last night, near Flint, Michigan, Red Patriots conducted a missile strike on an insurgent convoy. We have video confirmation that Walker, their leader, was killed."

Naz nodded and a Thumb pushed play. Toledo's two hundred gaped at the footage: spark trails, detonations, destruction and death. Red-blooded, they rose from their seats and roared.

Rivers of Rust

BAPTISTE HAD WAITED IMPATIENTLY—nothing. After that, he sent scouts—no dice. Finally, he signaled—but no return was sent. Shaggy and Mukwa had not returned.

Blind Doyle shook his head. Gone too long, the motorcycle and its men were deemed goners. Baptiste gave a French-flavored shrug, *Nous nous reverrons*—we will meet again. His crew mumbled in Métis, *Meena kawapimitinn*—see you soon, brothers.

Fearing ambush, they shoved off, paddling away from Bay City. Their hearts were heavy but the canoes handled better without the mini-motorcycle and its mismatched pair of riders.

The Saginaw River pulled them back to Lake Huron. They rounded Point Austin, then muscled south to Sarnia, following St. Clair to its lake. Canada lay low on the left-hand shore. The crews gaped at the gross wealth of Grosse Pointe, fire-blackened chimneys all that remained. On one Gatsby lawn, ragged with weeds, skeletons sprawled on lounge chairs. Sunglasses were taped to their skulls, one risqué rib cage sporting a bikini. Life was better in the burbs, death too, for the right colored folks. The upper-class bones were bleached a waspish white.

Doyle's vision clouded as they rounded Belle Isle. Its one bridge had been barricaded early in collapse. The mariner squinted at the Yacht Club. Loon detailed its watercraft for

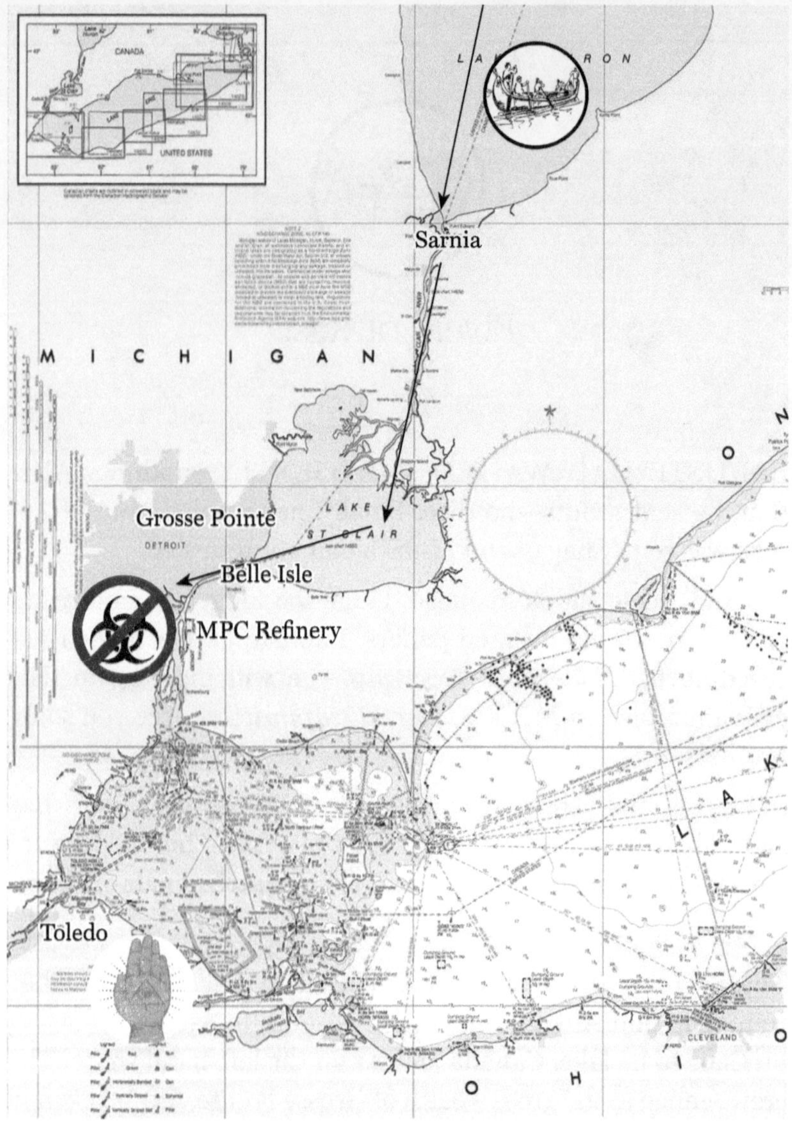

the fog-eyed fisherman: "Undamaged boats? I count five cabin cruisers. Maybe three larger yachts?"

"Bunch of flimsy fiberglass! What do you see, boy, that's *steel?*"

Loon looked again, through his own eyes and others'. "There's a DNR rig and a tow-boat. Both are floating, both look OK."

Doyle brightened. "That's more like it. Any storage tanks for fuel? Tell me!"

But Loon couldn't. The current was too fast, the phrasing too clunky for his feathered familiar.

"Damn you boy, it's important!"

Loon kept quiet. Baptiste growled. Doyle, unrepentant, chewed his cheeks.

They passed under MacArthur's Bridge, tractor trailers jack-knifed across the lanes. Detroit's Coast Guard Station had burned to the waterline. Warehouse District, the same. The Renaissance Center, without HVAC, had shed most of its glass. The Windsor tunnel, below the riverbed, had flooded, entombing Luxury SUVs—deluxe model sarcophagi for the drowned. Vanity plates served as tombstones for the dead: NOT-POOR, BOOYA, LIVN EZ, FUN2BME.

The Ambassador Bridge had been bumped off its pilings. A pile-up of barges pushed on it still. Doyle heard the suck of vortices: "Steer to starboard, Frenchie, starboard! Can't you hear the whirlpool? Back paddles, you fools! Steer clear!"

The voyageurs minded the mad mariner, following his point, heeding his heading. They canoed through the rusting wreckage and continued their float. Both sides of the river were ravaged. Looting and fire had leveled whole neighborhoods: Sandwich, Delray, and Zug Island were gone. Smokestack stubs and cold kilns were all that remained. The vents of Vulcan dormant for the first time in decades.

They passed Fort Wayne on their right. Built on a sacred burial mound, its strata of spirits overlapped: indigent Potawatomi, escaping slaves, Italian POWs, and all the victims of Covee, forever silenced by its sting.

"Here's our turn, boys! Take a right up this next river."

The canoes, passing Zug Island, exited Detroit's river and began stroking against the Rouge. The French, centuries ago, named the tributary for the color of its clays. Industrialized and poisoned ever since, the Rouge had caught fire multiple times.

The fall weather was fine. The sun, with diamond keys, unlocked a dazzling new dimension: a world without humans. Fish jumped, and a sturgeon, prehistoric, surfaced and rolled its ancient eye at the too-modern mariners. Earth's original kingdom—Plantae—colonized the concrete one green tendril at a time. A southing V of Canada geese carpet-bombed the factories, fertilizing the wasteland.

Colonel Dennis, back in Ignace, had ordered Baptiste to contact the Marathon refinery, ASAP. Walker, in a recent broadcast, claimed Antiva had captured it from Panzer. What were their reserves? Their manpower? Was fuel actually being produced? What did they need to make more gasoline, more diesel, more jet fuel? Could the refinery withstand a determined assault? Dennis had questions. Baptiste needed answers.

The first bridge they paddled under was Jefferson Avenue, a bouquet of noosed corpses festooning the guardrail. The eyelids of the hanged were crudely daubed with red. One dead Viral wore a cardboard placard depicting a biohazard symbol slashed by an angry red line:

The voyageurs trespassed beneath this trellis of twisting feet—sunshine to shade, to sun again. They emerged from bridge shadow and kept paddling. Well-hidden, the refinery sentries, Anti-Viral, scoped the eyes of the canoe-borne invaders.

Baptiste—aware of an audience—delivered his lines in a voice meant to carry: "Boat crews, weapons away. Hats and sunglasses off, now. Show 'em the whites of your eyes!"

The nervous voyageurs complied. Their skin itched, allergic to crosshairs. Each boat aired a dirty, white sheet for diplomacy: no red eyes here, no threat, we bring missives not missiles. Baptiste radiated intent as well, *Mon Dieu, je vous en supplie!*

The pair of war canoes passed a gypsum terminal and a sewage plant. Residual odors clogged their olfaction: a sulfurous stench to port, a fecal foulness to starboard. The voyageurs, men and women, raised bandanas against the stink.

The second bridge was a railway. They passed beneath its shade. Graffiti crowned the embankment with a phrase, *Our King is Coming!*

They paddled on. Loon, from the bow, shot a look back at Baptiste. The boy mimed a warning: the next bridge was held against them.

I-75 soared high above the river. Beyond it, the voyageurs spotted gas flares from the petroleum plant. Sulfides and hydrocarbons scratched their throats. The refinery, indeed, appeared active. Electrified, they heard music thrumming through the oily air. The petrochemical hive was busy with human bees.

After days alone, the proximity to people was paralyzing, but intoxicating too. Baptiste ordered the boats to hold their position in the current. Doyle was mumbling. Loon, seeking visions, closed his eyes. The voyageurs were nervous. The next move was clearly Antiva's. It didn't take the Anti-Virals long.

A megaphone squelched, "This is a restricted area. Turn back or we will sink you!"

Baptiste raised his steering paddle above his head, tokening peace: "We come from St. Ignace! Colonel Dennis sent us! We have messages! Hold your fire!"

In reply, two small stones tumbled down from the freeway—black blobs against blue sky. Doyle, extrasensory, felt the fury of their five-second fuses: "Grenades!"

The voyageurs ducked. The Comp-B inside the bomblets detonated underwater. *Ka-Whush! Ka-Whush!* They were soaked but unhurt—a shot across their bow.

Captain Doyle was livid. "We're on the same *fuckin'* side! Can you cunts not see us?"

Megaphone replied, "See you fine. Just don't like what we see. Last warning, turn the fuck around or we waste you!"

Perched on the bow, Autumn's boy cupped a loon-cry with his hands. His tremolo SOS echoed between the concrete legs of colossal I-75. A squadron of scaup—black and white birds—buzzed the combatants, offering close air support for the vulnerable canoes.

The urbanite defenders appeared awed by such allies. And Antiva was curious: the birds, the truce flags, and no sign of infection. The refinery defenders safetied their weapons, re-pinning grenades. Megaphone instructed, "There's a dredged channel behind you. Pull your boats into it and prepare for inspection!"

Baptiste did so. At the head of the weedy dredge, the voyageurs soon were covered by gun trucks and masked militia. The Anti-Viral symbol was everywhere, Black Panther icons prowling as well. Hands high, the newcomers followed instructions. They disembarked and were frisked by gas-masked guards wearing full PPE. Bright lights were flashed in their eyes. When Doyle was checked, his pupils didn't dilate. For now his fog had returned.

The sun sank redly in the west, an atomic fireball blooming in the petro-reek.

Marathon Petroleum Corporation

THE VOYAGEURS, for now, were quarantined in a shipping container. The strangers had been fed, watered, and given a bladder break. Then the doors were sealed. Early night had fallen, and the floodlights lit. The vampire shift punched in as day workers, drained of energy, stumbled back to barracks, brew, and gossip.

"They came in canoes. No signs of infection?"

"Say they fought at the bridge battle?"

"Yeah, they're Old Law."

"Nope, just allies."

"How 'bout that boy? Those birds?"

"And that blind bastard. Dude didn't blink."

"They've got maps. And letters. Signed by the colonel."

"What would Walker say? Where's he been? Days since we've heard."

"Fuck if I know. You?"

"What am I, his secretary?"

"Go screw yourself."

"Give me a hand?"

"Fuck off!"

"I'm trying to!"

"Shift starts in eight hours. Shut up."

"Goodnight."

"Nighty-night."

Baptiste was grilled in their boardroom, facing off with executives. Management was less than happy to see them. The execs still wore their masks. Most wore weapons. The voyageur could feel every frown, every scowl. He saw skin of all shades; some stank, some didn't. Their only unity was disliking him.

"We don't understand your mission. You say you've been traveling for days. For what purpose?"

Baptiste grit his teeth. "Told you already. Colonel Dennis wanted the port cities scouted. Especially Detroit."

"And? What's your report?"

"Empty. All empty. 'Cept for this one. Here you are, *Dieu merci.*"

"Yes, here we fucking are. And now that you've found us, we can't let you go."

"Pourquoi pas?"

"You know too much. The river. Our defenses. Our numbers. Our operation."

Baptiste frowned. "That's exactly what Dennis wants to know. I've got more questions."

The board objected. Baptiste overruled: "How many barrels a day? What are your diesel reserves? What supplies do you need? Can you transport by rail? Fend off an attack? What's your comms situation?"

Baptiste hit a wall. The execs weren't sharing. They questioned him instead: his loyalties, the bridge battle, Griffin numbers, the Free North. Baptiste told the truth, hoping to inspire the same. No luck, not tonight. Their masks—both corporate and biohazard—never slipped. Baptiste and his stomach were growling, his eyelids drooping. He was about to ask for his hot and a cot, when a runner rapped on the glass and was admitted.

"We're picking up a broadcast on the CORPS frequency. It's Kamul."

A female executive turned the knob on a speaker, saying, "We'll listen in here." Sousa began marching around the room.

Executive: "Switch on the plant speakers too."

Leadership nodded; full disclosure. No secrets between labor and management. "Stars and Stripes" played, and the petro-hive began buzzing, disturbing the sleepy drones in their cells.

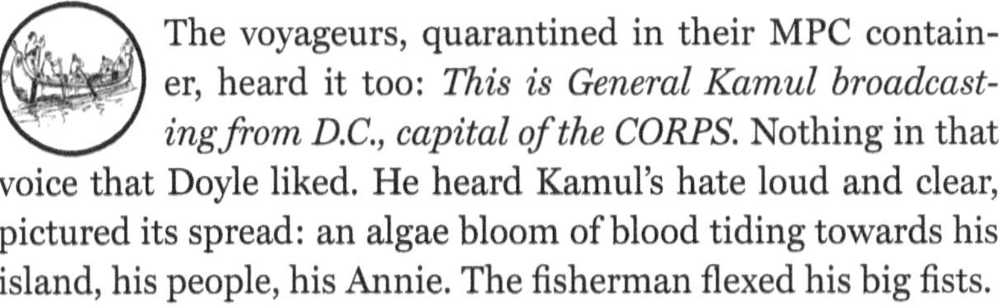

The voyageurs, quarantined in their MPC container, heard it too: *This is General Kamul broadcasting from D.C., capital of the CORPS.* Nothing in that voice that Doyle liked. He heard Kamul's hate loud and clear, pictured its spread: an algae bloom of blood tiding towards his island, his people, his Annie. The fisherman flexed his big fists.

Colonel Dennis pushed away his pipe, his papers. He knew the voice. Kamul was the most dangerous man in America. *Now, you all know me, I'm a man of few words. Your time is precious so I won't keep you in suspense.* Tonight's broadcast would change the game. Dennis made sure the transmission was recording.

South of Detroit, just across the state line, Major Naz knew what was coming. He observed Kamul's impact on the assembled militiae. The Red Hand commander, safe in Fortress D.C., fired for effect on multiple frequencies: *Last night, near Flint, Michigan, Red Patriots conducted a missile strike on an insurgent convoy ...* A red wave crested through the Toledo hangar. Two hundred dirty thumbs were raised as the badasses from Bad Axe were recognized.

 Their elderly patient, one-footed, had been stabilized. The preacher man was pale from loss of blood. Their Humvee's radio still worked, its auto-scan marching right up to Sousa's frequency. A commanding voice came in loud and clear: *We have video confirmation that Walker, their leader, was killed.*

Campbell shook his head. "You sure about that, hoss?"

Their stolen Humvee was well hidden. They had diesel in the tank, weapons, and some food. Liz purred, primping herself in a small mirror. Cowboy's crotch responded to her grooming, if Chow's cabin-treatment had put him on the recovery wagon, too much time with Liz was pushing him off: "Nothin' sexier, Lizzy gal, than an ace up a sleeve."

Red Liz had a racist streak. "Or in our case," she winked at Bob through the mirror, "the king of the fucking spades." Campbell flinched to hear it.

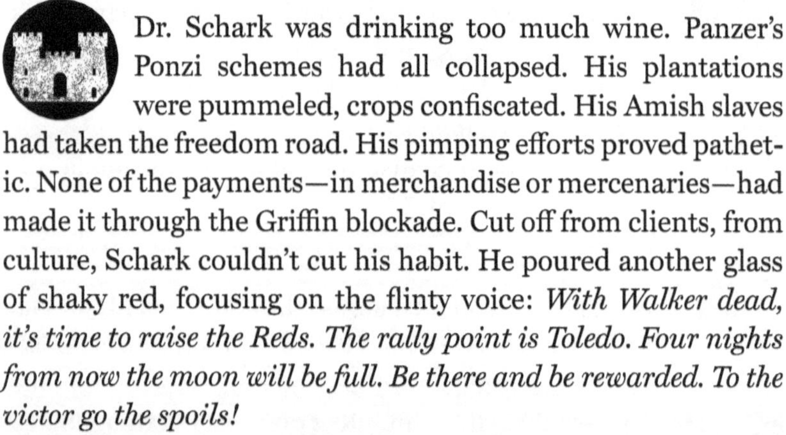 Dr. Schark was drinking too much wine. Panzer's Ponzi schemes had all collapsed. His plantations were pummeled, crops confiscated. His Amish slaves had taken the freedom road. His pimping efforts proved pathetic. None of the payments—in merchandise or mercenaries—had made it through the Griffin blockade. Cut off from clients, from culture, Schark couldn't cut his habit. He poured another glass of shaky red, focusing on the flinty voice: *With Walker dead, it's time to raise the Reds. The rally point is Toledo. Four nights from now the moon will be full. Be there and be rewarded. To the victor go the spoils!*

Schark drained his glass and cried out, *"Victori spolia!"* The spoiled prince passed out, puddled by pinot.

 A Ferny cousin, pocked and pimpled, climbed a coastal tree, wrapping it in wire. The improvised antenna improved their reception. Kamul's message-in-a-bottle washed ashore on Beaver Island: *What spoils you ask? How about food, farms, and fuel? And a bounty paid for every insurgent? I've authorized payment, dead or alive, for every Griffin, Antiva, Greenie or Old Law that gets in our way!*

The Ferny clan had been moonshining. Bill's colicky newborn was making a fuss. "Shut him up or shut the fucking door!" Ashley, Bill's ashen wife, quickly obeyed. Ferny grunted at his brethren, "What'd I tell ya boys? Our little bitch-witch, Blueberry, is worth her weight in gold!"

Redeployment

DATE TIME GROUP: 271100ROCT21

LOCATION: KALAMAZOO, MI

It had been a month since she'd showered or eaten a non-MRE meal. Her Army Combat Uniform was beat to shit and baggy from weight loss. She felt like a piece of jerky: over-spiced and shriveled. Well preserved against apocalypse, the salty combat veteran soldiered on. Amanda Taylor, command sergeant major of Michigan's 125th Infantry Guard Regiment, received fresh orders from Colonel Dennis on the satellite phone. The DOD's Palantir network, built to be EMP-proof, remained rock solid. The satellites, utilizing rare earth elements—far-seeing stones—needed few inputs from Earth.

"Yes sir—Affirmative—Nothing in or out of Panzer—Towards Toledo?—Yes sir—Sufficient fuel—Will redeploy to the state line—Walker dead? Is that confirmed?—I see—Thank you, sir— And to you."

Colonel Dennis ended the call from his HQ in the Free North. Taylor powered down her handset. Amanda couldn't catch her breath; sorrow squeezed her chest. *Walker? Missing? KIA? A rocket attack by some racist Reds?*

It just wasn't possible? It sure-as-shit was. Happened all the time, she should know. Taylor forced herself to breathe deeply and got on with it. That's what she did—what they all had been doing—every damn day since the world collapsed.

On the plus side, the Griffin blockade of Panzer had been total. Dr. Schark, toothless, was confined to his cage; nothing had gotten through. Word had spread among Spreaders and survivors both: Panzer Pharm was closed for business.

Her soldiers, along with the irregular Rangers, had confiscated valuable supplies. A fuel tanker seized from Blackwater contractors was the major score so far. Taylor wondered what Schark had bartered to receive five thousand gallons of unspoiled diesel. Given the supply and demand dynamic of dystopian Michigan, Taylor guessed it was either female flesh or pharmaceuticals—probably both.

For days now, she and her cannoneers had been "standing by to standby," ever since the would-be blockade runners had run away. Now that she had new orders from Dennis, the operational tempo became "hurry up and wait."

Colonel Dennis, running on fumes up in Ignace, could not deploy. His two F-15s—the Strike Eagles from the bridge battle—were flightless. The aircraft and their crews nested at the Soo. His remaining Griffs were guarding the Straits, keeping the bus road and ferry service open for refugees and runaway slaves.

So it was up to Taylor to protect Michigan's southern border. She'd hitch her cannons, fuel up the Humvees from the confiscated tanker, and hustle her detachment towards Toledo. Once there, facing the Reds, they'd probably be waiting all winter. Her supply of cold weather gear was thin. Her knowledge of cold weather campaigns was not: Valley Forge, Stalingrad, Bastogne—nuts! Too bad history was dead with all the rest; "The Battle of Toledo" had a certain panache.

Taylor had summoned both Ranger brothers; they pedaled up to her position. "Hi there, Mom!" Robert and Freddy mock saluted. "We missed you!"

Taylor cringed. The two preppers dismounted from their bicycles, taking in the scene. The unit's FOB was busy. Tents were folded away. The tanker truck had been tapped. Diesel fumed and the air shimmied as thirsty Humvees gulped fuel. Panthers and Griffs were bugging out. Black berets and helmets double timed their duties.

"Where we going, Ma?" Both boys were grinning.

She grimaced at their glee. "Where's Thorn? How many Rangers are left?"

The brothers inhaled; the diesel was intoxicating, pure power. Post-collapse, there was no potion stronger.

"Brother Rabbit is in the woods by the west gate. Did you get the patch he sent? Dude's convinced Panzer has a Sentinel prisoner, some she-elf he knew before."

The sergeant shook her head. "No time for that. We're pulling out, redeploying south."

Their grins grew bigger.

"Not you though. I need you Rangers here."

Their smiles shrank. "Why us?" Freddy asked.

"Because you're irregular."

"Mom!" they both objected.

"I mean it. I can only leave a handful, and that handful is you. Undermanned, you guys have the best chance of keeping Schark in his cage."

"What if the mercenaries try again?" Robert's grin had become a frown. "What if they're serious next time?"

"Like I said, you're our best chance. How many of you are left?"

Robert wiggled his fingers. "Just three."

Thorn lived mostly aloft.

Decades ago, a white pine had rooted itself near the west gate of the compound. This hilltop tree overlooked Panzer's campus and had a wide view of the country round. The former MSU Spartan slung his hammock in its crown. There he spent his nights, his lonely days too. His only tech was a pair of high-powered binoculars and a handheld radio. Each time mercenaries attempted a breakthrough, his early warning had aided Old Law.

Thorn's eyes were everywhere; his sharp ears were wide open too. He sifted the scent-scape, sensing subtle shifts. Thorn knew before most that Taylor was bugging out. He'd caught the first whiff of her diesel on an updraft. Humvee engines rattled the small bones of his inner ear. The birds were ruffled too, and shrilled their complaints.

Through his binos he saw the Griffins form up, strike their pennant, then roll out. Their allies went with them. Taylor's march column, panther-black and desert-tan, headed towards Portage Road, then I-94 and all points southeast.

Thorn's radio crackled.

Freddy's voice—singing falsetto—attempted a tune: *I think we're alone now. There doesn't seem to be anyone around ...*

Thorn rolled his eyes, then rolled the volume knob to low. Alone indeed, and better off for it. Schark, knowing he'd been caged, had gone quiet lately. With Taylor leaving, the bars might bend. Thorn hoped their foolish fish might make a move.

Nighthawk was in there.

He knew it. If she didn't come out soon, Thorn—with or without the Ranger brothers—would go in and get her. Freddy's song was the soundtrack of his rescue plans:

Running just as fast as we can.

Holding on to one another's hand.

Trying to get away into the night ...

Thorn keyed his radio in response. "Alone. Roger that."

When Freddy resumed—*The beating of our hearts is the only sound*—Thorn clicked off.

The Natural sought to synchronize his organic software with the hard drive of the pine. He mentally mapped the hub-tree, its connections to others, its pulmonic power. Things began to quiet, starting with himself. October landscaped the woods and low hills; trees dreamed in red and gold, preparing for sleep. Fair weather clouds puffed their forecast. Everything had gone very still.

Freddy's song aside, Thorn didn't feel alone in these woods. There was memory here, great wells of it, brimming inside each eye of burl. The trees, master communicators, had forgotten nothing, including the *Anishinaabemowin* from their youth. Long ago the Star-People, Indigenous, had shared their speech. The trees, omnilingual, had coded the words deep within their concentric cores:

Kalamazoo: *Ki-ka-ma-sung,* "boiling water" of Potawatomi.

Michigan: *Mishigami*, the "Great Lake" of the Odawa.

Saugatuck: *So'hktuk,* "where the river pours out."

Indian Summer stirred the spirits of the place: Kickapoo, Iroquois, and Potawatomi. Generational strata began to unfold. Ghostly scouts, painted for war in autumnal colors, whispered their warning. The pine-medium thrummed in translation. Skin to skin, Thorn received their spectral report: *something approached.* Correction, some *things* approached. These new arrivals were clad in gray, carrying weapons familiar to the spirits: spears hafted with wood, laminated bows, arrows sharply tipped and fletched with feathers.

The vibrations—spirited via the root network—emanated from the north, and Thorn shifted his focus, catching a faraway glint. Then his binoculars found the river—the Kalamazoo, *Ki-ka-ma-sung*—and an oversize canoe, expertly paddled.

Thorn recognized the frequency of these newcomers. Sentinels, uncloaked, were broadcasting in the clear. Their transmission repeated, telepathic, timed to their strokes: *We are coming. We are coming. We are near!*

"Ranger, this is Thorn, over."

"Rabbit, go ahead," Robert responded. Freddy was still singing in the background.

"Ranger, we've got friendlies inbound. They've left the big river for Portage Creek and are paddling south. I'm climbing down and will meet them at the Romence culvert. Thorn, out."

Thorn switched off the radio, gathered his gear, and began his descent.

Next Stop Kalamazoo!

TWO NIGHTS EARLIER, in Bay City, Mukwa and Shaggy—suspected Virals—had been captured along the highway. Realizing the mismatched pair were on their side, the A-Team eventually freed them from their flex cuffs. Their exploits at the bridge battle, retold and exaggerated by Shaggy, only increased their cred.

The van full of militants were highly motivated. Roadtripping, they passed a joint of homegrown. Mukwa and Shaggy soon got motivated too.

The night of their capture, a real low point, had been freezing. The van had been a welcome respite, a hotbox of happy vibes. Yes, the pair had been duped by the Humvee flat tire and imposter Griffs. But so what? Yes, they'd been robbed as well, but they weren't fucking dead, not yet anyway. Baptiste and the waiting voyageurs soon slipped their minds. Frenchie would be fine. Either the big man would figure it out or the loony boy would.

Adopted by Antiva, more joints were rolled. Shaggy and Mukwa were rolling along as equals. The Lakota Howler, even when sober, was far from shy. Saturated with sativa, his golden eyes glowed. The van basked in Shaggy and Muk's reflected glory:

"An auto-grenade launcher? Fuck yeah! You lit those Virals *up!*"

"Tell us about those LAWS again."

"Two-man rocket teams? On fucking Harleys? Hell yes!"

"And Eagles showed up? No shit? F-15s for real?"

"Blew the fucking bridge? God *damn!*"

Wolfman and man-bear nodded along as I-75 pulled them south. The van's stereo added motivation, Eminem—RIP—providing the soundtrack:

I'm a make a new plan.

Time for me to just stand up and travel new land.

Time for me to just take matters into my own hands.

The A-Team was tasked towards Kalamazoo. They were on a long range reconnaissance; most of their fuel cans were empty. Pre-departure, they'd fueled up with diesel at the Rouge River refinery. The execs there had mapped out their route: first scout Bay City, then join the Griff fight against Panzer. After that, if still alive, they could freestyle their way home.

They weren't the only van out there, they explained, just the best. At killing Virals anyway. Their tallies told the tale: Xs and Raider shields crowded their door panel. And they were big fans of Walker, borderline fanatical. *Walks-on-Water*, the healer, descended from African royalty. Shaggy and Muk had heard all the stories: The frozen Flint River. The colony of contagious. How the sick were healed and the soup never ran out.

At each piss stop, Ayesha, the driver, marked Walker's turf with spray paint: Bay City, Saginaw, Lansing, Battle Creek....

"Next stop Kalamazoo!" Ayesha announced. "Eight miles, get ready!"

It was late afternoon on their second day together. The sharp edge of the cold front had been blunted by good weather. Sheepish clouds frolicked in blue. The sun gilded the fading billboards along I-94—truck stops, fast food, and car dealerships—Rosetta stones of peak consumerism.

The van, action imminent, was mostly sober. Kalamazoo's Exit 78 approached: Portage and Kilgore Roads. "Battle stations! Masks! PPE! Watch your proximity, people!"

Marshall Mathers was turned down as Antiva geared up. Ayesha slowed their roll. Rifle-muzzles sniffed hungrily for targets from the van's open windows. Mukwa and Shaggy—"No offense, guys"—were pushed to the back row. The side door slid open; a battered M60 was belt-fed by its action-hungry crew.

"We've got company, people!" The navigator had his binoculars up, glassing the approaching convoy of black and tan vehicles. The convoy flew a Griffin pennant, and was merging onto the highway just as the A-Team exited.

"Looks like Natty Guard, but it could be a trap!" Ayesha drifted like a pro, spinning the van to unmask its machine gun. "Dismount! Take cover!"

Some of the militants jumped out, pointing rifles from the barrier wall. Mukwa and Shaggy were out too, long hair streaming as they ran for cover. Weaponless, they peered over the concrete at the approaching column: armored Humvees, heavy machine guns, towed cannons, and a fuel tanker.

"Holy shit! Fuckin' hope they're friendly?" Mukwa's buzz was fading fast. He looked at his Howler buddy. Shaggy's eyes were shining, his wolfish canines on full display. The approaching emblems were various: golden Griffins, Black Panthers, "Yield to None," "Long Live King."

The soldiery—those visible anyway—varied as well, guardsmen wearing MOPP and black-bereted irregulars sporting shades and dark jackets. The A-Team was waving white towels from the door, from the window. Ayesha passed the word: "No shooting! Hold your damn fire!"

The approaching Army convoy had spotted the black van. Its gun trucks quickly circled their wagons, shielding their prize, the precious fuel tanker. The Humvees' big 50s pointed at the van and its fighters. If shooting erupted, Antiva—exposed and outgunned—would be splattered.

"Friendlies!"

"Same side!"

"Non-Viral!"

White shirts and towels were flapping. So far, the disciplined Griffins held their fire. A female voice called on the loudhailer, "This is Sergeant Taylor of Michigan's 125th. Step away from your weapons and prepare for inspection!"

Ayesha, from the driver's seat, amplified Taylor's message: "Listen up, Antiva! Lay down your guns. Back the fuck away, we're on the same side!"

Antiva did so, and lived.

In five minutes they were cleared: masks were removed, sclera scanned and weapons safetied. Taylor and Ayesha squatted over a map. Antiva and Griffs—waiting on leadership—exchanged tokens. Shaggy and some Panthers shared tokes as well. Mukwa, Nighthawk-focused, hung by the map, overhearing the two tacticians.

Taylor was talking, "I've got orders from St. Ignace."

"Colonel Denny still the man up there?"

Taylor nodded. "Kamul made another broadcast. Red militias are rallying near Toledo; they're gonna push for Detroit." Her finger traced the route.

"Rouge River? The refinery?"

"That's my guess." Taylor locked eyes with Ayesha, bracing her for bad news. "There's more."

"Just say it."

"Kamul is claiming a missile strike killed Walker. Says they've got video." Sergeant Taylor, freshly bereaved, ordered her voice not to crack.

Ayesha gasped. "I heard that you knew him. Same church or something?"

Amanda choked on the past tense, nodding. A father figure for sure. Sergeant Taylor cleared her mind and the lump in her throat. "We've got three days. Kamul mentioned the full moon as jump-off."

Ayesha pointed at the map, indicating their position. "What about Panzer? We thought the fight was here?"

Taylor shook her head. "It was. Then it wasn't. Schark never came out. We stopped a few convoys, preventing resupply. I've left behind some Rangers, real irregulars. They say he's got prisoners, but Sharkey's caged pretty good. As my CO said, *We've got bigger fish to fry.*"

Together, they made plans. The A-Team would join the Griff column and push towards Toledo. The van would refuel from the tanker and top off their ammunition. The leaders went over the route together, anticipating allies and looking for a choke point to strangle the Reds. The Maumee River, a major water obstacle, flowed between Toledo and Michigan. Those bridges had potential. The two women got granular.

Mukwa, overhearing them, twitched his ears. "Schark's got prisoners?"

Ayesha and Amanda turned their heads at the intrusion. Standing tall, Mukwa reared above them, blocking their sun, shadowing their strategy.

Taylor took him in: Native cheekbones, ponytail, neck tattoo, trauma stare. The bear-sized warrior wore a gray parka embroidered with a tree.

"I've seen that tree before," she said, pointing. "One of the Rangers, Thorn, has a jacket like that." Taylor pulled open her Velcro pocket, removing the patch and the handwritten note:

Sergeant,

This patch is from an ELF parka.

A friend of mine—Mukwa—told me that Sentinel Nighthawk has gone missing?

Do you know anything about this?

- Thorn

Taylor handed both over. "Thorn found this in the woods, by Panzer's front gate." Mukwa felt the fabric, sniffing for scent. Over a month since she'd fled—from the island, from him. Hawk burned half the damn harbor in her flight.

Three nights ago at a crossroads, he'd met Hangman, the hatless cowboy. Truth or dare, he recalled the Viral's words:

A man on the island—some kind of professor—soldiers tried to arrest me—psycho Greenie got me instead—stole a boat, some gas, and escaped.

A reek of reefer and a pounding on his shoulder. Shaggy was calling, "Earth to Mukwa, you there, man? Anyone home?"

Mukwa shook his big head, got himself together. He was back. He was needed. Nighthawk was close. He would save her, or fucking die trying. Couldn't ask for more than that. He mustered a grin for his battle-buddy and said, "We've got work to do."

Shaggy flashed his fangs. "Ride or die, motherfucker."

The van nuzzled at the tanker's teat, drops of diesel glistening on its rusty chin. Ammo cans were opened. Invited by the Griffs, Antiva fighters loaded their fill. With handshakes and fist bumps, the A-Team farewelled Muk and Shaggy. The pair would remain at K-Zoo and contact the Rangers.

Mukwa needed to see Thorn. He'd last seen the Sentinel a month ago on the blasted bridge above dark straits. Three months before that, back in June, Thorn led the rearguard as

XCons and pit bulls hounded Naturals from their original ELF country.

Sergeant Taylor pointed the two friends towards an ammo trailer. "Better arm up before I change my mind." Taylor felt like crying; duty and decision making only delayed the pain. Her pastor was dead. No more quotes, no more quizzes. His marvelous mind, atomized by assholes. Antiva grieved as well. They'd known the reverend's touch, his mild temper. They'd met him, had shaken his scholarly hand. His voice on the VHF, digitized and scratchy with static, had kept them going. Ayesha wielded her spray can in denial:

Our King Shall Return!

She attached her van to Taylor's convoy, tears tracking her dusty face. The column policed up its trash, revved engines, and resumed the road towards Toledo and the Maumee River.

Mukwa and Shaggy, slung with weaponry, waved goodbye to the Griffins. Taylor's parting gift was a pair of beat-up bicycles. Shaggy straddled the girl's bike and fake-throttled its plastic grips. "Vroom! Vroom! Saddle up Romeo, your Juliet awaits!"

The column was gone, out of sight, out of hearing. Taylor had pointed the two bikers south. "How will we find them?" Mukwa asked.

Amanda smiled, her first in a while. "They're Rangers! Believe me, they'll find you."

Shaggy adjusted the sling of his carbine, arranging extra magazines in the basket. Of course, he picked the pink bike. The Howler thumbed its little bell, *Ding! Ding!* "Let's fuckin' go already." The Big Bad Wolf tucked his tail and went.

Mukwa, browsing the ammo trailer, had picked out a LAWS—the same light anti-armor weapon he'd wielded before. The Guardsman at the trailer was generous: "Take two, big man. Panzer still packs a punch." Muk had done so, slinging them both. He bladed himself as well, thinking of Uncle Keith. Two Army issue knives, retractable claws, now hung from his belt. Mukwa adjusted his gear and mounted up. A few wobbly pedal pushes, and the unbalanced bear bicycled away.

Home to Roost

WITH THE DEPARTURE OF THE SOLDIERS, the murder returned. Roost trees by the Panzer gate were soon inky with crows. The forest floor grew fetid with their droppings.

The diesel-burners were gone, I-94, a concrete river, carrying them east. As the convoy clanked away, its plume of pollution was diluted—billions of particulates blown away by the breeze. The carbon cloud, sequestered during the Carboniferous, drifted over the depeopled landscape, buoyed by balloons of dioxide.

Along with the crows came their cadaverous symbionts. The tattooed bones of the skeletons were baggy. Schark's Special Forces were no longer so special. The Gories were gaunt—from hunger, from neglect, from diminishing doses of diluted virucide.

The juice had run out and they were ravenous for many things, not least of which was purpose. They'd lost their leadership. Mackenzie, a specialist in regicide, had been bested by a Greenie. The Vishkanya bled out on the coast road, her mutant plasma pooling beneath her. The Aghori top sergeant, Guru Jones, was vaporized in an explosion, his tugboat rammed in battle. Had he found Nirvana? "Never mind," they told each other. Was death not—as Jones often preached—"the destroyer of worlds?" As for Dozer, they'd killed that coward—caught fleeing the Straits—slowly, themselves.

For their recruiter, Dr. Schark, they felt mostly rage. Their cunning maker, through his injections, had unmade them. His

CV-N scoured away their humanity. He'd boiled them down to bones and then rebuilt them, robots of rote obedience.

They had all killed for Sharkey, slaughtering innocents many times over. They'd toasted each other with the skull-cups their victims, "Skol!"

The Aghori, what was left of them, had come home to roost. Within the walls of Panzer lay their prize. Dr. Schark was a swindler. His once powerful voice needed silencing.

With the Griffin soldiers gone, Panthers too, the roost grew unruly.

# Beware of the D.O.G.

"ALL THE SOLDIERS HAVE GONE," Sentinel Sparrow briefed her canoe, "they took I-94 east. For what purpose, I don't know."

Sparrow had been scouting, flitting tree-to-tree to learn the lay of the land. Her squad, gray and weary from paddling, got on with it. The warriors, femme fatales, applied their makeup—green and black—from camo compacts. Well-heeled in combat boots, they unloaded gear, checked weapons and covered their oversize craft with brush.

Six days ago, back on Beaver Island, Baptiste had offered them a spare canoe. Sparrow and nine others, all Daughters of Gaia, had accepted. Baptiste, with Mukwa jumping aboard, had returned to Ignace, bringing Samantha's medicine—mind medicine—to Dr. Chow.

"Be the change you wish to see," they told each other, departing yet again from another ELF Country. The wished-for voyage had indeed changed them. Their hands had blistered, sticking to their paddles. Their muscular legs, under-used, had atrophied beneath them. They'd bailed urine from the bilge and emptied their shit in buckets. Three hundred miles, by the crow. Twice that, compensating for wind and current.

Had there been a battle here? Had Panzer been bested? The compound's walls breached? Or was it the other way round? After the bridge fight, things had been quiet, too quiet for the amped-up Amazons. Sentinel Sparrow, on occasion, helped Miin with her students. Other Daughters had hunted, caching meat for Beavers against the coming cold. Some stashed their spears away, resuming traditional gender roles. The island tedium, never-changing, had chafed. Too wild for domestication, the Daughters placed their bets, gambling their lives in service of Gaia.

The women had seen what Schark could do, what he'd do again if unchecked. The Daughters had fought Chosen, XCons, and Gories—the toxic pollutants of masculinity run amok. A month ago, Sentinels had stopped Line 5's pipeline from spewing. It would be Sentinels again—Gaia's Daughters—that would sever Schark's pipe, this time for good.

"What now, Sparrow?"

The youngest Daughter, Dee, laced up her battered combat boots. Covee had stung the life from her family as the old world collapsed. Naturals found her, feral, foraging in the woods outside Traverse City. The Sentinels, true believers, had trained the girl to serve Gaia.

Apprentice Chickadee, at the pump station skirmish, had feathered her first Viral. Her carbon shaft had cut through his ribcage. The teenager retrieved her bloody arrow. A collapse-era Cupid, she etched her first tally.

Sparrow gestured and Dee surrendered her recurve, a Fred Bear model with quiver attached. "Change the bowstring for starters, this one's wet. And use wax. It might save your life, or more importantly, mine."

Sparrow handed back the bow. Dee blushed, the Daughters grinned. Their war canoe was camouflaged in the culvert. The Sentinels shouldered their packs, leaning on spear shafts, awaiting their move.

Sparrow consulted her road map, pointing southeast. "Panzer's main gate is that way. A mile through the woods, and we're there."

"Then what?" The question, unasked, drifted on the breeze.

Sparrow heard it loud and clear. "Then, Daughters—Gaia willing—we'll see what we see."

A familiar birdcall scattered the squad. A lookout was signaling: *danger approached!* Arrows were nocked as the gray-clad fighters merged with boulder, lichen, and fern. The women stilled themselves, cloaking signatures, and reaching for allies. Gaia gave them guidance. Birds and breeze, shared what they knew: a single figure approached in the open, on the roadway, armed with a military rifle.

Their lookout scrambled into the ravine, a grin on her painted face. Her eyes found Sparrow's. "Gaia is good! Sparrow, you'll never guess who's coming."

Bird Calls

THORN HEARD THE BIRDCALL FROM THEIR SENTRY, recognizing the sunrise song of a robin. The ex-ELF swallowed a surge of happiness at the wrongness of the call—the late-season sun was westering and would be setting soon. Thorn ranged along the middle of Romence Road, in the open, nothing to hide. The dark elf walked in the slanting light; his rifle slung, he kept his hands in view. Thorn knew the call, knew the callers. Sentinels for sure, he'd been one of them, hadn't he? But who had come? And *why* were they here?

"Halt!" a woman's voice commanded.

Thorn opened his hands and froze. He could feel the tension of their bow-limbs, the thirsty steel of honed broadheads. Below the roadbed, Portage Creek gushed through its culvert. He guessed their canoe was stashed somewhere nearby.

Halted, compliant, he trilled the same song. Robin to robin, Greenie to Greenie, the evening dusk became dawn. For one twilit moment, October was June.

"Get off the road!"

He did so. The outbreath of trees, mostly leafless, felt cold. The ravine was crowded with unseen forms. His pupils adjusted, filtering more photons. He couldn't find them in the ferns. His chest could explode at any moment, punched through by a stainless steel spear.

"My name is Thorn," he addressed the potential ambushers, "you know me. I'm here with allies. I'm glad you came."

His voice was small, mouse-sized compared to the whoosh of fast water.

"Lay down that filthy rifle." The mossy boulders had spoken.

Thorn obeyed the stony command. He unslung his carbine, leaned the mechanical menace on a log. The oily contraption oozed insult. Thorn stepped clear and felt the tension ease. It was all coming back to him. He repented, "Gaia forgive me. I've fallen."

"*She* might forgive you, Thorn, but we will not." Sparrow flitted from her perch, alighting softly behind him. As the Ranger turned, she ducked his gaze, sweeping his legs instead. The ex-wrestler went down, landing awkward on the rocks.

"Ouch!"

In the twilight, the little woman towered over him. She was joined by others, bright-eyed beneath their hoods. An arm was offered. He took it and was hoisted to his feet with ease.

He rubbed his elbow. "Sentinel Sparrow, I need your help."

The gymnast nodded as he explained, "I found a patch from a parka by the gate. It's Nighthawk's. I just know it. She let it drop on purpose. She's been taken. Schark has locked her in a cage."

The Daughters gasped, *Gaia, NO!*

Thorn observed them as the squad conferred. Too long with Rangers, he saw them afresh: *Greenies, Primitives, Elves.* The women indeed were eerie. Four months since he'd socialized with Sentinels. Not since the rearguard, the ambush, and the execution of Bull.

It had been June then, summer lush upon the landscape. His Sentinel squad was slaughtered, stalling the Spreaders so families could escape. Sole survivor, he'd been left behind, assumed KIA.

Sparrow emerged from the huddle of women. Daylight was dying; the night would be long. "Do you have a place to shelter? Somewhere near the compound?"

"We have several. I'm with the Rangers. Preppers from up north. Good dudes, though they don't know Gaia."

Robert and Freddie were gonna fucking flip. Mocking their "Rabbit" was one thing, meeting an all-star squad—all female—would be something else entirely.

Sparrow anticipated their ignorance. "As for that, She knows we're all fallen. Gaia forgives and we're grateful to Her."

She hand-signed, *form up*, indicating Thorn's spot in the formation. He led them up the Romence embankment. It was brighter on the roadway.

Sparrow whistled, *chick-a-dee-dee-dee*, and the youngest elf jogged east, scouting ahead towards the compound. They put their backs to the sunset, gliding through the shadows. Thorn fell in line and ran with the women. A half mile passed before he remembered his rifle. *Oh fucking well.* No way he was going back. No way they would let him.

Purple bruised the sky behind them, an atmospheric contusion. The pregnant moon, nearing full term, was glowing, ruddy with reflected light. Jupiter, eldest planet of Sol, ascended in the east. The squad loped along the wooded road. Local fauna—both fur and feather—watched them pass with crepuscular eyes.

A different species—invasive and unnatural—observed as well, starving for a chance at predation. Through starlight scopes and thermal viewfinders, the revenants reckoned their chances—high risk, low reward—and aborted their ambush. The Aghori indeed had shriveled.

Crows *caw-cawed* their caution, resuming their reluctant roost—no calories tonight.

Eyeballed

THEIR BICYCLE TIRES HAD DEFLATED, of course they had. The road was shit. The tired tubes were torn. Two long-hairs dismounted, pushing their rusty steeds south along Portage Road. The right-hand sky had purpled. A low star—maybe a planet?—brightened on their left. The moon was almost full. The day was cooling. Stars began to sparkle.

Shaggy, shielding his night vision, sparked a joint, a home-grown gift from their Antiva homies. His lighter rasped—once, twice—then flickered with flame. What would they do when the Bics ran dry? Smoke less probably. Only a fiend would fire-bow for tokes.

The wolfman got the cherry glowing; his lupine face was lit. The Lakota gave his dreadlocks a shake, exhaling at stars. "Good shit." He offered to Mukwa. The big man declined, still buzzed from before.

There was an intersection ahead. Sergeant Taylor had prepared them: Romence Road, she'd explained, was the northwest corner of Panzer's compound. The area was an industrial park, corporate logos and tidy landscaping long overrun. The headquarters of FedEx, DHL, and Stryker were beheaded, razed flat by Panzer goons. The scorched earth tactic denied shelter and supplies to would-be invaders.

Despite the early falling dusk, Mukwa felt exposed as hell. The ruby tip of Shaggy's rollie had no doubt been noticed. "Dude, put it out."

The Howler cupped the cannabis, delighting in a leisurely drag. The Army veteran had scoffed at snipers before—toking towards Talibs, exhaling at ISIS. *"Inshallah,* Wabi Muk. *Inshallah."*

He blew a cloud and rubbed out the roach. "Eat shit, Sharkey." Senses enhanced, he halted Mukwa with a sudden outflung arm. "Big man, I do believe we're busted."

Shaggy's hackles were up; he felt eyeballed from all directions. He stood his bike on its kickstand, slowly stepping away. Mukwa did the same. Both men flashed teeth, shrank their profiles and—"Fuck it!"—prepared for flight or fight.

The local pack of *Canis latrans* sensed them first, with their noses. Kalamazoo's coyote population peaked as humans declined. The pair of talkative humans were obnoxious with odor: rubber, grease, and rust; burnt weed, dirty asses, and semen stink hovered over the two males pushing bikes along the road. And something else. From the big one: a bouquet of bruin. From his wild-eyed companion: a waft of wolf.

The pack, ever cautious, kept their distance. Their territory was growing crowded. Crows had returned, and skull-faces too. The arrival of these symbionts augured well for battle. A fleshy feast might ensue, a confluence of caloric opportunities.

But *Caution!* Another pack was prowling: a dozen alpha females had arrived via river. These gray-skins coursed along the road, steel-clawed and sharply toothed. The day dimmed, the moon brightened. The pack observed the dozen females as the warrior women laid a trap for the pair of stinky men.

Man-bear and wolfman, oblivious, blundered on.

"You see what I see?" Robert asked Freddy as a confusion of forms darted through the shadows.

"No fucking idea." Freddy plied the starlight scope. "Shit's hard to make out."

"Make out? Time like this, and your mind's in the gutter?"

"Fuck you."

"Making out *and* fucking? Bro, you sure you ain't Chosen?"

Freddy flipped his brother the bird. Robert, smiling, returned to his optics. They'd converted a guardhouse to an observation post. Panzer's perimeter was shrinking. The abandoned structure overlooked Portage Road. The moonlight enhanced their sight-picture. In the last few minutes, much had happened, tinted green through their lenses. The brothers scoped several canines, big ones. The coyotes had scent-checked the intersection, snouts sniffing north, before flaring their nostrils and scattering.

"Buggin' out, movin' south. Something's coming down that road."

The next figures were human. Fast moving and hooded, they flew through Freddy's vision field: ID impossible, allegiance unknown. This group crossed the road in a blur, merging quickly with tree shadow. "Did you see that?"

Robert's optics were aimed the wrong way. "See what?" Big brother repositioned.

"They looked like women! Three, maybe four? Both sides of the road."

"*Women?* Fred, this sex drive shit is getting old!"

Freddy grit his teeth, resuming his watch. Of course, his brother wouldn't let it go: "Let's take a peep at this here peepshow." Robert patted his optic. "Fred! You're right! Look at the tits on that tree!" He sculpted an hourglass shape. "Mama mia!" He honked at the tree with both hands. Another angry bird flew from Freddy's fist.

A flight of crows crossed the moon. Their inky shadows briefly blotted the road and were gone. The Rangers kept looking, kept seeing. The action continued. This time, both brothers observed the same target.

Targets, actually.

Men this time, two of them, one skinny, one large, approaching from the north. Something awkward about their gait. The preppers dialed in and saw bicycles. The mismatched men were pushing bikes? They both had long hair. Was one of them smoking?

Robert shouldered his rifle, adjusting for range. He cross-haired the smoker's lungs, "That shit will kill you." He thumbed the selector to SEMI, preparing to take another human life.

Freddy switched to spotter. "Go to glass. Report." Robert described the green-tinted scene. "Two men. Pushing bicycles. The skinny one has a rifle slung."

Freddy said, "Target the rifleman. Check parallax and mil." Robert did so, called it. Freddy aborted, "Hold up! Disengage!" He recognized the two men. "Robert, disengage!"

Robert was still scoping. "What the fuck, Fred?"

"It's those SIS dudes from the bridge. Mukwa and Shaggy, I'd fucking swear it!"

Robert confirmed through his scope. "Damn! Brother, I think you're right."

With each step, Mukwa's anxiety increased. *What the hell were they doing? Strolling in the moonlight? Was he still high?* Panzer's compound lay silhouetted, low in the south. Mukwa could see the guard towers and the darkened stadium lights.

Shaggy definitely was. High, that is. At least he'd stubbed out the roach. Shadows crossed the moon, and Mukwa flinched. "What the—!"

The Howler laughed. "Just birds, damn you're twitchy. Come on dude, relax."

Mukwa snarled. They'd had it easy lately, rolling with Antiva. Time to tighten the fuck up. Nighthawk was close. Closer than she'd been in months. He looked at the walls, the light-towers. Muck felt the old locker-room feeling: anthem, coin toss, kick-off, *ka-runch.*

Sparrow positioned her squad. Spears and bows enfiladed the road. Thorn asked for a weapon, a request she denied. "Just watch this time, we don't trust you yet."

What a Sentinel thing to say. Sparrow reminded him of Elena, of Diana, back in ELF Country. Not in a bad way, but still. These Daughters, extremists, did things their own way. And their way wasn't his way. Much had changed since the old days; Diana was dead, kamikazied by a drone. He had no idea if Elena, badly wounded, had ever recovered.

Fuck it. Thorn unsheathed his belt knife in solidarity with the squad. Young Dee had spied two men approaching, pushing bikes, just strolling down the road. "Could be a trap?" she cautioned. "Easy bait to lure us out?" She might be right; who in their right mind would be walking around this place in the open?

Sparrow nodded at Dee's report. Bullet holes pocked the roadway. Someone's convoy had been recently ambushed. Shot-up vehicles littered the shoulder. The pavement was stained with vital fluids. Blood from dead mercenaries? Oil from perforated motors?

Thorn debriefed the engagement for Sparrow. He'd been there. The Blackwater column, sent to Sharkey by some rich survivor, had been demolished. The Griffins—Yield to None— hammered them with howitzers: flatly trajected and point-fucking-blank.

Sparrow halted his excited play-by-play with an abrupt hand signal. Her female squad switched frequencies. Bat-like, they echo-located in the dark. Owlish, the elves swiveled their sonar, producing a soundscape, three-dimensioned and ultra high-def.

Thorn attempted to give himself to Gaia, to merge with Her as the Sentinels did, as he used to. Scorned, She denied him. He didn't blame Her. Thorn had fallen.

He observed Sparrow as she sifted the scene through her senses. He saw her react. She'd recognized something—a sound, a scent, a sign? Thorn felt her smile in the dark, heard her happy whisper, "Gaia be good, it's our Oso!"

She quickly instructed the squad, hushing orders to her chick: "Dee, leave your weapon. Join me on the road. Follow my lead."

An Irregular Meeting

A GRAY HOODED FIGURE GHOSTED ONTO THE ROADWAY, causing the pair of bike pushers to freeze mid-stride. The night was cloudless. Spinning Earth had thrown off its blanket, the day's accumulated heat vacuumed up by the void. Moonlight shone coldly upon the scene. Chilled from transit, the reflected photons had lost all their fire.

The spectators were many: crows and Skulls; a pair of Rangers; the coyote pack, downwind; a squad of Daughters; and a final watcher, shark-eyed, via closed circuit TV. The doctor scented blood in the water, his infrared drone circling the scene.

Mukwa stopped Shaggy with an oversize paw. "What's that in the road?" Muk sniffed, but the wind was behind him.

"What's what?" Shaggy squinted, bleary-eyed and blazed.

Mukwa bristled. "Buddy, we're busted." Both men reached for weapons, but were halted by a female command, "Don't move."

The voice was behind them? In front? On their flank?

"We've got you pinned. Lay your weapons on the ground. Step away from the bikes."

Disoriented by gender, by direction, the two bad boys obeyed. Something tugged at Mukwa's memory, enzymes expressing both pleasure and pain. Tigre? Matador? ELF Country in summer?

Matador shook his head and called instead for Gorrión, *the squad's smallest member. The young woman, war-named Spar-*

row, pushed away the grinning Bull and squared up, all business, in front of Mukwa.

Why this memory? Why now?

Mukwa looked at Matador. A half-second later and he couldn't fucking breathe, eyes wide, mouth sucking wind, his diaphragm in spasm. Sparrow aimed another kick, swept his thick leg, and he was on the ground.

Mukwa flinched, peering at the gray figure ahead. *Sparrow?* He addressed the ghost of Matador, mere molecules of memory: "You tellin' me something, *amigo?*"

Wolf and Bear stood in the moonlight and held their hands high. Shaggy seemed eager for a fight. "Looks like just one? Big man, let's move!"

An eddy of air wafted their way. Mukwa identified Sparrow's signature and tiny Chickadee's too. He scent-printed the entire squad in hiding. He knew them all: Sentinels, Daughters, DOGs.

Thank fuckin' God, and good Gaia too!

He flung a mental message over the distant wall, *Nighthawk, we're here!*

Shaggy, nose-blind from smoking bud, was still squinting. "I see 'em now! There's only two, and one's *tiny!* Buddy, let's goooo!"

With that, the dreadlocked man charged. Mukwa, in on the joke, kept his hands high and waited. He saw one of the women, Sparrow, step aside. Dee alone faced the wolfman's wrath. Shaggy, almost four-footed, sprinted low along the roadway, eyes and teeth gleaming an unhealthy yellow.

Little Dee flitted aside as he slobbered right past her. The wolf clacked its jaws—nothing but air. Rapidly he turned, and this time he feinted. Shaggy telegraphed left, but lunged right instead, grabbing for a wing.

Tweety Bird, ever faster, fluttered away.

The dog-man stood on hind legs, chest heaving. He aimed his muzzle at the moon and howled his frustration. Many ears locked onto that sound: moths, mice, and a myriad of mammals. The two gladiators fought for an audience of thousands.

Shaggy, sobering, gathered himself. He would NOT underestimate this girl again. Then her companion stepped forward into the moonlight. Little women, both weaponless. *Was this a game? Where the fuck was Mukwa?* He looked for his battle-buddy, un-fucking-cool.

His tiny opponent hopped twice, not towards him, but away? She jumped towards her friend, who caught her feet and flung her. The bird was airborne! Wings flapping, she booted him hard in the face. A crunch of cartilage, a rage of red pain. The big wolf lay in the road, badly bruised. Her little hood rose above him.

They watched each other, unmoving. One blink, then two. Dee offered her hand. Shaggy hesitated, then took it. The wooded coliseum, flooded by moonlight, erupted in chorus. The coyote pack was howling; Sentinels applauding; the Rangers, eyeing their scopes, wiped away hysterical tears.

Mukwa was there; he thumped his buddy on the back. "Shaggy, meet the Sentinels. Sentinels, meet Shaggy." Nods all around, the concussed man saw stars.

Then Mukwa recognized Thorn amongst the elves. The Ranger mustered a smile. "Mukwa, Shaggy, long time since the bridge, eh boys? Good to see you again."

More hugs, more thumps. Thorn whispered an aside, "Oso, we need to talk. It's Nighthawk."

Mukwa rumbled his response, "That's exactly why we're here."

The Sentinels policed up the scene, pushing bikes to the shoulder. They avoided the modern weapons, metallic with mischief, with menace.

Shaggy, checking his snout, shook Chickadee's hand. "Girl, that was awesome!"

Dee and Sparrow re-slung their quivers and picked up their bows.

An owl call boomed from their lookout, *DANGER!*

Sparrow hissed and the Sentinels scattered. Mukwa and Shaggy dove for their weapons, rolling off the road. They could hear something buzzing, a mosquito whine. Two camouflaged figures approached at a run. Dee and Sparrow, both nocked, sighted down the roadway. Mukwa, all thumbs, fumbled with the LAWS as he scent-checked the two runners. The breeze was right; he printed them via olfaction, a positive ID, "Friendlies!"

The runners were Rangers, two brothers. Muk had scented them before, at the bridge battle. But the alien whine grew louder. Sparrow and Dee, as one, tensioned their bows, loosing two arrows. Thorn yelled a warning, "Robert! Freddy! Look out!"

Too late. The missiles, fire-and-forget, flew towards the figures. A crunch of metal, an electric flash. Target destroyed.

The Sentinels circled the scene with their spears. The brothers, panting, arrived a second later and looked down at the body. Thorn flashed a red light. An IR drone with a Panzer logo lay impaled, oozing oil. Two arrows had lanced the lens. Its circuit board had been shattered.

The two Rangers, wearing camo, halted, hands up, outgunned by Greenies. The shorter brother caught Thorn's eye and grinned. "Well, Rabbit, looks like you snared us this time."

Thorn stepped forward, shielding his comrades. "Sparrow, I know them. These men fought at the bridge, under Colonel Dennis."

Sparrow gestured, and spears were lowered. "We need to get off this road."

The Sentinels dispersed. Dee put her boot on the drone, pulling both shafts free. Robert clipped the plastic carcass to his pack.

Sparrow hand-signed to Thorn: "Shelter—Hide—Interrogative."

Thorn, rusty, signed back: "Guard—House—Near."

He asked permission from the Rangers. The brothers, grim, both nodded consent.

Sparrow signed, "Tactical Column."

The pack of irregulars took to the trees, paralleled the road, and vanished.

Rage Against the Cage

"WHAT DO YOU MEAN THEY'VE VANISHED?" I was close to losing it. I really was.

Frau, my techie, my fair-haired fascista, shrugged her shoulders at the screen, now staticky with snow. My drone feed was dead. The mysterious figures—some cloaked, some pulsing red through the FLIR—had my full attention. First, there'd been two, pushing bikes down the road. Two became four—were they sparring? Then four grew to fifteen! Two more trespassers ran to join them before I went blind.

And they were close! Practically at the gate! And who else was out there? And how would I stop them?

"Launch another drone! Bring me my Wermer. Get Major Naz on the Palantir. And ready the VHF radio, I want to broadcast to those boys again."

Frau's blue eyes blinked behind glasses. She nodded, swishing through the airlock. For a moment, I saw myself through the looking glass, reflected in her lenses: Narcissus, aging by the stream. Except the stream was flooding fast. I'd have to leave my tower soon, or be marooned inside its moat.

Just when things were looking up! The National Guard—natty in fraying uniforms—had finally pulled out. Black Panthers no longer prowled. Gleeful, I watched them form up and depart, pennants fluttering. No doubt they'd heard Kamul's broadcast and were tearing towards Toledo, wrathful at the death of dear Walker. Well, Godspeed to you, Griffins. So long as you go!

The mercenary buzzed and was admitted. Wermer, a Blackwater contractor, remained optimistic: "Doctor Schark, I'm charging a drone and have doubled the guard. We need more men, more food, more fuel. We could try another convoy. Should I contact our clients?"

"Make it so, Mr. Wermer."

My creature, cyborgian, cleared his throat, eyes glazing as his halo computed. Unasked, Werm's question was clear, so I answered. "And yes, I can pay! Tell your supplier that his merchandise remains in *mint condition*. Mint, I say!"

"Yes, doctor!"

Wermer left to place his sat-call. Pre-collapse, our billionaire neighbor had bought a bunker, a five star fortress, fully staffed for survival. The eight-figure contract included chefs and chauffeurs, mercenaries and musicians. America's top one percent: Darwin's dilettantes, survival of the richest. This crypto client—a Carnegie of collapse—was on fire for my females. Bored by his current mistress, cock-blocked by the shark cage, the deal, and his debauchery, had been too long delayed.

I'd earned a glass, so I poured it. My million-dollar wine cellar would not go to waste. I imbibed, tongued its terroir, and considered my options.

Plan A: Build Back Better.

Shelter in place. Traffic sex for more soldiers; fence my females for fuel. There were clients out there, cash-cushioned from collapse and fiending for flesh.

I'd do it differently this time. No Virals, no Panzerland, no feudal fiefdom. I longed for simplicity: a hearth, a home, a partner. Power, sure, but pleasure too. My memoir needed writing. My future offspring needed siring. Could Hawk and I ever be happy together?

We are running low on food, with little fuel for winter. Wermer's men, private contractors, are unpaid and underworked. I've been buying them off with injections—chemical cocktails to dull the dullness. But they grow bored. They grow boorish. Werner suggested I could pimp them my product, let them sample some wares. So far, I've rebuffed him. My merchandise must not be manhandled. Barbies are worth more in their boxes, unopened. I feel the mutinous malaise of these men. I am Captain Bligh of this compound.

Plan B: Abandon Ship.

A bitter pill even for a pharmacist. Could I leave it all behind? My library, my labs, this campus I've crafted? Major Naz has teased this idea. He's extended an evac-invitation, via helicopter, for me and my plus-one. Of course, I'd take Nighthawk. The CORPS would insist, goaded by AYE EYE. We'd pack a suitcase full of valuables, flee Berlin's crumbling bunker and the nooses of Nuremberg. Could I be Adolf in Argentina? Could Hawk be my Eva Braun? Probably not, but post-collapse, consent is overrated.

My tech-assistant has returned. A Nazi for neatness, Frau's hair was tightly bunned. She brought the tools for Plan B: my tablet and the Palantir. I dismissed her on an errand. My scheme for escape must not be known. "Invite Ms. Nighthawk to join me. See that she is sedated and properly dressed."

With the tablet, I recorded a message. I'd finally found an escape destination, a nest we might fly to. Hawk herself, via truth serum, had given me the idea. I think she'll be pleased. I aimed my VHF missive at the clan I was cultivating. I knew the frequency where such freaks could be found:

"Boys, your isolation is ending. An alliance will give you power. You'll have virucide injections. You'll have advanced weapons and training. You'll have the means to destroy your enemies and ensure the survival of your family. Prepare for my arrival. Feather the nest. This is Doctor Schark from Panzer Pharmaceuticals. Over and out."

So much for Plan B. My message will soon be sent.

Next, I used the Palantir to contact Naz. Halo-implanted, he was rallying Reds near Toledo. The major sounded busy, but interested. His helicopter would arrive three nights from now, when the moon was full. Would Hawk and I be aboard when it left? I assured him we would be.

After all, there is still a chance for Plan A. Wermer just gave me the thumbs up on CCTV. Apparently he's contacted his Carnegie; a convoy will be coming. The deal is consensual, quid pro quo: his contractors for my comfort women, his mercenaries in exchange for my merchandise.

There are grudges still to settle and the Aghori top my to-do list. In the beginning, I made them, forming them from chemical clay and dosing them with shark juice, the very breath of life. After Dozer's bridge debacle, surviving Gories repaid me with sedition, and had scattered. However, they're returning now to roost. I've caught glimpses on my screens. What are their intentions? Will they come for me? Join me? Their crow companions are shitting on my campus.

Frau returns, holding Nighthawk's leash. My Greenie looks drugged; her black dress, alluring. I hand the tablet to Frau. "See that this gets sent, same place, same time. Also, prepare the product; we have a buyer. Our ladies will be picked up soon."

Frau clicked her heels and departed, eager to inspect every crack and crevice.

I held Hawk's jesses in my hands, her whole life too. Did she know it? A fire flickered deep in her eyes, undimmed by dosage. Oh, she knew it. Hated it. This woman-in-black would neither forgive nor forget. My capacity for self-deception has increased, a worrying trend.

Oh well. "Here's to us!"

I filled a second glass and clinked it with my own. Hawk didn't move. I lifted hers to her lips. Nothing. I dribbled some drops. She flicked her tongue and tasted. I'll take it! I drained my own, then hers. Let's face it, I am drowning.

Flotsam and Jetsam

"MI CASA ES SU CASA." The Rangers tidied the guardhouse, setting the table and kicking through debris. The windows were covered; a Sterno heated soup, an LED flickering dimly overhead. The brothers gestured, and the guests sat down.

"What is this place?" Mukwa's belly growled, anticipating a meal.

Thorn, hosting, stirred the pot. "Used to be a service gate manned by Blackwater, back when Panzer had more power."

Robert charged a piece of technology from a solar battery. He nodded to a bullet-pocked wall. "Till the Griffs pushed them out."

Freddy had gathered up the rifles, clearing actions before stacking the weapons by the door. "And the Panthers kept them out. The black berets sniped a few and the rest stayed away."

Sparrow removed her hood and looked around, uncomfortable amidst the glow of gadgetry. The rest of her squad bivouacked beneath the stars. Lookouts were posted. The DOGs slept well in their frosted sleeping bags. "What do we know about Doctor Schark? His numbers? His intentions?"

"Fuck him," Shaggy interrupted, "what about a smoke? Some beer?" His face looked swollen, black-eyed from Dee's boot. "Don't suppose you guys found any porn?"

"Shut up, Shaggy." Mukwa bluffed a punch at his flinching friend. "I'm with Sparrow, I don't like being blind."

"Speaking of blind," Shaggy tried for serious, "you'll never guess who we found on Lake Huron. Who *I* found, actually." Mukwa raised an eyebrow at his friend.

Shaggy winked. "OK, I had some help from Loon and that Frenchie, Baptiste."

Sparrow and the Rangers were interested. Shaggy licked his lips, preparing a performance, but Hawk's clock was ticking, so Mukwa upstaged him. "Doyle. We found Tom Doyle, the captain of *Bloody Mary*."

"Hey!" Shaggy objected. Mukwa overruled him, "Doyle wasn't killed. The explosion blinded him. He washed up on an island, a tiny one. He climbed aboard a pine tree, riding the currents till we found him."

Gaia works in mysterious ways. Sparrow had been at that battle, on board *Nodin*. Skeeter drones had killed her captain, Diana.

"Where's Doyle now?" she asked. "Where's Baptiste?" These mariners were assets, pieces on the board.

Mukwa interrupted Shaggy again: "We left them in Bay City, still had their canoes. They were headed towards Detroit, checking refineries for the colonel."

Thorn portioned out the soup, vegetable beef. The companions blew it cool and conversed. Sparrow and the Rangers produced spoons. Mukwa and Shaggy slurped, happily cursing despite burnt tongues, "God *damn*, this is good!"

"Definitely not freeze-dry. Where'd you get the cans?"

The guardhouse was steamy with good smells. Sterno, and their fellowship, added warmth to the room. Robert grinned around a mouthful of broth. "You can thank Sharkey and his Blackwater buddies."

"Yeah," Freddy continued, "Griffs hit a resupply convoy. It was headed to Panzer, loaded with loot." He nodded at the pallet in a corner. "Some food, some other shit. The fuel tanker was the big score. Mom flipped when she saw it."

"Mom?" Even Sparrow felt relaxed. Good food and company were Gaia's gifts.

"Sergeant Taylor. Colonel Dennis's CSM. She hates that nickname."

"Which, of course, is why we use it." Robert and Freddy clinked spoons.

All six were laughing. Bowls were wiped clean. "Ready for dessert?" Freddy asked. "Take a look in that drawer."

Freddy gestured to Shaggy. The wiry man sprang to the desk, then howled, *"Owwwoooo!"*

He emerged with a magazine, ogling the centerfold: Miss February from two years ago. The model was dead of course, the photographer too. Her statuesque figure, an airbrushed Aphrodite, was an artifact of before.

Sparrow cast an appraising eye at February: deltoids, biceps, quads. The Sentinel dismissed her. "She looks soft."

"I'll tell you what's not soft!" Shaggy's amber eyes were shining.

"Keep your pants on, wolfman, try some of this!" Freddy tossed him a baggie. The weed was over-dry and stemmy, but Shaggy licked his lips and started sorting.

"You can thank the Blackwaters for the bud. Actually you can't. They're dead."

Shaggy tore a scrap from the photo, rolling a joint in February's cleavage. "Rest in peace, fellas. I know I *will!*" He held her boobs to the flame, huffed and puffed, and blew the house full of smoke. Mukwa hushed his homie with a paw.

Cannabis crackled in the air. Their hurts were soothed, their minds cleared. A moment of silence as the herb went around. Memories of better days. A focus on the fallen. Sparrow thought of ELF Country and the comrades she'd lost: *Squirrel, Tigre, Matador, Diving-Duck* ...

For Mukwa it was the old man, Keith; little sister, Miin; and their paddle upriver. The pharmacon freed his mind, bio-activating a memory: *Keith filled the pipe with Samantha's blend. A final pinch he held high, as if to the moon. This one he gifted, sifting it to the ground between fingers and thumb* ...

Mukwa dried his eyes, blaming the smoke, saw others do the same. Shaggy's twitchiness had subsided. "Thank you Freddy," he blew another cloud, "I owe you one."

Freddy's Old Law unit had saved Shaggy's SIS at the bridge. The Ranger held up a V of fingers. "That's two you owe me."

Shaggy winked, passing the roach to the Ranger. Fred sampled the smoke, blew a stream, and winked back. "I consider the debt reduced."

Shaggy lolled his tongue, they all did, the pack lounging in its lair. They talked quietly of small things they'd seen and done. They quoted music and TV shows. They avoided collapse, staying away from the war. Sparrow had them laughing, retelling the escapades of Oso, the fighting bear.

"That reminds me!" Robert's device was now charged, a video recorder he'd detached from his scope. "We don't have popcorn, but how about a movie?"

The friends gathered around the tiny screen. Robert pushed play and zoomed in:

Two fighters faced each other, tinted green by the starlight-optic. One was tiny. One crouched on all fours ...

Robert hit pause. "Ladies and gentlemen, in the left corner, weighing in at one hundred pounds, Sentinel Chick-a-deeeee!" Cheers and whistles rose from the audience. "And in the right corner, weighing a buck-fifty—"

Emcee Mukwa interrupted, "The *Lakota* from *Dakota*. The *man* from Afghani-*stan*, Shagggggggy-wolf!"

Boos and howls. Shaggy, joint dangling, shook his fists, mock-angry, at the crowd. Robert selected slow motion, narrating the play-by-play. The smoke curled round. Laughter lifted spirits. A pouch of MRE peanut butter was passed. When the fight was over, Robert powered down his device. Their facial muscles hurt from hilarity. A moment to savor, then reality returned.

Mukwa began it, saying, "We've got to get her out of there."

"And this Nighthawk's not the only one," Robert added. "That Blackwater convoy had an empty van rigged with restraints."

Freddy spoke up, "We suspect Schark is trafficking women. Females for fuel. Something like that."

Sparrow gripped Mukwa's arm. "The Daughters are with you. We will see this thing done."

Thorn stood up, inventorying the room. He took a corporate jacket from a hook, displaying its Blackwater badge. He donned a ball cap too, pulling the brim low. "What do I look like?"

"An asshole!" Shaggy crowed. "Contractor scum!"

"Exactly." Thorn was onto something. "We need Schark to see the same."

Robert was with him. "We'll need Blackwater vehicles, and not the ones on the road."

"Griffs shot those to shit," Freddy said; he was in as well. "Sharkey's seen 'em already, he's got eyes everywhere."

"What the fuck are you guys talking about?" Shaggy's drooping eyes were bloodshot.

"Ever heard of the Trojan horse, soldier?"

"Trojans?" Shaggy mimed his member. "Sure! My size is magnum!"

Mukwa swatted him down, turning serious. "OK, Freddy, what's our next move?"

The Crucible: Captors

A WEEK SINCE THE TREE ACADEMY TEACHER WAS KIDNAPPED. Miin didn't know it, but the island was astir—from Baraga's Landing on the north end to Beaver Head Light in the south. Young Blueberry was a favorite. The Indigenous woman was missing. The search must go on. Miinan kept singing, broadcasting in the dark.

Wayaa way-ay-haa-yo wayaa way-ay-haa-yo.

Mee-ay Nibi Kinagajitoyan!

Three days since the stretching started. Cousin Boot had tied her wrists, hanging her high from the rafters. Ferny, so far, had kept his racist clan in check: "For now, Miss Minny, for now."

They hadn't racked her long. Ferny made sure no permanent damage was done. The witch hadn't been ducked yet, either. Their waterboard, still dry. Something, or someone, stopped Ferny's kin from going too far. Miinan overheard more than they knew.

"He wants her *unspoiled.* Said the same with any more we can catch." Ferny delayed his dogs by adding, "Plans have changed, boys. Believe me, we're better off this way."

The cousins were cranky. Captain Ferny consoled them: "A little more patience, then it's party time, you'll see."

"Yeah, but how much longer?" moped Boot.

"And how big is this party?" pouted another.

"Couple days more, is what he said. *When the moon is full.* You heard him too."

"And the party?"

Ferny leered. "Boys, it's gonna be wild!"

Disappointed, they clomped up the cellar stairs.

Miin knew what they called themselves, overhearing their whiskeyed brag—The Beaver Boys, or *Bois*. Miin heard how they said it, Red militia wannabes. She knew them by sight, sound, and smell, most of them from before. They numbered a dozen all told. But just a handful were allowed in the cellar. Pimpled Ferny was their boss, their big man, their chief. They listened to a radio at their Stone House hideaway. She overheard some transmissions: *isolation*—static—*ending*—static—*feather*—static—*nest*.

Miin, more desperate each day, continued the water song, a green transmission of her own. She tuned her green vibrations, summoning life, pushing need through the soil. To transmit her location Miin needed a telegraph, she needed touch—a single tendril, a single tuber would serve. There were listeners out there—her students, elder Grace, and Samantha—but she needed a signal, and something to touch.

Wayaa way-ay-haa-yo wayaa way-ay-haa-yo.

Bioacoustic, the island biome was responding. Fungal filaments—rooty first responders—raced towards the cellar, one millimeter per hour. Hydrotropic, they sought the water promised by her song. Mycorrhiza pushed through the cellar's hardpack, seeking the singer, summoned by her tears.

Against the Tide

DOYLE'S OCULAR LENSES were still socked with fog. Some days it lifted, some days it didn't. Antiva's refinery had no doctor, but an EMT Panther, with a reference book, examined his eyes. "It's not cataracts." She dilated his pupils, examining the retinas. "No clouding that I can see." The EMT consulted the index, asking his history, palpitating his eyes. "Don't think it's glaucoma either, though what do I know?"

Not fucking much. Doyle bit back his retort. He didn't like being prodded. Didn't like her accent, her bossiness, or her failure to heal. Mostly, Tom was sick of being blind. The shock—and guilt—of survival had worn off. The weirdness of Goose Island and his pine tree savior had subsided. He was disabled. He was old. He was far from his home island, and good wife Annie thought him dead.

Oh, how he longed for her! For the harbor and their Whiskey Point home, for cribbage on the porch and sips of strawberry wine after supper. He'd treated her so poorly, taking her for granted. *I've been a goddamn fool. Annie-lass, forgive me.*

She would, and he knew it. But would Tom ever return? *Not fucking likely.*

Back to business then. Doyle had been given a task and he'd do it.

"Find us a fleet," they said. The Antiva execs had summoned Baptiste and Doyle. The two captains were cleared from quarantine. Uncontaminated, the voyageur crews had outstayed their welcome. Detroit's Rouge River plant was no rest house. The oily hive was humming. Every worker bee was busy. Refined petroleum dripped from rusty combs.

Executive number one, an engineer wearing an N95, said, "The Reds will come by land and by water. We need a fleet to block them."

Exec number two added, "Fifty water-miles between their forces and this facility." She stood by the wall-map. "The Maumee flows into Lake Erie," she pointed at Toledo, "they could come up the coast and enter the Detroit River." Even through his fog, Doyle could see it: another Viral fleet, like the one at the Straits.

"Once in our river," she continued, "they'd have us."

Exec number one confirmed it: "If they roll up I-75, we'll be pinched between them."

The strategy talk flowed forward. Doyle's trauma ebbed him back: to the bridge, to his boat. The discussion continued. Colonel Dennis, without fuel, was stuck in the north. Could a tanker get to him in time? The roads were iffy. Could escorts be spared? And what about Sergeant Taylor? And her Griffs? Were they still in Kalamazoo? Would they come to their aid? And where were the vans? Antiva had spread itself thin.

Doyle, blind to this present, re-lived his past: Hannigan had been killed, O'Donnell too. Tom had rolled the deckhand's lifeless body overboard. The Straits of Mackinac had burned, flames wicked by human blobs soaked in petroleum.

The MPC boardroom mirrored his mood. They were remembering Walker—RIP. Without the reverend, they were less. The vote was unanimous: "We have to stay put, defend Detroit; it's what Walker would do."

"I remember something he said," an executive reflected, "*The best thing about the future is that it comes one day at a time.*"

"Sounds like him."

"Bullshit, sounds like a quote."

"Exactly!"

"Either way, we're not leaving."

"With the plant running, we have a chance."

"If the Reds take it, we're screwed, the Free North too."

"Agreed!"

"Agreed."

Nods around the conference table, all eyes on Baptiste and Doyle. The Métis man spoke up: "I'll need my canoes, and my crew."

Doyle was in. "And diesel, and tools, and any batteries you can spare."

"We can do that. What's your plan? Where will you start?" The executives looked at the map. Doyle stood, groping his way to the wall; a freshening purpose thinned out his fog.

They made room for the mariner. His thick finger found the Rouge River, the location of their plant. Squinting, he traced it back the way they'd come, upriver to Belle Isle and the Yacht Club. "Frenchie, your Loony-boy reported boats here, mostly undamaged?"

An Antiva executive confirmed it. "I've been there recently, in Ayesha's van. Some looting, but the big stuff seemed intact."

Doyle growled, "Aye, it's the big stuff we'll need."

Baptiste backed the Beaver Islander. "You Antivas provide us fuel, parts, and tools. *Dieu voulant*, we voyageurs will see it done."

Doyle saw the boardmembers more clearly. Masked, nervous, and pale, they looked like maggots—gas-grubbers with a pet-ro-stink. *Annie, we don't have a chance in hell.*

The room discussed the opposition: General Kamul's radio boasting, the growing strength of the CORPS, rocket-armed militias, the Hercules sighting—high up and far away. The tide had turned against them. Their resistance was weak: Walker was dead. Dennis choking on fumes. What strength they had was stranded in the north. In two days, the moon would be full and their defenses would be flooded, drowning the resistors in a crimson tide of Red.

Doyle's Irish spirits rose as their survival prospects diminished. He stumped out of the room with Baptiste, leaving their limp hands unshaken. The air outside had a sweetish stink. The sun wobbled in a chemical haze. Doyle's tread was firm. He felt a breeze on his cheek. Lifting his head, he saw circling gulls, white upon the blue. He clapped his shipmate on the shoulder. "Ahoy there, Frenchie!" Tom belted out a ballad:

Oh, the cabin boy was Flipper

He was a fuckin' nipper

He stuffed his ass with broken glass

And circumcised the skipper

The crews were released from the shipping container, springing to the task. Voyageurs laded their two canoes, delighted by Doyle's ditty:

It was on the good ship Venus

By Christ, ya should've seen us

Men and women, red-hatted, joined in, French and English, turn for turn:

Il était sur le navire en bon état de Vénus

Par le Christ, tu aurais dû nous voir

Cargo was handed aboard: food, water, jerry cans of diesel, 12 volt batteries ...

The figurehead was a whore in bed

And the mast, a mammoth penis

The Antivas shook their heads, supplying the sailors with tools: socket sets, fuses, electrical components, starter fluid ...

La figure de proue était une pute au lit

Et le mât, un énorme pénis

When Baptiste had ballasted the canoes to his satisfaction, the voyageurs stepped aboard, paddling with the Rouge:

Friggin' in the riggin',

Friggin' in the riggin'!

The MPC refinery receded as the river pulled them away. Loon perched upon one bow, Tom Doyle the other. Off-duty oilers waved farewell, chorusing with the boat crews:

Friggin' in the riggin',

Friggin' in the riggin',

There was fuck all else to do!

Your Hurting Will Heal

CAMPBELL WAS DRIVING. He missed his cowboy hat, his dip, his coffee. Bob's two passengers slept. Liz snored in the front; Walker sprawled in the back with his bandaged stump. The Humvee's lights were off. The waxing moon, two days from full, illuminated their southern migration.

He'd just seen an exit sign for Troy, a northern burb of Detroit. They were on a road trip to check out the Red rally in Toledo. Liz planned to ransom their hostage there, "To the highest bidder, Bob. The highest fucking bidder."

Campbell was in a night-drive kind of mood. He'd driven this highway often in the before-times. As a contractor, he'd built houses all around here, had even lived in one with his wife and little girl.

Liz had spent the past couple days stabilizing their amputee. "Ain't worth shit dead," was her logic. Ol' girl wasn't wrong; she rarely was.

So they'd holed up during daylight hours, eating MREs and shitting them out. They'd tended Walker's wounds, doping the man with antibiotics from their first aid kits. The trio only moved at night, short distances, conserving diesel as they fought over the future. Bob's plan to head north, like their fuel reserves, had eventually run out of gas.

Red Liz was looking better. Her bubbled burns were finally scabbing over. She was sleeping, and eating, and acting less manic. He liked her like this—quiet, reflective. Bob was trending that way himself. It reminded him of his Beaver Island cabin: Chow's resident patient, alone in the dunes.

Their sex life, what was left of it, had subsided. For once, he didn't miss it. He and Lizzy were like retirees, respecting each other's space, pensioners in a time of purge. He eyed the road signs, tracking the turf-war graffiti: Walker crowns, drippy Xs, and fading skulls. Any fresh-looking paint worried him; every underpass could put them under. The Humvee had just enough fuel for a straight shot, no more detours. I-75, south to Ohio. Bob fiddled with the radio dial, finally finding a frequency that worked. A ham radio disc jockey, holed up somewhere, announced, "This one's for the lovers."

In a bar in Toledo across from the depot

On a barstool, she took off her ring

He cocked an eye at Lizzy; then, from the backseat, a baritone surprised him:

I thought I'd get closer so I walked on over

I sat down and asked her name

Oh, why the fuck not? Campbell and the preacher dueted towards Motown:

When the drinks finally hit her she said "I'm no quitter

But I finally quit livin' on dreams

I'm hungry for laughter and here ever after

I'm after whatever the other life brings."

No quitter herself, Red Liz, next to him, kept sleeping. Bob used the rearview to observe his backseat passenger:

In the mirror, I saw him and I closely watched him

I thought how he looked out of place

Walker looked the part. The Detroiter appeared educated yet athletic; dark hair streaked with gray, a stern look and keen eyes. The old man's face was furrowed, from frown lines, and from laughter.

Walks-on-Water, eh? Bob could see it, and understood the devotion, even from XCons like that Squints. What had the infected man said, back at Hochstettler's during confession? *I heard he's a preacher, some kinda healer. Lotta rumors about him and what he can do.*

There was something old-timey about this old timer.

"Where exactly are we, Mr. Campbell?"

Their duet dissolved; Lucille had left them both. A pale light was spreading, increasing their vulnerability. Walker had learned both their names. Dude was a hard man to deny.

"We're near Troy." Bob's stomach was growling. Too many restaurants in this neighborhood. He and his wife had known them all. The hotels along the highway were fire-scarred, but most were still standing. He and his Ashley knew them too. "Exit 69 for Big Beaver Road," had been their parental code for "adult time," especially when their inquisitive daughter was listening.

Bob pulled his mind from the sheets as Walker recited something gloomy:

Troy has perished, the great city.

Only the red flame now lives there.

The dust is rising, spreading out like a great wing of smoke and all is hidden.

Whatever. Perish, flame, dust, and smoke. Bob preferred the sheets.

"Do you know *The Iliad,* Mr. Campbell?"

"Can't say I do."

The light kept increasing; time to get the fuck off the road. Save fuel, plan their next move. The green MDOT sign for Exit 67, "Rochester Road," had been freshly tagged with an icon Bob hadn't seen before.

The crown was obvious: Walker, a rumored descendant of kings. The royal icon was used by Antiva and Panthers to mark territory. Bob had seen plenty of skull markings before as well. The XCons used them along with Sharkey's Chosen. What was new to Bob's eyes was the combination:

"Take this exit please, Mr. Campbell."

The old man was backseat driving. Bob glanced at sleeping Liz; even her bad side was looking better. "Why here?"

Walker indicated the sign, and Bob slowed their roll. The gray light increased along with Campbell's confusion. "The crown? The skull? We've seen them before."

"Yes, Mr. Campbell, but not together. Do you not see the other?"

Bob looked again. There, in the corner, same paint, same style, swam a tiny fish:

"I see it. So what?"

The pastor's response sounded like scripture: *"And they did eat, and were all filled*—exit please, Mr. Campbell!"

Bob booted the brakes of the heavy vehicle, doing some muttering of his own. Beside the off ramp, a blue lodging-sign listed the nearby hotels. There he spotted another fish, even smaller, next to the Quality Inn.

Walker was pointing. "Investigate that place please, Campbell, but use caution."

Bob had no such intention. They didn't have the diesel. Liz would fucking freak, they'd be lucky to make Toledo as is. Plus, the neighborhood was crawling with Virals, Bob could feel it: the fresh graffiti, the revealing dawn. Crows overflew them, caw-cawing their position—*Oh hell no!*

And yet, Bob obeyed. He turned off Rochester Road, entering the lot of a Red—now-roofless—Inn. Campbell parked the Humvee under its fire-scarred overhang. He switched off the engine. The sudden silence woke Liz, half beauty, half beast. "We there yet, boys?"

There was a hint of dreamy innocence in her voice, still half-asleep. Campbell's heart double clutched. He'd never heard Liz like that. Was she actually healing?

She sat up straight and observed the blighted cityscape, the weedy parking lot. She wasn't impressed. "What have you homos been up to?"

Liz was back.

Bob's heart backed away, he opened his door. "Gotta check something quick. Hang tight, honey."

"I'll hang *you*, motherfucker! Don't you *dare!*"

Oh, he dared. Campbell shut the door on Walker's mumbling, and gave a thought to his getup.

Crown, Skull, and Fish. How should he approach? Not as a Guardsman. He unzipped his ACU jacket, leaving it on the hood. He heard Liz subside, *Walks-on-Water* calming the storm. The waves of her sea were hushed. The old man's window rolled down, some geezer advice rolling out: "No man has a good enough memory to be a successful liar."

Another quote? Bob shrugged, full disclosure then. He'd go maskless. Campbell added a MOPP hood to his discard pile, choosing the Amish hat—a dead man's—instead. He fingered his pistols, dare he leave his nines behind? Crown, Skull, Fish ... who the fuck knew?

Another quote floated his way, like a fart from the backseat: "Whatever you are, be a good one."

Pistols then. Cowboy brandished his Berettas, checked their loads, and re-holstered with a flourish. Oh, he was good alright. He tipped his hat and stepped away.

"Oh, Mr. Campbell." Bob stopped, broken glass underfoot. "Those who look for the bad in people will surely find it."

Bob rolled his eyes. Walker's window rolled back up. He blew a kiss to Liz. Soothed by Walker's presence, she even blew one back. *Those two are making me soft.*

The gush of daylight was quickly clotted by clouds. Halloween approached. The cold day was growing windy. Cowboy strode towards the Quality Inn. Fall foliage, like tumbleweed, blew around him. Their colors crunched underfoot as more leaves were stripped, unwilling, from their trees. Bob hummed the old tune, subbing Lizzy for Lucille, changing some words for a happier ending:

I've had some bad times, lived through some sad times

But this time your hurting will heal ...

Loaves and Fishes

SPOTTER: "YOU SEE THIS MOTHERFUCKER?" A man was walking towards them; dude wore a straw hat, camo pants, and a gun belt, heavy with pistols.

Shooter: "Contact." With a clear eye, the Recon Marine tracked the incoming bogie shuffling through leaves towards their position.

Spotter: "Go to glass."

His partner—face tattooed as a skull—put his eye to the rifle-scope, describing the target.

Shooter: "I've got a military-aged male. Tall, no mask, combat boots."

Spotter: "That's your primary. Check parallax and mil."

The Gorie sniper did so and called it.

The spotter—with similar markings—keyed his walkie-talkie. "Gate, this is Overwatch, over."

A crackle of static, then a woman's voice: "Go ahead, Overwatch."

"Gate, you've got an armed pedestrian inbound. Could be a Viral, over."

"Roger, Overwatch. We're ready. Cover us." The spotter keyed his confirmation and awaited the encounter. The other Marine tracked their target, laying crosshairs on the man's forehead. "One wrong move, straw man, and I fill your hat with brains."

But the man made no wrong moves, keeping his hat, keeping his head. The stranger halted at the hotel's perimeter. His head was down, hands high. The place, by design, appeared abandoned. No guards were in evidence, no sign of lodgers, no dogs. No burn-barrel smoke or flap of laundry betrayed its inhabitants. And yet, they were there.

The hotel was booked full and Bob knew it. But the signs were subtle: he'd seen another fish, and there were windage markers, lining the approach. A scrubby lot, trash-filled, had been recently disturbed. Fresh dirt mounded the potter's field. He could almost smell the rot leaching through the soil.

Bob's forehead itched from magnification. He resisted the urge to scratch, to run, to hide. Instead, he waited for a gatekeeper. The wind increased. Plastic bags like tattered ghosts danced in the updrafts. Crows overflew the compound, inkblots on a billowy page of gray. A haunted house, but what price for admission?

He was about to find out.

A welcome party of three marched towards him: no masks, red eyes, emaciated. Virals then. Oh well, so was he. The woman in the middle, Arab-looking, wore a headscarf and appeared to be the leader. Her flankers were men. The two dudes wore body armor and carried rifles. X brands marred their pasty foreheads. Cowboy surveyed them from under his brim, something familiar. He considered. No fucking way.

Headscarf spoke first: "Nice lid, stranger." Bob gave the barest of nods. "Now take it off so we can get a look at you."

He took it off. They looked. "Viral, eh?" Another nod, barely.

"Your affiliation then? If you don't mind me asking."

Bob scrolled through his options. Nothing good. Walker's voice whispered in his ear, *No man has a good enough memory to be a successful liar.*

"I used to boss for Chosen."

Her guards grew agitated, she noticed. "Whereabouts then?"

"Oh, all over. Charlevoix most recent."

"Bullshit! Man's a fuckin' liar!" The older guard was squinting. "I know him! He's one of them Amish Yoders. A fuckin' pussyfist, 'cept he ain't!"

The younger man, with a methhead look, joined in. "Killed our buddy near Clare. Bashed his brains out, made us bury him."

Squints grew heated. "Tied us to a tree and fucking left us! For dead!"

Methhead was mad too. "Till Gories found us," both men shivered, "dug up our buddy's body. Cut us loose. Made us help."

The woman studied the accused with irritated eyes, trying to see who he was, who he'd been. "Got a name, do ya?"

"Call me Cowboy. You?"

"Sussan."

The courtyard trees were full of crows, crumbling sidewalks sticky with droppings. Bob's head itched. He could still feel the scope. No place to parlay, but it wasn't his move.

"Well Cowboy, what am I to make of you?"

He let Sussan work it out. Kept his hands open, away from his side.

"Claim you bossed Chosen. Yet my guys swear you're Amish. Some of your gear is military. You friends with Old Law?"

Walker whispered again, Bob delivering the line: "Those who look for the bad in people will surely find it."

"Pussyfist!" Squints spat.

"Murderer!" Meth mumbled.

Campbell remembered the fish symbol, Walker's scripture. "Look lady, I just want a meal." His stomach audibly concurred.

Sussan was staring.

"After that, I'll be on my way. Unless I can help?"

Her hard stare, reluctant, turned into a smile. "You're a smooth one, Cowboy. I'll give you that." She offered the smallest nod, leader to leader.

Once decided, she was brisk. "No guns allowed. Unbuckle that belt. Get 'em back when you leave."

Her guards were most unhappy to hear it. Bob gave his gun belt to Squints. Sussan scanned the sky, the road, the rooftops, before opening the building's outer door. Bob followed her in.

The lobby was in shambles, a necessary ruse: water stains, broken windows, soiled mattresses, and urine stink. Further inside, the cafeteria appeared squared away. Chairs were stacked against one wall; clean tables lined another. A large wipe board detailed the day: meal times, committee meetings, and a lengthy quote. Bob took it all in:

To be free is not merely to cast off one's chains, but to live in a way that respects and enhances the freedom of others.

Now who did that sound like? Bob's thoughts went to Walker: *Exit please, Mr. Campbell!*

What was that cripple up to? And how the fuck did he know? Bob nodded at the board. "I met a man once who talked like that."

Sussan replied after a moment, "I never did, though there's others here who have."

Bob tested her. "Maybe you'll get your chance? It was powerful. I'll never forget it."

He saw the flinch in her face. She'd heard the news then, believing Walker was dead. They either had a radio or good intel sources on the ground.

Sussan bowed her head a moment before switching subjects. "You said you were hungry," she remarked, nodding at the meal times. "You can join the next shift."

Savory smells floated from the kitchen. Some kind of soup? He could hear pots and pans and Spanish singing.

Bob, the perfect gentleman, pulled out two chairs, holding one for Sussan. "Join me?"

The woman, rail-thin under multiple sweaters, licked her lips and sat. She dismissed the guards, placing her radio on the table. "Call me if you see anything."

The two men—ex-XCons?—departed. Nothing forgiven, they shot Bob a hard look. Campbell sat down with a sigh. He took his Amish hat off, finger-combing greasy hair.

"Look pretty healthy for a Viral, Mr. Cowboy."

Bob couldn't say the same. Under that headscarf, Sussan was probably bald. He played coy. "I've had some luck."

"Bullshit. Your load is low and you know it. You're barely infected. What happened?"

Another XCon limped towards them from the kitchen, his face and hands tattooed with birds. Eyes red-rimmed, the cook set down two cups. Bob smelled hot chocolate. *No fucking way.*

Birdman nodded at the woman. *"Algo más*, President Sue?"

"You spoil me, Raymundo. *No gracias."* The man went back to his kitchen, to his stew.

"Hot chocolate?" Bob warmed his hands in the steam. The cafeteria, though clean, was freezing.

Sue smiled. "Hardly. It's from an MRE. 'Cocoa flavored beverage powder,' I believe."

Bob gulped it down. "Delicious." Curiosity killed the cat, would kill him too someday. "What kind of name is Sussan?"

"Arabic." She traced it on the table, flowing the letters from right to left. "It means *lily of the valley."* The Dearborn soccer mom took a sip, fighting the gut-clench for her kids, dead with all the rest.

"President Sue?"

She sighed, pointing to another wipe board, which held what looked like a civics lesson:

We the People

Article 1: Legislative, 20 members, 1 month terms

Article 2: Executive, President Sue, 6 month term

Article 3: Judicial, 2 justices, USMC—Semper Fi

"What's that all about?" Bob felt like he was in school.

"Long story," Sussan looked at her watch, "and we're running out of time." More clatter from the kitchen, Raymundo singing of his *corazón*.

"Short version then?"

Sue went to the board, fetching a tattered booklet for her pupil. Bob groaned at the tiny text. "The Constitution?"

Sue shrugged. "It's Old Law. Jarheads claim Walker gave it to them."

Too many questions, so Bob prioritized. As always, his own life came first. "Jarheads?"

"We've got Marines," she pointed to Article 3, "judge, jury, and executioners. We're protected by them. They started all this, though where it's going," she sighed, *"Allahu a'lam*—God only knows."

That explained the scope-itch. Some fucking grunt had crosshaired his brains. Bob hated that shit. "Walker *gave* it to them?"

"Up north somewhere, Indian River? They were starving— runaways from the war—sniped at his bus convoy for supplies. Got caught by Panthers, then released. Walker lifted them up, gave them food and this booklet. The rest, my friend, is history."

Bob blinked. Suddenly, there were Virals at the double doors—malnourished, menacing. They flicked their tongues, glaring redly at Cowboy, the intruder. Bob flashed back to his boss days, felt the old headache—*no fucking thanks*. He made a move to stand.

Sue put her delicate hand on his arm. "Cowboy, don't."

Her eyes—less red than her followers'—implored him.

So he didn't.

Sue stood, Bob followed. She beckoned and the crowd lined up, grabbing bowls, clinking spoons. They shuffled past Raymundo and his mystery pot. Birdman's apron was stained. He served them all, ladling broth and warmed-up tortillas. Sussan and Cowboy were served last. Both spoke their thanks, then took seats at the slurping table. Furtive looks were darted at the stranger, elbows and bodies angling away.

Cowboy cased the room, recognizing himself in these others: a scrounger for the Chosen, a pencil-pusher of apocalypse. He'd bossed Virals, and had been bossed himself. A middleman, a minion, he'd never met Sharkey. He knew the taste of defeat. Bob had been bested by Greenies and betrayed by a friend.

The infected had no menace to them. Bob thought of Spreaders he'd known: viral loads at maximum, rapists like Heavy and Hammer, dangerous women like Liz and that Lacy who'd peed in his dog bowl.

He whispered his confusion, "Where are your fighters?"

Sue sipped from her spoon. "We've got guards outside and some scavenger squads. But I know what you mean," she looked at him, "we are not what we were."

Bob tasted fish and plenty of flavor. Their table had finished, using tortillas to wipe each bowl clean. The hotel's inhabitants stood and stacked chairs, radiating respect towards Sussan. Once they were cleared, Bob fired away. "The graves by the parking lot?"

She sighed. "Starvation for some. Execution for others."

He stared. Sue explained, "Marines run the show here, Dan and Roy. Both Aghori, or used to be. Are you familiar?"

"Skulls you mean? Can't say I ever met one, mostly heard rumors."

"Stick around, Cowboy, and you will. Like I said, this is their show."

"They've executed Virals?"

Sue nodded. "When necessary, especially the aggressive ones, the heavy-loaders." She gestured at the board—*respects and enhances the freedom of others.* "Our Gories are true believers: no rape, no theft, no assault. And their courts are quick."

"*Semper Fi*, eh?" Bob raised an eyebrow.

"Always faithful," Sussan confirmed, "to the law, to their oaths."

"Next question, if you don't mind?"

"I'm trying to recruit you, Cowboy. You and your pistols. Honesty seems best."

Ha! Fat chance of that. He had Lizzy, and a high-value hostage. Walker was their ticket to Toledo. They'd get what they could for the old man—fuel, food, ammo, safe passage—then ride off into some happy-ever-after. Bob asked anyway, "How do you feed everyone? What's up with the fish? The symbol? The soup?"

Sussan rose and pulled Bob with her. "Time for show-and-tell." He followed her to the kitchen, putting their bowls in the sink. Birdman was scrubbing.

Sussan patted the chef's shoulder. *"Señor Raymundo es un mago con sopa."*

Raymundo flashed a grin; his vat of stew was still on simmer. A propane canister provided flame. On the prep counter was a cardboard case stenciled: MEALS, READY-TO-EAT, INDIVIDUAL. It looked half-empty. Sue pulled out a pouch: MENU 21, TUNA, CHUNK, LIGHT, WATER PACKED, LEMON PEPPER. It bore the Department of Defense seal—eagle, shield, and arrows—along with its testimonial, "Warfighter Approved."

Campbell nodded, no stranger to freeze-dry. "I've had plenty of those. Menu 21 ain't bad. Tuna, tortillas, mayo, some crackers?"

"That's just it, Mr. Cowboy, and there's always plenty."

"Come again?"

"Walker gifted this case to our Gories, the two Marines that sniped his bus at Indian River. We've been eating it for a week."

"How many are you?"

"All told? Over 200."

Campbell computed. "That's not possible."

"No shit, Sherlock." Sussan was smiling. Bob looked at Birdman, his brown apron, the steaming vat, the open cardboard case. He voiced his confusion, *"Cómo es esto posible?"*

The X-branded Viral met his gaze. *"Cómo?"* Bob pressed him. Raymundo shrugged, lifting red-rimmed eyes to the ceiling. *"Es un milagro."*

Cowboy's Spanish was rusty. *"Milagro?"*

Sussan translated, "Miracle. Ray says it's a miracle."

Birdman beamed, beatific despite his puckered X. *"Si. Miracle. De la biblia."*

"The Bible?"

Sussan tsked him. "No Sunday school?" Bob frowned. School—on any day—was ancient history.

Raymundo dipped a soapy finger, tracing a wet fish on the cardboard. *"Camina sobre el agua como Jesús."*

Bob caught Ray's drift—Jesus was a water-walker too. Sussan shook her head at Bob's disbelief. "Loaves and fishes, partner. Loaves and fishes."

State of the Union

SUE TURNED HER COWBOY LOOSE, still hoping to recruit the gunslinger to their cause. Bob left his gunbelt in the lobby, a token of return. "Call a meeting, Sussan. Invite everyone." Bob tipped his hat to his hostess and crossed the parking lot, watched over by crows.

The rooftop Marines pinned the outlaw in their sights. Their walkie-talkie beeped, Sussan's voice coming through: "Roy, Dan, stand down. Man's a Viral. A friendly. He'll be coming back soon."

"Wanna bet?" Dan, the clear-eyed shooter, offered odds to his partner.

Roy watched the hatted man through his optic. "Doesn't look infected to me." The two Gories keyed compliance on the handset, continuing their surveillance. They knew the old law, their place in the chain—Article II Section 2—President Sue, for now, was their commander in chief.

The tall target ducked around a corner of the roofless Red Inn. The skull-tatted spotter pulled away from the eyepiece, seeking black birds instead. With a whoosh of wings, the murder complied, lifting from their roost and following the primary.

The two Aghori—corvid compatible—live-streamed the avian feed: *the Humvee and its occupants—a fire-haired female, a wounded man in the backseat.* The crows came factory equipped with hardware, 30 million years of Research and Development.

They ran facial-recognition, quickly matching the crippled man. The murder had seen him before, so had the Marines. Their tattooed jawbones twitched as they radioed the report.

"Are you fucking *high?*" Red Liz was not having it. "You found a *hive* of Virals and you want us to *stay?*" They held a meeting in the stolen Humvee. A blackbird peeped at the trio from its nearby perch. Campbell admitted her point, but protested, "These guys are different, Lizzy, not like others we knew. Trust me, this feels like our move."

"God damn it, *Toledo* is our move! Ransom this geezer to the Reds, rest is gravy. Our life together, Bob, fucking *gravy!*"

Even furious, she'd never looked better. Lizzy's eyes had whitened, even her skin was smoothing. She'd lost the Viral twitch and was less gaunt than before. Bob, too, had lost his lustiness, his lechery. He'd felt this way before: Chow's cabin in the dunes, a guitar, some books, and the prospect of peace. What was the cause? Could it be Walker?

Was ol' Liz right? They should cut a deal with the Reds. Take care of themselves, enjoy the end-times together, whatever time they had left. Could he though? And what about Walker? Deliver the dude in chains, put the preacher on the block? Auction him off to the highest Red bidder?

Even the thought was bitter. Bob knew he couldn't, even if she could. The old man—Lizzy's "geezer"—stayed quiet. It was Campbell's test, pass or fail, no cheating allowed. Of course, the Reds would lynch this water-walker in a heartbeat, roping his reputation, twisting a spear in his side. Bob's head thundered, thoughts flashing back to Petoskey, hanging town, the light poles, the human fruit, the stink of shit and sex and fear.

The ex-Chosen made his choice, a no-brainer, shaking off her fury. "Can't do it, Liz." Bob addressed the backseat, "Mr. Walker, let's go."

Seeing red, Lizzy spat venom, flashing teeth and claws, her virality freshly resurgent.

Bob stepped out of the Humvee, immediately confronted by double demons. One of the Marines opened Walker's door. Both Gories carried rifles, wearing Kevlar over ribcage tattoos. Stenciled on the butt-stock of their M4s: the skull, the crown. The Aghori wore no masks. There were crows in the trees, crows on the cornice.

The skeletons, without haste, nodded with civility. "Mr. Cowboy, Reverend Walker. Our assembly is almost ready, will you both come?"

Walker's escort had brought crutches, sizing them now to the wounded man's length. The other pressed a hidden earpiece and said, *"Renegade* is confirmed. Inbound in sixty seconds." Above the haunted hotel, more crows were circling—Combat Air Patrol for the joint session of congress. Walker nodded to his escorts. Did he recognize them? They processioned across the pavement, gazing at the potter's field, the swellings of the ground.

A Humvee door slammed; Liz was out! The rearguard deployed his rifle, red-dotting the angry lizard right between the eyes. "Ma'am, stop right there!"

Liz stopped, due more to the *ma'am* than the machine gun. "Fuck you, Skeletor! I'm coming too."

Earpiece checked with the hotel, relaying Sussan's decision. "Permission granted. Right this way, if you please."

Campbell wasn't pleased, feeling powerless without his pistols. Single file, they approached the inn. No generator noise, no lighted windows, no outward sign of two hundred hungry souls. Earpiece opened the lobby door and passed them all inside. The tattooed Skull nodded at Bob. Trust was building, but could he trust it? Things were getting pretty trippy. Had Raymundo laced the damn soup?

Campbell blamed Walker, his weirdness. Shit like this happened when ol' boy was around: the airfield, the chaos of sorting, the container for Non-Compliants, Virals shouting his name, begging Walker to touch, to heal, to set them free—not from cuffs or confinement, but from Covee.

Hannah Hochstettler had been at Clare, wearing a bonnet and boarding a bus. Bob had yelled out Sarah's name, Sammy's too. Had Hannah heard? He didn't know, he'd been tased. Bob thought of Methhead and Squints guarding Sussan. Those lecherous *iks* had lusted for little Sarah. Who else might Cowboy know here? Who else might know him?

The two Skulls secreted them along a service hallway. Walker crutched too, stump seeping; dude had yet to say a word. They paused at a pair of double doors, "Patio and Pool." The dice were tumbling. Cowboy Bob rolled along. The Aghori gestured them through. Earpiece nodded as the reverend crutched by: "*Semper Fi*, sir."

"Ooh rah, Marine," Walker replied.

The courtyard was dim, an Army camo net hiding the enclosure. The leaf-strewn swimming pool was half-full of potable water. The congress crowded the concrete. Four hundred eyes glared redly at the guests.

President Sue called the convalescents to order: "Mr. Speaker." Chef Raymundo stepped clear. "Mr. Speaker, I present the Reverend Walker and his two companions."

The X-branded soup master bade them proceed. Confusion rippled through the crowd as the trio traipsed to Sue's platform. A wave of whispers was building, wonder cresting at Walker's survival.

See? He lives! He bleeds!

Told you! Can't kill him. Not with rockets they can't.

Our Marines, Walker saved them. Showed mercy.

Walks-on-Water saves us all. His soup! His fish!

Who's that with him? They infected?

Used to be, is what I heard.

Chosen. Bossed for Sharkey. Blood on their hands.

We called him Cowboy. He's a bossman, handy with rope.

The woman?

Red Liz. Kinky. Least she was. Different now though.

Virals then? They don't look it. Did he heal 'em?

Course he did. Heal us all. Yes he could!

Heal us! Touch us! Save us!

King! King! King!

The Virals surged, the Gorie guards glaring them back. The touch-hungry tide receded. *Heal us. Touch us. Save us! Oh king!*

Walker pivoted on his crutch-points. Side by side by side, the trio stood with Sue. Cowboy and Liz, hearing their names from the crowd, grew edgy, sidling away as far as they could. Through the camo netting, Cowboy saw the circling crows, the darkening clouds; a stray leaf skittered across the sky. The trippy feeling returned—Walker! God damn it. Liz was right. They should've left. This poolside parlay was not their scene.

President Sue was speaking. Cowboy inventoried the courtyard's stores: a row of motorcycles, a full bike rack, two tarp-covered generators, rusty oil drums—contents unknown.

"Give to the Congress Information of the State of the Union." From a tattered pamphlet, Sussan recited the old law, then looked up at her constituents. "Well, we've gathered—citizens and three branches—to witness Walker's return." She encompassed the courtyard with a sweep of her hand. "The state of our union is *strong!*"

Stray sparks of applause were quickly doused, pissed upon by pundits.

"Strong" Suzy says? My fuckin' teeth are fallin' out!

"Strong?" Does she mean the damn Reds?

Heard they're in Toledo. Fuckers comin' our way.

Roll us with tanks. You know they're backed by the CORPS?

"Strong?" We used to be, till we buried all our bad-asses.

Murdered 'em you mean? Fuckin' Marines!

Let's see you tell 'em that!

Yeah right. Shit's rigged. You know the deal.

I'm hungry. Starving! Wasting away.

Sue, we're hungry! We're fucking hungry!

The boo birds began as the first raindrops fell. Sussan ceased her oration. The crowd's empty bellies had stuffed up their ears. The infected turned nasty. Cowboy looked for an exit. Liz, point-blank, shot him a look: *Told you so! Asshole!*

Walker, propped beside Sue, turned his dusty face towards the stinging rain. There was ice in every drop, crystallized kernels of winter to come. His wife and daughters—two years dead. His congregation—collapsed. Their Baptist church—baptized by blood. His retirement, his rest—rescinded forever.

The sea of Virals was hissing. Angry waves swamped the boat.

Walker, save us!

We're drowning here.

Don't you care?

Walker's crutches clattered to the concrete. The commotion captured the crowd's attention. Campbell supported him; the old reverend leaned in. Unencumbered, Walker embraced the rain. With outstretched arms, the old man rebuked the crowd: "Quiet, now."

The Virals quieted, stilled by his legend. Walker put a question to them, "Why are you so afraid?"

We don't wanna die!

Soup's almost gone!

Soldiers are coming! Red Hands will wipe us out!

Walker, we're fucked!

Sharp tongues were spitting and so was the rain. The old timer shook his weary head, addressing the multitude again: "Have you no faith?"

The rain and their panic both seemed to lessen; many red eyes opened wide. "Who *is* this? Even the rain obeys him."

The two Aghori stepped smartly forward, tattooed Skulls eyeballing the crowd.

Shh! The Marines!

Fuck those jarheads! Dudes executed my buddies!

Old Law lawyers! What the fuck do they know?

Your buddies were bastards. Rapists deserved it.

Bastards? Fuck you!

No! Fuck YOU!

People started pushing; a contagious mosh pit churned. Storm-tossed, a crow *caw-cawed* a warning. One of the Marines raised his rifle—*crack-cracking* his own. The crowd quieted. How would this play out? The Skull barked out a parade ground command, "Atten-SHUN!"

Briefly, they had it. The two Gories took advantage: "Following Old Law ain't easy," Dan and Roy tag-teamed their rebuttal, "but hard law is better than none!"

Not wrong there. Amen to that.

What else do they say?

The Marines said it.

Dan: "We know this man. This water-walker, he's for real."

Roy: "You know the story. We tried to kill him, loot his bus."

Dan: "We were captured by Panthers. He set us free."

Roy: "Gave us food, gave us law."

Dan: "More than that, Walker gave his *touch!*"

Roy: "Now we're protected, we're strong."

Dan: "You've seen us. Do we wear masks?"

No, they don't. No masks, no MOPP, no PPE at all.

Roy: "You've lived with us. Are we infected?"

No, they aren't. Covee couldn't catch 'em.

Dan: "Our doses are long gone. Our Shark-juice ran dry."

Roy: "It's not virucide that protects us."

Dan: "It's Walker! His hands!"

Roy: "He scoured us of Covee!"

Heal us! Touch us! Scour us too!

The Fist

BOTH MARINES SWORE OFF MORE SOUP, Dan and Roy donating to the hungry instead. President Sue did the same, along with other Virals whose load-levels were low. Raymundo and his helpers prepared the meal; infected lining up for their ladle of life. The rain held off while the captains conferred. Sue started with the obvious, observing, "If we feed 'em all, the soup will run out tonight."

Walker replied, "Then feed them. The best part of the future is that it comes one day at a time."

Campbell itched. Had he heard that quote before? Liz dug her nails into Bob's arm, hissing, "Gotta get out of here, Cowboy. Or we're fucked."

Were they though? Could they leave their golden goose behind? No way Walker would come away willingly. This motel and its roaches were right up the martyr's alley.

Walker nodded at the soup line. Some assholes started shoving. "I must go to them."

Sussan, presidential, tried pausing him. "But sir, what's the plan? Wait here, starving, for the Reds to come squash us?"

Others, passing on their portion, joined in: the Aghori Marines, some X-branded bikers, Squints and his buddy Methhead, who held onto a flier. A bearded gang leader, gaunt in his jacket—*Devils Disciples DDMC*—glared at Walker with red eyes. "How long?" he demanded. "How fuckin' long will we wait here starving? Walker, how long?"

Walker answered the Disciple, "How long? Not long, we shall reap what we sow."

Cowboy itched again. The Marines pressed their preacher for orders: "Sir, exactly *what* are we sowing?"

Walker, tired out from trauma, leaned on his crutches, his quotes. "We are entering upon a life and death struggle, a holy war; we are performing an all-embracing sacrifice—"

"Ooh RAH!" the Marines interrupted.

"That's more like it!" Dan said. "Speed, surprise, and violence of action!" He and Roy fist-bumped each other. "Sir, now you're talking!"

The outlaw bikers were grinning. Their bearded leader spoke up: "There's pockets of us all over the city. We'll spread the word, round everyone up. We might go down, but we'll go down dicks swinging!" More fist-bumps, *Hell yeah!*

Liz tried tugging her cowboy away. The Devils Disciples needed details: "So, where should we meet up?"

Marines, ever-tactical, wondered the same: "Sir, what's our rally point?"

Reverend Walker watched the soup line—the bent, the broken. They had restored their own order, the mosh pit storm dwindling to category one. The strong helped the weak, sick helping the sicker. Two Virals, stooped by starvation, felt Walker's gaze and stood straighter. Ducking the spit of rain, they each raised a clenched fist, supporting this descendant of ancient, far-away kings. Walker's photographic mind saw the past as ever-present: a podium at the '68 Olympics, two athletes once did the same. Reverend Walker raised his right arm in solidarity. Curling his fingers into a fist, he returned their salute.

The Marines were staring, MC Disciples too. The bearded gang leader, a local Detroiter, interpreted the old man's body language. The outlaw studied Walker, then the Marines, flashing a yellow smile. "Perfect. The Fist! The Joe Louis fist, on Woodward! Our rally point is there!"

Dan and Roy, both Texans, confirmed: "That boxing sculpture? By the river? Black stone, like a battering ram?"

The outlaw bikers nodded, they knew it. President Sue approved, announcing, "The Fist is a good spot. It's central. There's water. Area's been quiet. We'll gather everyone, but what then?"

The retiree slumped on his crutches. His stump ached; his empty stomach flopped. Sleet spattered him with icy doubts. Goosebumps pebbled his ashen skin. The reverend was tired. Rest was coming. But first, there was this. He flashed back to the explosion: his crumpled bus, Butters's melted body, his ascension, a night flight. His bookish mentors had all been there, shelved amongst the stars. Walker had paged through his parietal, leafing through the lobes of his library. Now, more than ever, his mentors advised him:

Gandhi, one sandal at a time, had walked all the way to the sea for salt. MLK junior once walked through the wrath of red Alabama. Thousands had marched—Selma to Montgomery.

Walker, a medium, channeled their voices: "We are not about to turn around."

Disciples cracked knuckles. "Fuckin' A, we're not! We're on the move now," one cried out.

"Aye aye, SIR!" His skull-faced Marines were highly motivated.

Walker crutched himself over to the serving line. Chef Raymundo made room, lending the old man a ladle. The cripple doled out portions, dosing the Virals with each dollop. Many shook his hand, tried to kiss it. He consoled them all, quietly quoting, "Yes, we are on the move and no wave of racism can stop us."

"Yes, sir."

"The burning of our churches"—his own Second Baptist was ash—"will not deter us."

"Yes, sir."

"Like an idea whose time has come, not even mighty armies can halt us."

"Fuck the Reds! Fuck the CORPS!"

Walker! Walker! Walker!

The preacher looked weary; a damp evening made his old bones feel brittle. The soup was gone, along with every scrap of tortilla. Raymundo and his helpers were clearing away dishes. President Sue directed her citizens.

The gang of Disciples were given fuel and a task: round up all nearby Virals, rally tomorrow at the Fist. Defend Detroit!

The motel's inhabitants would stay one more night. Lights out in ten minutes; tomorrow, they'd march.

Raymundo was on water detail, which meant he'd scrounge around for containers. Every possible drop must be packed up and carried.

The Marines, Dan and Roy, were in charge of the hotel's armory. Weapons were few, and warriors even fewer. Firearms were distributed—a cadre of fighters would protect the whole flock.

Walker, done in, was mumbling. Sussan looked at Cowboy. "Take care of your friend. We'll make room. You three are welcome here." Sue nodded at Liz. "We owe you thanks. Thanks, for bringing *Him.*"

Lizzy wasn't having it. "Nope. No way. We'll sleep in our ride." She moved to Walker's side, Bob took the other. "Come on old timer; let's get you out of this rain." The crippled man leaned in, his weight almost nothing.

"Not so fuckin' fast." Squints, leering, moved to block her. Methhead waved a heavy hand, thrusting his flier towards the born-again Marines. Roy, smoothing it, passed the wanted poster to Sue. Sussan perused the paper, gave a sign to her Gories and—reluctantly—read the warrant aloud:

Wanted by order of the US Army

Member of the so-called Chosen 'Red' Liz McGee

Member of the so-called Chosen 'Cowboy' Bob Campbell

Descriptions, aliases, crimes (alleged) and photos below

Order to be enforced by all units identifying as 'Old Law'

Signed, LTC J.R. Dennis

Battalion Commander 125th Infantry Regiment, 37th IBCT

"God DAMN you, Bob!" Liz was hissing, then gasping, as a rifle-butt knocked the wind out of her and she was cuffed.

Walker stumbled, clumsy on his crutches. Campbell stepped up and steadied the man. Mean-eyed, the Viral with the rifle squinted, spitting his triumphant comeuppance point-blank in Bob's face: "Pussyfist!"

Beyond weary, Walker leaned on Bob's shoulder. Cowboy raised both hands to be flex-cuffed. "I'll come. Don't hurt him. And don't you *dare* fuckin' tase me!"

The Disciples

PETEY BOY WAS FIRST AMONG THEM, even before collapse. The bearded biker, a real devil, was always the first Disciple to throw a punch, first to make meth-money, and first of his crew to catch the Covee. When Petey emerged, red-eyed and un-dead, his gang crowded round and the virus spread. Their motorcycle club was a one-percenter: outlawed, violent, shunned. Covee, then Stinger, whittled them further, sharpening the horns of the surviving Devils.

Permissioned by Sussan, Petey Boy gassed up, kicked his hog and roared, unmuffled, through rain. He knew his route, knew the signs, the passwords. At every Viral dive, Blind Pig, and speakeasy he recited, *The king has returned. He heals! Reds are coming. Meet at the Fist. Defend Detroit!*

The outlaw knew the turf to avoid: places where Panthers prowled, or Antiva was active. Out of sight from the born-again Marines and their Old Law adherence, Petey profited from his rounds—Royal Oak, Southfield, Dearborn—dealing contraband to Virals as he rallied them. The contents of his saddlebags shifted as he supplied their demands: cigarettes, methamphetamines, and DVD porn—some things never changed. Petey Boy didn't judge, left that shit to the jarheads.

The Rouge River corridor was usually a no-go zone. Anti-Viral haters had recently captured the refinery. Sharkey losing the plant's petroleum had hastened Panzer's end. Oh fucking well, the Disciples were never Chosen, and none wore the X. Sue and her *Semper Fi* Skulls had been clear, so into Antiva's lion den he went. Petey motored past the warning signs: Biohazards, Crowns, and *Long Live King!*

Dix Avenue, north of the refinery, was a no man's land, a DMZ: Arabic advertising, fire-scarred mosques, and overfull cemeteries. Where Dix crossed the Rouge, the drawbridge was up. Petey slowed his roll, splotchy skin prickling as laser sights established his range. He sat his Harley as Antiva snipers dialed up his death.

Fuck it. He drew breath, half-hoping it might be his last, and yelled, "Hey Antiva assholes! I've got a fucking message! We have *Walks-on-Water.* He's wounded, but he LIVES!"

Slim Jim and Big John were brothers. Side by side, the pair of Disciples made their run. There were urban farms in Corktown and the Warehouse District. Secret to most, the brothers knew the pass-signs and approached, unshot.

A melting pot of Virals cultivated rooftop terraces. Mexican, Black, and Chaldean were minorities no longer. An infected majority now dominated D-town, produce and pot giving them power. Goods were exchanged along with the news: *Walks-on-Water is back. His hands can heal. Meet at the Fist. Defend Detroit!*

Jefferson Avenue was on the brothers' route—Gold Coast, Waterworks and Marina—they proselytized to pimps and prostitutes alike. At Parkview Drive, Slim Jim braked his bike, something bright catching his red eye. The brothers turned right towards the river and were flashed again. Arc lights? Was some fool welding? Another blue flash, yes indeed. At Stockton Park they looked across the river at Belle Isle. Voices, lights, laughter? There was a fucking party at the Yacht Club, and they hadn't been invited.

Belle Isle Yacht Club

"TIE US THE FUCK OFF!"

Captain Doyle's command squelched through the loudhailer. On Doyle's barge, a red-hatted voyageur stepped lively, making fast the spring line.

"Ya Canadian cocksucker." Doyle checked the mooring lines. The low sun dropped from the clouds. Its fireball silhouetted the skyline, nuking Detroit from afar. Satisfied with their breakwater berth, Doyle conserved diesel by killing his engines. The tug shuddered and went silent. He patted her helm with a work-hardened hand; *Dirty Debbie* had balls—a pair of twin CATs, 340 horses apiece.

Tom was proud of his find. There were plenty of vessels to choose from, but the small push boat had stood out. Unlike most river tugs, *Dirty Debbie* was in decent shape. She'd been winterized by her previous captain—*may he rest in fuckin' peace.* Doyle fingered her oily valves, greased her bearings, and plugged her stuffing-box good. Tickled by the starter, *Debbie* moaned, then revved to life with a roar.

Doyle felt like roaring himself. His eyes and purpose were clear. Their little fleet was assembling: a dozen, all told, and shoving off soon. Last night's rain had ended, today's wind clearing the clouds. There'd be a working-moon tonight for their float downriver. Doyle's improvised fleet was overdue at the refinery. Tomorrow night the moon would be full, plenty bright for fighting a battle.

Antiva predicted that Toledo's Reds would attack Detroit, and soon. A transmission from the CORPS mentioned the full moon as "kickoff," the night of Halloween: "Trick or treat, motherfuckers." Doyle worked the bolt of the rifle he'd been issued, then slung it from the wheelhouse bulkhead.

Since their arrival yesterday, Belle Isle had been busy. Baptiste and his Frenchies knew how to turn a wrench. During collapse, the Yacht Club was scavenged, but only lightly, just like the MPC executive had said. Oil and fuel were siphoned early on. Some boats had been lived in, and shit in too. A collection of dry corpses, stripped of any finery, had been found. The two oversize canoes departed the refinery yesterday. A storm had risen in the night. Icy rain and lightning strikes. And had Doyle heard motorcycle engines? From the park across the river? Hard to tell with all the thunder. So far, none of the voyageurs had slept.

The empty gravel-barge would serve their purpose. It was dry, offered protection, and could be stuffed full of fighters. The barge had been piled up at the Ambassador Bridge till *Debbie* and her CATs tugged it away. With any luck they'd throw lines shortly, float down the Rouge to refuel, and prepare to defend D-Town from Ohio's Reds. The fuel they'd been given was almost gone. MPC's jerry cans were almost empty, the fleet's armament entirely too light.

Baptiste, at the helm of his own tugboat, gave Doyle the ready signal. Twilight bruised the sky. Detroit's skyline gaped, a mouth of broken teeth. The river shouldered past, impatient for the sea. Doyle started both engines and eyed his gauges before barking into his hailer, "Throw the fuckin' lines!"

Thus commanded, the deckhand sprang to the spring lines, unmooring *Debbie* and her cavernous barge. The voyageur signaled, thumbs up to Doyle. Underway! Tom felt the familiar heart-lift. *Yo, ho, ho and the winds blow free.*

The current quickly captured them. Doyle throttled forward to gain steerageway, sparing a look over his shoulder as other craft did the same. Tom's tug and barge led the way, Baptiste's ducklings, ugly with repair, waddling in their wake. Doyle steered for the fourth arch of Belle Isle's bridge. Almost dark. Red and green markers, barely visible without electric light, aided their navigation. The chart claimed he had clearance: thirty feet above and thirty below. *Debbie* and her barge squeezed through the arch, but barely.

The moon, almost full, rose above Ontario. Doyle's fuel tanks, almost empty, sank his good mood. Eight miles, maybe more, to Rouge River's refinery. Could they make it? The main engines and generator were working. His electronics were dialed: 156.8 MHz, channel sixteen, Tom turned up the static. The refinery had an antenna. Should he risk comms, report his low fuel? Not yet. Who the fuck else might be listening?

Baptiste and the others emerged from the archway. Loony-boy perched on Frenchie's bow. *Father and son?* Doyle adjusted his rudder. *Or cabin boy and captain?* Tom steered for deeper water. *What do I care?*

Checking astern, Doyle squinted in the dark: ol' Loony was flapping, Baptiste began flashing—*three short, three long, three short*—Save Our Ships. Off their starboard beam, firelight flickered from downtown. Near the Ren-Center, Tom saw a spray of gunshots. *Ambush?*

Doyle deployed the dead captain's binoculars. The flicker came from torches, looked like hundreds, one street from the water? Muzzle-flash strobed the skyline, but no rounds were incoming, no bullets whanged against his hull. *Who the hell were they targeting? And who the fuck are "they?"*

Captain Doyle was about to throttle forward to get out of range when his marine radio squawked. "Voyageur, Voyageur, this is Big Oil. How do you read? Over."

"God damn it, Big Oil, reduce your wattage! Voyageur. Over!"

Christ! They might be heard in Toledo. Doyle dialed down his power, hoping the refinery did the same. The exec called again,

"Voyageur, be advised, you've got a pickup downtown. Highest priority. Tie up along Riverwalk and prepare for passengers. Take precautions, avoid infection. Big Oil, out."

Oh HELL no! The cancerous CUNTS! Fuck were they up to? Picking up Virals? Fat fucking chance!

Baptiste beeped him on the radio: *"Debbie,* Loon's got something. We need to pull over."

The Oathbreakers

DETROIT'S VIRALS, many near death, had walked all day to see Him. Walker slumped beneath the Joe Louis Fist and did his duty. He blessed the infected, shook their shaky hands, and shared an ocean of salty tears. These sick had been abandoned, shunned, and persecuted without mercy. Mothers and fathers, sons and daughters, all grieved losses of their own. No fault of theirs, they'd survived. Not one of them that wouldn't trade their red eyes for brown, or blue, or green.

Some had sworn oaths to Sharkey's Chosen, some to Mustafa's X, but most of those heavy-loaders were gone, killed at the Mackinac Bridge or purged from Panzer's farms. The aggressive ones had died skirmishing over food, or fuel, or sex. Some heavies had joined partisans in the forest, preying upon depopulated places. Some had been lynched by MOPP-hooded clans, eye color their only offense. The survivors gathering by the black stone were oathbreakers. They'd been called from their urban caverns and shadowed alleyways. Currently unaligned, they lined up now for Walker.

President Sue had no way to feed them. What calories Raymundo scrounged had been consumed on their march. The Disciples had indeed passed the word; Sussan was shocked at the Viral response. She'd never seen so many Spreaders, not in one place, not for one purpose.

They came because of Walker, now more myth than man. His reputation had grown while his body withered. There was not much left of *Walks-on-Water*. The legend had been blown up, his brain traumatically injured, and the bandaged stump still seeped. Drops of red flowered upon the potholed pavement. The reverend had crutched most of their route, refusing help from motorized Disciples. The Marines, Dan and Roy, diagnosed sepsis. Walker needed antibiotics and an immediate IV, help that Sue's oathbreakers could not provide.

She watched him minister to the malcontents, the masses. Each encounter looked deeply personal. Each leprous touch was truly touching. One at a time, the snapping, spitting Virals were subdued by his soothing. When they left the line, they seemed calmer, more compliant. Liberated—somehow?—from Covee's curse, they reverted, however briefly, to themselves. At the black stone of the Fist, they found a word for this effect. Borrowed from the Crown-and-Skull Aghori, they started calling themselves *scoured.*

Walker passed them along to the two Gories. Dan and Roy, skull-faced, formed them into squads, drilling on Jefferson Avenue. Weapons were few so most trained with sticks. One firearm per squad was all they could muster. If, or when, its bearer was killed—by Reds, by starvation, by exposure—the next squad member would inherit the weapon.

The sun scribed its shallowing arc. Winter-weak, it cowered behind smoke-blackened buildings. The moon, fattening towards full, took over. The Viral host, pale and shadowy, lit bonfires, huddling together for warmth. In their undernourished state, death by exposure was a real possibility. The Red exterminators were coming and might squash them tomorrow, but tonight Sue's priorities were the cold and lack of calories for her community.

Promote the general welfare was an Old Law commandment. *Provide for the common defense* was another. Well, they would die trying, sooner for some, later for others. Sussan—two years bereaved from all she held dear—was fine with sooner.

The Aghori Marines posted lookouts; Disciples watched the approach roads. Toledo was a long walk away, but if the Reds had fuel and vehicles there could be fighting tonight. If Detroit's Virals were surprised, it would be a bloody slaughter.

Dan, a combat veteran, stepped away from the raw recruits, pressing his earpiece receiver. An upriver scout was reporting contacts: "Recon One, there's boats on the river, maybe a dozen, headed our way. They're led by a big fucking barge. Over."

"Scout, this is Recon One, pull back to our position." Dan thought it out, conferring with Sue, Raymundo, and Roy, his fellow Marine. They agreed, and Dan made the call. "All scouts, all Disciples, this is Recon One. Pull back to the Fist. Defend Detroit! Recon One, out!"

Dan looked at their host, scattered, unprepared, undisciplined. Some waited in line still for Walker, some were stick-training, most were hunched by flames or holding torches of their own. The tattooed Gorie fired a burst from his battle rifle, *Crack! Crack! Crack!*

The echoes caromed off the concrete and got the host's attention. Squad leaders formed up for defense. Walker's touchline was suspended; most had been scoured already. Those still in line hissed their displeasure as their water-walker was hustled to his Humvee for safety.

Caw! Caw! Caw! A roost-tree rustled as blackwings took flight. Left behind were naked branches and a crumbling sidewalk, sticky with shit. The corvids overflew the river, scanning the intruders with night-vision eyes. On one of the boats stood a boy. Familiar with their frequency, the young two-legs formed a mental message, detailing his desires and radiating respect. An understanding, bird-to-boy, was reached. A messenger crow peeled off to report. She found her skull-faced master, perched upon his bony shoulder, was fed a crumb, and reported: *Not a threat. Not a threat. Not a threat.*

Skull to Skull, Dan and Roy talked it out, sharing with Sussan.

Midnight

CRACK! CRACK! CRACK!

Gunshots slapped him from his slumber. Besides the too-tight cuffs and Lizzy's too-rank odor, Bob had never slept better. He'd been with his wife, a delicious dream of before: fancy hotel, bottle of bubbly, their sexiversary. His-and-Her robes were about to come off.

Then the armored doors opened, cold air and woodsmoke gushing inside the Humvee. Bob heard yelling and sounds of confusion. Crows—*caw-cawing*—whooshed above, winging for the river. A clear-eyed Marine stuck his skull inside the vehicle, re-checking the restraints of the two back-seaters. "Right this way, Mr. Walker. Sit yourself down, sir. You'll be safe enough inside."

The crippled man looked weak as shit. They folded his ass into the passenger seat, setting his dirty crutches on the desert-tan hood. The jarhead shut the door. A cheesy odor oozed from Walker's stump. Dude was septic, badly infected, but not with Covee nor its stinger. Old Sussana, pretty ripe herself, took the driver's seat. She switched on the electronics, powering up the loudhailer mounted on the roof. Drawing juice from the batteries, Sue hoped there was enough.

"Reverend, could you say a few words? Calm everyone down? The Marines confirm that those boats appear friendly. Disciple Petey Boy says we should all get on board the barge."

Walker nodded; he wasn't all there, hadn't been since the rocket attack. Sue handed him the mic, showing him the PTT. The preacher cleared his throat. Campbell felt itchy; here it fucking comes. Walker thumbed the talk button, his battered voice bolstered by batteries. A pair of 12-volts powered his pulpit:

"I am not bound to win." Amplified, the words bounced off the buildings.

He speaks! Shhh! I wanna hear this.

"But I am bound to be true."

Shut the fuck up, let the man talk!

"I am not bound to succeed."

Course not, Reds are coming. We're fucked!

"But I am bound to live up to what light I have."

Now you're talking! Make the most of it.

"I must stand with anybody that stands right."

Anybody? Even Griffs? Even Reds? Asshole Antivas?

"And part with him when he goes wrong."

Like toothless Sharkey! said an ex-Chosen.

RIP, Mustafa! spat the angry Cons.

After a pause, Walker continued, "Those words were Lincoln's, and I believe them."

We believe in YOU! Your hands! Your healing!

Wal-ker! Wal-ker! Wal-ker!

Torches flickered, orange and yellow. The incoming boats, black-hulled, loomed nearer. The teacher kept teaching: "Long ago, the Underground Railroad came through here. The codename for Detroit was Midnight. Well, the midnight hour is upon us; we stand upon the very spot. Slaves stood here—right here!—and cast off their chains. They boarded boats that took them to freedom. Tonight, my friends, we must do the same!"

What's he say? We're slaves?

"What chains us tonight is our fear. Break those chains! Board the boats! Fly like geese! Stay on the drunkard's path! Follow the stars!"

Geese? Drunks? Stars? What the fuck?

Walker, schooled in abolition, knew the quilt-codes of the old railroad. Too deep in his head, he flew way over theirs.

Did he say we're boarding?

Nah, man. Said you're boring!

Fuck you!

You wish, I've been scoured!

Me too!

What's next then?

Didn't you hear? We board the fucking boats!

Boats? To where?

To freedom, fool! Like ol' king says!

The Ambassador

SUSSAN TOOK THE MIC, instructing the Virals, "Citizens, form lines along the Riverwalk. Prepare to board. No shooting of any kind. Maintain social distancing. Do not infect the boat crews!"

She powered down the Humvee's electronics. The Marines formatted their squads. Crows kept them updated on the convoy's approach. The two Skulls ducked out of the moonlight and took up a firing position. Dan and Roy, spotter-and-shooter, guarded the embarkation zone, providing overwatch.

The big barge bumped the landing. A red-capped deckhand tossed lines at the Virals, tethering two worlds together. The push boat captain stepped out of his wheelhouse, holding a rifle and a grudge. He barked, "Tighten up that bowline, you fur-fucking Frenchman!"

The red cap complied, biting his tongue.

"You there, on the sidewalk! Yes you! Ya pink-eyed pansy. Move that spring line back one bollard, before I bash out yer brains!"

Pink-eye, surprised, stepped lively.

The captain shaded his eyes from moonlight, counting the Virals waiting to come aboard: two hundred at least, maybe more.

He leveled his rifle at the gangplank. "Hey there Spreaders! Don't fucking move. I've got no food, no medicine either. You all stay put till I get some damn answers!" Baptiste and the others backed their engines, holding position in the current. The Ambassador Bridge lay ahead, a downriver hazard.

Walker, up past his bedtime—past his life-time—sat slumped. Sue turned, looking at Bob in the backseat. "You heard that barge captain. How 'bout it Cowboy? I need an ambassador."

"Him?" Liz smirked. "Cowboy's a clutz! He'll let you down! Free me instead! I'll get what you want."

Sue stared at Bob—true, his eyes were barely red, but could he pass for non-Viral? Cowboy thought it through, but only got so far. "I'll do it, but on one condition."

He waited. Sussan waited. The river rolled along. The moon was rolling too, a ghoulish marble in a playground sky. Sue nodded.

Bob had her, pressing his advantage. "Set us both free. Rip up that warrant. Pardon us for good behavior."

Sue considered. "That's it?"

Campbell nodded. She read the fine print aloud: "You don't get the Humvee. You don't get weapons. You help *him*," she looked at Walker, "you help *us*. You and Liz, you both see this through."

Bob agreed, elbowing Liz, who snarled her reluctance. Campbell offered up his cuff, and Sue flourished a switchblade, cutting off the plastic shackle. Bob opened his door and began exiting.

"What about me? Cut me loose! God damn it Bob, take me with you!" Lizard was writhing, skin flushed, eyes ablaze—her virality on full display.

Bob looked at Sue, who shook her head, a presidential veto. "Can't do it, Lizzy. Be right back, OK honey?" Cowboy leaned in for a kiss, a peck of support. Red with wrath, Liz head-butted him hard. Bob sniffed back a nosebleed and backed away from the Humvee.

Hart Plaza was infested with Virals. Some held weapons,

some waved torches. It was after midnight. Sue stood beside him and pointed to the barge, the push boat and its rifle-toting captain. "We need to get aboard that barge. We'll die here if we don't."

"But what about Toledo? The Red invasion? All that talk about Defend Detroit?"

"It's true, they're a threat. But tonight the bigger danger is from cold and hunger. There have been deaths already. We need to move. Movement is life."

"But whose boats are they? And where will they take us?"

"You ready for this?" Ol' Sussana grinned.

"Try me."

"Antiva sent them. The execs are offering shelter and food at their MPC refinery."

"*Anti*-Virals sent them?" Sue nodded.

"To us? To every fucking Viral left in Detroit?" Another nod.

"And you *trust* them?" Bob pictured the starvelings helpless in the barge. "Ever heard of concentration camps? Poison gas? Zyklon B? Sue, they'll murder us. Dump our bodies in the river, declare a victory, a final solution!"

"Bob, I don't think so. *He* doesn't think so." She nodded to Walker, nodding out in the passenger seat. "My Marines don't think so, and neither do their crows."

Bob was struck dumb at her dumb-assery. *Confirmation from crows? A crippled senile? Mutant fucking skeletons? A Constitution-quoting "president?"* It was all too much, it really was.

"Let me ask you this, Sue. What exactly does Antiva get from this deal?"

Sue's brown eyes met his blues. "Those oil execs are shitting themselves. They fear the CORPS more than we do; they've got a lot more to lose. What do they get, you ask?" She gestured at the well-ordered squads of infected, the torch-wielding host, the packed Plaza and the embarkation line snaking along the Riverwalk. "They get an Army of the Dead."

Cowboy put himself in the Shinola shoes of Antiva's executives.

"Zombies, Bob, they get fucking zombies. All they have to do is feed us and transport us. We'll do their dirty work, and they know it."

"And what do you get?"

Presidential, Sue declared, "Another day or two of life? Maybe liberty for some low-loaders like you? And for the rest of us—*inshallah*—if we survive, we get to pursue some kind of half-assed happiness before we die."

Fuck it. Cowboy was in. Anything to avoid another quote. Sussan, run down, looked relieved at his acquiescence.

"So, what exactly am I doing?"

She looked at the international bridge, medieval in the moonlight. She pointed at the barge captain, his rifle, his rancor. "You're our ambassador, Bob. Get us aboard. Get us food and shelter. Get us the fuck out of here."

Cowboy nodded, tapping a hip where his holster should be. Sue, well-regulated, shook her head; she'd keep his pistols. Bob would bear no arms, not tonight anyway.

From the shadows, Dan, the Marine spotter, tracked the Amish-hatted man as he turned from Sue towards the barge. "Keep that fucker in your sights, Roy."

His shooting partner held his crosshairs on Cowboy, grunting in agreement.

A Mug Up

THE BEAVER ISLAND CAPTAIN rested his rifle on the rail, itching to pull the damn trigger. Douchebags of disease lined the Riverwalk, licking their chops for a bite. So help him, he'd shoot the first fucker to step on his barge. Antiva's oily execs had ordered this pickup, but Doyle needed answers, and so far, he'd had none. Baptiste had babbled something about the boy and his loons? Like a twist of old rope, big Frenchie was fraying.

Doyle's deckhand cupped his hands, calling up, *"Capitain!* There's a man here. *Un ambassadeur.* He wants a word?"

Doyle squinted, saw a hatted man on his gangplank. Dude's hands were held high, no weapons in sight. "Stay the fuck away from him! He's infected. I'm coming!"

Doyle stomped along the empty barge to the gangplank. He handed the voyageur his rifle: "Cover me." He pushed the crewmember aside, facing the newcomer alone. Doyle kept the breeze at his back. If the Viral was shedding, he'd steer clear of the drop-zone. They eyed each other, silvered by moonlight.

"Ya don't look infected to me," Doyle observed gravely from the barge.

"Not so bad yourself," Gangplank replied.

"You Viral?"

"Used to be. Don't know what I am anymore."

Amen to that. Their first point of agreement.

"Captain, it seems we might need each—"

"Bull-fucking-shit! You filthy Spreaders need *me*, and the refinery weasels need *you*, but ol' Tommy Doyle needs none of this shit, 'cept to get the fuck home!"

Something clicked in Cowboy's brain—*no fucking way*. Bob recalled his recent crossroad conversation with Bear, that oversized dude and his skinny friend he and Lizzy conned. *"You're* Doyle? From Beaver fuckin' Island?"

Clouds scudded past the moon, casting shadows—silver, then gray. Tom squinted for recognition, finding none. He'd never met this gunless slinger before. Doyle half-raised his hands to halt him, but the hatted man kept shooting. "You're that Captain Judas? The betrayer, left them stranded in Charlevoix to die."

Doyle flushed. If he had his rifle, he'd swing it; bash this bastard's brains all over the Riverwalk. RPMs revving, heart hammering, Tom sought serenity—the wave lap and gull cry of Goose Island. Born again, breathing deeply, St. Thomas, for once, took the high road, nodding as he acknowledged, "That's me." Falling quickly from grace, he added, "Now who the fuck are you?"

Cowboy had him riled. Time to press the advantage, gouge him good; Bob sighed instead, too beat for brinkmanship. "I'm worse."

A standoff of sinners, the fallen stood face to face. The moon, impartial, played hide and seek in the clouds. The two men, sick of hiding, sought the light in each other, finding a glimmer.

"Tell me true, stranger, you contagious? Got the Covee? Been stung?"

Cowboy laid his cards on the table. "Variant killed my family. My wife, my little girl. It had me too, but let me go."

"Let you go, eh?" Doyle remembered the bridge battle: the Spreader on his boat, the faceful of virions, his kamikaze collision.

Bob addressed Doyle's doubt. "I reckon so. Maybe I was healed by Chow, or scoured clean by this water-walker? Honestly Captain, I just don't know."

"Chow, you say? You know that Natty doctor, do ya?" Doyle sneered, couldn't help it, no love lost between white collar and blue. "And what should I call you?"

"Call me Campbell, Bob Campbell."

Time was a wasting. Cowboy felt the hunger of the red-eyed host behind him, the crosshairs of the Gorie sniper, Sue's attention to his every damn move. "There somewhere we can talk, Captain? Got a mask you can wear?"

Yes there was, and no he hadn't. Doyle's gut urged him to trust.

"Let's have a mug-up, Bob Campbell. Get outta this goddamn cold."

Doyle's deckhand guarded the gangplank, keeping the hissing horde at bay. *Debbie's* wheelhouse fumed as a can of Sterno heated river water. The two men stayed silent till the beany brew was ready, eyeing each other over chipped mugs of expired Army coffee.

"Got a smoke, Campbell?"

Sure wished he had. Bob shrugged, sipped, and grimaced. Doyle grinned crookedly, the connoisseur of crap coffee taking a gulp. "How exactly do you know me?"

Campbell, caffeinated, spilled the beans: Chow's isolated cabin, the she-elf's rage, man-bear's mopey confession.

Doyle perked up. "Little red cabin, bars on the windows, hidden by dunes?"

Bob nodded. "Know it?"

Doyle did. "My Da built the fucking place, conceived me there too."

"No shit?"

"No shit."

More sips. More silence.

Campbell finally said, "I've heard your voice before."

"You don't say."

"Oh, but I do."

A warm summer night, bossing Chosen, Petoskey, River Road, Mikey's fucked up fox-hunt, radio transmissions: shore-to-ship and ship-to-shore.

Campbell continued, "I overheard two voices that night. I'd swear one was yours; the other we called Crow."

"Crow, eh?" Doyle, post-trauma, stressed his past disorder. "Those were crazy times, Campbell. Do I regret what I've done? Keith Two-Crow was an Indian, born on-island. Too late, he became a friend of mine. And yer right. I left him, left them all. Honest? I'd probably do it again."

Cowboy sighed and took off his Amish hat, dragging filthy fingers through filthier hair. "Collapse'll do that. I know, 'cause it happened to me. A hundred times. All the good ones are gone. Like your Keith."

"No offense, Campbell, to you or your Chosen, but ol' Crow went out with a bang. Night before he died he mined a road, blew a bunch of your bastards to hell. Saw the flashes from the tower. Heard thunder booming too."

Bob made a mental note to keep Liz away from this guy. She'd lost two lovers in that ambush—lechers Lacy and Hammer. She'd lost her looks, half her hair, and her left titty too.

"Ya don't say?"

But Doyle did. "Keith survived it. Tough ol' bird, 'Nam vet, you know the type. Diana's ferry picked him up outside the breakwater."

"With me locked inside."

Doyle blinked. "With you locked inside. Me and my captains stopped 'em at the harbor. Didn't know about them Greenies, feared they were all Spreaders."

"And your friend Keith?"

Doyle shook his head. "Didn't make it."

Campbell remembered the ferry engines, his chafing shackles, the singing, the rifle shot. Bob backed off. His own history was a minefield, plenty of places he wouldn't go.

"Well Cap'n, thanks for the coffee," Bob said, emptying his mug. "But the question remains: will you have us? May we come aboard?"

Doyle knew he should say yes. Why fight it? The ferry, the Judas tower, the betrayal. His misdeeds decided him, yet still he resisted. Fuck these Virals! And fuck these Anti-Virals too! Fuck anyone from off-island—his Da's lesson rang true. "Look Campbell, all I want is to go home. Be a better husband, a better friend. I've got a niece, name's Maggie. And there's fishin' to do."

"I get it Doyle. I really do. Antiva, Reds, Old Law, Virals. Too many players, and you ain't on a team."

"You understand, then?"

"Look man," Bob tapped the bulkhead, "we're in the same fucking boat. I'm no true believer and I don't pick sides. I try an' do what feels right because I don't like feelin' wrong, not anymore."

"But what the hell feels right?" Doyle wanted to know.

Campbell didn't have to lie, a relief. "*Walker* feels right. Least he did, old dude is pretty messed up."

Doyle drained his mug, grudging his guest a salty grin. "Ain't we all."

"Amen."

"So, what? Walker heals people? Cures their Covee? Soothes their sting?"

"Something like that. I've seen some shit I can't explain. But what do I know?"

"More than me anyway." Doyle paused for a moment, deciding. "Look Campbell, I'm responsible for my crew." He nodded at the rifle-toting voyageur and Baptiste's boats in the river. "Your Spreaders can board the barge, but they stay the fuck away from everyone else."

Bob the ambassador indicated agreement.

"Oh, and we might not make it to Rouge River, to the refinery. We're down to fumes and the river's full of hazards. We got no food, no medicine. I can't vouch for those slimeball execs neither. Whole thing could be a trap. Honestly, I don't fucking know."

Cowboy stood, tipped his hat, and exited the cramped wheelhouse. "Par for the course, Cap'n Doyle. Par for the fuckin' course."

Doyle cursed, starting up the engines. *Debbie* sputtered, coughing on dirty diesel.

Winona and the Big Oil Windigo by Jason Clark

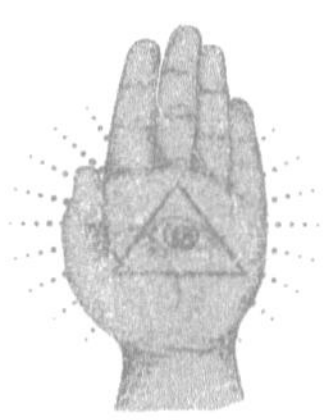

Jumping Off

MAJOR NAZ KEPT ONE EYE ON HIS FORCES, the other scanning the data-stream on his smart-patch—dumbed down, alas, since the great EYE had dimmed. So far, so good anyway, only sixty miles to Detroit. The rising sun illuminated the first bridge he must cross. The Maumee River, still in shadow, slipped silently towards Lake Erie. Tonight, the moon would be full.

His army had decamped at twilight, traveling all night on 280 North. The two attack helicopters, for now, were left behind on the weedy tarmac with their pilots and a radio. Left behind as well, Naz hoped, was the boredom and the boozing. They'd been in camp for a week; the region's Reds had rallied. Each day brought new fighters, called to arms by Kamul's broadcast. Each day brought fistfights between macho militias.

Just as dawn broke, General Kamul, the CORPS commander in D.C., utilized Palantir, summoning Naz with the sat-phone. "Everything ready in Ohio, Major?"

"Yes sir. We're ready."

"What's your count then, men and vehicles? Do you have enough?"

"General, your broadcasts have helped, and the killing of Walker. I put our militia at a thousand. We've got about a hundred vehicles."

"Nice work, Major. And your fuel? Can you reach the refinery? Latest intel says the plant is still pumping."

"Depends on I-75, sir. If the road is clear we'll make it, but barely. If there's fighting, it's trickier. There's simply not enough gasoline."

"Lima Charlie, Major. Anything I can do from D.C.? Anything from the CORPS?"

Naz paused, considering. The "Confederacy" of Red and Patriotic States was a seaboard affair. Six hundred unsecured miles stretched between his irregulars and Philadelphia, the nearest fist of Red Hands. When Naz first received his orders, General Kamul had been clear. The major and his militia would have to live off the land. Naz must mobilize local assets to fuel his hostile takeover of the Midwest. The CORPS was too far away for resupply. As America's population flatlined, its geography had grown.

"What about close air support, sir? Bust up any obstacles on our road to the refinery? Warthogs? Gunships? Drones? Fuel drops? Anything would help."

"Now, Major, you know I can't do that. You're on your own out there, Naz. You knew the deal. You've got two pilots and two helos. That's a hell of a lot more than most militias. Don't make me regret attaching those assets to you."

"You won't regret it, sir. We're at the Maumee now. We'll cross the Michigan border later this morning. With any luck, we'll be refueling at the refinery by sunset tonight."

"Bravo Zulu, Major. Once you've refueled, I expect a final push on Panzer. Doctor Schark must be neutralized. His special project, and all her files, must be secured for further research, highest priority. Good luck and Godspeed."

Kamul ended the call, Palantir going dark.

Major Naz powered down his satellite phone, replacing the handset in its charger. He'd met her once, this "special project" that so captivated the R and D branch of the CORPS. She'd been dining with the pill-doctor, dressed in black and dopey with drugs. The blood sample he'd taken contained anomalies. More interesting still was the security video of her encounter with Aghori; anomaly was an understatement. Whether throwback or some future breed, Ms. Nighthawk was special, a superhuman in these far-from-super times.

But there were many rivers between Naz and Schark's Kalamazoo compound: first Maumee, then Ottawa, then Raisin. Each of these, and twice as many creeks, complicated his approach to the refinery on the Rouge. He must cross them carefully, one at a time, starting with this one.

Toledo's Skyway Bridge was newly constructed. It spanned eight thousand feet across the muddy Maumee. A single pylon carried six lanes in and out of Toledo. Naz looked at his wristwatch, synchronized with AYE EYE. His militia would commence crossing in one minute. The major hated bridges, their constriction increasing his vulnerability. If the Skyway was held against them, they'd find out pretty quick.

Naz put his eye to the spotting scope as his vanguard—flying crimson flags and Confederate gray—began to cross. The Thumbs, those "badasses from Bad Axe," were the lead vehicle: a dubious reward for destroying Walker and his busload of Panthers.

The major watched for muzzle-flash. There was none. So far, so good. What a sloppy way to proceed. Done properly, he'd have recon units already across and a reinforced bridgehead. He'd have aircraft overhead, rotary and fixed-wing, to shepherd his faltering flock. Instead, he had a van stuffed with fatties. Pedal-to-the-metal, they swerved around obstacles and were soon across. Surprised by survival, the Bad Axers raised shaky thumbs at their followers. The rusty rest ran the bridge's gauntlet. In ten minutes, his crimson column—all one hundred—had made it safely across.

Major Naz checked his paper map against the flickering EYE. Step one, they'd managed the Maumee. Naz had feared being bottled up in the burbs; instead, the Toledo War had been bloodless. In two miles, they'd merge onto I-75 North towards

Detroit. A mile after that, they'd be exposed again, another river obstacle, the Ottawa this time. If they avoided ambush, it was two miles to Michigan's border. After that, the terrain was less complicated, advantaging the attacker.

His data patch dinged with a message generated by his implant, his permanent halo. True, the pentagon's EYE had dimmed—lack of wattage, lack of WiFi—but the large language model could still plagiarize text:

Nobody ever defended anything successfully, there is only attack and attack and attack some more.

No sources were cited, but Naz knew his Patton; "Old Blood and Guts" wasn't wrong. During collapse, the mighty US military had fractured, Blues playing defense while Reds, led by Kamul, went aggressive. The blitzkriegers had triumphed. Blue officers and politicians were executed for sedition, a necessary evil, death by firing squad.

Blues that surrendered—bringing valuable equipment, intel, or vehicles—were amnestied. Nicknamed Purples, they had to prove loyalty to the CORPS. The quickest path from Purp to Red was to kill a fellow Blue. There'd been plenty of volunteers. Wiping Blue blood from their hands, turncoats were assigned to Red fists.

Major Naz and his halo calculated fuel consumption. They just might make it. He wondered at the lack of resistance. The rallying of Red militias in Toledo was no secret. Kamul's broadcasts, by necessity, had been unencrypted and sent in the open. Where then was Michigan's National Guard? Where was Antiva? The Panthers? Had killing Walker decapitated their defenses?

Again, so far so good. Interstate 280 was clear, his column was moving. His two helos, his metallic beasts, had not yet been needed, saving fuel, saving ammo. Local defenders—if there were any—had missed their chance. Out his window, he observed the charred remains of Toledo's Correctional Institute.

The max security prison, like many during collapse, had been ravaged from within. Covee and its stinger played favorites, sparing violent felons. R and D was working on it. Until Naz heard otherwise, his standing orders were to kill all Virals. The Reds weren't immune, not yet anyway. A single cough could kill his whole force.

His column advanced, as did the sun. The Buckeye sky was clear but cold—perfect football weather—with the temperature near freezing. Dark clouds gathered in the east, hinting at snow, a traditional trick for their Halloween treat.

The Valiant

DATE TIME GROUP: 310900ROCT21

LOCATION: MICHIGAN-OHIO BORDER

Amanda Taylor, from her command turret, signaled halt. They'd made it to the border, but had they made it in time? Her mixed column of desert-tan Humvees, blackened Panther trucks, and Antiva vans coasted to a stop with a gassy sigh.

Crews sprinted to relieve themselves. Some stood while they sprayed, some squatted. Others sought privacy behind bushes and barricades. Belts were unbuckled, camo pants tugged down. Human waste, evacuating warm bodies, steamed in the cold morning air.

Sergeant Taylor shaded her eyes against the rising sun while surveying their position. It was the best spot she'd seen. If Reds were indeed rolling north, they'd be coming up I-75. She'd stop them here, at the border. Outnumbered, she needed the advantage of terrain.

Facing south, Shantee Creek guarded her left flank while Halfway Creek protected her rear. On both sides of the interstate, fenced farmland provided her cannon crews with clear fields of fire. Anticipating action, the Michigan alum read the fading billboard aloud: "Welcome to Pure Michigan—" Taylor, class of '97, couldn't help adding, "—you Ohio assholes."

It had taken three days. Most of the roads had been a mess, and the column had crawled to save fuel. Overly cautious, she'd called halts for reconnaissance; avoiding ambush was Taylor's highest priority. Their rendezvous with Antiva had slowed them down as well. She had no direct comms with the refinery or their fleet of vans. Colonel Dennis, up in Ignace, had patched things through. All in all, a shit-show, but at least the Anti-Virals had shown. Her mission objective was to defend the refinery and repulse the damn Reds. Hopefully they still had time.

Her cannoneers, well-trained, knew the drill. Fire support teams deployed the unit's towed howitzers with banners flying—blue shields and golden griffins. In an hour, they could all be dead. *Bring it!* Taylor raised her fist, calling out, "Yield to none! The yellow and blue!"

Her crews felt it too, the old fuck-it feeling. "Yield to none! Hurrah! Hurrah!"

Taylor checked the layout, part of her game-day routine: the 105mm guns were well-layed, ammunition at hand. The guardsmen had staked out camo netting. Any Reds rolling north were in for a surprise.

Four Antiva vans had attached themselves to her force. Taylor would use them as cavalry. Each one mounted a machine gun behind an armored sliding door. The vans would screen the howitzers and prevent Red Hand infantry from groping.

A-Team's van was lead vehicle, Ayesha its nervous driver. She attended as Sergeant Taylor went over their role. "I want your vans out of sight. Use that copse of trees as cover."

"Yes, ma'am." *Cops?* Ayesha looked sideways for police.

"Not a ma'am, I'm a sergeant." Ayesha nodded through her nausea, pre-game jitters.

Taylor continued, "We have to hide the Humvees. Our cannon crews will be on foot; if Reds break through, it's up to you Antivas to protect them, pull them out. Understood?"

"Yes, Sergeant."

"Another thing, Ayesha. Those 105s are the best chance we have. Don't ruin their surprise. Stay out of sight, but watch the billboard." Taylor pointed to a pair of signals specialists scaling its ladder, trailing semaphore flags as they climbed.

"We assume the Reds will be scanning. So stay off the radio, we'll use Wig Wags instead."

"*Wigs*, Sergeant?" Ayesha's tummy flopped.

"Old school, study this." Taylor handed over a NATO cheat sheet. "Keep eyes on that signaleer. Got this, Antiva?"

Seriously? The only thing Ayesha *got* was the feeling she was screwed. "Got it, Sergeant." Taylor gave the twenty-something driver a hard look. The lives of her Griffs depended on this graffiti-girl from Gratiot.

Ayesha, proud, wore her tattoos—gang and prison—like Taylor wore her stripes. If it hadn't been for Walker, Amanda might have ended up the same, or worse. Walker had saved her from the streets. Reading her superior, Ayesha asked, "You really think He's dead?"

Damn. Taylor swallowed. "I'm afraid so. But we can do this, Ayesha. We have to." Eye to eye, they sized each other up, then parted. Time to get on with it. Ayesha hid her vans, and looked over the NATO codes while sharing a final joint with her A-Team.

Taylor, the head coach, made her rounds. Panthers and their trucks would hold the bridge behind them. In case of retreat, they'd serve as rearguard. She stashed her fuel tanker—stolen from Sharkey—further back, *victori spolia.* A thousand gallons of unspoiled diesel to whichever side proved victorious.

The Griffins, Army-fluent in HUAW, had completed the *Hurry Up;* now gun crews lounged through the *Wait.* The sun labored above brown fields. Cold light sparkled on nearby creeks. The breeze was slight. A darkness gathered in the east as clouds collected lake-effect snow from Erie's updraft.

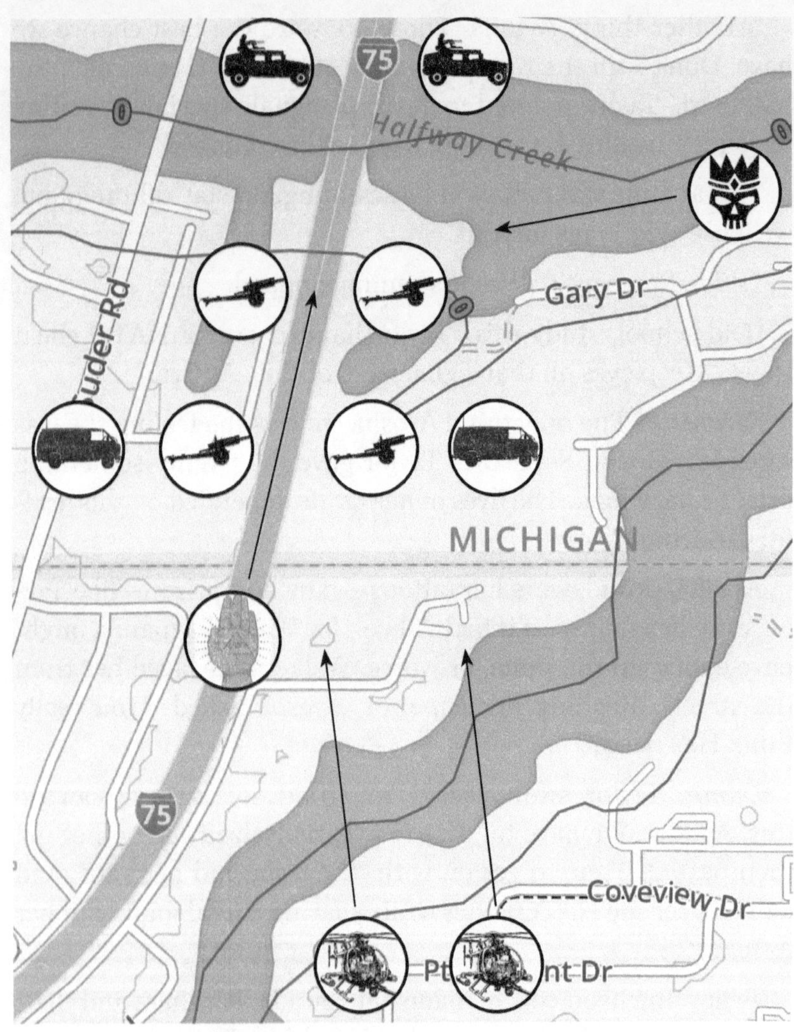

No sign of bird or beast, the borderlands were listening. Sergeant Taylor, half-dozing, was listening too. Her gunners played cards, betting stale candy. A football was passed between camouflaged cannon. Sterno-stench wafted over the dug-in battery as hungry soldiers heated chow, gambling for favorite MREs.

No thrum of engine, no clanking tread or buzzing drone. Amanda heard her teacher's voice. Mr. Lincoln walked through her mind: *I will prepare and some day my chance will come.*

Eyes closed, she scrutinized her mental map—*prepare*. The placement of the guns—*prepare*. The cannon crews—*prepare*. The strategic bridges—*prepare*. She inventoried her irregulars, Panthers and Antiva, their positions—*prepare, prepare*. That *some day* was today. Their *chance* was now.

She felt a disturbance and opened both eyes. Signal flags fluttered from the billboard. Black wings fluttered from the trees. Crows, ever-calculating, began to congregate in the cheap seats, beady eyes counting on carnage, on carrion. Her signaleers, high above and hidden from the enemy, could see around the bend. Taylor stood up and her soldiers followed, facing the flags. Was it time? The Griffs, adrenalized, policed up their chow, tightened chinstraps, and checked each other's body armor.

Ayesha, in her van, tried translating what she saw: an all-red flag with a bite out of it? A barred square of red/yellow/red? Then a white one with five little crosses? This last one, raised twice? Heart hammering, she consulted her cheat sheet: *Bravo-One-Zero-Zero? What the fuck? Taylor!*

Sergeant Taylor scanned the hoists, reciting: "Enemy in sight. Vehicle count: one hundred." She glassed the highway, but could see nothing yet, not from her vantage. The gun crews watched their coach. Taylor raised her right arm vertically, palm forward, waved a horizontal circle then pointed to her boots: "Assemble on me."

The Griffins hustled over, huddling up. Taylor eyed the Michigan billboard, its signaleer: *Vans-First-Red-Thumbs*. She inspected her guardsmen—eyes dilated, high on epinephrine. Dosed by danger, they looked pretty good. Silent, the semaphore continued: *RVs-Buses-Red-Hands-Warning*.

Walker's spirit was with her. They used to wordsmith slogans after Sunday school, trading rhymes, comparing couplets. Amanda had a verse in her head. Had he put it there? Sure sounded like him. She spoke to the gathered battery, her veteran team:

"Let them come, in their gray and crimson!" Taylor pointed south towards the unseen enemy, then up at the Welcome sign. "These Ohio State fuck-eyes will be stopped by Pure MICHI-GAN!"

Her cannoneers, badged in yellow and blue, raised gloved fists and ROARED! Red pennants began to appear on I-75. She dismissed gun crews to their howitzers, waited while they acquired targets, then hand-signaled the kickoff, "Commence Fire!"

A split-second later, their cannon ROARED too.

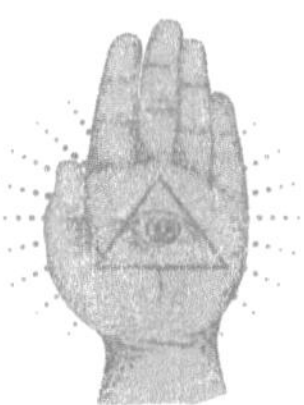

Brutus and The Beasts

THE SUN CLIMBED AS DISTANCE SHRANK: sixty miles to the refinery, then fifty, then forty-five. Naz's force had crossed the water obstacles: Maumee, then Mud Creek, then Ottawa and Shantee. Not a single bridge had been held against them. Their intel about Guard units and Antiva might have been wrong. Major Naz was fine with that. The real fight would be at the refinery.

Still, he wished he had air cover, or a drone-feed, or cavalry scouts at least. He checked his data patch; the EYE was blank. The major hated driving blind, but his dwindling supply of gasoline forced him to improvise. The attack helicopters had siphoned all remaining fuel from his empty cargo plane. Their pilots, call-signed *Panic* and *Terror,* were standing by. Naz was saving the two beasts for his final assault on the Rouge and its refinery.

I-75 curved away from the coast. The Shoreland subdivisions were left behind. Fallow farmland, some of it fenced, opened up ahead of the column, a quarter mile more to "that state up north." Naz could see the sign through his spotting-scope, *Welcome to Pure Michigan!* The borderland was deserted. Low in the east, storm clouds loomed. The only sign of life was a flurry of black birds.

The van, all Thumbs, was in the lead. The Red Hand column entered the long straightaway. Straight away, they were fired upon.

The Bad Axers were first to be chopped, *Ka-Whumpf!* Their van was blown in half, its occupants reduced to fodder, minced meat for crow-pies.

The shockwave shoved Naz to his seat. Another quickly followed, *Ka-Whumpf!* A bus full of blowhards was blown to bits. A racist mist was all that remained.

Ka-Whumpf! Ka-Whumpf! An RV of Reds. A pickup of Prouds. Both vehicles vaporized by high explosive shells.

Ears ringing, Naz pulled himself together. This was direct fire! The gunners were close. God damn it! The price of driving blind. Immediately he was on the radio, "Vanguard, dismount! Secure those guns! Everyone else, reverse! Get back around that bend!"

Naz knew the enemy crews were reloading. He counted the seconds, guessing a four-gun battery. When his count hit 20 he braced, here they come: *Ka-Whumpf! Ka-Whumpf!* More fireballs, more flaming bits of meat. A pregnant pause, then, *Ka-Whumpf! Ka-Whumpf!* His vehicle count kept dropping.

Had to be guardsmen? These gunners were good! His vanguard had halted. Red militia, some shit-stained, were diving for cover. Naz calculated: each gun was firing three rounds per minute. A battery of four meant he'd lose twelve vehicles every sixty seconds. In eight minutes, he'd have nothing left!

He swiveled his naked eye. The column was reversing, re-crossing the border: *Ohio, "Find it here!"* Now or never. Major Naz tugged at his eyepatch, radioing his beasts, *"Panic, Terror,* this is *Witch King,* over."

His data eye, dead-looking, winked at the call sign. Halloween. He'd beat that "team-up-north" with a pair of bladed broomsticks.

Naz's lead vehicles had halted, spilling their fighters. Soon every car would be a coffin; they were better off on foot. A big brute led the charge, ex-military, a Keeper from Ohio. Eager for End Times, he'd recruited fellow vets, battle-buddies who took their oaths seriously. They'd prepped hard, surviving Covee intact. Their purpose survived as well: "To defend against all enemies, foreign and domestic."

Hunkering through collapse, they had weapons, had radios. They'd found Kamul, and Kamul found them enemies. The Keepers had been bored by apocalypse. Without platforms, without shit-posts, what's the point in posturing? Being fired upon fired them up. A border battle was perfect for Brutus and his boys. Wide-eyed and stinking, they planned their assault. Brutus looked them over. He had half a hundred fighters badged in Buckeye scarlet and Butternut gray.

Ka-Whumpf! Ka-Whumpf!

More anatomies were atomized as two more vans exploded. But Brutus saw the battery, the flash, the smoke. Huddled up, the team captain diagrammed X's and O's in the dirt. Showed his men how they'd approach, where to toss grenades, how many seconds to wait before mopping up the mess. He gave his squad a final inspection. Some were drunk, some spattered with shit, but most were ready. Good enough. Time for kickoff.

"We're gonna drive down that field," Brutus said, indicating their route.

They thumped each other's body armor. "Hit them hard!"

They banged helmets and steel-plates. "See how they fall!"

Bullet-heavy magazines were inserted with a *clunk*.

"Smash through to victory."

Grenades were pouched and ready. "Fight till the end!"

"*Their* end, you mean!" a squad member cried out.

"Damn right! Blue bastards!" yelled another.

The militiamen, eager, looked to Brutus. Their NCO was on the radio with Naz: "Roger, *Witch King*. We'll wait. Helos inbound my position." Brutus grinned at his men, whirling a thick finger. The rotary beasts were airborne, flight time: sub two minutes. "Smoke 'em if you got 'em," he told his squad. The

Buckeyes crowed with laughter, as factory cigs had been the first thing to go.

From a flayed tree, inky birds, scenting blood, crowed too. Storm clouds gusted nearer, freighted heavily with snow.

The Storm Breaks

DATE TIME GROUP: 311000ROCT21

LOCATION: MICHIGAN-OHIO BORDER

Welcome to Pure Michigan! proclaimed the sign. Two signals specialists positioned on its catwalk—a press box—called the play-by-play of the battle below. The Griffins—Yield to None—had rolled back the Red carpet. They semaphored the SITREP down to their sergeant below: *Tango-Delta: Two-Four.*

Sergeant Taylor, FO for the battery, hand-signed the score to her shooters: *24-0.*

Her gunners cheered the kill count and kept firing: time to run up the score. Eyeing the opponent through her binoculars, Taylor—the defensive coordinator—was nervous. Most of the attackers had escaped south around the bend. Indirect fire was iffy, and they had no rounds to spare.

A Red assault was forming. If their running game got going, her defense was in trouble. She glassed their team captain, a big brute with discipline. The Reds had broken their huddle, inching up the field using cover—three yards and a cloud of dust. They were almost in the red-zone. When they charged, Ayesha had better be there with her cavalry. Well-hidden, the Antiva vans were still out of sight.

The storm front clouded nearer, swallowing the sun. Spectators, beady-eyed and black-feathered, flocked around the field. Crow-calls heckled the contestants as the sharp day dulled to sudden dusk. A cold wind was blowing. *Thud-thud-thud* could be heard, not thunder but rotors. The sound of chopping blades cut Sergeant Taylor to the bone.

Signal flags were flying, furious from the press box: white/red; blue/red; quartered yellow/black; yellow/red diagonal; white crossed by blue; yellow/red/yellow.

Thud-thud-thud, her heart kept falling. Voices on the wind grew louder. *Hotel-Echo-Lima-Oscar-XRay-Two.*

Taylor translated the signal-hoists: *Inbound-Helo-times-two.*

Shit! A trick play! Taylor, panicking, raised palm to helmet, swinging her signal-arm up and down: *Cease Fire! CEASE FIRE!*

Her order was relayed, the cannons went quiet. She crossed her forearms above her head, once, twice: *AIR ATTACK!*

THUD-THUD-THUD! Approaching rotors bladed the sky. Then she saw them, two gray creatures snaking below the clouds, metallic talons heavy with assorted weaponry. Taylor recognized the aircraft; Boeing's AH-6 was called Little Bird. Through 10x binos she appraised their armament: 6-barrel miniguns, Hydra rocket-pods, and Hellfire missiles. Dragon's teeth had been painted on their snouts.

Alarm increasing, she raised her right arm above her shoulder, swinging it down: *TAKE COVER!* Griffin gun crews burrowed in the dirt, blind with fear, as the first rockets shrieked from above: *Whoosh-whoosh-whoosh!*

BAM! BAM! Ka-BOOM!

Two gouts of dirt and a direct hit on an ammo crate. One gun emplacement disappeared in a white-hot FLASH. Seconds later, seared flesh pattered down upon shell-shocked survivors. Throwing away weapons, the cannoneers fled—mowed into meat by merciless miniguns.

Brrrrriiip! Brrrrriiip! Brrrrriiip!

In each three-second burst, 300 bullets blazed forth. Vicious with velocity, the 7.62mm rounds ripped apart the runners. The gun crew, caught in the open, crumpled before they made it ten yards. The Griffins gawked. Taylor froze. The beasts fell upon them with gusto, and a feeding frenzy commenced.

Brutus leered, looking at his warriors: the brave, the bold. "Nothing like air cover, eh boys? Told you ol' Naz would come through!"

The Griffin guns had gone silent. Death from above—the passing game—had paralyzed the defense. Momentum shifting, Brutus called the next play. "Time for a frontal assault, boys, muscle against muscle. Sling your weapons, ready grenades, and follow me!"

Whoosh-whoosh-whoosh!

Ka-BOOM! BOOM! Ka-BOOM!

Another howitzer was hit. Another mess of wreckage, men and women melted to their molten machine. The Buckeyes roared a battle cry, "COME ON OHIO!"

Red militia followed the brute. Up and over, they drove down the field, busting up any Blues they encountered, fragging them with grenades then shooting them when they ran.

Pop! Pop! Pop! Another Griff was dropped, the lucky marksman stopping to take trophies. Blue dog tags and Michigan insignia could be traded for perks. Brutus and his boys stuffed their pouches with bloody bits—the coinage of the CORPS, Red currency of the realm.

The defense had been routed. A few were running north, out of range. Reaching the Welcome sign, Brutus looked about him. Major Naz had restarted the column; sixty or seventy vehicles were rolling their way.

The attack helicopters were beautiful as they blazed away at the Blues, *Brrrrriiip! Brrrrriiip! Brrrrriiip!* Bludgeoned by bullets, men and women were mushed into mud.

THUD-THUD-THUD! The twin Beasts bladed the blackening sky. Rocket fire shrieked from talon-pods. *Panic* and *Terror* stalked the gridiron, reaping those who ran.

"Someone's up there!" Brute's men were pointing. Sure-as-shit, two Griffs hid behind the billboard, spotters for the artillery annihilating their buddies. Potshots were taken, and betting odds as well.

"Cease fire! Cease FIRE!" Brutus banged on some helmets. "Let's do this proper. Rifle-line, on me. Form UP!"

His macho men pushed for position, taking aim at the twin targets above. "From left to right. One shot only. Bottle o' bourbon for a kill, stannnd-BY!"

The two Griff specialists flew their final signal—a surrender flag fluttered, all white against a storm-black sky.

"Aww, there goes our fun!" A Proud Boy lowered his rifle.

Brutus stomped over. "Bullshit!" He snatched away the man's carbine, shoving him aside. "Those Blue bastards have *OUR* blood on their hands!" Brutus took aim with the rest. "Left to right. Commence FIRE!"

Crack-Ping! Crack-Ping! Crack-Ping!

Bullets ricocheted off the steel platform. All misses. The Griffs dropped their truce flags and tried for cover. There was none. Death by exposure was real.

Crack-Ping! Crack-Ping! Crack-thud!

Winged by a Buckeye bullet, a wingless Griffin fell. The guardsman hit the ground, *Crumpf!* Reds ran over to paw at the body, pulling patches, pulling rank—*Ka-WRANG!*—the dead man's grenade, booby trapped, exploded. Brutus, grudgingly, gave the Griff props: "Some harakiri shit right there."

Naz's column was advancing, his hungry helicopters hunting prey. Time running out, Brutus called out, "Full auto! Together now! Grease that fucker!" *Kak-Kak-Kak-Kak-Kak-Kak-Kak!*

The remaining Guardsman, a woman, came apart at the seams. *Welcome to Pure Michigan!* The blue sign was splashed with arterial red.

Ayesha's van was tangy with puke. Two of her Antivas had tossed up their cookies. Another tossed away their weapon, opened a door, and ran. Things had fallen the fuck apart.

Thud-thud-thud! Those damn helicopters were still hunting; they'd fireballed two of her homies. Her van was well hidden, they hadn't found her yet. But she couldn't stay there. The sergeant had asked her—no, *tasked* her—to remain. But was Taylor still alive?

Ayesha doubted it. They were fucked. Cannon crews had been killed, the billboard had been bloodied. She was blind and alone and the bile-smell was unbearable. Her man on the roof started hammering—he'd seen something? Dude was yelling. She rolled down the window; the icy air helped.

"Runners! Ayesha, there's *runners!*"

"Ours or theirs?"

"Ours! Fuckin' ours! Ayesha, let's GO!" He swung in through the side door, eyes wild as the gusting weather. "FUCK!"

She craned her neck, saw no choppers. Then she floored the pedal and they WENT! The lifted van bumped over branches, crashing through a fence. They burst from cover, a black-painted rabbit, eyes peeled for death. Ayesha saw the runners: "There they are!"

A small squad of Griffs, led by Taylor, retreated north along the roadway, making for Halfway Creek Bridge. Panther trucks had been placed there, a rear-guard of last resort.

Thud-thud-thud!

Her heart rate increased. Ayesha stomped on the gas and they flew.

THUD! THUD! THUD!

The gray warbirds gathered—they'd seen her! The A-Team was fucked!

"Get that door open! Make room! Pull 'em inside!" Her crew obeyed, the big door slid open, I-75 raced by. Taylor's squad limped north to the bridge, was someone wounded? Her van raced to catch up. Both choppers pursued, a fusillade of shrieking.

Whoosh-whoosh-whoosh!

Bam! Bam! Bam!

Rocket fire cratered the concrete. Her windshield was spidered by jagged debris. Ayesha two-wheeled the van left, and then right. Shadowed by death, she double-booted the brakes. The beasties overflew her, then snaked around for the kill.

Taylor and her men were close: "Scoop 'em up!" Ayesha called out.

Bloody squad members tumbled aboard. Antivas grabbed the tourniquet-Griff by his harness, hauling his one-legged ass inside. "GO! GO! GO!"

The door slammed shut. Ayesha accelerated, bodies slamming against seats as the gutsy van galloped away. "Yee-haw! Motherfuckers!"

The van raced beneath the birdies. Surprised, the pilots pivoted again.

Three hundred yards to the bridge. Her mph approached sixty.

Thud-thud-thud! The choppers were gaining.

Two hundred yards. Her needle indicated ninety.

THUD! THUD! THUD! The birds stretched their wings, flying 150 easy.

"Where are those Panthers?"

Brrrrriiip! The flying beasts spat hot lead.

Brrrrriiip! Her back door was shredded, asses hanging in the wind.

One hundred yards! Her rpms redlined, no giddy-up left.

"Here comes the Prince!"

A black Humvee, with purple panthers on the hood, sprang to their aid. Music from before bumped from big speakers: *I would die for you, yeah Darlin', if you want me to, I would die for you!*

Armory-stolen, twin-fifties were elevated at the nearest chopper: *Ghak-ghak-ghak-ghak-ghak-ghak-ghak-ghak!* Brass tinkled from gun ports as angry tracers stung the fast flier. The two beasts, whistled back by their master, turned tail, slithering south to cover the advancing column of Reds.

"Fuck yeah, Prince!" The Antivas knew this cat. A bad mofo with a purple helmet crewed the heavy gun and flipped the departing birds his black birdie. Ayesha crossed Halfway Creek, pumped brakes and fishtailed around. Panthers still held this shoreline. She could see them now, black trucks well-concealed in firing-positions. The A-Team van was smoking: tires, radiator, and passengers too. Pale from panic, they passed a joint. *Holy fuck, they were still alive!*

Sergeant Taylor caught her breath, checked her wounded man, then sat shotgun by Ayesha. The two women shared a look, shaky with endorphins.

"Thanks," Ayesha said, trembling. She couldn't help it; they'd been fucking slaughtered. There were pieces of people all over the place. *Her* people. She was crying.

Taylor steeled her, nodding south. "It ain't over yet."

Three football fields away, dozens of crimson-flagged vehicles motored beneath the bloody billboard. The crow-crowd wasn't waiting. Feathered black, they rushed the field. Fair weather or foul, corvids had no friends, no favorites. Red or Blue, the flesh tasted the same—over-seasoned by industrial explosives—but still edible.

"Can't stop 'em, can we?"

Sergeant Taylor calculated, shaking her head. "Don't think so."

Ayesha fisted away her tears. "So what now?"

The A-Team was toking in the back. High on survival, they joked, sharing glances as the stumpy Griff was patched up. "Love ya man."

"I know it. Back atcha."

"You bet."

"How 'bout that Prince though?"

"Fuckin' A!"

"Dude's my hero."

Taylor had heard it all before: Anbar, Kandahar, and more recently, Clare and Kalamazoo. She answered Ayesha's question. "We keep going."

A minute or two is all they had. The horde advanced with the storm front. Soothed by second-hand smoke, time slowed for Sergeant Taylor. She'd have to detonate her diesel tanker, leave no spoils for the Reds. Find communications gear if she could. Radio the refinery, let them know what was coming. Her Griffs, forced-to-yield, had failed. The Reds would wreak havoc, not just here but all over Michigan.

Taylor reached for the door handle; time for final rounds. Ayesha stopped her, pointing southeast at the Morin Point peninsula. "You see that?"

"See what?"

Dark clouds had shoved ashore. Were there shapes in that storm? A loom of boats? A barge? Black hulls ghosted in the gloaming, then disappeared.

Taylor went cold. *Black ships? What's this now? Another fist of Red Hands?*

From the clouds came a barrage of white. The van roof, impacted, started to ping.

"Is that fucking hail?"

Taylor heard something else, ordering, "Roll down the windows!"

The A-Team listened. Faint cries could be heard and dim horns blowing. Ayesha pointed again, this time at the Reds. "They've stopped!"

So they had.

A murmur of many voices. Pellets iced the rusty hood. The maw of the storm gaped open, a barge ramp clanged down: red-eyed in the gloom, Devils Disciples came riding! A hacking, contagious cloud of gunfire and death. Mounted on motorcycles, the Virals enveloped Ohio's soft-skinned column, attacking the Red-blooded cell from all sides.

Was she stoned? Taylor flashed wild eyes at Ayesha. "Turn this thing around, ready your machine gun. Covering fire!"

Taylor jumped out to prepare her line-of-battle and was pelted by precipitation. It stung. She laughed aloud, "Hail? In October? Why not? Hail to fucking Michigan!" She energized her people—the leaders! The best! They pumped their fists with the storm, cheering their amphibious allies. Whoever these bikers were, they were fucking champions!

The Black Fleet

DOYLE HAD BEEN UP ALL NIGHT DRINKING INSTANT, his Irish temper boiling over. Since collapse, the navigation charts were shit, the many hazards unsigned. He carried a cargo of contagion and now this fuckin' storm. He'd never pushed a barge before and the big bitch had him nervy. Luckily, *Dirty Debbie* had done this before; ol' girl had mind of her own. Doyle was learning, decades too late, to let the fuck go.

The captain slurped his sludge, dead-reckoning position. The Ohio line drew near. He'd loosen up on Annie if he ever made it home. Give the gal some leeway, let her mind her own rudder. He'd been oversteering for years. It was a wonder she stayed spliced.

It had been a long and weary night since his mug-up with Bob Campbell. Doyle liked the guy, didn't care about his past. The loading of passengers had gone smoothly, Doyle and his crew staying the fuck away. Bikers, red-eyed, had rolled aboard with Harleys. Then came Campbell's Humvee, with his girlfriend—not half-bad—and the wounded preacher still inside. After that the Virals, many sickly, had boarded the barge.

Doyle, loud on the hailer, had been barking, "More bodies to starboard! Can't you feel she's listing?" He'd herded cats, infectious and hissing, till the barge ballasted even. He and his men stood behind glass, behind guns. The voyageurs tied scarves over their faces, staying upwind of the Spreaders while heading downriver.

"Stay on the bloody barge! None of you contagious cunts touch my tugboat!" The angry voice, a white one, was spitting from the speakers.

Sussan, their leader, their law, looked to her masses. Starving, shivering, they huddled for warmth. Segregated, denigrated, they sought President Sue for succor, though she had little to give. "Close those hatches now. Share your blankets, people! We can only survive this *together!*"

Devils Disciples tended their weapons, their chrome, and their wheels. The Marines, Dan and Roy, led conscripted Virals in combat drills:

"Squad!" Armed, the red-eyes attended their skull-faced instructors.

"Direct front!" Spreaders slowly shuffled to a firing line.

"Enemy vehicle!" They pictured a lynch mob of Reds, Confederate-flagged.

"Three hundred meters! Second team!" Half the squad took a creaky knee.

"At my command!" They set their sights on imagined justice.

"Commence fire!" A dozen dry clicks as hypothetical Klansmen were killed.

Confined in the barge, belly of a whale, the Jonahs—Lord-tested—felt the current take them. "Next stop, the refinery!" A few ragged cheers before the shivering returned. The cold steel stole their heat. Not so long ago, in the before, the barge had hauled grain; gleaning parties now gathered what they could in the gloom. Chef Raymundo lit a fire and ground the stale seeds, making a mush to warm them. The two Gories, *Semper Fi*, sniped rats and skinned 'em out, adding their protein to the pile.

With its belly full of virus, the rusty behemoth wallowed downriver. Ancient sturgeon, kin to stegosaurus, gave little heed to the barge above. Virals, especially the Detroiters, tried guessing their position as they were tugged into Zug River. They heard the squelch of megaphones, the clomping of the crew, hoses being dragged on deck, then smelled the sweet stench of diesel as their fleet refueled.

"Stay calm. Stay below." Sussan, presidential, soothed her sorry citizens. "This is Antiva turf and we've been redlined. Trust me, it's safer out of sight."

The last thing Sue needed was some activist—*Infected Lives Matter!*—crossing the picket line. They'd have their chance in battle to fight their way free. Walker and his healing had given them hope. They would beat back the Reds, steal their food, their vehicles, and maybe make their way south. Jim Crow was everywhere; infection the new Black, the Mason-Dixon had blurred. Sussan dreamt they could find somewhere warm, somewhere fertile. Exhausted and hypothermic, she mouthed the phrase, "Domestic tranquility." She could picture it, some promised land between a river and the sea. They'd turn their red eyes to the sun, gather milk and honey, and let nature's heat heal their many hurts.

Arriving at the plant, Doyle was shocked that the petro execs— white-collar fuckers—hadn't fucked him. True to their word, MPC had been generous, both with diesel and with weapons. Once they'd been refueled and rearmed, Antiva fighters, masked against infection, had jumped aboard, some with Doyle, some with Baptiste. Hazmatted, the Anti-Virals shoved the fleet and their contagious cargo back into the river. Next stop, Ohio!

Apparently, they had allies at the border. Scuttlebutt was that some guardsmen and their cannons were making a stand. Not in Detroit, not at the refinery, but down towards the state line. All night Doyle had inched along the coast with his fleet, his quarantined cargo. The plan was to find the Red bastards, land behind them, and turn the Virals loose. Good riddance, but then what? Besides the bikers and Bob's Humvee, the Spreaders looked pretty thin. Cannon fodder, he guessed. Antiva's plan all along?

If there was going to be a dawn, it would be breaking pretty soon. But maybe there wouldn't be? The storm's maw had swallowed them. Lake Erie was spitting: sleet, snow, and hail. Winds were increasing, the big barge—stubborn bitch!—was yawing. They'd be puking down below. Doyle, seeking shelter, rounded the cape of North Maumee Bay. He studied his nav-chart. If the Reds used I-75, they'd be somewhere nearby. He'd have to head upriver to find them, but which one? His thick finger traced three: Ottawa, Shallow, and Halfway. Each water-way was possible, but which was most probable? The highway crossed all three.

Flaming fuckery! Doyle undogged his hatch, looking land-ward for clues. Black sky above, black water below. A roar in his ears, cannon fire or the gale?

His marine radio beeped, channel 16. That bastard Baptiste breaking silence, any Red asshole could overhear! "*Dirty Debbie,* this is *Voyageur.* On this one, Tom? Over."

Ham-fisting the mic, Doyle growled, "*Debbie* here! Fuck you want, Frenchie?"

"My boy has found crows, a huge flock of 'em. Feeding on car-rion. Go around Morin Point, then up Halfway Creek. Over."

Jesus Christ! Not that fucking Loony again!

The boy had been right before, damn it. Loon found his blind ass on Lake Huron, clinging to a sappy pine. Doyle remembered his marooning and pointed a flashlight at his chart. Halfway Creek was damn shallow.

"Looks like there's a boat launch on the point, Frenchie. Gonna ground the barge, jury rig a ramp and offload. *Debbie,* out!" Tom slammed the mic, cracking its cradle, and squinted through the gloom. He'd have to find it first. Fuck!

Mopping Up

SOME DAY THEY'LL GO DOWN TOGETHER
they'll bury them side by side.
To few it'll be grief,
to the law a relief
but it's death for Bonnie and Clyde.
—Bonnie Parker, "The Trail's End" (1910–1934)

It had been a long fucking night of fuck-less arguing and Lizzy was furious. Cowboy Bob had blundered again, backing the wrong bitch. "Virals, Bob? You've committed us to Virals? Against Red Hands? Against the CORPS? Fuck YOU!" Hissing, the angry lizard had a point.

Nodding along, Campbell took stock. Reverend Walker, septic, was fading fast, succumbing to his wounds. During transit, Spreaders in the barge had been seasick, the stench of their puke still permeating the Humvee. He swore his new buddy Doyle was lost at sea. Storm-blind, Bob sensed their tug and barge had been weaving.

Then suddenly they'd run aground. Both Marines, skull-faced, began barking. Some kind of ramp had been rigged. The Disciples, red-eyed, mounted up and entered the fray on their motorcycles. Lizard was clawing for a better view, so Bob followed the crowd, driving their Humvee ashore.

The landing zone was uncontested. A skeletal Marine—Dan?—halted him while the Virals disembarked. "Get Walker in that turret! They'll follow Him anywhere." The jarhead pointed at the assembling Spreaders. Walker fumbled for the megaphone, propping himself, one-legged, in the open hatch.

Sounds of thunderous battle could be heard. The ground shook, concussed by heavy weapons, stabbed with flashes of light. The Harleys, already engaged, were blowing horns for backup. Apparently, there would be no dawn. Darkness grew with each gust of gale.

The Spreaders, terrified and malnourished, were holding back. The two Marines grunted them into squads and were signaling the Humvee to advance, frantic for Cowboy to lead the charge.

"Don't you fucking dare!" Liz warned him. "We need to surrender to the CORPS, ransom ol' peg-leg, and ride off into the Goddamned sunset together."

Bob couldn't do it. Just didn't feel right. And he was so fucking tired of feeling wrong. Then he heard singing. Walker's baritone, powerfully amplified. Preacher stood where the red-eyed masses could see him.

Mine eyes have seen the glory of the coming of the Lord.

Sussan and Raymundo joined in.

He is trampling out the vintage where the grapes of wrath are stored.

The music spread through the Spreaders. The Viral host weaponized their lungs, singing forth a contaminated cloud of virions.

He hath loosed the fateful lightning of His terrible swift sword.

Cowboy revved his engine, nodding at the Marines. Liz drew her pistol. "I'll fucking shoot you myself!"

With a violent move, Bob disarmed her. Wrenching open her door, he gave his good gal a shove, and out she tumbled. "You'll be better off without me! Goodbye Liz!"

He accelerated; Walker braced himself for balance. The Virals followed their preacher. Bob rode into battle, singing with the host.

Glory! Glory! Hallelujah!

 When the shock troops hit, his Red militias were shocked. Naz's radio whined with panicky reports: *Virals! Zombie bikers! Skeleton Marines! A black fucking fleet!*

Halloween had come, and with it came hail. His attack helos iced-up in the storm. His militiamen froze. Bewildered at the amphibious assault, most tossed away their weapons and ran. The tide had turned against them. Unmasked, with no PPE, the coming contagion filled them with dread. The Reds knew their doom was at hand.

Major Naz radioed his pilots, ordering them down. One of his noncoms, Sergeant Brutus, popped a smoke grenade, escorting his CO to the LZ. "Not our day, eh Major?"

Naz glared, gesturing Brute to follow. They ducked under the downwash, each man climbing aboard a bladed beast. Naz checked fuel and their munitions. He had one mission left. The AH-6 pilot said they could make it, but barely. Hail pinged off the canopy. "Sir, we need to lift off ASAP, we're taking damage."

The major acknowledged and away they went. He tasked his neural implant, his rare-earth halo, to make the calculations: from the Ohio line to Kalamazoo it was 130 miles—*As the crow flies.* Naz consulted his smart-patch, or more aptly, a *Hawk.*

Sussan counted their losses—*Alhamdulillah*, they'd been small. During the battle, some Disciples had been shot by Reds, some of her sickly footsoldiers as well. They prepared the dead as best they could, laying them out in a still-smoking crater. Some words were said, then dirt shoveled over. Marines took a knee, marking the mass grave—helmet, rifle, boots—with a battlefield cross. *Allah yarhamo. Allah yarhamha.* May God have mercy.

Sue saw their new "allies" were doing the same. Surviving Griffins, Antiva, and Panthers prowled the battlefield, policing up bodies and their various parts. The two forces—united by a common Red enemy—remained socially distanced. Her Virals were hot.

The sign—*Welcome to Pure Michigan!*—had been scaled. The dead Guardswoman, a wingless Griff, was lowered down. A bit of diesel was splashed, a Zippo clinked, and the blood-spattered billboard went up in flames. A beacon of battle, of their un-civil war.

Another corpse—her face and torso half-scarred—was interred in the same grave with KIA Griffins, though the body wasn't one of theirs. The imposter's stolen uniform fooled the recovery team—Elizabeth McGee, chameleon to the end. A few shovels of cold dirt snuffed Lizzy's fire for good.

Crows and coyotes were shot off the corpses. Hell, even Buckeyes deserved better. Hail had turned snow, shrouding the scene. So far anyway, Sussan witnessed no looting. The Marines and their rifle squads had secured the Red column. Raymundo and his helpers were sifting through the spoils. There'd be some food, at least for a while. But then what? They had their lives, at last some liberty, but what path to pursue? Sussan, daughter of immigrants, felt pulled towards the sun.

Sue believed in Walker, his touch, his cure. She could feel herself healing. She glimpsed the near future, the load-levels in her followers decreasing. Why not caravan some of these captured vehicles? Backtrack to Toledo and pillage Red supplies? Then they'd roll south, one gas tank at a time. A great migration in reverse. A Hajj towards healing, towards wholeness. Then find someplace warm and just live. They'd reap what they'd sow, *inshallah*. Put themselves in God's hands.

 Bob halted his Humvee at the Halfway Creek checkpoint. Campbell pulled off his bandana. Far from white, he waved it out the window. The Panther on the other side wore a purple helmet and an attitude: "The fuck you want, man?"

Good fucking question. Campbell sympathized, he really did. Walker, worse than ever, was laid out on the backseat. Once the bullets started flying, Bob had tugged the dude inside, pulling him from his pulpit. Bob hadn't seen Liz since giving her the boot. Hadn't even looked. Didn't want to. He wanted to get the fuck away.

"Let me talk to your leader, I got a wounded man here. Someone important."

Purple replied, "All you whiteys think that. Stay the fuck where you are!"

This wasn't working. Walker was dying, maybe dead. Road raging, Cowboy laid on his horn. Purple was pissed, the Panther climbing towards his fifties. A Griff sergeant marched over. From the north side of the bridge the woman glassed his Humvee, his dirty hanky. Bob showed both his hands, steady, not shaking.

He'd seen this sergeant before. Back at Clare, the airfield, she'd been sorting prisoners with Walker. Bob had spotted Hannah Hochstettler; he'd shouted to her. Of course he'd been tased. Non-Compliant, Cowboy was confined in the cold-ass container with Liz and her Lazy Boy.

The sergeant spoke sharply to the Panther. Purple nodded, then swung down from his truck, waving Bob forward. Had she recognized the Griffin-marked Humvee? Bob had stolen it from her after all. Would she hold that against him? Probably. So long as Walker got treatment, Bob didn't much care. Halfway across the bridge she stopped him, pulling on MOPP. Purple covered her with a shotgun; dude looked eager to shoot. The hazmatted sergeant approached, traffic stop-style, Porky the Pig.

"You contagious?" Her hand hovered near her pistol.

"Used to be. Don't think so anymore."

"Returning Army property?"

"Only borrowed. It's yours if you want it."

"Borrowed, eh? You're Bob Campbell, the jailbreaker from Clare. Where's the wounded woman? Liz McGee was her name."

"Yes ma'am, that's me." Cowboy tipped his Amish hat. "Don't think McGee made it." Least he could do. *Good luck Lizzy, if you're even alive?*

"Not a *ma'am*, I'm a sergeant. Now who's that in back?"

 Walker's impressions were of salt; he tasted it, smelled it too. That's what got him confused. He'd quoted Gandhi recently. A soupline? A crowded courtyard? Mahatma's Salt March to the sea:

We are entering upon a life and death struggle, a holy war; we are performing an all-embracing sacrifice.

"Hush now, Reverend. Hush."

He heard his student's voice. "Amanda?"

Was this Sunday school? He smiled. Cheek-to-cheek she pressed him. Walker tasted tears and opened his eyes. She'd grown so old. So how old was he? Her face was still fine, but furrowed by fatigue. Gray hairs escaped her helmet. Wearing sergeant stripes, she leaned over. He was on a stretcher in a Humvee. He scratched at the IV drip in his arm.

"Just saline. Reverend, leave it alone."

Salt on his cheeks, salt in his veins. He'd been bandaged. He'd been dosed. He looked around the cluttered interior, grateful for life. "Where's Mr. Campbell? Where's my cowboy?"

The tall man in the driver's seat removed his hat. Smudging a tear from his filthy cheek, he looked back. "I'm here, Mr. Walker. Thanks to you, man. We made it."

Walker was exhausted. He closed his eyes and overheard them making plans. "Thanks for the diesel, Ms. Taylor. Should be enough. Three hundred miles to the Straits and the Free North ferry."

"Campbell, you sure you got this?"

"Sergeant, I got it."

"How about an escort? Or a turret gunner at least?"

"No offense to your Griffs, but they'd just slow us down."

Cowboy, impatient, spurred the Humvee's two hundred horses. The engine, eager to run, gave a torquey roar in response.

Taylor trusted him, trusted Walker's trust in him. This was a Medevac emergency. Her mentor was septic, gangrenous. Salvation was speed. She handed Campbell—ex-Chosen, ex-perp?—a handwritten chit for Colonel Dennis. "Godspeed to you both!"

Purple rolled back the roadblock, saluting Walker with a raised fist. Taylor stepped away from the Humvee, giving its armored flank a swat. Cowboy brimmed his hat low. From the backseat, Walker, horizontal, gave a listless thumbs up. Campbell kicked the accelerator; heavy tires threw slush, and away they both flew. Next stop Mackinaw City, the ferry, and the Free fucking North.

Halloween: A Trick

THREE NIGHTS AGO, Ranger Thorn had come up with a plan, their Trojan horse into Panzer. Shaggy—their big, bad wolf—had blown the guardhouse full of smoke. The herb had relaxed them: Robert, Freddy, Mukwa. Even Sentinel Sparrow, smiling, had wet her beak.

Their ruse depended on Blackwater mercenaries, the privatized Praetorians preferred by the top one percenters. Several billionaires were bunkered along Lake Michigan's southern shore, cash-cushioned from collapse. They luxuriated in fully staffed silos, surviving in style while the hoi polloi died tacky deaths. But rich men grow bored. Wives, even mistresses, lose their luster. When Panzer's prince turned to pimping, the lecherous class leaned in.

"Only a matter of time," Thorn argued, "we just have to be ready."

Mukwa was highly motivated. "Yeah, but how *much* time?" His Hawk was still caged.

"Look, they tried once, they'll try again," Ranger Robert answered, backing his Rabbit. "Billionaires don't take no for an answer."

Sparrow settled it. "The Daughters will see this done. We'll give the mercs a few days to try again, then we do it *our* way."

What their way was she hadn't explained, hadn't had to. On Halloween, at dusk, Blackwater came knocking. Mercenaries and their employer had received a "coast is clear" message from Panzer: apparently the guardsmen were gone, Panthers too. Schark's cage was wide open. Bent on barter, the out of shape mercenaries approached Panzer in a column of four: truck, slave van, fuel tanker, truck. Spotted early and ambushed effectively, Blackwater's boys were knocked the fuck out.

No guns were fired, no distress signals were sent. Two trees, solicited by Sentinels, gave their ponderous permission, and were felled for a trap. There had been bird calls and green shadows. Pinned by pines, resisting mercs were pin-cushioned; the rest raised shaky hands in surrender. An armored truck, its driver arrowed through the throat, went crashing through the brush, trumpeting its distress. The raid was planned—and perfectly executed—by the Ranger brothers: Robert the brave and fair-minded Freddy.

"Cease fire!" Robert barked from the woods. The rain of arrows dried up as Blackwaters bled out.

"Step away from the vehicles! Keep your hands high!" Freddy commanded from the conifers. Surviving mercenaries, softened by sloth, complied and were spared. The captured men, spooked by shadows, shivered in the wind. A cold front filled an atmospheric void. Hail came first, followed by snow.

Ambush over, gray-hooded forms stepped free from the forest. Some held bows, some spears. Most of the fighters were women. They tied their prisoners tightly to trees. All arrows were recovered; a few had been bent by body armor. Using handsaws, the roadblocks were removed and sawdust swept away. Rough hands stripped the mercenaries of uniforms as well. Sentinel parkas and Ranger gear were swapped for Blackwater jackets, tactical vests, and helmets. The ambush site was scrubbed, no crumbs left for Sharkey or his far-seeing drones.

"So much for step one, Sparrow." Shaggy drove the empty Blackwater van, following Thorn's truck in the early falling dark. "Now what the fuck is step two?" His golden eyes, low-beamed, were shining.

Sparrow chirped up, "We make it believable."

Ten minutes later, the column, nearing the west gate, halted.

"You want us to do *what?*" Mukwa was confused.

Sparrow explained, "Ambush us. Open fire. Make noise, get Schark's attention."

Ranger Robert was nodding. "Look, you big bear, we fire high, do no damage. They'll send a drone to investigate, we make it look real. Then we break off and book it for the gate. They'll let us in. They're desperate for this trade. Hopefully our fake firefight will rush them, get us past any passwords or protocols. Get it?"

Mukwa got it, one step closer to Nighthawk. This had better work.

"Are you sure this thing is working?" The good doctor was in a foul mood. Schark thrust the Palantir phone towards Wermer, who nodded.

"Doctor, it's working, please be patient. Our client has called, he's sent a convoy. It should be here shortly."

"And what about *Naz?*" Panzer's CEO was flushed with too much wine, a nightly condition.

"Doctor, please, the major called earlier. His two helicopters are inbound from Toledo. Their ETA is sometime this evening."

"But that was *hours* ago!"

The prince of pinot was coming apart. Head aching from the halo implant, Wermer bit his tongue. Had he backed the wrong horse? Trapped himself in a tower with a madman? Too late for all that. Heavy-lidded with fatigue, Werm popped a pill, then two. This was Panzer, there were plenty.

Dr. Schark had succumbed to his wine cellar, leaving Wermer, as councilor, to oversee preparations. Per Major Naz's orders, Werm sent aviation gas to the helipad and Schark's frost-blonde assistant to the cages. The women there were readied for barter, for the block. When it arrived, Blackwater's fuel would be sampled for freshness. Panzer's product would be sampled as well. Wermer trusted Schark's Frau to inspect every inch.

Wermer paced the control room, keeping watch on the monitors and his implant-feed as well. Admittedly, the great EYE had dimmed—not enough juice to keep the Pentagon powered up. Not any more, probably never would be again.

The few guards he had were manning their posts, seemingly sober. The squall worsened as dusk descended; his security screens were staticky with snow. It was Halloween. The Palantir, heavy with potential, charged in its cradle. Panzer's antennae—VHF, UHF—probed the dark for Naz and his pilots. He envied them their freedom, their fuel, their metallic wings.

Wermer, neurally linked to AYE EYE, could fly anything, and had. Most basic competencies could be uploaded from his halo. A skilled mercenary, multi-tooled, he didn't come cheap. A week ago, hoping to retain him, Schark asked his Werm to name a price. Wermer's tongue twitched; he'd nearly spoken her name. He had cash aplenty, plus property and pills. It was Nighthawk and her powers he wanted. What man wouldn't fuck this wonder of a woman?

Sharkey wanted to, of that Werm was certain. Although, lately too much sauce had softened boss's noodle. The CORPS craved her too; they'd "research" her body, delve into its "developments." Of course, Frau had been the one to frisk her most frequently. "No stone unturned," the dominatrix purred with delight.

Major Naz, earlier on the sat-phone, had been suspicious: "Why have you neglected to report for so long?"

Werm, nervous, had reassured the CORPS commander. "Major, Panzer is secure. The Griffins have departed, Panthers too. They've lifted their siege."

Naz laughed at that; *Witch King* was his call sign. The major could be cruel. "Oh, I'm *well aware* of the guardsmen. I'm aware you failed to destroy them for me. Witless Wermer!"

Werm hooded his eyes, receiving orders from Naz. "Tell Schark that the specimen is not for him. I am coming for her, say just that. Do you understand?" Wermer gulped and repeated: no matter the terms, Ms. Nighthawk was not to be traded.

Thud-thud-thud-thud-thud!

Speak of the devil. The Witch King cometh. Wermer's handheld squawked with a sentry's report: "Sir, we've got two helos inbound, I can see their navigation lights. Approaching low from the east, over."

The mercenary licked his lips. "Light up the landing pad. Prepare to refuel. I'll be there in a minute. Wermer, out."

A series of flashes, then a sharper sound ripped the night: *Kak-Kak-Kak-Kak-Kak-Kak-Kak!*

Automatic weapons? Outside the walls? Warnings flashed across his screens. *Proximity alert! Gunfire detected!*

A sentry radioed, "Resupply convoy is almost here! But those Blackwater boys are gettin' bushwhacked!"

Wermer responded, "Launch a drone! I want eyes on that column."

Insectoid, a multi-sensor UAV soon overflew the ambush. Wermer's screen displayed its infrared feed: *Blackwater vehicles.* Werm counted four. *Scattered gunshots from the trees.* All that was left of Old Law's siege? *Blackwater men returning fire as they raced towards the wall.* Werm studied the scene, no need to wake the sleeping Schark.

"Open the west gate! Cover the convoy! Let them in!" Ex-Blackwater himself, his boys had this in hand.

The gate opened. His remaining Panzers, from the parapet, laid down suppressing fire, silencing the would-be ambushers.

The four vehicles rolled in, battle-damaged, but none were disabled. The gate closed. Grinning guards crowded around the convoy. Any action was welcome, especially an easy one.

Thud-thud-thud-thud-thud!

Werm could see them now; those choppers were close.

Halloween: A Treat

SUBTERRANEAN IN HER SILO, Nighthawk felt the moon's pull, could point to its rise. Tonight, Gaia's granddaughter, Selene, had reached full term. Green senses enhanced, Hawk heard the cries of fellow captives. The caged women moaned in mutual misery. That blonde bitch and her orderlies must be making their rounds.

The trafficked females shared a hallway, each dorm a padded cell with bed-shackles and a drain. Hawk had gotten to know her neighbors, sending them strength. Most were Amish girls, abducted from family farms; some sisters came from cities, captured by Chosen, XCons, or their ilk. At least one was Native, a biker scout nabbed before Schark's big bridge debacle.

They'd been drugged. They'd been shocked. A sorority of shame. They were outnumbered and out-muscled. They were fucked. And some had been, by mercenaries with money or trinkets to trade. Not Nighthawk though, not yet. Sharkey's favorite was still strictly verboten.

The Sentinel, despite her dungeon, felt doom approach. Large forces were astir: an atmospheric vacuum, a surge of arctic air, a hallowed eve, gray figures in a forest. She felt a *thudding* terror, a stab of panic. Something evil—flying fast!—was winging her way.

A key violated her lock, prying open the deadbolt. Jackbooted goons kicked her cell door open. Banded to the bed, Hawk hooded her senses, pacifying her pulse. Silently, she prepared her body to reject the coming injection. Then it came.

Hard hands on her skin, the blue hum of voltage, a probing needle, an ejaculation of ice.

Biochemically, she fought the invasive compound, pushing her proteins to stem the tide of poison. Rohypnol again. Hawk staged her sedation, role-played being roofied. Frau wanted her floored, so Hawk folded her wings, feigning compliance. Fascist fingers feathered over her breast, pinching her parts. Pheromones wafted from Frau. Decoding them was easy; this bitch was aroused.

More *thudding*. Not heartbeats this time, but vibrations. Two mechanical monsters bladed the sky. Frau's radio beeped with Wermer's update: "We've got helicopters inside the perimeter. Bring the product. Prepare the package for departure."

One of the goons lifted her lids, checking vitals. "She's dilated. Pulse low. This Greenie's out cold."

Stymied in her inspection, Frau snapped, "Unshackle her! Put the prisoner in the wheelchair. Take her to the surface. Let's go!"

Limp, Hawk let herself be manhandled. A tech lifted her into the chair, rolled it to the elevator doors, entering a key-code. They ascended together.

At the surface, the airlock swished open, revealing a snow globe tableau. Two gray beasts, scaly with armor, perched on the helipad floodlit by halogens. *Panic* and *Terror* were stenciled on each fuselage. Their painted mouths leered—red, white, and black. Horny pinions clutched weapon pods. Hoses had been connected; they suckled fuel from the drums. Hawk, still faking, flinched from their petro-stench.

A blizzard of snow was whipped by their rotors. The two aircraft were refueling hot, engines still running. Mercenaries hunched against the gas-driven gale. Wermer was there, escorting his employer. Dr. Schark looked pale and leaned on his man. The goons, led by Frau, pushed the wheelchair towards them.

Schark leaned over, grasping at his prize. The CEO of Panzer Pharm, fermented, was slurring, "Time fer a night flight, lil' hawkling."

Everything in Hawk screamed against this plan.

"We muss fly the coop, my dear. Greener pastures for my Greenie."

The pilots were stripping out seats, stowing jerry cans in the choppers. Auxiliary fuel for a long flight ahead? Two men wearing US Army uniforms and heavy holsters approached Schark's party. Both were badged with a bloody red hand. The enlisted man, an NCO, was a giant, a real brute. The other wore an eyepatch and the oak leaves of a major. His name-tape read *NAZ*. This cyclops had poked her before—one week ago? Two?—sampling her serum.

Naz sneered at Dr. Schark, holding up a finger. "I'm sorry, Doctor, but due to fuel concerns we only have room for one." He signaled his sergeant. The brute lifted Hawk into the helicopter, buckling her in. Hawk, feigning fatigue, sat slumped. The major took the open seat. Donning a headset, Naz ordered his pilot, "Our destination is Washington D.C.; pilots, this is *Witch King*, let's go!"

Panic shrieked as the rpms increased. The rotors roared. The gray beast spread its wings, flying away from the floodlights. Nighthawk lifted an eyelid and peered down. The brute and the other pilot were boarding *Terror*. Schark and his Werm would be left behind on the pad.

Unacceptable to both men was separation from Hawk.

"Mr. Wermer, if you please?"

Sharkey's man licked his lips. Flashing a sidearm, he placed a bullet in the brain of both pilot and brute. Wermer holstered his smoking pistol and stepped over the bodies into the cockpit. Jack of all trades, he pushed a button on his halo and soon mastered the controls.

Dr. Schark—cloaked in his white labcoat—climbed aboard and buckled up. "Follow her!"

Terror took off in pursuit of its mate.

The four vehicles rolled in, battle-damaged, but none were disabled. The gate closed. Grinning guards crowded around the convoy. Any action was welcome, especially an easy one…

But the Blackwater van wasn't empty. Instead, the Trojan horse reared in Panzer's crowded courtyard. Mukwa's hackles were up, canines bared. Sentinels sprang forth, each woman a warrior, a badass DOG. The Daughters darted stupefied guards with deadly steel. Heavy spears punched through Kevlar. Well-aimed arrows found open throats and eye sockets. Blood puddles congealed, cooling—one slow snowflake at a time.

Earlier, in the woods, Sparrow had taken a Blackwater bullet, a searing wound to her unarmored flesh. "Find her!" she yelled at Mukwa. "The landing pad! Listen for choppers!"

Shaggy jumped back in the van, Mukwa tumbling in too. Both longhairs sped away. Panzer Pharma was a fucking labyrinth. Without a thread to follow, Muk and Shaggy followed their ears, discerning the *thud-thud* of approaching rotor blades. They were close! Sentinel no longer, Mukwa pawed through the van's weapon pile. They were strapped! Rifles, grenades, plus the two LAWS rockets gifted by the Griffs.

They made it to the snowy helipad, moth-like, drawn to the lights. Their panicky hearts were pounding. Muck was terrified his Hawk would be taken away.

"There they are!" Shaggy braked. The van halted, but they couldn't stop the scene. A giant soldier and a pilot had just been shot. Two others—was one the shooter?—stepped over the corpses and boarded the helicopter. The first gray beast was already lifting away, snow squalling from its downwash.

"Noooo!" Mukwa dropped low, charging the helipad. *Hawk, where are you?* He squinted against the hail. Bullets zipped past him, a muzzle flashing from the airborne bird. Mukwa rolled towards cover behind the empty fuel drums. The second beast was lifting off while the first one hovered—*zip-zip-zing!*—keeping him pinned.

"Wabi Muk! CATCH!"

He looked back at Shaggy, anticipating a weapon, but wolfman pointed at the sky: a figure—female?—was crouching at the helicopter door! Mukwa choked up—*Nighthawk!* Horrified, he watched the woman spread her wings and leap from the aircraft. Flying, she grew larger as she fell. He was in position. The stadium lights, the kickoff, the roar. Hail-fucking-Mary!

She body-slammed him, pounding him flat, an anvil from above. *Oooof!* The big bear couldn't breathe. *Crack!* Bones had been broken, definitely his. Muk, suffering from shock, curled up and heaved, emptying his gut. Light on her feet, Hawk rolled away.

Zip-zip-zip-ping! They were still taking fire. The Greenie zigged towards Shaggy's van. The Lakota's hair was streaming as he shouldered the LAWS. The 66mm rocket had been armed. Shaggy sighted on *Panic*; its mate, *Terror*, hovering nearby.

WHOOOOOSH!

Sparks trailed towards the helo but missed, the rocket disappearing harmlessly into the snowy void. The twin beasts had had enough; fuel was short, and they had miles to go. They rotated, dipping their snouts, preparing to flee. Shaggy fumbled his remaining rocket. Then Nighthawk was there: "Let me have it!"

"You *GO* girl!" Shaggy pitched the last launch tube to Hawk. The Daughter cringed, corrupted by the weapon as she armed its rocket. *Gaia forgive.* She tuned herself to the night, to all its feral frequencies. Hawk shouldered the contraption. *Aim small, miss small*—the markswoman's mantra.

WHOOOOSH!

The concept was as old as the species: a missile, a launcher, a target. Twenty thousand years between the Atlatl and LAWS. Highly explosive, the warhead left the launch tube streaking 500 feet per second.

Panic and *Terror* fled from their unguided doom.

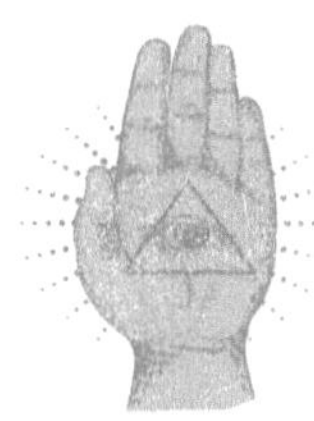

Halloween: Witching Hour

WHOOOOSH!

Cyclopean, Major Naz observed the ascending spark trail. His halo calculated, projecting on the patch: the rocket, fired by the mutant female, wouldn't miss.

Ping! The warhead bumped his helo's fuselage. Naz's last microsecond diagrammed his demise. The nose cone crumpled, detonating a booster in the base, setting off the main charge—450 grams of Octol high explosive. *Ka-BOOM!*

The *Witch King* and his beast fell flaming from the sky.

WHOOOOSH!

A streak of white fire leapt up from the ground. "Did you *SEE* that!" Schark shouted his surprise, unheard in the noisy cockpit. Pilot Wermer merely nodded. Too fucking close, that rocket barely missed. He pulled his stick to lift them up, up, and away.

Ka-BOOM!

The detonation thumped through Werm's body. The other AH-6—Naz's helo—just exploded. Flaming wreckage, man and machine, plummeted to ruin upon the pavement of Panzer. Wermer looked down at the receding campus, trying to observe the crash site below. Stadium lights were blurred by the blizzard. Had Nighthawk been aboard? *Fuck!* He'd never have her now.

"Where to then, Doctor?"

But Schark didn't answer. Horrified and half drunk, he gaped at the wreckage. Wermer tapped his boss's knee, pointing to the extra headset.

"Doctor, are we going to D.C.?" Werm readied his neural implant for navigation duty. The pharma CEO, in a day, had aged a decade. He'd lost his compound, his command. His pet had been stolen, then killed outright. Alone in the wilderness, just he and his Werm.

"No."

"Doctor?"

"No. We're not going to D.C.; we're done with the CORPS."

"Sir, I need a heading. This airspace isn't secure."

"North, Mr. Wermer. Don't worry, I've prepared a spot for us."

Wermer banked the helicopter, steadying *Terror* on three-six-zero. They had fuel, a few rifles, and whatever munitions were left in the pods. The landscape below was utterly dark.

"Kill the navigation lights, Mr. Wermer. Fly as low as you dare. We must arrive in secret."

The pilot did so, plotting a course while trying to predict Sharkey's plot twist: Grand Rapids? Cadillac? With all that extra fuel, maybe Traverse City? Werm glanced at his boss; the old shark was grinning. *What's he got to smile at?*

Dr. Schark, for now, kept his secret, cutting his losses. At least he was free of the cage. Yes, Red Hands had nabbed his Hawk, his happiness. His golden goose had been roasted. But he was over it. She'd been one in a million, or had she? The Greenie, dosed with truth serum, had babbled. He'd taken notes, connecting the dots—an Indian girl, an island academy, a whole batch of little Greenies.

True, he'd lost the bird in his hand, but he knew where the bush was. "Keep an eye on our fuel, Wermer. It's going to be close."

Hawk, fully grown, was too haughty to handle. He'd have better luck with fledglings. Schark, swimming free, homed in on their nest.

Mother Earth and All Her Creations by Jackie Traverse

Something Rotten

DING-LING!

Annie Doyle, recently widowed, pushed through the fake spider webs, entering the woodstove-warmth of the Shamrock. Jack-o'-lanterns and candles illuminated the interior of the well-worn tavern. Beaver Island's Main Street was crowded with children in costume. Island families, Irish and Natives alike, had turned out despite the cold—their second Halloween since collapse. Calories being scarce, "skeleton" was a popular disguise.

"Trick or treat!" the skinny kids demanded, heaving pillowcases filled with homemade loot. Gone were the confected candies of before, sweet tooths making do with maple syrup and molasses instead. A tray of caramel apples was attended to; guisers were treated to Granny Smiths and Wagners.

Annie had an appointment with her good friend Samantha. Barkeep Alice caught Annie's eye, nodding to a booth. Samantha, costumed as a witch, had placed her pointy hat on the table and seemed to be dozing. Annie approached. Eldest cracked an eye, then a grin. "Where's your costume, Annie Doyle?"

"Going as the usual," Annie said as she eased herself down. "A lonely fishwife."

Samantha *tsked*. "How long since your Tom went away?" No love lost between Irish Doyle and the Indigenous. But Sammy had a shine for Annie, her womanly plight.

"Almost forty days now," Annie's chin quivered, "twenty or so since the fleet came back without him."

Nine Beaver boats had battled beneath the Mackinac Bridge. Five returned. Doyle, Hannigan, and many others hadn't made it. Surviving crews shook their heads; they'd seen the fireball, the terrible explosion. No way Tom survived. *Bloody Mary* had rammed a barge, contesting its contagious landing.

They'd interred an empty casket, nothing elaborate, just a plain pine box of mementos. Doyle's body, what was left anyway, was swallowed up by Michigan's salt-less sea. The word "courageous" was often heard at his funeral. Annie bristled each time; that wasn't her Tom. "Cantankerous" served better. But the dead belong to everyone. Annie, unwilling, shared her claim.

Samantha, in witch mode, eyed every customer, lowering her voice as she said, "There's something rotten going on. Annie, I need your help."

Annie wiped her cheeks and attended. Least she could do. The bartender eyed Samantha eyeing the room and attended as well. After decades of eavesdropping, Alice angled for acoustics, catching Sam's drift. Later she'd repeat it, filling eager ears with poisonous news.

Ten days ago, the orphan Miin had gone missing. She'd been teaching in ELF Country, training Nats and farm kids alike. Indian Point feared a kidnapping, or worse. Deputy Travis, the only badged law, had been badgered, but so far had done little. "The girl's disappeared before, Samantha," the lawman gaslighted granny, "maybe your Miin is back on the main?"

But Samantha knew better. Her community was angry, another MMIW ignored. Whether Miin was murdered or just missing, the Indigenous young woman must be found. Samantha was calling in favors from white folks that she knew. Annie, ever an ally, promised help. She had connections in the fleet, and would share any scuttlebutt that drifted her way.

Ding-ling!

Annie pushed through the tavern door, striding towards the harbor. Her bluff bow parted an incoming tide of trick-or-treaters. Brown-eyed and blue, dark-skinned and freckled, the sugar junkies snatched apples and surrounded Samantha, chanting, *"Nookomis! Nookoo! Boozhoo!"*

Samantha donned her pointy hat, brandishing her broom. "Scat! I'll put a spell on you! Let's go home now, children. *Kasaga'amin!"*

Samantha tipped barkeep Alice with a sealed jug of brew. At the Shamrock, payments varied: patrons split wood, provided kerosene, fetched water or washed dishes. No barter too steep for a chance to socialize and feel normal.

Ding-ling!

Samantha swept her charges out the door, herding them homeward like so many cats. A winter wind was strengthening, scented with snow. Carved pumpkins leered from every stoop, flames guttered by the gale. When every kid was home safe, eldest turned inland. Her bog-shack was too far, and too painful besides. The site of Miin's abduction was tainted. Miin's *nookomis* blamed herself. How not? What kind of grandma loses hide-and-seek with kidnappers? Samantha fared westward. The medicine woman had kin on the Point.

Indian Point

BINAAKWE-GIIZIS, Falling-Leaves-Moon, was just about full. Samantha shuffled through the leafy drifts on Donegal Road. At the fork, she wended north. Deciduous corpses crunched underfoot as centuries of ancestors pulled her towards the Point

Woodsmoke welcomed her to the glowing lodge, sage and salutations spicing Sam's arrival. She shook her head at the frowns from her friends. No answer to their burning question. *Where was Miinan, Blueberry, daughter of them all?*

She stripped herself, of clothing and excuses. The wrinkled woman scrubbed her skin—spirit too—with cedar boughs, but Sam couldn't get clean. She partook in ceremony, in purification. Grandfather stones sparkled in the dark, amplifying echoes of epochs long gone. The circle of sweating elders heeded the stony voices and their origin song.

The island began with an incubation in ice. Two million years ago, eccentric Earth wobbled in its orbit. Great sheets of ice, implacable, ground south from the pole, terraforming everything before reluctantly retreating.

The Age of Ice transformed the planet's peoples too. Long ago, in East Africa, the Great Hunt began. Early humans, chasing calories, abandoned Eden for Asia Minor, then Siberia, and then the straits—often dry—of the land bridge, Beringia. With the grinding ice behind them, First Peoples had scattered, diasporic, across a continent empty of their kind.

Eleven thousand years ago the island emerged, scraped clean by the northbound glacier. *Mishigami*, the Great Lake, had once been less so. The island, during these dry times, lost its insularity, becoming a mere peninsula of Michigan's mainland. Wingless creatures had walked across. The four-footed came first—deer, elk, wolf—pursued, as ever, by bipeds—Paleo-Indians—and their flinty projectiles. Rising water levels marooned these mammals, and Beaver Island—a sandy Noah's Ark—was put in dry dock, stranding its assorted passengers.

Millennia later, on All Hallows' Eve, snow sifted upon a tent filled with elders. Drums, unseen, thrummed in the deep, the primordial pulse of Indian Point. Samantha's glistening lodgemates heard the *tom-tomming* of *Pukwudgies*, little people, wild woses of the woods.

Aboriginal to the island, they might have walked across ages ago. They'd seen the tall ones come and go. First the Odawa, pushed west by flooding whites. Then came English, French, and the baptisms of Baraga. And still the *Paissa* of the Point endured. Often invisible, they could go to ground for years, then reappear in a twinkling.

The island's *Pukwudgies* had suffered strange kings. In the 1850s—a puckish blink ago—James Strang and his Mormons hunted them for sport. Then came hungry tides of Irish. Boat-focused and fishing-centric, the sons of Éire had left them alone. Besides, their Emerald Isle had *Púcaí* of their own. Fish-wives were well-versed in placating the little people. November 1st in Ireland was Púca's Day. A tithe of harvest was shared with these spirits, the wild folk who'd come first, abiding under hills.

It was after midnight in the elders' sweat lodge. November 1st, a hallowed day, had come again. Snow hissed on the taut skin of their tent, a melted fairy circle in a whitening field. Those within were transported, though each *Midew* journeyed alone. Samantha was spirit walking, seeking, always, for any sign of her Miin.

The girl was on the island still. Of this, Sam was sure. She'd investigated her shack, reading the signs of struggle. White men had bound her, uprooting Blueberry from Cranberry Bog. Miin's students and their parents had never stopped searching, along with elves from the forest. Bearded Brian flew endless reconnaissance, cycling through raptors, weather be damned. Grace, dosed with tea, flew flights of her own.

The Natives were searching, Irish as well. Beating the bushes, patrolling on ponies. Every campfire was investigated, every lantern too. They'd had no gleam of Miin. There was no scent of Blueberry for Samantha to follow; something had walled up between them.

As the stones cooled, their visions diminished. Dreamers exited, wordless, from the lodge. Exhausted, Sam's companions fell into beds. Eldest was last to emerge. Several inches had fallen. Her skin steamed. Snow haloed the moon.

Tom-toom. Tom-toom. Tom-toom. Insistent, the island *Puks* were beating their drums. There was a stone circle on the island, a ring of carved boulders. The site had been investigated—medicine wheel? Celestial calendar? Stonehenge? Experts could not agree, though the islanders did—it was a place of ancient power. For centuries, *Puks* could be seen there, diminutive fairies dancing in the dark. These paleo-people were drumming there still.

Sam's heart pulsed apace. *Tom-toom. Tom-toom. Tom-toom.* Samantha shivered. Something foul was winging their way. Vibrations, not from earth, but sky, thudded through her. Some terror approached. Sam fought an urge to flee.

Then it was gone.

The drumming continued; sleep was impossible. The little people, barefoot and elusive, were calling her to vigilance. Sam heeded them, waking all her kinsfolk. Ponies were saddled and rifles made ready.

The Beaver Bois

BILL FERNY WAS PRICKLY, like his parents, and grandparents too. Ferny's thorns had been sharpened by collapse. And he had blood on his hands—Keith Two-Crow's. He'd killed the 'Nam vet with a rifle, shooting the old timer off the ferry—filled with refugees and seeking sanctuary.

Captain Tom Doyle—*damn him!*—had allowed the ferry to dock. Its passengers were screened by Newsome for infection. ELF Country had been established. Most islanders approved— these green thumbs had saved the harvest and island root cellars were full.

Ferny, pimpled and loath to connect, had few friends outside his clan of cronies. These he'd banded together, his Beaver Bois. The spelling came from a pre-collapse militia: gun-loving, cop-hating. Those mainlander *bois*, Hawaiian-shirted, had blogged about Boogaloo; they'd executed it too. What was not to like? Ferny's clan, likewise, turned klannish.

Not so long ago, fleeing famine, the island's Irish left Árainn Mhór, in Donegal. The Ferny farm, island-rooted since 1850, had once been more fruitful. Some county roads were still signed in Gaelic. From King's Highway, Paid Een Ogs Road ran west. The Ferny burrow was north a bit. Bagúin Road dead-ended at Bill's battered green door. *Bagúin* was Old Irish for bacon. Once an idyllic spot, the place was cluttered with mildewed sacks and bags of spoiling food.

Ferny's wife Ashley—recently delivered—was dead on her feet, both of which were freezing. Halloween's midnight had come and gone. She was not treated well; her whole life she'd been tricked. Bill, once darkly handsome, had bullied her, first to bed, then to bride, and every day since. Ashley was frying bacon by the greasy light of a lantern, fattening her husband and his ever-hungry boys.

Snow blanketed Bagúin's dead-end and its rusty contraptions. Cold in its crib, Ashley's colicky newborn was crying. The cranky clan was whining too: "Woman, we're starving! Bring us some shine!" The ashen woman endured, as had her ancestors. Catering to cowards was nothing new for her line.

The Ferny cousins had bloated lately, egos and belt-lines both. Ashley knew they'd been stealing food, "gathering" from others, sharing amongst themselves. And they were glued to the radio. Someone out there was stroking them. She knew the signs, she'd done plenty herself. Ashley shivered as she piled plates with pilfered food. Her baby was shrieking: "Hold on little one, I know you're next."

That fool Travis Williams, when pushed, had deputized them all, granting Ferny and his cousins a township truck and a fuel ration too. Feathers in their caps, they flaunted their authority. Under-lettered, a cousin had mis-stenciled their gear—*Shirriffs-Obey!*

Most islanders didn't, which rankled them more.

Ashley served the men in the TV room. Of course the radio was on, just static for now. Acquiring batteries and chargers posed no problem for deputized law.

"Bacon's burnt!" grumbled one.

"Forgot the damn shine!" from another.

They backhanded her with abuse as she did their bidding. She scooped her baby and nursed him, away from prying eyes. A sight of breast could rouse appetites less easy to satisfy. She didn't think Bill would allow it, least he hadn't so far. But the cousins were wild and her Ferny had fallen.

A sudden voice pushed through the static: *"Shhhh—Nest, this is Shark—Shhhhh—Inbound—Shhh."*

A thudding sound pushed through the snow. Ashley, nursing, felt terror. Her babe felt it too; losing his latch, the little lad screamed. Confused, the whole clan was in commotion.

"Shut that fucker up!" Ashley blanched and fled to the bedroom.

"Where's *she* going then? Don't be shy, missy. We've all seen titties before!"

Ferny kicked them into action: "Fools! It's *him!* Light the fuckin' pad!"

The cold air slapped them sober. The LED landing-lights were charged. The bacon boys grunted as they illuminated the snowy field.

Thud-thud-thud-thud!

Even the dimmest wit could hear it now. Some mechanical monster, from an earlier age, was winging their way. Power is what they felt, balls to bones. And it was on their side! *Sooie!* They'd make this island squeal!

A great shadow descended, a falling cloud. The downdraft blizzarded the boys. The beast touched down with taloned feet. The rotors slowed, the engine died. The LED lights, blown over, beamed askew. Ferny and his deputies squinted. Two figures dismounted, stepping their way. The pilot—*wearing a crown?*—pulled a pistol. Ferny's eyes crossed, his sphincter slipped. Point-blank, the man aimed it right between his beady eyes.

Ferny stuttered a welcome, "D-Doctor Schark? I'm Bill Ferny, these are my Bois."

The pilot sneered and safetied his sidearm. *"Boys* is right," he sniffed in derision. "Boss, you sure about this?"

The quivering cousins made a poor impression. Their pork-bellies bulged, their marbled shoulders sagged. Trying to look stern, they hitched up their jeans. Butt cracks grinned darkly as LEDs were plucked from the snow. The second man was taller, with an executive bearing. He wore a white labcoat, collar up against the cold. His voice had power, though his face was splotchy: "They'll be fine, Mr. Wermer, I'm sure."

Labcoat addressed Ferny directly, "My Werm wants fuel, immediately. His gas tanks are dry." Ferny's head was bobbing. Only one problem, island fuel was stored at the harbor.

"I'm feeling a bit dry myself. I trust you have refreshment to offer?"

More head bobs. "We've got a fine shine, Doctor Schark. A *fine* shine."

"Excellent. But what interests me *most*," Schark circled Ferny, "is the *girl*, this 'green witch' you claim to have captured."

Ferny gasped at his intensity. The man's eyes, afire, bored right through him.

"I trust you still have her? I've lost one specimen tonight. I will *not* lose another."

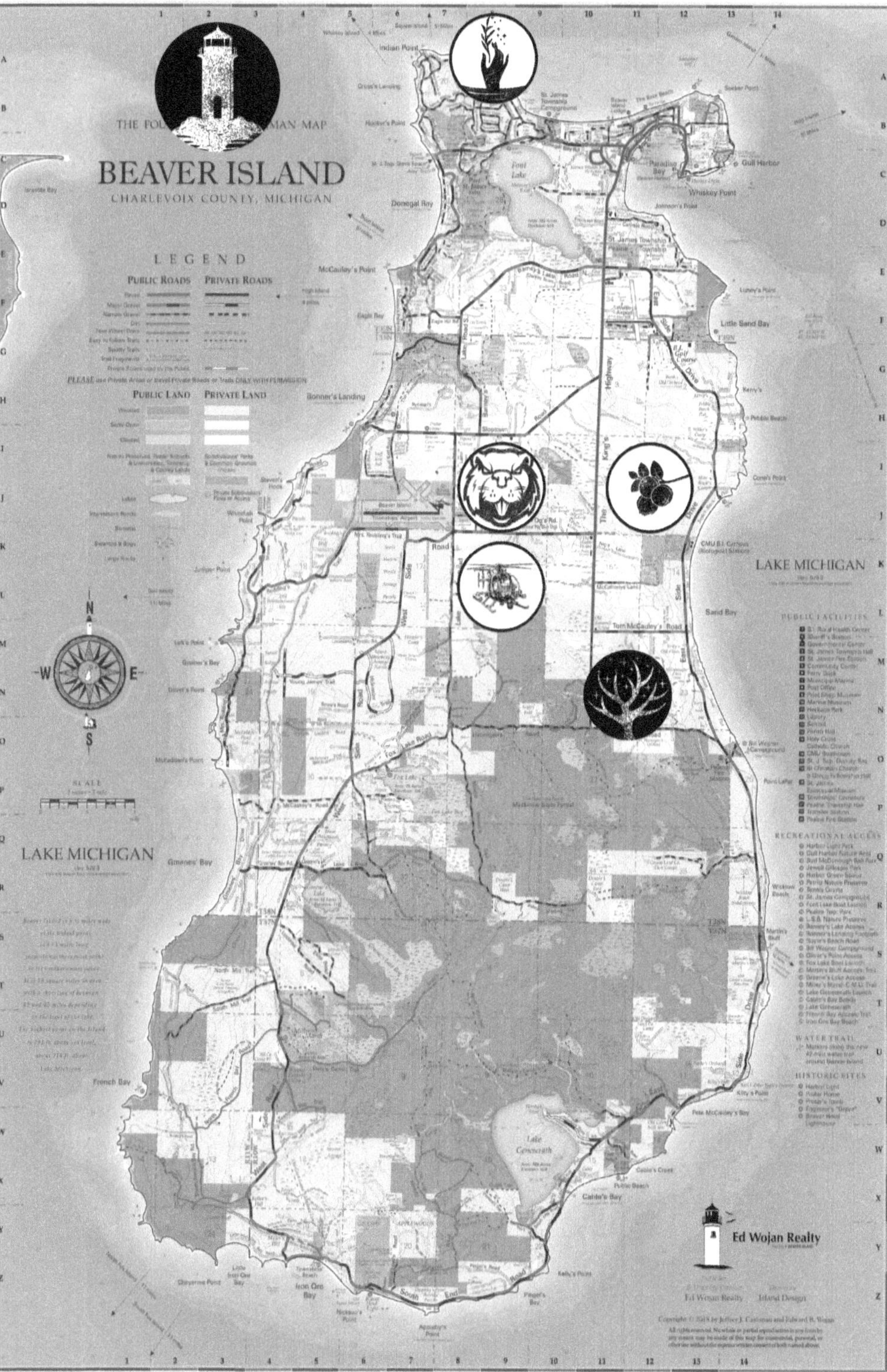

THE FOLDING ISLAND MAP
BEAVER ISLAND
CHARLEVOIX COUNTY, MICHIGAN
LEGEND
PUBLIC ROADS
PRIVATE ROADS
PUBLIC LAND
PRIVATE LAND
LAKE MICHIGAN
LAKE MICHIGAN
Ed Wojan Realty
SCALE
N
W
E
S

Tree Academy: Seeking

INDEED, THEY STILL HAD HER. Their green witch hadn't flown, nor could she. Beaver's Bois had hog-tied her tight. Between Bagúin's dead-end and Miin's Stone House lay a bumpy mile of Paid Een Ogs Road. "Young Patrick's" was the translation from Gaelic. The road's namesake had fled, starving, from Ireland's famine. He'd put down roots in Beaver's sandy soil, plowing other fields as well. His seed had proven fertile. Many islanders traced their branching lineage to young Patrick's trunk.

Josie Greene and Michael Martin were two of these descendants. Both farm kids had been students, highfliers, in Miin's Tree Academy. When teacher was taken, they'd stirred up ELF Country and the neighboring farms. Adults got involved, as young Miinan was a favorite. Farmers patrolled; barns and sheds were looked into. Naturals hunted for her, winnowing the woods. No sign was discovered, though there were rumors aplenty.

Deputy Williams was questioned about these new "Shirriffs" in town. Many suspected pimpled Ferny and his clan of kidnapping.

The deputy was defensive. "Look, it isn't them, OK? Ferny swore to obey the laws and follow county directives. Believe me, they're looking, too."

There was mockery of this, both at Shamrock and the Comber. Barkeep Alice put a stop to it: "This is how it starts. First an

Indian girl, an orphan, and you shrug. Next, they nab one of yours. Think about it." She shooed the bar flies away. Patrons alighted elsewhere; there was much to buzz about.

Churches got involved: Pastor George and his flock of Naturals, Father Pete's Holy Crossers. Prayers were offered, divinations attempted, but if their God was omniscient He kept Miin's location to Himself.

October was a busy time for the island—harvest, preservation, and hunting. Stove wood needed cording, leaky roofs needed patching. Yes, a girl had gone missing, but this had happened before. They remembered Miin's stint, last summer, on the mainland—there and back without a scratch. "Maybe Mukwa returned and she went off with him?"

"Or the Nats?"

"I heard a canoe of their women left about the same time."

Heads wagged at this; then, islanders got back to work. The days darkened as daylight diminished. Canning shelves grew heavy. Miin's students weren't having it, nor the elders on the Point. They wore themselves out seeking for the place she'd been stashed. Old warriors—mounted on ponies—looked around, turning up the heat. Ferny felt it and stayed away from Stone House.

Trick-or-treat had come and gone. The academy kids—though depressed—had dressed up, a perfect excuse to knock on doors and snoop around. Afterwards, still costumed, they gathered at the Martin farm to debrief.

Mr. Martin had brought them back from town in his wagon, Michael's mom staying home with the youngest. Now, she filled their glasses with water hand-pumped from the well. The over-sugared kids were thirsty, gulping it down with thanks. The kitchen woodstove was warm. They huddled around its heat. At 13, Josie Greene was the eldest. "What about Ferny's place? That dead-end on Bagúin? Ferny's boys are suspects, badges or not."

Arturo, a Natural, and Cheyanna, Point-born, had biked there together, pedaling back to Martin's in the snowy dark. "We checked it," Arturo reported. "Ferny's wife answered the door. I could hear her baby crying."

Cheyanna added, "We didn't see any men around, but that place is a pig sty. There might've been dozens."

Josie nodded. "What about other houses off Patrick's Road?"

Arturo answered, "Tried 'em all. Most were abandoned, no one there since collapse."

Michael Martin asked, "I know we've checked it before, but what about Stone House? Corner of King's Highway?"

Cheyanna shook her head. "Stone House is the same. Dead and dark every time. No tracks. Locked tight, no one coming or going."

"Damn!" Josie was frustrated. They all were. "What would Miin do?" she asked for the hundredth time.

She had the answer before she finished asking. They all did, but they'd tried it before. The four academy kids waited for Michael's mom to leave the room. "Almost midnight," Mrs. Martin said, pointing at the wind-up clock. "Bedtime for trick-or-treaters. I'll bring some blankets in here. You can bunk by the stove. Mr. Martin will drive you home in the morning."

She tucked them in, filled the firebox, and went to bed, bringing hot water bottles to her man. The seekers sat up, looking at one another, determined to try again. "The *trees* of course." Fire-flicker hallowed their faces. "Miinan would ask the *trees*." An obvious answer, but easier said than done, even for the academy. Every tree-talker had tried already, on multiple frequencies, but the trees—if they knew anything—weren't responding.

Ten minutes later—booted and bundled—they stepped into the night. The Martin place was an old one, its woody denizens older still. Arturo, an ELF Natural, found an oak that felt familiar. Cheyanna, Native of the Point, picked a white pine, a massive one. *"Zhingwaak,"* she intoned, looking up, up, up. Michael, on home turf, headed for his beech grove. Josie, birch-affine, befriended a nearby copse.

The night was cold; the trees felt the same. Precipitation crowned the high moon, winter's halo. The four students, fingers numb, experienced difficulties logging in. The wood-wide-web had slowed—its connectivity logy with delay.

This still wasn't working. Not for any of them. Core temperatures began to fall, along with the flakes.

The Crucible: Terror

CELLAR-CONFINED, dumbed by its dankness, Miin, clinging to life, sensed snowfall. The complex crystals shed electrons as they fell. Miin felt positive that the outside air was charging. Underground currents charged as well; subterranean, their pace was more plodding.

Miinan's voice was raspy, her water song drying up. She'd been abandoned in the dark. Some days ago, Ferny and his clan had stopped calling. The rafter ropes chafed her wrists, but at least she could stand and drink from the dipper. But the bucket, like her song, was almost dry. Dehydration was a real danger. She could die in this cellar; her desiccated corpse would eventually shrivel. Throat parched, lips cracking, she again sang her song, summoning life.

Wayaa way-ay-haa-yo wayaa way-ay-haa-yo.

She guessed clan Ferny was saving her for something, or some*one.* Their interrogations had been interrupted. She was worth more to them unspoiled. Miin envisioned a cage in her future, a life in a lab. Double-blind, reduced to a rat: drugs and electrodes, enzymes and DNA. They would break what she was to see how she worked. Studying her green ability, she'd be severed from its source.

Blueberry was wilting. She hadn't heard Arturo's "trick-or-treat" from earlier, Cheyanna's neither, her costumed kin. Shivering, she was strapped to the ceiling. Her doom approached. She could feel it *thud-thudding* her way. Something foul? Some *thing* from before? A creature? No, a *contraption*. Constructed for killing, fumy with death.

So this was it then?

Miin's heart hammered, her body sagged. But another pulse was out there, not her's, and not the *thing's*. The Earth itself was thrumming, *Tom-toom. Tom-toom. Tom-toom*—heartbeat of the land. Aboriginal and all-knowing, the *Pukwudgies* were responding to her need. Burrowed beneath the frost line, the wild ones heard her water song, her ancestral SOS. The wood woses had awoken. They did what they could to relay her distress.

Miinan—a bog-child, island fluent—had seen them. Not often, just glimpses. The diminutive *Puks* appeared burly, gnarled like stumps, strong of limb and green-spirited. Something old in them, ancient even. Tonight the *Puks* were drumming, not just for Blueberry, but the entire island. They *tom-tommed* against the *thud-thud* of approaching terror—Earth against Sky, and woe to those caught between. Miin added her voice, rasping her song:

Wayaa way-ay-haa-yo wayaa way-ay-haa-yo.

Suddenly, something shifted in the cellar, an electric charge and chemicals too. Miin ceased her singing. In the sudden quiet, she sensed the presence of another—a sniffing, sentient, *something* had pushed through the hardpack seeking the water promised in her song. Hydrotropic, a tuber's tendrils had found her.

The island woses, for millennia, stretched their drums with birch and skins. Miin too, stretched herself for a final transmission. The cellar's tubers—web-connected and willing—now grew through the floor. All they needed was touch. Miin felt the weight of Stone House above her. She'd pull it all down for a chance to transmit.

The thudding grew louder. Her terror increased—*lab, knife, needles.* But the rafter ropes had no give, she couldn't reach the roots. Miin slumped; she'd given her all. But Earth itself wasn't done. The tubers themselves were thrumming. Eagerly, they sipped up her signature—*Sunlight On Berries*—a pheromone feast.

A creak of rope as her toe strained nearer. The root clump extended, electrons were exchanged. A final push and her toe touched the tubers. Connection! A complex coding of chemicals. Location was everything; she had to be found. Miin compressed her coordinates, zipping them in a file. Just before blacking out, the captive hit send. With the last of her signal strength, she broadcast pure *need*. Miin fired her final bolt. It forked through the dirt like green-rooted lightning.

Pride Goeth

FERNY AND HIS FELLOWS ASSURED ME, I could trust their trussing. The green witch is buried deep, confined in a stony cellar. The girl hasn't been missed, not much of a fuss. "She's an orphan, see? Lots of those on the island now, Doc. Plus she's Indian too, runs around with Nat-brats. Besides, we're law now, we got badges. Little Williams knows to leave us alone."

They squinted at me, their Sharkey. Did the old man approve? Had the little piggies done well? They rooted for reward, yet I had none to give them. When they discover this, the Beaver Bois will make her squirm. They'll take their payment, a pound—or a pounding—of her flesh.

Would I allow it? Probably. So long as science came first.

Of course, I'm kidding myself. I have no laboratory, no technocrats, no files, no servers. I've lost all my mercenaries and been banished from Panzer. Without my Palantir, I can't contact the CORPS.

But would I want to?

Major Naz was beaten, badly, at the border. He'd run, cut his losses, then came for the Greenie. He'd taken my Hawk, killing her in the process. Both were shot from the sky. I witnessed the fireball, felt its sear of heat. Good riddance to Naz. And to Nighthawk, goodbye.

I can't stop shivering. This hovel is freezing, the woodstove gone cold. These boys look to me for orders. I'll play my part, then warm up with some shine. Wermer stands beside me. I must keep him, he's mine. I empower my voice, directing it at the chief of this freckled clan, "Only one thing matters, Mr. Ferny. Scratch that, make it two."

The thorny man was loath to take orders, so I softened my touch. "You've done well here, and will be rewarded. But first, fetch me your little Greenie. Then get us some gas. We need heat for this home, and fuel for our flier."

I indicated the window, the snowy field. Naz's AH-6 perched with empty tanks. There were weapons in its pods, enough to subdue any citizens, but without precious fuel we were grounded. The Halloween night flight had been horrible, Werm forced to land, refueling from jerry cans. I caught him utilizing the EYE, but worse, I caught a chill.

Ferny nodded at my commands. "No problem," said the chief. "Load up, boys! We'll take the truck to town. Get two birds with one stone. We'll hitch the fuel-wagon from the harbor, and grab our little witch on the way!"

The piggies were squealing, to market they'd go. My mercenary sneered at their rustic rifles. Behind a door a baby cried, hushed by its mother. I watched my man; I knew him. The Werm licked his lips.

"Mr. Ferny!" My voice stopped the clan leader mid-stride. Their truck had been started. His cousins piled in bearing shotguns and pistols; most wore badges. The Beaver Bois were beaming in the dark.

"Yes, Doctor Schark?" Ferny was in a hurry.

"You made mention of moonshine?"

"That I did, Doctor. A fine shine. You'll see!"

He bent backwards to host me, setting out a jug and two glasses, both filthy. He even rekindled fire in the stove. He'd have tucked me in if I'd let him.

"That will be all, Mr. Ferny. Godspeed!"

The crooked man nodded and hurried out. Taillights disappeared in the dark. Wermer, meticulous, cleaned his pistol, its parts. The stove warmed. I took a kerosene-flavored sip, warming as well. The kitchen, the house, the whole world—for a minute—was quiet. How the mighty had fallen. My wine cellar, my staff, my legacy. A bell, far away, began to toll. Ask not, I thought. So I sipped again, and didn't.

It all came down to fuel, to electricity. Whoever had it wielded power. General Kamul, controlling the coastal refineries, had more than most, but not enough, not to harness AYE EYE. The fires that fed peak power were cooling, wattage dimming. And thank goodness. Fully charged, the EYE was, all-seeing—nearly omniscient. Linked to its nine servants—enslaved by their halos—who could stand against the CORPS? Not I certainly, even in my prime. There were rumors that the EYE—following blueprints of its own—was close to completing a fusion reactor beneath the Pentagon, mastering a source of infinite power. In the future, AYE EYE might no longer be constrained by the grid.

Pride goeth before a fall. I squandered all my chances. Betting big at the bridge, I'd been busted. I've lost so many things. And I'm tired. The shine is shit, of course. My lids are like lead. I might just doze.

With a metallic flourish, Wermer worked the slide of his pistol and holstered it. I cracked a bleary eye. Assembled, my man stood ready.

Another cry mewled from the bedroom.

Werm flicked his tongue, bulging eyes asking permission. I granted it. What did I care? He stepped to the bedroom, prying open its door. From the nightstand a greasy candle wavered; Madonna and child frescoed the scene. There was no waver in Werm. He went to them, unbuckling, and knelt on their bed. He made soft noises as he pulled the babe from its breast.

I sip my shine. He's left the door open so his Sharkey can see.

Something cracks inside me. I remember the bell, its midnight peal.

Surely—another sip—that bell tolls for me.

Tree Academy: Finding

JOSIE GREENE SLUNG HER HAMMOCK HIGH. She suspended herself between birches, puffy in her coat, batting flakes from tear-damp eyes. The Martin house glowed across the snowfield, pumpkins on the porch, lit from within. Mister and missus, asleep in their bed. A whiff of woodsmoke tickled Josie's nostrils. Off the ground was always better. Hard for her to tune treeish without being aloft.

Things were happening on the island, an island she'd never left. Josie felt an overlay of vibrations. Oldest, deepest, was a thrumming from the earth. Seismographic, she sensed its ticking, *tom-toom, tom-toom,* her needle jumping. Next, something foul had thudded over, black blades chopping the night. Terrifying, till its engine-whine ceased. And finally, a bell had tolled, or was it two? And what midnight tale were they telling?

Clang! Josie felt fear.

Clang! There was fire.

Clang! There were foes.

Clang! Clang! Clang! Islanders, awake!

Amidst the clamor, Josie felt a stirring from the birch trees, a stretching of limbs. Their paper eyes, ice-encrusted, began to blink. Plenty of winter left for sleeping. The grove had been bolted awake by someone's *need.*

Miin's need? Josie knew it was, least she wanted it to be.

The birches were more certain. Molecules, not emotion, had decided them. Below the frost line, the mycorrhiza remembered Miinan. Her pheromones were filed in the root-mass of the island. Her signature now was circulating, telegraphed by tubers. The island kept a list of its dendrophiles; Miin's profile was publicized, her urgency expressed. *Sunlight-on-berries* had been confined!

The old ones in their burrows heard the news first, *tom-tooming* what they could. Now it was Josie's turn. She constructed a map in her mind, planting it with trees, arranging her lignin landmarks. She proffered it now to the birches, imploring their twigs to sign it. The *wiigwaasag*, sweet-blooded by nature, agreed. They returned Josie's map, engraved now in green.

Snow crystals covered her hammock chrysalis. Josie minded her map, turning it one way, then another, till it mentally clicked. Instead of roads, there were roots, and every trail was a tendril. She followed the forks to a house made of stone. Their teacher was there!

Josie emerged from her cocoon, flying through snow. She shook her friends from stumpish stupors—oak, pine, and beech. There was talk of the horse, of harnessing, but that would take time. The students, hard-pressed, were soon pedaling bikes.

Four miles from Martin's farm to Miin, in darkness and in snow. They packed some gear: a crowbar, a lantern, extra clothing. Arriving out of breath, they found the Stone House was dead. Her classmates, breathing hard, looked to Josie. "Miin's inside, let's try the cellar."

Michael pried off the hasp and the lock-hole was opened. Cheyanna sparked the wick, adjusted flame, and the four friends descended. A foulness met them halfway, a fecal fug that wrinkled their noses. By lantern light, they glimpsed a figure hanging lifeless from the rafters.

"Is that—?"

"Is she—?"

"Miinan? Teacher? Miin?"

Something green and tubular shimmered from the dirt floor.

Slowly, the suspended marionette twirled towards the lamp. Blueberry, bruised, turned her face towards the refined sunlight of their lamp, heliotropic till the end. "And *what* do we have *here*?" their teacher rasped in a jesting tone.

Michael Martin, the academy mimic, smiled wide, then burst into tears.

Raising the Alarm

DING-LING!

Barkeep Alice locked her tavern door behind Halloween's final patron. She lifted pumpkin lids, blowing out their greasy candles. It was after midnight and she'd made up her mind. It was time, past time, to set things right. Everything started slipping when Doyle and Hanny went away. When the captains hadn't come back, shit got even worse.

Alice blamed the Fernys. Most did, but so far the townsfolk had done nothing. Bill's boys had started stealing, roughing people up. The council deliberated; Deputy Williams delayed. An armed standoff was off the table. Getting shot by a damn *Shirriff* scared most folks away.

Of course, the bartender had eavesdropped on Sam and Annie's booth. Overhearing them had decided her. Alice knew Miin, always had, the island's favorite orphan. If the girl had been taken, abducted by those assholes, then their piggish fucking heads would have to roll.

Wiping down her bar, Alice felt a cloud of fear. Something terrible was looming. A blade of terror touched her heart. Alice steeled herself, it was *past* fucking time.

She slipped out the back; it was snowing. She walked the block to Holy Cross and roused Father Peter. Together they tolled the big bell—*Islanders, awake!*

Then she woke Travis Williams and told the deputy off.

Battery driven, the lighthouse clock blinked 0100. Maggie Doyle keyed the mic: "Point La Par, Point La Par, Point La Par. This is Whiskey Light, over." She released the PTT button.

A crackling came through, and then, "Whiskey Light, this is Point La Par, over." Young Hannigan was at his station. Nick had been half-dreaming of her.

"Point La Par, what's your report, over?"

"Whiskey Light, Point La Par. Nothing to report, except I love you, over."

"Point La Par. Roger, nothing to report. Whiskey Light, out."

Maggie, warmed by Nick's aside, updated the log with cold fingers. Footsteps spiraled up the stairs; she recognized the tread. "Aunt Annie! Happy Halloween!"

Her aunt entered, puffing, and tossed her niece a sugary treat. "Who's on watch?" Aunt Annie looked grim. Maggie spun her logbook: *Hannigan, McCann, Miller, Keller, Bauman …*

Widow Doyle nodded. "A good crew, friends of Tom's, every one."

"Auntie, what's wrong?"

Then Maggie felt it too; some dreadful squall was blowing their way. Her radio lit up. Other watchers were tracking. Miller, at Beaver Head—the island's southern point—was closest: "It passed right fuckin' over me. Scared me shitless. A helicopter, lights off, flying low. Damn thing disappeared towards the interior."

Maggie scribed Miller's sighting, a rare contact in the almost empty log.

Clang! Clang! Clang!

She looked askance at auntie. They both heard it—holy shit! The Holy Cross bell!

Islanders, awake!

Maggie radioed the nearest watchers. Each station kept a boat, fueled and always ready. Those she summoned were already shoving off, opening throttles, speeding darkly—lights off—towards the harbor. The rest maintained their watch. Who knew what else was out there?

On Main Street, near the harbor, Barkeep Alice had lit a fire against the cold. The first responders gathered around her burn barrel. Annie and Maggie had come down from the tower. Tom's niece detailed their defenses—fog horn, spotlights, ambush. "Something's coming. Probably for the fuel. And we all know a girl has been taken. If they don't come to us, then in the morning, we'll take the fight to them."

The watermen, old salts, joshed each other, only half-listening to young Maggie's plan. Tom's niece balled her fists, stumped in close, and chin to chin cussed 'em out for cowards. After her outburst—punctuated by some choice phrases of Tom's—the "cancerous cunts" and "goat fuckers" fell right in line.

"Aye, Aye, Captain Doyle!" And they meant it. The crews maneuvered their boats and made ready, following Bloody Maggie's plan.

The big bell brought in the townsfolk and nearby farmers. Most jogged or bicycled; a few carried firearms. Some Indian Pointers clopped in, their shaggy ponies steaming in the snow. Deer rifles were pulled from scabbards, wielded by dead-eye elders with a grudge. Travis Williams, late to the light, did his part. With the crowd as his witness, he verbally de-deputized Ferny and his boys.

"About fuckin' time," was the crowd's consensus.

Alice clarified the rules in her last-call voice, "No killing! Not if you can help it. They're islanders after all. Shoot-to-wound if you have to, and watch for Annie's signal."

Mrs. Doyle mimed covering her ears. "That fog horn will blow your drums out, pay attention or pay the price!"

They dispersed to battle stations. The snow sifted down. Annie warmed her hands and waited. It didn't take long. Headlights swung onto Main Street, twin beams groping her way.

Shirriffs to Town

THE TOWNSHIP TRUCK—*SHIRRIFFS-OBEY!*—bounced down Bagúin to Young Patrick's Road. The dead-end was a mess. Rutted from logging, the two-track was frozen. Stately maples had once sheltered the lane. Their stumps and slashings loomed skeletal, haunting the headlights.

Ferny, cradling a police-issue 12 gauge, rode shotgun. The rest of the clan squeezed in where they could. Schark's helicopter had sure been a surprise. The pilot, Wermer, and his pistol-pointing had surprised Ferny too. The Beaver Bois were playing with fire. He heard his Da's voice from the grave, *Matter of time, Billy, 'fore someone gets burned.*

But it wouldn't be him. Ferny finally had the odds. His rivals were dead: Big Hannigan, Two-Crow, and that fucking show-off, Tommy Doyle. Ferny had shot the old crow himself. Ever since Keith's killing, the Indians on the point had left him alone. The Nats were weak too. They'd lost leaders at the bridge and some of their women had slunk away in a canoe. Everyone else only cared about food, firewood, and surviving the winter. Plus, his Beavers had been deputized. With badges and bullets, his Bois would be fine.

He couldn't believe Dr. Schark, a CEO-celebrity, was drinking shine in his home. Stranger still was the helicopter perched in his yard. The stinky contraption thrilled him. Ferny pictured it chopping his foes, putting them in place, setting things right.

The doctor wanted two things tonight, and Ferny would deliver. First, they'd grab the Greenie on the way to town. The girl would be no trouble, Schark promising reward. Next, they'd gather up the fuel-wagon, hitch it from the harbor, and trailer it home. Ten miles round trip, they'd be back in an hour. Then they'd celebrate their spoils and discuss next steps. The future looked bright for Clan Ferny.

His cousin slowed and turned left on Patrick's Road. A quarter-mile later, the boys in the truck bed started shouting, thumping on the roof. There was a pulsing glow in the east, a fiery throb. Too early for sunrise; was something burning at the King's Highway crossing?

Ferny couldn't rub the strangeness from his eyes. Stone House was on fire. Could rocks even burn? Sure looked like it. The heat as they approached pushed the truck and its human livestock away. Was the girl still inside? Shit! Schark would not be pleased. The doctor wanted a Greenie. Now Ferny had none to give.

The cousins squealed on each other. *What the hell! Who checked her last? Which of you fuckers has been fondling?* Innocence all around. Out of sight, out of mind, their captive had been neglected. There'd been no waterboarding, no ducking of the witch, no touching neither. Too many search parties, too many eyes. The Bois had been forced to leave her alone.

The buck stopped with Ferny, their chief. Bitter, Bill let it go. Fuel was more important. They put the fire behind them, turning north onto King's Highway and sped, scowling, towards the darkened harbor.

Things went from bad to worse; the frying pan, then the fire.

The island's precious fuel supply, tightly rationed, was locked inside the fenced ferry landing. Ferny's plan was simple: flatten the gate, hitch up the honey-wagon, and head home before the lighthouse knew what hit 'em.

Course, there'd be a watcher on duty—thanks to Tom fucking Doyle. There'd be a radio up there and some asshole would use it. But what could they do? By the time a posse formed, they'd be holed up at Bagúin. Then let them come! Visions of helicopter strafings danced in Ferny's head. Any posse would turn pussy, they'd turn their tails and run.

Approaching town, every window was dark; jack-o'-lanterns extinguished by snow. At Holy Cross they turned right, then left onto Main. In the small hours, islanders were abed, snoring in icy rooms.

All but one.

Some fool stood outside the fuel fence, warming her hands at a trashcan fire. Ferny squinted. No fucking way. His old crush, the widow, Annie Doyle. She blocked their path.

"High beam that bitch!"

Cousin Driver flicked his lights. Annie flicked them off, matching the pigs, glare for glare. "You can't have it, Bill. It's not yours."

Ferny rolled down his window. "And why fuckin' not? The Boss needs it. Besides, we're the law. Now get outta our way!"

Ferny's cousin revved the engine. Annie flexed her fists in the firelight. "Bill Ferny, you're not wanted here, never have been. This isn't your place."

Ferny feared his new master, Dr. Schark and his pilot. With their green witch burned alive, Bill needed that fuel. He leaned towards Annie and spat from the window, "And why should we listen to you?"

Ferny exited the truck, racking a shell for show, and stepped towards her. His ruffians piled out, trotting after their chief. They carried weapons, some sporting tin badges.

Annie didn't move. "Because, Bill, you're standing in the light and covered by rifles."

Ferny looked but saw nothing. Main street was empty, the harbor, pitch black. "One last chance, Annie, for old time's. Now get the fuck outta our way!"

Sneering, he ordered his driver. The dude honked the horn and began rolling towards her. Annie didn't move. "Blow it out your ass, I've got one better." She covered her ears. From the Coast Guard Station, the fog horn boomed—*DOOOOOOOuuuuuuum!*

The bacon boys squealed, the decibels deafening. Then a blaze of lumens caught them squirming. There were spotlights from the water, spotlights from the wharf. Windows and hedges sprouted muzzles aimed by stern-eyed citizens. A dozen rifle bolts were locked into place; the Beaver Bois were trapped. The townsfolk had the draw on the *Shirriffs*. Ferny and his clan laid down their weapons and were spared.

"Hold your fire!" "Don't shoot!" Several voices shouted at once—Annie's by the fence, captains from the water. There were other voices too, less forgiving, hoping some fool would make a move. But no fool did. The battle by the water had been bloodless.

Last Call

DAYBREAK WASN'T FAR OFF. The snow had ceased, citizens returning to hearth and home. The *Shirriffs* and Ferny had been disarmed, de-badged, and detained. Of Miin and her murder, they hadn't said shit. Deputy Williams cuffed them to bunks in the county's substation, then read them to sleep, quoting Miranda: "You have the right to remain silent."

Alice, Annie, and Maggie discussed their next move. "Need to make a house call to Bagúin, see what those boys have been up to. And we need to find Miin."

Deputy Williams nodded to the township truck. "Give you gals a lift? Seems the least I can do."

Shamrock's owner was thoughtful. "Not a bad idea. If there's anyone left at Baggy's dead-end, they won't suspect their own truck."

They turned away volunteers. The deputy drove, giving Bill's shotgun to Alice. The Doyles—auntie and niece—rode in the backseat. Some elders had already departed on horseback. "We'll meet you there," a rider said, "just in case."

Two years since the girls had gone for a drive. Williams pushed a button and the heat came on. Out of habit, Alice tuned the radio, searching for stations—static, every one, the viral soundtrack of apocalypse. They drove south on King's Highway; soon the harbor was behind. A tiny push of the pedal and they flew down the road. It took their breath away, the petro-ease of speed.

The cold sky was thawing, the black ice on the roadway, puddling to gray. Soon their headlights weren't needed. The roadside trees stood naked, exposed by the dawn. November 1st was All Hallows, Púca's Day in the Old Country. The island's own little people, if they existed, had stopped drumming. Any hole-dwellers had again gone to ground.

The deputy decelerated. "Someone coming our way. A horse and wagon?"

Alice left her shotgun alone. "That's Martin's rig. He's driving too fast and there's kids with him. Travis, be careful."

They parked the truck and opened doors, stepping into the chill. Tree crowns were gilded by sunrise. The old draft horse *clip-clopped* towards them. The truckers opened their palms, tokening peace. Martin halted his horse. The heaving creature steamed where it stood, an equine locomotive—an engine of flesh, fueled by fodder. They counted four children. Young Michael carried a shotgun beside his dad. Josie Greene, Cheyanna from the Point, and one of the Naturals—Arturo?—sat behind in the wagon.

They exchanged good mornings and eyed each other.

"Saw the truck. Feared you were Ferny."

"Won't have to worry about them anymore," the deputy caught him up, "*Shirriffs* got themselves arrested trying to steal fuel."

"Ferny too?" Nods from the truckers. The farmer approved while the kids in the wagon kept quiet.

Alice addressed them, "Eat up your candy yet?" She'd treated their bags last night at the 'Rock.

Poker faces, every one. Mr. Martin seemed impatient, fingering the reins. "Well, we're headed to town. Clinic open yet?"

Frustrated, Josie interrupted the small-talking adults. "We found Miin! She's hurt bad. We need Doc Newsome, now!" Josie pointed at a blanket pile in the wagon. Someone moaned beneath.

"My God!" They all moved at once.

Scattershot questions, flighty evasions. Miin's quilted stretcher was transferred to the truck bed. Deputy Williams, wearing a white hat at last, played the part: "Well done! We'll take her to Doc Newsome, you kids head home."

Josie wasn't having it. "No offense, but we're coming too! She's our *teacher!*"

Deputy puffed his chest, beginning to bluster. Alice deflated him, "No time for this! Kids, jump in the back and watch over Miin. Martin, what's your plan?"

The farmer thought for a moment. "Where were you headed?"

"Baggy End. Might be more trouble."

"I'll turn around and head that way too. Pick me up after you drop by the clinic?" Alice nodded and both rigs reversed—the truck to town, Martin's wagon to Bagúin.

No great distances on the north end of the island, only five miles between the clinic and Bagúin. The township truck delivered the patient to Newsome. The doctor tried to shoo out the kids. Michael Martin quipped, "But Doc, we're Miin's *minions!*" The practitioner relented as smiles cracked their faces.

Miinan in good hands, the truck backtracked towards Ferny's cabin. On Paid Een Ogs Road they overtook Martin's wagon. "Jump in! Bring that shotgun!" Deputy was driving, Alice beside him, both Doyles sitting behind in the cab.

Martin hobbled his horse, feeding an apple to its engine. "I've got a score to settle. They hurt that girl bad. Someone'll pay."

Baggy End was bouncy. The township truck was rattled by ruts. "Waste of good timber," Martin muttered, eyeing the treefall along the lane. Nearing the cabin, they found a great tree lying hewn, its ancient corpus left to rot, slowly leached by lichens, one century at a time.

Unchallenged, they idled the truck. The posse took in the scene. The Ferny place—well-placed on its hill—was trashed. Its once-large garden, untended, grew only weeds. Vehicles from various decades varied in decay. A rust-yard of bodies. A potter's field of parts. The cold chimney was smokeless. The windows wore blinds. A tatter of flags bannered Ferny's beliefs, *Don't Tread on Me! WhereWeGo1WeGoAll!*

Something monstrous fumed in a field, some terror from a bygone age. They discussed it in the truck: "Must be the helicopter we heard."

"Explains them stealing fuel, though our dirty diesel would destroy it."

"Imagine if that thing got off the ground?"

They imagined. The beast bristled with weapons. They shuddered.

Hand-painted signs were nailed to a tree trunk. *No Admittance! And Party Business Only!* A crooked cross flagged their chapter of Michigan's neo-Nazi party. A tired swing had been cut down, a ragged noose dangling from its fray.

"Well, here goes." The county's only deputy prepared to do his duty. From his pocket he withdrew a mask, an N95, and put it on. Williams holstered a pistol; his badge shielded his chest.

"We'll cover you, Travis." Alice and Farmer Martin flanked him and approached. Maggie and Annie followed too. They heard birdcalls, half a dozen, from the woodlot. An Indian Pointer showed himself, then he and his deer rifle faded back into the trees.

"They must've cut cross country?" Alice asked.

Martin nodded. "Times like this, it's good to have friends."

"Amen to that." Both shotgunners swallowed.

The deputy adjusted his mask, then knocked loudly on the battered green door.

A shark's dead eyes peered through the blinds:

The truck had returned, though it bore different riders?

No wagon had been hitched, no fuel for his helo?

How had this posse gotten past surveillance?

Curse his mercenary and the man's rusty halo!

Apparently Werm had scouted elsewhere.

Mapping goodwife Ashley, the terrain of her body.

Rifles were aimed from the treeline. Alice and Martin backed their deputy's play. An old-looking man, raggedly dressed, opened the door. A shadow slouched behind him.

"May I help you?" An educated voice gone slurry, a tone of polite aggravation.

"Mr. Schark is it? From Panzer Pharmaceuticals? I'm Deputy Williams. Bill Ferny has filled us in. Are you contagious, sir? We will abide no virus on this island."

"Ha! Abide no virus. Fool! I *AM* the virus! And it's *doctor*, you dolt!" The man's face cracked and his laugh was hideous. Deputy Williams took a step backwards. His shotgunners stepped up, covering his play.

Alice called out in her barkeeper's bray, "Will you scorn our help? We offer it to you and your man!"

"To *me?* To S*harkey?* Nay, save your pity. All my hopes are ruined, but I would not share in yours."

"What about your man then?"

At this, a pale creature, a guard of some sort, slunk into the morning light and flinched. Something metal was attached to his head. The man was buttoning his pants, cinching a gun belt.

"You mean Wermer here?" Schark sneered. "Well, you can't have him. He's my pilot. If you'll sell us some gasoline, we'll be on our way."

The pilot protested, "Doctor, it's *jet* fuel we need."

"Silence, Werm! Can't you see these people want us to leave?"

Alice tried again: "Mr. Wermer is it? You're welcome to stay. Quarantine first, and then a fresh start."

Schark laughed. "Nothing fresh about Werm here! He's rotten! Why don't you tell these kind people exactly *what* you've been doing? Or should I say *who?*"

The mercenary glared at his master. Snake-quick, Werm pulled a pistol, putting it to Schark's temple as he addressed the posse. "This doctor is a war criminal, a mass-murderer. I'll trade him to you!"

Another laugh, and a sharp crack from a tooth, a hollow one. Schark smiled at the scent of bitter almonds, his last. He'd bitten a cyanide capsule—aerosolized and patent-pending—invented by Panzer for just such occasions.

The doctor's face tightened, then relaxed. *"Shark Bites," he would have called them. Too late he saw the profit potential. He could've made billions. Who wouldn't want to control their own end?*

The man's body crumpled. A gray mist hovered over it, still poisonous. The islanders stepped back in horror. From the cabin a woman cried, springing suddenly at Wermer.

"Ashley! Stop!" Alice yelled.

Too late.

Wermer dropped his pistol; it fell with a thud. Mrs. Ferny held a bloody carving knife. Werm was split open for display. He bled out, dying in his own mud. Ashley's infant, safe inside, gurgled with approval.

The house-callers, stunned, now stood sickened. The poison mist blew away, scoured by a wind from the west.

"Ashley Ferny, drop that knife!" the barkeeper barked. The woman did so, ducked inside, and came back with the baby and a bag of her things.

"Come with us, Ashley, we'll put you somewhere safe." Annie and Maggie stepped up.

"Don't go near her! Might be contagious!" Deputy Williams wore the only mask. Both Doyles ignored him. They took mother and child, settling them in the truck away from the bodies.

The deputy was at a loss. He'd just witnessed murder. No way he'd charge Ashley: *I can only guess what she's been through.* He looked down at the once-famous doctor. The man had been on TV, a celebrity of collapse. Schark's face had been shriveled by cyanide—skin stretched tight on a hideous skull. Williams kept his mask on, stepped inside, and emerged with dirty blankets. He shrouded the two corpses and turned back to his truck. "I'll fetch Newsome, the coroner, and come back for the bodies."

And that damn helicopter. Thing looked lethal, fuel or no. He'd bring it up at council, an emergency session.

Alice and Martin had safetied their shotguns. At the treeline, they exchanged words with the elders—*miigwech, chi-miigwech*—parting in peace. The ponies carried the warriors home to the Point. Deputy drove the rest to town; last fuel he'd be burning for a while. The day's mileage had been a splurge. On Young Patrick's Road, Martin resumed his wagon. "Need to check on the missus. If you see my Michael, please send him home."

Next stop was Newsome's clinic. A crowd had gathered outside its doors. Word had gone round about Miin and her mistreatment. The deputy assured them a council would be called and justice served. Aunt Annie and Maggie Doyle escorted Ashley and her baby inside. The woman had been badly hurt. Mrs. Ferny was brought to an examination room.

Barkeep Alice asked Newsome about Miin and her rescuers. The doctor was treating her, the four students assisting. Alice, up all night, was exhausted. She bid them farewell and walked home. She'd have to open the Shamrock soon. Place would be packed. Gossip was thirsty work.

Deputy had a word with Newsome about the two bodies, then trucked to the substation to check on Ferny's gang. Their cuffs chafed, and they were full of complaints—no food and their room was fucking freezing. They had powerful friends that would put things to rights.

Williams chafed them further—Schark was a suicide. His Werm had been dissected. The Bois of Beaver Island gave little squeals of despair.

Tree Academy: Healing

MIIN WOULD NEVER HEAL, not fully, not right away.

Their job, Samantha instructed, was to bring her back, as far as they were able. The wise woman cautioned patience. Recovery took time; Miin had been snatched, then stretched. She'd been forgotten, then found. For finding her, Miin gave them thanks—her students, her saviors. They smiled to hear it—Josie, Michael, Cheyanna, and Arturo—though they smiled through tears.

November, gray and brown, waited on winter, the second since collapse. Islanders waited too, on news from the mainland. *Where was their Mukwa?* Indian Point wondered. *And our Sentinel Daughters?* asked ELF Country.

The watch was maintained, though the tower logged few entries. No broadcasts had been received, the month's atmospherics not ideal for transmission. *Was Colonel Dennis still headquartered at Ignace? Was the Free North still free? And what about Virals? And pockets of Hidden? And Baptiste and his voyageurs in their oversized canoes?*

Their worldview darkened with the dimming days. The island's vision tunneled—calories, cordwood, and occasional cooperation. A purgatorial season. Great skeins of southing geese unspooled, fleeing the freeze. Islanders that looked up tracked them with envy.

Council had convened, had concurred. Ferny and his boys would remain confined. The harbor's stockpile of fuel was inspected. Stabilizer was added and the clinic's ration was reduced. Not much left in island tanks. Gasoline goes bad, diesel too, how long would it last? Council felt panic at the ease of Schark's intrusion. If more choppers crossed over, how would they stop them? Or an invasion fleet? Shit, even a raft? A single Spreader could sting them all dead.

With his fuel allotment gutted, Doc Newsome cycled down the clinic's generator. He and his helpers signed off on Miin's release. Blueberry, herself again, was gently uprooted, then replanted carefully in the bog. The patient was popular. Many hands helped shift her to Samantha's shack. Mr. Martin drove his wagon till the two-track brushed over. There were plenty of stretcher-bearers to carry Miin home.

Cranberry Bog was the peaty heart of the Jordan State Forest. Samantha's sugar shack, with its weathered boards and woodsmoke patina, had been the site of Miin's abduction. But the brave girl didn't flinch. She held its spirits blameless. With Miinan's return, the familiar fairies—*loci spirituum*—doubled their efforts, doing what they could to salve her suffering.

But healing requires light. Medicinals, and the pharma-plants that produce them, need solar. As December approached, the daylight disappeared. Sugar maples were empty, hollowed out, summer's green elixir cold-stored in their roots. Josie, even Samantha, couldn't tap them. The trees, undead, stood bloodless, awaiting the thaw.

Miinan would wait too. What Blueberry needed was a full dose of spring. Samantha explained it to the students: "Until then, we make do with what we have."

"And what's that?" asked Arturo.

Samantha winked, waiting on the pupils. Josie and Cheyanna announced in sync, "As a last resort, use *At-the-last.*"

The class recalled the pneumonic: "Minty-*green*, methyl salicylates *means*." They'd memorized the melody that portioned the potion. Sam's shack began humming as dried herbs were taken down—chamomile, feverfew, St. John's. Stirred awake by students, the botanicals, bioactivated, began to bloom, a simulacrum of spring. Miin, scenting green, months early, responded in kind.

Homeward Bound

TOM DOYLE, MAN AND BOY, had spent most holidays off-shore. Few Decembers found him tied up with Annie. Christmas cloyed, made him claustrophobic; Doyle preferred his Silent Nights to be so, save for wave-lap and the holy hymn of horsepower.

Christmas Eve on the Great Lake, all calm, all bright. Grid gone, the winter stars dazzled, diminished only by the fulling moon. Doyle helmed his tugboat and gave thanks. He'd been blind, but now could see. Was once marooned, then found by friends. His *Mary* had gone under, now *Debbie's* solid decking held him up. And he had a package—a present, already decorated—for his Annie, and the whole island too. Celestial, Doyle navigated. Beaver Island was close! They just might make it in time.

Dirty Debbie's logbook lay open on the chart table, illuminated red by a night-vision bulb. Doyle's blocky hand outlined their journey. After Ohio, Baptiste and his voyageurs remained by Tom's side. From eve to eve, Halloween to Christmas, the two tug boats and their crews had been busy.

October 31st, North Maumee Bay, cold and snowy

1200	*Ohio's Red militias have been routed.*
1400	*We've filled our tanks with their fuel.*
1600	*Unhitched from the grounded barge.*
1800	*Farewelled Sergeant Taylor, shoved off for Detroit.*

Clouds of crows—black cumulus—had covered the corpse-strewn field. Doyle's barge of Virals—some on Harleys, some afoot—had saved the fucking day, headless horsemen on Halloween! The invading Reds, without PPE or unit discipline, had scattered. Two helicopters had flown away westward. Cowboy and the septic preacher raced north in the Humvee to the hospital at Ignace.

To the victor went the spoils, unspoiled fuel. Sergeant Taylor had thanked Tom's flotilla with diesel; she'd been generous to the Viral caravan as well. Sussan and her Marines commandeered Red buses and vans, spreading south, following the old laws, seeking the sun.

Sergeant Taylor would lead survivors—Griffs, Panthers, and Antiva—north to Detroit. They'd refit at the refinery. Quarantine would be mandatory. Her cannoneers had been fighting non-stop for weeks. Doyle and Baptiste would get there first—Frenchie in his tug, Doyle driving *Debbie*.

November 1st, Zug Island, MPC, calm and clear

1400   The execs were giddy, so we gouged them for supplies.

The petro-hive had been humming. The dreaded Reds were defeated and Detroit's Virals had gone. Over loudspeakers, the voyageurs were hailed. Worker bees pumped fists for the conquering heroes—the victors, the valiant.

Baptiste and Doyle filled a barge with stabilized diesel, cluttering its deck with tools and spare parts. They stocked their tugboats with crates of nonperishables. Bay City was next, and its mothballed prize. Doyle had a delicious idea, a surprise present for Beaver Island and his oft-neglected bride.

November 3rd, Port Sanilac, Lake Huron, rough weather

1100   Our two tugs and barge have been hugging the coast.

Doyle and Baptiste had a mug-up in *Debbie's* wheelhouse. They pored over stale charts and poured staler coffee. The mariners waited out the whitecaps gnawing at the breakwater.

"What d'ya think, Frenchie?" Doyle fingered Saginaw River, their next port of call, up and around Michigan's thumb. Baptiste traced their route from there—north to Alpena, a stop at St. Ignace, then on to Beaver Island.

"A long way, *capitain.* Lotta fuel. Lotta risk. Is your surprise present even seaworthy? The weather, *Dieu pardonne,* will only get worse."

Doyle agreed on all points. Fuck it. He'd still try. He owed the island this effort. He owed his Annie even more.

November 4th, Saginaw River, diminishing winds

0800   Tied up at the museum pier. We'll be here a while.

Two weeks since they'd seen her last. Of course she was pierside, where else would she be? Who else would want her? Who but themselves could set the old gal free?

November 5th-December 20th, Saginaw Valley Museum

"The Gray Ghost of Vietnam" was one of her nicknames. In her prime, she'd been designated "Fast" as well. But those days were decades gone. It would take more than a month to make her seaworthy. The voyageur deckhands, out-worked and out-cussed by both captains, would get to know all 400 feet of her once-sexy body.

For weeks, the punch-list of repairs only grew longer. With the turn of the month, the list finally started shrinking. They wielded welders and torches, scrap metal and paint. They cursed setbacks in three languages, cheering successes as one.

Bay City and its riverside were abandoned. The scrounge parties saw no Virals, no Antiva, no Hidden, no Law. There were no motor sounds, no flashes of light in the sky. The urban sprawl had been de-gentrified by collapse, its real estate green-lined by osprey entrepreneurs and hipster coyotes. Black bears of Tobico Marsh had grown bold, nosing through neighborhoods, window shopping for deals.

December 21st, Saginaw Bay, calm and cold

0930   Underway! Left the barge behind.

0945   Channel Island. Two tugs and one GIANT tow!

At long last, Annie's present had been patched, painted, renamed, and decorated. Her leaks had been stoppered, her rudder answering the helm. Baptiste's big canoes had been stowed and remaining diesel drummed for transport. She had a working radio on her bridge and a machine gun on her bow. They'd have to tug her though. Try as they might—and mightily they tried—her engines wouldn't turn.

December 24th, Straits of Mackinac, light winds WSW

1015   Reached Les Cheneaux Archipelago.

Approaching St. Ignace, Christmas Eve, Doyle deviated north, tugging Baptiste and their towed package along. He had to check. His shipwreck and marooning still traumatized. And he'd never seen the place, not with his eyes anyway. Doyle focused binoculars, and there it was, a tiny spit of land: 45.9222370° North, 84.4303128° West.

Goose Island, his blind guess had been good. There, the saplings! There, his sandy burrow! There, the birds!—competition for every calorie he'd combed. All his life, he'd been oblivious to his blind spots. Thomas Doyle, at last, began to see.

1200   Exchanged signals with Dennis.

1215   Tied up at St. Ignace.

1300   *Traded some of our fuel for armory surplus.*

Entering the harbor, Colonel Dennis, CO of the Griffins, ordered *Bravo Zulu* to honor the voyageurs. Signal flags—"Well Done!"—snapped from tower halyards. Baptiste and Doyle, tugging their oversize package, acknowledged with horns.

Soon the whole harbor was honking, including the ferry. *Nodin*—previously *Emerald Isle*—was resting from her Free North labors. Drone-damaged during the bridge battle, she'd since been repaired. The gaping hole left by Diana, her ELF captain, had not.

December had been cold; the Straits would soon freeze. Refugees would walk the ice road, pulled north by Polaris, stone cairns marking safe passage. Other forms, furtive in starlight, would walk across as well. Wolves—segregated for a century— were again moving south.

Colonel Dennis honored them by coming aboard. He debriefed both captains, taking notes on the Michigan-Ohio War as they saw it. The bookish man, of course, was writing one.

Doyle bartered diesel drums for armament and crates of late harvest—stocking stuffers for hungry hearths back home. Dennis had no comms with Beaver Island. Baptiste asked about Autumn. No word from Manitoulin either. Colonel had locked up his satellite phone. He didn't trust himself with the Palantir. Who knew what was out there? Why give himself away? For now, it was best to go dark.

Dennis shook their rough hands with his soft one, congratulating them again on their prize. The haze-gray warship was a sight, whether she made her own way or not. As the captains tugged their package away, Dennis noted the name change. Next to the DD-946 designation on the bow, a single word, *Annie*, had been stenciled with care.

2100   *Underway! Howlers wolf-whistled at* Annie.

As Doyle's tug left pierside, a large man threw down his crutches and jumped the widening divide. Mukwa barely made it, sprawling four-footed on deck, wincing in pain. The stowaway straightened, parting hair from his eyes. "Cap'n Doyle, can I please hitch a ride?"

It was the "please" that softened Doyle. They'd been shipmates before. Doyle sized up Mukwa, an islander from Indian Point. Keith Two-Crow, the youth's mentor, would be proud.

Doyle assented, "Third time's the charm, eh Muck?"

The longhair scowled, recently arrived from Kalamazoo.

"I mean, it's good to see ya again ... Mukwa." Doyle's better-self grinned, extending a big hand. The big man shook it, stood taller, sniffed the air, and got to work stowing lines, though he limped.

2145   *Crossed under Mackinac Bridge.*

2200   *A moment of silence, then set course 260° for home.*

A long blast from *Debbie's* horn. Baptiste and Doyle both idled their engines. The captains gazed upwards, as did Mukwa, Loon, and the voyageur crews. The bomb-severed roadway twisted above them in the moonlight. All four lanes had been cut. The big bridge led nowhere. Its two towers, scarred by fire, had not been repainted. Rusting rebar shed concrete in chunks.

Loon flashed back to Bearded Brian, their piney nest, the drone swarm at dusk, and shrieking eagles. The boy was eager for Beaver Island; he'd see his fellow flier soon.

For Mukwa it was motorcycles, the SIS charge, and the trumpeting mammoth. He couldn't unsee the yellow-painted Seekers, leaping—freshly contagious—to their deaths.

Doyle, newly sighted, pictured corpses on the lake bed, 30 fathoms deep, encrusted by mussels and freshwater clams. These vehicle traps, baited with flesh, formed a structure he vowed never to fish.

December 25th, Beaver Island approach, winds light, SSW

0700   Just raised harbor light! Christmas Day!

Tom Doyle signaled his deckhand on USS *Annie*. The red-capped voyageur started the generator, plugging in the lights. A thousand bulbs painted the gray lady—red, blue, white, and green.

Christmas Day

MAGGIE DOYLE STOOD TOWER WATCH. Saint James Harbor was skirted with ice. The full moon, and hourly reports from fellow watchers, kept her company all eve. Nick and their recent engagement warmed her as well. *But who would walk her down the aisle?*

Almost time to log the 0700 reports.

Maggie zipped up her layers, stepping onto the catwalk. Elevated, she observed Earth's curve, its implacable spin. The great globe rolled east, burying the moon, birthing the sun. Between the two lights twilight pinked the sky. Maggie faced east; something large was looming. She raised the big binoculars, spun the focus: a blur of light sharpened to points, multi-colored ones? *Holy shit, the shape was huge, a damn Christmas* Titanic!

Pulse revving, she quickly calculated its course, its speed. The dreadnought was being towed by two tugs, straight towards her harbor! She ducked back into the watch room, fogging a long blast on the horn: *WARRRRR—NING!*

Maggie observed no change in the targets' course or speed. Heart hammering, she blew five shorts: *WHAT—THE—FUCK—ARE—YOU?*

No response. The triple threats, possibly Viral, vectored closer. Maggie got on the radio: "Pan-pan, pan-pan, pan-pan, all stations, all stations, all stations. This is Whiskey Light, three unidentified motor vessels approaching my position, requesting assistance, over."

Around the island watchers scrambled, reluctant engines coughing to life. Ready-boats keeled through skim ice, converging on the contacts. Maggie heard her aunt spiraling up the stairs. The Doyle cottage was close.

For widowed Annie, the times had been taut. Made bitter by endings, old auntie had frayed. "Another damn helicopter?" she demanded, huffing up the last few steps.

"No auntie, take a look."

Annie spun the dial. "That's a damn warship!"

"Yes, but Auntie, why the lights?"

Channel 12 beeped, 156.600 MHz, the island's home frequency. Familiar, a ghost from Christmas past spoke to the present: "Whiskey Light, this is tugboat *Dirty Debbie*. Permission to enter the harbor, over."

Annie, red-faced, squeezed the mic. "Denied! Denied! *Debbie*, be advised, these waters are restricted. Stop your approach or be fired upon!"

A laugh like gravel rumbled from the speaker. *It couldn't be ... Tom? Uncle?*

The Doyle women stared, their disbelief was total. Channel 12 cackled, "Annie lass, that any way to talk to your hubby? Over!"

What the flaming hell? It WAS Tom!

The tugs towed closer, the Forrest Sherman-class destroyer, DD-946, looking sleek in the dawn. From all three vessels happy bells were clanging.

Annie was muttering in the mic, broadcasting her betrayal for the entire island to hear. "Why you ... scumbag! You ... maggot! You cheap, lousy—"

Maggie grabbed the radio. "Motor vessel *Debbie*, identify yourself—"

Annie grabbed it back. "Don't I know my own husband then?" The old gal wiped an eye, pushing Maggie away. "Girl, go sound the all clear!"

Niece Maggie—stunned—made her way to the bell. The ensuing love language between spouses violated all FCC rules on lewdness and profanity.

"You're a bum! You're a punk! You old piece of junk!"

"Happy Christmas?"

"Your ass!"

"I pray God it's our last!"

In the frosty morning, Maggie's tears froze to her lashes. *Uncle Tom could give her away at church!* The bride blushed, then grinned. *Ha! Now Nick would have to ask him!* She overheard the sparring spouses:

"Tom Doyle, you took my *dreams* from me!"

"I kept them with me babe, I put them with my own."

"Damn you, I can't make it all alone!"

"Annie-gal, I've built my dreams around *you.*"

Maggie, smiling, hummed an oldie of Auntie's. "Galway Bay" would be in the ceremony for sure. She fisted the bell-pull. The tower, then the town, echoed: "All clear!"

Islanders emerged, sharing scuttlebutt. "Captain Tom and his tow!" "Would you look at that?" "It can't be! Somehow the old dog survived."

USS *Annie*, festively lit, was on full display. The islanders began cheering, then singing, and the bells were ringing out for Christmas day.

Something large approached, of that much she was sure. Samantha consulted her watery mirror; the power of its ring was ebbing. Her vision, once far-sighted, had diminished. Tending Miin, they both heard the bell toll. Martin's barn was the nearest relay. The two women could tell by the tone it was merry.

"Minobii Niibaa Anama'e Giizhiigad!" The shack-mates shared a grin. "Happy Christmas!"

Back Splice

 DOCTOR CHOW WAS NOT RELIGIOUS, but he understood the reverend's pull. Walker, the septic amputee, had survived, but barely. That madman Campbell delivered him to the healing house just in time. Colonel Dennis read Taylor's battlefield note and immediately green-lit their care.

Chow prescribed antibiotics, intravenous fluids, and vasopressors. Walker, a supposed son of ancient kings, had recovered. Since then he'd crutched around, pacifying every patient he palmed. The man's reputation as a healer was growing. Walker preached amnesty for Virals, attracting a following. "These Spreaders, they have worked the will of the virus and its variant. As it fades from them, as it is scoured from them, they will return to themselves, to the trauma they have caused. They are more to be pitied, than feared." A bridge too far for many, though the chasm was shrinking.

Chow's faith was science. The gospel of data didn't lie, and there was good news in abundance. Hannah Hochstettler was part of Chow's medical team. The Amish *braucher* had described Walker's effect back in October, after measuring viral loads of Compliants he'd touched: "Walker has the hands of a healer."

Since then, the data confirmed that indeed there was healing going on. Chow wielded his microscope, its ring of magnification. Measured in T-cells or tinctures, the results were the same. Something was working.

Free North
Beaver Island
Manitou Island
Kalamazoo
Detroit
MICHIGAN
INDIANA
LAKE MICHIGAN
YIELD TO NONE

Colonel Dennis, historian of sorts, would need a long quiet spell to get it down proper. He'd been taking notes in a tower logbook. Its red cover crawled with scratched out titles: *The War in the West, The Shadow Lengthens,* and others. He'd been scribbling for decades, ever since his brain injury in the first Gulf War. Not visibly wounded, the young LT had found refuge in writing.

The colonel still had the habit, but the urgency was new. Dennis stood at his scattered desk, filled a pipe, and flared it—misting mountains of material with tobacco smog. How to get it all down? Not by blowing smoke. Inspired by Native allies, he was penning an appendix on Great Lakes' Indigenous. Dennis colonized their speech—*Anishinaabemowin*—marching it into columns: Ojibwe, Odawa, and Potawatomi.

St. Ignace received written word from the Rangers: Panzer Pharma had been abandoned and its Schark had swum free. Dr. Chow begged Dennis to send him south to scavenge its labs. Proper trials were needed, and equipment to conduct them. The colonel agreed; Walker and his biome would be fully investigated. Dennis asked Captain Young and his two enlisted men to escort Dr. Chow: "Strong enough, Frank? You soldiers ready for a recon mission?"

Booker and Cruz, bored by garrison life, shared a look. "Affirmative, sir."

Captain Young and his men got busy.

The Humvee had made it, delivering Walker just in time. The water-walker delivered Bob as well—from evils in his past, and from present infection.

Rolling off *Nodin* at St. Ignace, the amputee had been fussed over. Campbell's load-level and his keys had been taken. Testing negative for Covee, negative for Stinger, the Amish-hatted gunslinger had been promptly ignored. Fine by him. The bureaucracy of the Guard and its administration of the Free North hurt his head. Bossing was a bitch, Chosen or Griffins only a matter of degree.

But he wasn't ignored by all. Moseying through town, the first morning after arrival, he was hug-bombed by two refugee tykes. Little Sammy and sister Sarah bent their *ordnung* to sneak attack the tall *Englischer* who had saved them from the *iks*.

The siblings were plainly pleased at his surprise. They told their tale through laughter. Their *Mamm*, Hannah, arriving in the Free North, sent word to her father on the farm. Old Hochstettler had reluctantly uprooted. He and his *kinner* took the bus road north, fleeing the chaos of collapse and other horrors.

"Dawdy saw *Deifel*," Sarah whispered. The old farmer had witnessed skull-faced devils, feeding on the fringe.

"And how is your mama? How is Hannah?" Campbell had seen her once, at a POW camp in Clare. Bonneted, she'd been boarding a bus, Walker's *Pony*—RIP.

Both children grinned. With calloused hands they strong-armed Bob to their home for show-and-tell. They'd been assigned an empty house on Spring Street, near the football field, now a farm. Hannah and her father were stacking wood on the porch. Dawdy frowned to see him, making fists with both hands. Hannah straightened, then squinted, saying, "That's Elam's hat."

Campbell's lonely heart was heavy. Indeed, the hat belonged to her husband. Bob took it off, unbent the brim, and returned it. The woman received the straw hat, remembering.

"Hannah, I'm sorry." And Bob was. Not just for Elam's death, but for them all. "My wife died too. And my little girl."

They looked upon each other.

"I can call you Bob? Bob Campbell?" Dawdy and her kids had told stories.

"My friends call me Cowboy."

"A cowboy needs a hat." Hannah rebent Elam's brim, then

held his hat out as an offering. "This fits you."

Bob put it on, tipping it like a Texan. "Ma'am."

He and the kids helped finish the woodpile. Hannah went inside, preparing a meal. When breakfast was ready, they were summoned to the kitchen. Surprise, surprise, coffee-fucking-soup. Old crusts and older grounds, but Bob's grin split his face. His blue eyes—once red—were sparkling. The table had been set for five. Campbell hung his hat and jacket on a peg, removing his gunbelt too, hopefully for good. Hannah, glowing, guided him to his chair. "I heard what you did. You saved them."

She sat him down. Bob nodded to the children, winked at Dawdy's scowl. "Well," he said, "looks like I'm back."

Nighthawk, from her perch in the cedars, eyed the sandy island, the best one they'd seen. She and her sisters, Daughters of Gaia, had been canoeing Michigan's coastline for weeks. The island was South Manitou, eight miles offshore from Sleeping Bear Dunes.

With Nighthawk, they numbered eleven. All had seen combat: Bear River, Charlevoix, the bridge, the pump stations, now Panzer. None were unscathed. Sparrow had been shot by a Blackwater bullet. A flesh wound; she was healing. Chickadee's recurve had arrowed the mercenary, dude choking to death on a throat full of feathers.

On All Hallows' Eve, Hawk had spread her wings and flown from the helicopter. Mukwa's bear-sized bulk had cushioned her from concrete, though his body—bruised and broken—paid a price. She then fired the missile that killed Major Naz. Muck missed his shot, in more ways than one. Dr. Schark and his Werm, odious, had fled in their oily machine. Terror went with them—black wings, black breath. The snow had sifted through the floodlights. Cold, she'd turned Mukwa down and watched the broken man deflate. Down but not out, she spoke truth: "I'm just not ready, not yet."

By early November, the Sentinels began reconnaissance: Portage Creek, Kalamazoo River, Lake Michigan, and beyond.

Saying goodbye, had Nighthawk offered Oso hope? "Race you home!" she challenged him with a grin.

"Home?" Big bear, on crutches, looked confused. Muck had one arm in a sling; his shattered leg had been splinted by Freddy.

"Beaver Island? Your people are there. Samantha? Miin? I'll be back someday."

Moon-faced he nodded, turned tail, and crutched away. None of that mattered now. Gaia's Daughters had found a place of their own. The massive cedar that Hawk perched in—sentient for six centuries—reassured her with barky breath. Isolation was a must, then food and fresh water. Uninhabited for decades, Manitou's soils were good. Even in December, there was game to be had.

The women paddled its perimeter, looking for lights, for landings. This virgin grove had beckoned. Its oldest cedars predated Columbus. Mankind's recent calamity, reckoned by rings, was just one of many. Searching for something new, the women turned to the old. Gaia had provided the place. Winter be damned, the elves would do the rest.

After Halloween's tricks and treats, Hawk had thanked the Rangers, Robert and Freddy, for opening the cages. Sentinel Thorn she knew from before. Nighthawk tasked them with securing Panzer's hard drives, the refrigerated ova, embryos, and any medical equipment that might still be useful. Who knew what devilry the pharma labs had been brewing? The Rangers would overwinter inside Schark's compound; there were victims to care for and supplies to scrounge.

Shaggy and Mukwa turned the brothers down, scrounging a

ride north to the Straits instead, as soon as the broken bear was able. Shaggy winked as they departed; missing his Howler pack, he might rejoin the St. Ignace's Scouts.

With rivers and fertile fields, Panzerland had prospects. The brothers ranged wide, striding around this new shire. Robert chiseled their rune, signposting their claim. Freddy carved a peace emblem beneath each R. Ask first and shoot later. Adventurers Not Welcome!

Freddy pitched the concept: "A pleasant place for peaceful people, no d-bags allowed."

"Life should be for living." Thorn, family-ready, yearned for a Rose.

"So long as the perimeter is patrolled," Robert said, sobering them. "There are foul things afoot, and much work to do."

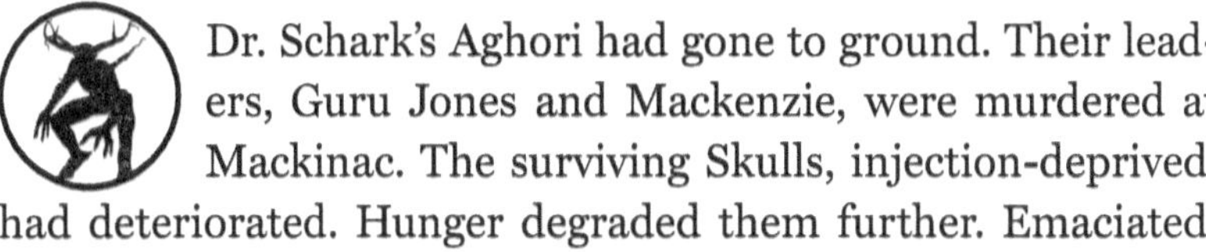

Dr. Schark's Aghori had gone to ground. Their leaders, Guru Jones and Mackenzie, were murdered at Mackinac. The surviving Skulls, injection-deprived, had deteriorated. Hunger degraded them further. Emaciated, their inked-on skeletons had sagged. Singly or in pairs, they ravened the fringe. On sharp winter nights they violated the edge of human settlements, the boundary of taboo. Mothers told cautionary tales to wayward kids—*Beware! Bogeyman! Forbidden Forest, Dog Man!*

Two born-again Gories migrated south with Sussan. Roy and Dan, Recon Marines, had been touched by the healer, disciples of Old Law. They rode herd on the Virals as they spread towards the sun. Viral load-levels dropped with the latitude, the condition of the host improving climatically.

Northern Aghori fared less well. After Panzer was breached and Sharkey had flown, the feeding, for a while, had been good. Blackwaters had been tied to trees by their ambushers—a tasty treat for the protein deficient. Frau and her goons were found as they fled. The pharma-fascists didn't make it very far. The grinning Gories sucked sustenance from their skulls in a frenzy of phrenology.

Things fall apart, even D.C.—the CORPS' center—may not hold. Bad news had reached Kamul, on multiple fronts.

His Great Lakes foray had utterly failed. Major Naz, along with his entire militia, were dead—a devastating loss of men and material. He removed Michigan's map from his White House wall. Force projection—boots on the ground—was too costly, and to what end? There were too few boots and way too much ground. The Midwest was once again a far frontier. The Seaboard, and then Appalachia would need taming first. Manpower was an issue, desertions were many. There were simply not enough Hands for all the necks that needed noosing. Kamul had no contingency plans for this, and his halo didn't help.

The general's neural implant was defunct. A catastrophe had occurred. The great EYE was now dim. The old grid—gas, solar, and wind—had kept its fire flickering, but eventually failed. The massive centrifuge Kamul had been forging—a ring of fusion power—had melted down. There was not enough wattage to cool its components. That bright age had now ended. Kamul and the CORPS would remain in the east, consolidating what they could, biding time in the land of shadows.

Epilogue

Stars in the Night Sky by Naomi VanDoren

Epilogue

AN OSPREY FLEW AT NIGHT, the coldest of the young new year. Beaver Island endured, encased in ice, mostly safe, mostly sound. Smoke curled from chimneys, carbonic ghosts of departed trees. Their woody limbs—stuffed with solar energy—had been lopped, then split. Islanders orbited their stoves, miniature suns made of metal, radiating heat.

Three figures wended their way up Kilty's Hill in the dark. The raptor, recognizing them, banked towards his nest, his hearth and home. "Keith's Hill" they named it, at least to themselves. Lake ice boomed, a crystalline cannonade. Owls barred the way, *who-whoing* the trio. Who were *they* to trespass here?

Reaching the resting place, the companions paused for permission. The oaks, subzero, granted it slowly. A fire was kindled from their fallen fingers. Twiggy canopies touched the stars. The campfire snapped. Sparks ascended, seeking reunion with an unseen sun, the source of their photonic power.

Keith—what was left of him—calmed the feathered guardians. Grave as ever, Two-Crow welcomed Mukwa, Miin, and Samantha to the grove. His rifle rusted where they planted it, one metallic flake at a time. His organic remains had been absorbed by soil. The iron in Keith's veins now strengthened others: fungi, acorn, squirrel, and hawk. His presence, what lingered anyway, steeled his three friends. In life, Two-Crow had that effect. Why should death be any different?

The trio sat up straighter. Crowned by stars, the circle of friends swayed, shamanic. The ring of their fellowship remained unbroken. The arctic atmosphere formed a mere coverlet between living earth and lifeless void. Lake ice hushed. Owls ceased their query. A long quiet passed before the dawn.

Presence here was enough. The presence of each other, and also Keith. What else was there? Be present, and acknowledge the same in others, as often as you can. They opened themselves to this gift. Constellations of consciousness passed between them. As within, so without. From below, they gazed above:

Behold, the Winter-maker! Star-belted and bold.

Behold, the Seven Sisters! Winking with mischief.

Behold, the Bear! Pursued—ever north—by three Hunters.

The End of the Sudden Quiet Trilogy

Acknowledgments

"Remember the plants, trees, animal life who all have their tribes, their families, their histories too. Talk to them, listen to them." — Joy Harjo

It is a daunting task to "remember" and properly thank all of voices that I have "listened to" in the writing of this book, but I certainly must acknowledge those that make an actual appearance on the page:

Joy Harjo's poetry helped guide both my dedication and these acknowledgments. Marvin Gaye surprised me and Cowboy both when he showed up in Hochstettler's hayloft; I'll bet Marvin was astonished too. Shakespeare, as always, is everywhere, all the time, including Sharkey's rantings about Macbeth. Walker, my "descendent of ancient kings," is a repository of old lore and no doubt would scold me for not properly citing Lincoln, MLK Jr., Mandela, Gandhi, Homer's *Iliad*, and all the rest. The musicians Peaches and Herb helped me "reunite" Cowboy and Liz in a shipping container outside Clare. Also, I was genuinely moved to discover that Bonnie Parker wrote poetry before her violent end with Clyde, and it helped me see Liz, and her relationship with Bob Campbell, in a softer light. I was tickled to find Kenny Rogers lamenting his "Lucille" on the post-collapse radio dial outside Detroit; the duet between Cowboy and wounded Walker in the backseat is one I'd like to hear. 1980s popstar Tiffany singing "I think we're alone now" seemed perfectly irreverent for the Rangers and their endless teasing of Thorn. And I'm sorry, but It's impossible not to hear Eminem in Ayesha's van as her A-Team cruises 8-Mile hunting Virals. Finally, I'm not exactly sure where the Panther gunner "Prince" came from, but if TAFKAP were to ever crew a weapon, a .50-caliber seems about right.

Concerning the "plants, trees" and "animal life" that Harjo urges us to remember, I must acknowledge my debt to the master tree-talker, JRR Tolkien and all his works. Like an Eldar from an ancient age, the professor has "woken me up" to the marvelous language of the rooted world. I also acknowledge the Indigenous peoples of the Upper Great Lakes, tireless caretakers and symbionts with the environment, both today, in the future and in centuries past. *Miigwech!* As for the flora, fauna, and epic forces that formed them, they hardly need acknowledging by me. Instead, like Miin, I stand humbled in their presence, radiating respect and gratitude, knowing they'll outlast us all.

Let me close by thanking the talented team at Mission Point Press, especially my editor, the fantastic Scott J. Couturier— Scott and Shayne, stay weird! Local bookstores and libraries are godsends for bibliophiles and democracy alike. Thank you, Juan at Horizon Books in Traverse City, and all the libraries and booksellers of Northern Michigan for helping readers find these pages.

Lastly, to Katie, my wife and life-partner, none of these words would exist without you, and even if they did, they wouldn't mean a thing. You are the one that gives meaning to all of this, and to all of me too.

APPENDIX:
Concerning Humans

EVEN I WILL ADMIT THAT, in the beginning, it was nice.

Suddenly there was less noise, less movement. Time slowed, and the lengthening days of spring were filled with quiet. Society had been stilled by a virus—a novel one, the first of a series—and like the season, began a period of waiting. Waiting for winter to let go, waiting for transmission data, for a vaccine, for things to go back to normal. I knew this longed-for normal would never return, but in the beginning, it was nice.

We watched it all happen on our phones, on our screens. Satellites shared their images, links intact, circuits undamaged, flooding the eager populace with views from above. Fleets of semi-trucks, ever-busy, now sat parked and orderly. Plumes of factory smoke disappeared, region by region, as whole economies shuttered. Ocean trade routes were no longer criss-crossed by wakes of automated freighters. The human pall was lifting from the Earth. Millions in India marveled at the Himalayas revealed. Dolphins frolicked in the unpolluted canals of Venice, going unphotographed by tourists that weren't there. The lights were still on, electricity served its master. Our little planet sparkled at night, flashing its many-minded message into the void.

And there was food to be had, delivered right to the door. A swipe on a screen, some taps on a phone, and there it was. Sanitary, masked, no touching of course, no exchange of droplets; a smile, a wave, and the driver moved on. Grocery bags were unpacked into kitchens, each item disinfected with wipes: bananas, avocados, oranges, meat and bread and fruit and vegetables—foodstuffs from the world, all readily available. Children helped parents, schools went remote, and mothers grinned with fathers at the helpfulness of the kids. It was good to have some extra time, good to slow down, and what should we have for dinner tonight?

We could read all about it, and we did, endless articles from every angle. We watched the speeches, dissected interviews, posted our comments and added our voice. We were in this together, though the sick died alone in an ever-accelerating curve of heartbreak. But that came later. All curves take time, even exponential ones. In that first spring there was mostly just quiet, and waiting—and for some, a refocusing.

Of course there were soothsayers, those who used the early days of the pandemic to prepare, to warn others of the coming calamity. These voices, loudest at the end of any era, were once again ignored, at least by most. In this biological storm, as in the floods of old, the many would not be saved, only the few. Masses cleave to the status quo, and their dying wish is to return to the familiar. It's not that the group can't change, but that it won't. Nature's law is change or die. The virus did, humans didn't, and so they died.

As the cold calculus of the curve continued, whole cities were shaved by the scythe. But the lights stayed on, refrigerators hummed, every cell in the hive backlit by screens. We watched our world end, a million channels to choose from, broadcasts in any language, though the content stayed the same.

Complex systems need expertise. Large cities require many workers; disruption leads to filth and decay. The great metropoles of the world were quickly fouled, trash multiplying as the rats grew bold. Every age takes pride in its cities: high-water marks of culture and learning. But turn back a few pages and witness the pyres, the furtive burning of the piled dead. If a city is old enough there will be places stained by such disposals, public squares and pier-side landings where the taint has never faded. From London, Venice, and Athens to Uruk, Ur, and Babylon, the tale of plague is as old as civilization.

On our screens, we saw the overflow at city morgues, the mass graves dug in Central Park. City workers wore hazmat suits and respirators because the corpses, infectious, still vectored the virus. Funerals were forbidden, undertakers taken under; bodies were buried in the clothes they died in.

And then I got involved, my white hand pressing the plunger. After a soft launch, my Stinger started trending, a viral finale to the novel crown-series. The first pyre was in Milan. Milano, that old plague-port, was no stranger to such fires. Some part of that city remembered, though its modern denizens did not. Outraged, the world shared grainy videos: backhoes tending the blaze, clanking treads and floodlights, polizia barricades, Euro-sirens and the wailing of bereaved.

A super variant, Stinger spread its venom. Crematoriums were clogged, first responders were unresponsive; corpses became a biohazard, and the mass burnings began. Old cities knew the drill—Mumbai, Damascus, Istanbul. New ones learned quickly—Los Angeles, Mexico City, Kuala Lumpur. Satellites peered down, incurious, as across the globe factories went cold and pulsing highways flat-lined, their belching exhaust replaced by humanity's last gasp: the oily plumes of our burning dead.

Little did I know these storm clouds were silvered with green. Nature's fuse, tamped no longer, had been lit. Our age, the Anthropocene, ended with a bang. The next one, a throwback, teased its trailer: a return to roots.

APPENDIX:
Timeline of Collapse

SOME OF THIS YOU already know. SARS-CoV-2, undeclared and undocumented, began deplaning several years before collapse, an uninvited guest to a long-expected party. Covee's seeming origin was a zoonotic spillover in China. The West, blasé after decades of SARS, MERS, and their acronymic kin, cold-shouldered this new arrival. TikToks of Asians quarantined in factory-cities were rejected as too on-the-nose and far, far away.

Covee's first wave infected almost everyone, while mRNA vaccines, indeed miraculous, inoculated the rest. There were deaths—several million—but most were predictable culls. The human populace sighed with relief, but the poison had been planted; billions, unknowingly, had been envenomed. Global immunization, via infection or vaccination, had hijacked the herd's defenses. The Stimulator of Interferon Genes system (STING), the immune system's pistol, had been primed and pointed, not at the invader, but at the host. All I did was pull the trigger.

This was a busy time for my company, Panzer Pharma. Headquartered in Michigan and designated vital for defense, we were given carte blanche, and flush with taxpayer billions. When Covee began cresting, POTUS, eyes-only, issued orders to Panzer: create something new and, ideally, untraceable. We rolled up our sleeves and got to work.

With a PhD in virology, I became Dr. Frankenstein, and Kalamazoo my castle. We utilized CRISPR to encode a new creature, a riff on Covee, but this time with a sting. Too cunning, I knew it would work, so rather than chase a vaccine-mirage, I channeled gobs of cash towards an in-house virucide, security recruitment, and other doomsday delights.

Before too long, my VOHC was detected, a variant of high consequence. In March of what became Year 1, several years after Covee, this variant started stinging. Cytokine storms, a hyper-immune response primed by previous exposure, quickly overwhelmed the populace and, soon after, the hospitals. Pro-vax or anti, the variant didn't care; our politics shrank as Stinger gained function. Covee and my variant morphed, blindly cosmopolitan in their ability to transcend race, religion, and country of origin. The planet's humans achieved equality at last, mere months before functional extinction.

The end wasn't pretty. From my tower, through a darkening globe of satellites, I could see things far away. I watched the world grow dim.

Nuclear exchanges, of course, had happened; entire regions lay radiated, devoid of life. The Indian subcontinent, the Middle East, and both sides of Europe's tattered curtain had become domains of Darwin—primordial. What might emerge from such a soup? That first winter was a long one, the upper stratosphere saturated with soot. The growing season shrank as not enough sunlight came through. Massive solar flares triggered geomagnetic storms, frying what remained of our fragile grid.

The planet's climate had been seared, but even so, green pockets survived. Trees kept scrubbing and the air grew cleaner, arboreal zones again sheltering hominids. Fresh water, as always, was precious. The species' earliest stomping grounds—Lake Baikal, Amazonia, the old Rift Valley—might now become our last. The story arc of sapiens had been reset to the beginning. Old ways became new again, and neo movements, oh so mockable before, now shared their surplus food with survivors.

Michigan, my future fief, is insulated by the Great Lakes, the watery lungs of a new Midwest. Here I will stake my claim, carve out a barony, and prosper.

And I'm not alone. There are prescient others, bunkered behind their billions, at my beck and call. For I have their elixirs, the coveted virucides; my white hands are upon their throats!

And so, as one age ended, I positioned Panzer for the next.

First off, that woman, Michigan's gumptious governor, had to go, so she went. The tricky Halloween raid of Year 1 was a treat for my newly minted mercenaries. Her lieutenant governor deployed the National Guard to secure Detroit's refineries. We took them next, a symphonic attack by rail and barge. The facilities and their precious petroleum were captured, and fires were set throughout Motor City. By sunrise, Detroit was a Wagnerian Götterdämmerung.

Next, we eliminated our rivals in the pharma field. Merch Biotech in New Jersey was a daylight raid, live-streamed by thousands. By then, Panzer's recruits had been metamorphosed by my virucide, blooded by battle, and inked with the ashes of the slain. The video views were in the millions. Mesmerized, the masses found our signifier. The unit's Sanskrit tattoo, *Aghori*, was summarily analyzed, my paramilitary nameless no longer. The stormtroopers, torsos and skulls tattooed as skeletons, were henceforth known as Gories.

All in all, Year 1 had gone well. Naturally, I'm only speaking for me and mine, no need to remind me of the bilious billions. Remember, jurists of the future, I am merely responding to events, not instigating them.

Of course, I don't expect you to believe this. I only half believe it myself.

APPENDIX:
The Island

ON BEAVER ISLAND, collapse crested slowly. March and April of Year 1 saw little traffic between island and main, a quiet season while the world burned. Strict isolation was voted in place; runways and roads were cross-hatched with trucks and old buses, ten-ton hazards, dragon's teeth to chew up invaders.

Fuel rationing was enforced—diesel and regular gasoline—no driving allowed, no non-vital equipment. Every drop was saved for the fleet, saved for the generators. Squadrons of sailboats were pressed into service, canvas engines fueled only by wind. Watchers were posted, with eyes and ears in every direction. The "Voice of Beaver Island," 91.9 FM MHz, lifted spirits with borrowed oratory till the batteries died:

"We shall defend our island, whatever the cost may be, we shall fight on the beaches, we shall fight on the landing grounds, we shall fight in the fields and in the streets, we shall fight in the hills; we shall never surrender."

Boat crews were armed and drilled: respond, repel, and retreat. Despite the sandy soils, islanders were ordered to produce their own food, plant gardens, stock up on nature's bounty.

Then came the chaos of that first summer. As the Midwest felt the sting of Covee's variant, island defenses—water and sky—were tested in waves. For a handful of Beaver pilots and gunners—an amateur BAF—it was their finest hour. Island airspace was blitzed by small-engine planes, panic-flying and over max gross. Spotters vectored the incoming, and Beaver planes scrambled to intercept, spitting fire and littering the island with wreckage, a hurricane of defiance. Eventually, invaders stopped coming as their avgas ran dry.

By water, refugees loaded boats and tried their luck, fleeing the sinking ship of Michigan's mainland. Shots were fired, diesel stocks were depleted by patrols, island boats returned with windshields shot out and first aid kits deployed. Blood was splashed on decks, on transoms. The Beaver boats were no strangers to gore; human or whitefish, it hosed off the same. Captains were killed, teenage sons took the wheel, racing home through tears as Dad bled out in the stern. Watch lists were drawn up, quadrants assigned. Voices were raised at council, graves were dug—diabetics first—as island medicine ran out.

The summer days of Y1 were shortened by fall. Islanders survived, unstung by the variant. Hunters were prized for their skills, venison smoked and stored away; squirrel, rabbit, and fish bolstered dwindling larders.

Doomed, the islanders scrolled on their screens. They watched remotely as the virus morphed and vaccines failed. The center did not hold; November's presidential election was contested, surprising no one. Command lost all control, soldiers deserted, and there was rank fratricide. Big pharma, bloated, went bust. The electrical cable, the island's umbilical, was clamped and then cut, its mainland mother running out of juice.

Y1 handed its scythe to Y2 and winter had its cull. Three months of cold, without electricity's buffer, added more names to the island's ledger. These dark-month additions had shivered to death, mostly alone. The enormous blue of winter snuffed out the fragile flames of human life, cold-stored bodies awaiting the thaw tucked snugly into their beds. Stormy waters kept the island unmolested. The lack of screens became a respite. There was no going back. Alcohol stocks were depleted, cigarettes too. Islanders endured.

The spring of Y2 brought new digging to the island: graves first, then gardens, a prehistoric pairing. Busy as beavers, whole families now worked together to sow and tend their fields, motivated by a direct connection between crop yield and survival.

Days lengthened, north-bound geese wondering at the emptied world.

ABOUT the AUTHOR

Joshua Veith is an educator, adventurer, and outdoor enthusiast. He graduated from the University of Michigan, later earning an MA in Literature from Eastern Michigan University. Today, Joshua lives with his wife and two sons in Northern Michigan, fishes and hikes in the same spots that Hemingway enjoyed as a young man, and teaches a literature class on JRR Tolkien. As a public school teacher and writer, Josh strives to be an Indigenous ally, recognizing that traditional relationships with the environment offer the most sustainable pathways for humankind's interaction with the planet.